PARK PLAZA

Previous books by Richard Cox

Hartman's Game
The Botticelli Madonna
The Columbus Option
Ground Zero
The Ice Raid
The KGB Directive
The Katanga Run
Sam 7
Operation Sealion

PARK PLAZA

Richard Cox

St. Martin's Press
New York

Designed by Judy Dannecker

Library of Congress Cataloging-in-Publication Data

Cox, Richard Hubert Francis
    Park Plaza / Richard Cox.
        p.   cm.
    "A Thomas Dunne book."
    ISBN 0-312-05490-4
    I. Title.
    PR6053.0969P37   1991
    823'.914--dc20

                                                90-49189
                                                CIP

First Edition: February 1991
10 9 8 7 6 5 4 3 2 1

This book is dedicated with gratitude
and affection to Bunny Pantchev

PARK PLAZA

Chapter

1

'O n l y Europeans and crooks have no credit cards.'

The remark stabbed at Barbara's memory when, as she'd instructed, one of the reception clerks slipped back to warn her that the couple were leaving.

'Five thirty-eight is checking out, Miss Andrews.'

'Okay. Just handle it normally.'

Only Europeans and crooks didn't carry plastic, Craig had said after the pair created a scene when they checked in. They'd resented the Park Plaza's regulation one-thousand-dollar deposit for guests without credit cards. In fact 'resented' was too mild a word for their reaction. She braced herself and went through to reception, holding a letter as if she had a query.

The Irishman was there, running through items on his account while the desk clerk watched attentively. He had dark, tousled hair and a Celtic swarthiness on a world-weary young face. He'd been in a brawl or two in his time, she thought, even if this morning he was wearing a neat shirt and tie under an English-style tweed jacket.

She fixed her 'Have a good day, sir' smile in place and walked along behind the counter to face him. To everyone else there, she was simply a tall, self-confident woman in her late twenties, with dark hair cut short and swept back, only a touch of make-up, and that 'straight out of a magazine ad' crispness to her blue uniform which the Park Plaza's General Manager insisted on.

'Everything all right, sir?' She wasn't going to be intimidated by the suspicion in his expression. 'I hope you've enjoyed your stay with us?'

'Sure and we would have enjoyed it more'—he gave her a twisted look, waving the bill with a show of disgust—'except for this part of the thing. Lucky we paid that deposit and all. Could have been down in the kitchens washing up otherwise, couldn't we? Us being without those cards you're so fond of.'

'Have a nice day, then,' Barbara said coldly, omitting the 'sir'. As she turned away she spotted the woman. She was in her mid-thirties, pallid, as faded as a flower that's been without water. She was perched awkwardly on a small decorative chair by one of the lobby's white marble pillars, like an unattractive girl desperate to be asked to dance. Even at this distance Barbara could see she was nervous. She kept shifting her position, as if acutely uncomfortable. Her physical attitude was screaming, 'Can't we get out of here!' Could it be just that she was picking up the tab and had gotten unexpectedly short of cash? All Barbara's instincts told her it was something far more serious.

Feeling conspicuously isolated among the people thronging the impressively vast, high-ceilinged space of the Park Plaza's lobby, the German squirmed on the small, hard chair. She was in a ferment of anger. When she'd noticed that woman spying on her from behind the reception counter her agitation had increased. Did the cow suspect something? What had been reported last night after the call from the night clerk? 'My husband and I have a little row,' she had explained. 'Everything is all right.'

All right! When the bastard had been half drunk and had just deceived her—deceived her without caring. In the beginning he'd talked about detonating the explosives with a fuse set off by a phone call to their room. Sophisticated and precise. He'd ended up relying on an eight-dollar alarm clock from a discount store. Before they arrived he'd impressed her with scientific explanations of how a bomb planted inside the surrounds of a bathtub would have its explosive force directed downwards through the room below: and then said it was not feasible after all. 'I can't do the same as we did in Brighton, me darlin'. They build the bloody hotels different over here.'

The offhand way he'd revealed all this, after extorting tens of thousands of her money, made her tremble with fury. Worse, after months of planning he'd taken absurd risks by disguising himself as an engineer to plant a reduced amount of the Semtex in the ballroom ceiling with only the alarm clock to set it off. She could scream. She doubted if it would ever work, let alone at the precise time she wanted, when they had none of his promised last-minute control. She hated him for the deceit and felt doubly humiliated because Horst's death might not be avenged.

The Irishman left the cashier's desk, stuffing a handful of notes into his hip pocket. The woman noticed, was relieved that the thousand dollars had been enough: and steeled herself to demand the change back. As he rejoined her she stood up, faltered from a twinge of excruciating pain and had to steady herself by grasping the chair.

'Everythin's fine, Birgit, me darlin',' he said. 'They're bringing the bags and we'll ask for a cab.'

Forcing herself to smile at him, she took his arm and they walked together towards the Fifth Avenue entrance, the bellboy following with their two suitcases.

Barbara watched as the couple left. She wished Craig had been with her and felt powerless to do any more, even though yet another incidental thing struck her as odd. On Saturday she'd seen the couple return with three shopping bags visibly heavy with purchases from Bloomingdale's, Bendel and Bergdorf. 'The big B's,' she'd reflected. 'They must be more loaded than we thought.' Yet now the bellboy was trailing behind them with only two smallish cases. Nothing added up about that pair, nothing at all. Even though they were leaving, she felt apprehensive without knowing precisely why. If only Craig had come down. He was the one person she could rely on. It seemed extraordinary that four months ago, in June, she had barely known him.

Chapter

2

'W h y can't you find a job nearer home, if we must live here? You're always leaving the moment I get back. What's so great about being in security at the Park Plaza anyway?'

There was irritable acidity in his wife's voice which Craig Clifford knew all too well.

'Because I'm trying to make this more than just a job, honey. I'm trying to build a career.'

'Then we ought to live in Manhattan, like my friends all do.' As Julia spoke she began loading the dishwasher, ostentatiously clattering the dishes in a way that asked, unmistakably, why Craig himself never did any clearing up. 'Well?' She paused for a moment and faced him, her wide blue eyes contemptuous. 'Don't say your great new career doesn't pay enough.'

'You know damn well it doesn't yet.'

'Not even with the pension from the famous Green Machine?'

'Not with both.' He gritted his teeth, knowing exactly what was coming next: he wasn't any longer the man she'd married; if he loved her he wouldn't force her to live in a dump like North Plainfield, New Jersey: Why couldn't he work in Quantico, Virginia, where they owned a house, instead of renting that out and themselves renting here? Why hadn't he fought harder to stay in the Marine Corps—at least they might get posted somewhere glamorous occasionally, like Hawaii. Or Jackson-ville, he usually joked.

He joked because he still had bad dreams about the Medical Board last year. The Board's senior officer told him, with sympathy, but no arguments permitted, that the injury to his ankle 'precluded him from performing his rightful function' in the Marine Corps. In other words: out. Medically retired four years short of the twenty necessary for a full pension. If time at the Naval Academy had counted he'd have been okay. He'd have made the exact number of years and, since he'd joined under the 'old system', he'd have received a full pension straightaway instead of this lesser medical one. It wasn't a good joke.

Anyway, today he wasn't going to start kidding or getting into a marital free-for-all about his alleged failings—not five minutes before he had to go to work, not this time.

'Listen,' he insisted, unwisely, 'as of Monday I become Assistant Director of Security, okay? More money, more regular hours. The training's over. I'm in management. It's like I've graduated.'

'At thirty-eight years of age. Fantastic. How do we celebrate? With a six-pack of Bud?'

Jesus, but Julia knew how to get under his skin! He stared angrily at her, ready for a fight despite his resolve. She'd been a looker when they met six years ago. Blond, even if it wasn't natural. Sexy. Horsing around the Allied Headquarters in Bel-gium, where she was a senior secretary, in a way that caught the Generals' attention and seemed pretty amusing at the time. A bit of a character, Julia, the British Colonel she worked for used to say, lives in the fast lane, don't suppose she'll ever settle down. She was flattered too, quoted him openly. But then for her the Brits could do no wrong. She just adored everything about them, from their accents to their titles: especially their titles.

Astonishingly, after going out with Craig for a few months she'd done the unthinkable. She'd married him—and he a mere major in a place where bird colonels were no better than errand boys. He never did know exactly why. Maybe the mission he'd been on when he hurt his ankle and which had qualified him, quite exceptionally, for an intelligence job at NATO, gave him a kind of glamour. Although it had been secret, she knew about it through her own work. And she'd been able to go back to her job after they had a baby. So during those three years at NATO everything had been fine. No reason it shouldn't have, with hindsight. She already had a neat apartment and a whole circle of friends in Brussels, and he had decent allowances. There was money, they could hire a nursemaid for the baby, they could afford to have fun.

Then he was posted back to the Fleet Marine Force at Jacksonville, training men for operations in northern Europe and eighteen months later, just as he was into the promotion zone for Lieutenant Colonel, he suffered the accidental fall that broke his damn ankle again. Zonk, someone among the heavies began asking if he had any future with the Corps. Was he fit to hold a field command? Within weeks he was up before the Medical Board and that was it.

For a man as quietly dedicated to the military life as Craig their decision was staggering. He'd been stunned. Their marriage had already begun to get rocky: Julia hated the officer's quarters they'd been allocated and, sure, Jacksonville was a very different lifestyle from Brussels—though what in hell she had ever thought living back home again would be like he couldn't fathom. Like 'Dallas' maybe. But he wasn't the quitting kind. He heard of the hotel job through a friend and seized it. The thought of New York revived Julia's enthusiasm. She had backed him solidly for once.

But New York had turned out less exciting and glamorous than she'd imagined, especially its New Jersey suburbs. All she talked about these days were the things that, in her constant British phrase, she utterly loathed. In North Plainfield those enlarged to damn near everything, from the New Jersey Transit to the slang their daughter, now five, picked up at school.

'I'm getting a promotion.' he said carefully. 'You ought to be glad.'

'I loathe North Plainfield, I loathe this house, I hate typing for a lousy eight fifty an hour, I don't want Antonia brought up in this kind of place. How do you think we like it being alone out here all the time?'

That 'we' was an ass-kicker. Whenever Julia really had it in for him she brought their daughter into the dispute, even though at this moment Antonia was in school doing whatever the first grade did at two-thirty in the afternoon. Shit, why had he ever gone along with giving the baby a name like that anyway? Antonia, for fuck's sake! Lady Antonia awaits you in the drawing room, my lord. That was what Julia dreamt about: and in reality her father was a goddamned Internal Revenue Service official living in a Chicago suburb no better than this one. He drained his coffee and heaved himself upright, catching a twinge from his ankle and almost stumbling.

'I have to go now.' he said firmly and without rancour. A shouting match would for sure make him late. But he did pause for a moment and look around, thinking that Julia didn't have things so bad. This house was basically pre–World War II and wooden, but on stone foundations, while the structure had been faced with brick in the 1960s. It was a decent professional family's kind of a house with three bedrooms and an attic—a solid and quite spacious home with lawns back and front o a thirty-by-ninety lot. Okay, so it wasn't an elegant, high-ceilinged apartment on the Square Marguerite in Brussels. But many of his contemporaries would reckon he was lucky and it cost him over a thousand a month in rent. Once he was fully into the new job he aimed to sell the Quantico house and transfer the Veterans' Administration mortage to buy this one.

As if to drown out his departure, Julia slammed the dish-washer closed. Water began to gurgle into it. This kitchen was fitted out with all the machines: dishwasher, refrigerator, freezer, waste disposal, blender, food processor, toaster, electric can opener fixed by the sink, a TV glaring down from a bracket high on one wall. He liked gadgets himself, but this was a bit much. This was a factory! And right now it was starting to reverberate like one. It was as if she'd read some magazine about what the ideal home ought to possess and gone and bought the store.

'Could be two in the morning before I'm back,' he said, with more consideration than she deserved. 'Don't wait up.'

'I certainly will not.' She had to half shout to be heard. 'Some of us have things to do tomorrow, even if you don't. Antonia has to have a new dress. She can't possibly go to next week's birthday party without a new one.'

Craig checked himself from replying. The children's party was being given by neighbours whom they'd only just gotten to know. Julia seemed to dislike them on principle, as if they threatened her arguments against living here. He went through into the hall, picked up his Burberry and left for the bus, deciding the hell with it, this weekend he'd buy a second car that he could leave at the Plainfield train station. As of next week he could legitimately start living like a manager.

As he walked to the New Jersey Transit bus stop he thought about that. These last six months while learning the business of hotel security at the Park Plaza he'd been working like any other security man there, clocking in for shifts, paid by the hour. He'd wanted to discover how it was for them, for guys who had only a single automobile, which was years old at that and which they repaired themselves at weekends. So he had travelled into Manhattan the same way they did. Julia had called him a fool and refused point-blank to take him to the train, let alone deprive herself of the Volvo when he had a late shift so he could drive the whole day. If he was honest with himself, he'd married a bitch. He ought to cushion himself any way he could.

He glanced at his watch: 2:33. She had delayed him. He hurried into an awkward run and arrived out of breath at the corner where the bus stopped with only seconds to spare. The driver joked about being late himself and Craig grinned back. There was a kind of comradeship about commuting into the city. By the time the bus was out on Route 22 and heading for the Lincoln Tunnel he had managed to put Julia's tantrums out of his mind, except for wondering briefly how she would have liked living in Union City or Newark.

Not, Craig thought, as he made his way down through the grimy cavern of the Port Authority Bus Terminal to the subway, that he'd ever have looked for a job in New York if this one hadn't been offered. A childhood in Wisconsin and sixteen years with the Corps did nothing to make the sunless canyons of New York appealing. To the rich it might be the hub of the universe. But who in their senses would want to be a blue-collar worker among the human flotsam of this city! An elderly-looking black beggar, a sign pinned on his shirt saying VIETNAM VETERAN, held out a paper cup at him. He saw from the man's face that he was having a hard life whether he was a veteran or not and dropped a coin in the cup. Half a second later, a young black in a baseball cap, shiny purple zippered windbreaker, jeans and scuffed trainers pimp-rolled up to him.

'Yo! How 'bout a dollar.' He faced Craig with unconcealed menace. 'Gimme a dollar.'

'Not today, friend.'

The young dude rocked to and fro on the balls of his feet. 'What yo think yo's sayin, man.'

'I'm saying "no".'

The curt authority of the answer made the boy buck his head and roll his eyes in anger. He danced in front of Craig. The old beggar began to shuffle away, sliding his backside across the floor and clutching his cup. Across the concourse another punk lolled against a wall, watching alertly.

'You jes' give a dollar, huh.' The words were what the boy intended. But the menace was fading. The more he looked at this whitey, the less sure he felt. The guy's limp had made him look like a pushover. Could be he wasn't some regulation Wall Street motherfucker. He didn't carry any briefcase. His face wasn't a city face, it was lean and weathered and, holy shit, the eyes were staring him out. They were cold grey eyes and they were boring holes straight through to his brain. He had to look away and as he did so he slid his right palm over the windbreaker's pocket, feeling for his knife.

'Don't go for it,' Craig said quietly.

The boy rocked some more, unable to look straight back, noticing that this guy's raincoat wasn't buckled, it hung open. And the man was relaxed. He was just too relaxed. He could have a gun under that raincoat. How else could he be so cool? The boy's nerve broke. He backed away, still balancing on the balls of his feet, forcing a laugh. 'Ain't got no small change, huh. 'Nother time, then, man, 'nother time.'

'Don't count on that.'

Craig stood still and let the boy retreat three yards or so, keeping watch on his hands, until he turned and pimp-rolled exaggeratedly across to the other punk.

'Is yo crazy!' exclaimed the beggar, looking back at him.

Craig grinned down. 'They do teach you something in the Green Weenies,' he said and resumed his walk to the subway.

But, he reflected as he waited for an E train, he couldn't rely on the cool approach succeeding every time. Trevinski, his ex–Police Captain boss, made a lot more outward show of toughness. Which way would be most effective if they came up against a gunman or a terrorist in the Park Plaza? Not so much 'if' as 'when', either. There'd been violent crime in the hotel before, as well as the endemic petty theft. With 2,500 on staff and as many well-heeled guests, with a lot of money around, with the protective anonymity of the hotel's size and several entrances, there would be again. Trevinski had told him so—and that any deputy he trained would learn his job in the firing line.

Chapter
3

'O h my God, how can—!' Father Vaughan checked himself. The office he worked in might be informal, but a priest still had to control himself. Even so, he was faced by the devil of a request, to put it lightly. Worse, it came from a man he had known for many years and held in high regard.

'Do you have to send an answer today?' his secretary asked, trying to restrain her curiosity. The airmail envelope with its Indian stamps and the superscription 'Diocese of Malabar' had arrived creased and dirtied: looking as though an elephant had trampled on it, in fact. Watching Father Gerard's face she guessed it contained some form of summons from the past.

'Give me a minute, Mary. Yes, I do have to answer.' He had to live by his own rules and those rules included replying immediately to every letter this charitable organisation received. You might not be able to help, but you could at least respond. Although, dear God, how either he or the charity could help with this one was another question. He picked up the slightly torn sheets of thin paper again, disregarding the hubbub of the small open-plan office, noticing it had been sent Express on June 4th.

'My dear Reverend Father,' the text began, continuing with a paragraph of good wishes and conventional enquiries. The typing alone jerked his memory back twenty-seven years, dissolving time. It was the unmistakable imprint of an ancient Remington and it carried him back to the intense humidity of southern India. The cracking stucco of the two-storey diocesan office was turning black under the constant damp and heat. The Indian typist, whose white shirt became more threadbare with every washing, always had a not too clean glass of lemonade on his desk alongside the piles of the Bishop's correspondence and the starkly upright, black enamelled, museum-piece Remington. Father Vaughan could imagine the energetic little man hammering away to produce these two pages of flimsy and sweat-stained typescript. Except, he realised on this second reading, that the Bishop must have typed them himself. The contents were too potentially explosive for him to have trusted a gossiping clerk.

Mary Jenkins watched, her curiosity mounting. She was not a Catholic herself—you didn't have to be one here, you simply had to be competent—and she wondered if not being of the Faith was why after several months in the job she still couldn't make her employer out. He looked more like a rancher than a priest. His beard was touched with grey and his skin was tanned and roughened from long years of labouring under a hot sun. His hands had none of the softness of the seminary. They were a worker's hands. Nor were his roll-neck sweater and slacks the usual dress of a priest. The most she could conclude was that Father Vaughan was as much his own man as a man of God. Yet for all his self-reliance, this letter had definitely caught him off guard.

'I know you will recall the extraordinary veneration with which the Faithful in Malabar regard the astylar Cross in the Church of Our Lady at Kottayam.'

He did indeed remember! Once a year that elaborately fashioned thirty-inch-high silver and gold fifteenth-century cross was carried out for the Easter procession, its plinth mounted on a six-foot pole so that the crowds could see it. The man bearing the pole often staggered under the weight: one of the minor idiosyncrasies of the Eastern Orthodox church was that if a man lacked the intelligence for spiritual anguish then the priests allowed his physical capacities to be tested instead. Before this particular congregation of Malabar Catholics were reunited with Rome they had owed allegiance to the Syrian Patriarch in

Damascus and they retained various Eastern customs. So, on these occasions, the cross swayed on its pole beneath a single staggering acolyte, while the pressing, heaving, sweating crowd of Indian faithful gasped and prayed as it passed.

They gasped and prayed because the cross was to them a legend. The silver-covered crossbeams terminated in square gold mounts, set with huge pale ruby-coloured stones, four in all. Beyond those spread swelling gold and silver fronds, like the Prince of Wales's feathers, by comparison with which the delicately wrought solid gold figure of Christ crucified seemed disproportionately small: until you realised that the figure's perfectly sculpted hands and feet were nailed to a smaller cross, set against the front of the main one.

Held high on a golden pole above an Easter procession, glittering dully in the sun, the cross was a spectacular sight: just as it dominated the very different annual service commemorating the birthday of Saint Thomas. But the subject of the Bishop's letter was not the gold and silver on the cross: it was the legendary missing jewel.

On the back, at the junction of the cross behind the figure of Christ, gaped the place where the diamond given by a converted Prince of Cochin had once been mounted. Whether the other huge stones remaining, like those on the front, were indeed diamonds, rubies and emeralds, or semiprecious, or just artfully made of paste Father Vaughan had never discovered. But then the Catholic liturgy had always been supported by theatricality. However, all Christians in Malabar knew that the great rectangular diamond had been genuine, just as they shuddered at the appalling retribution the Prince had endured for his conversion. Captured by a Moghul expedition, he had been tortured and then crucified. Together, the diamond and the cross had become the object of a veneration which this Oriental setting and the Indian temperament had transformed into much more than devotion: into something mystical, all-compelling, ecstatic.

More extraordinarily, the theft of the diamond sometime in the early 1700s, far from weakening the cult, had intensified it.

'This cult,' the Bishop went on in his grammatically perfect English, leaving Father Vaughan to imagine the accent in which he would have spoken, 'is of incalculable importance to the faithful here. They are simple people, easily influenced. Relatives returning from employment in the Gulf try to convert them to Islam. Hindus assail their Christianity. The Communists in the Kerala State administration teach that there is no God. It is something of a miracle that this remains the largest Christian community in the entire sub-Continent.'

Father Vaughan understood. Although his own first posting as a young missionary had been to Hyderabad, he had spent some weeks visiting Malabar and he knew the legends. The great diamond had been donated during the seventeenth century. The cross had probably been brought from central Europe via Byzantine Damascus a few years before. Personally he thought it originated from northern Italy. No matter exactly when. The history of the Thoma Christians of Malabar was complex. What mattered was that the cult and its associated miracles still held the imagination of the ordinary people: and did so to the greater glory of God, even though the diamond itself had been missing three hundred years.

'We may, some of us,' the Bishop added indulgently, 'be sceptical of some aspects of the cult . . .'

No thinking, educated, modern priest was likely to take the miracles of healing associated with the jewel at face value. Arab medical science was available to the rich in the seventeenth century and the Prince would have used it to retain his subjects' loyalty after his conversion. Was the mechanism important, Father Vaughan asked himself? The outcome had been the cult, and the cult was in no sense evil and it helped sustain the church. And now he was back at the climax of this letter.

'Nonetheless the return of the diamond would be an event of immense significance to all Christians in Malabar. This is where you can perhaps assist us. Word had reached me that a stone named the Malabar Angel is being offered in London. It may be unconnected with our church. But if it is our diamond, then somehow, through God's grace, we must secure its return.'

'How can . . .' Father Vaughan repeated, drew in his breath and shook his head again at the enormity of the task. The Malabar diamond must have been huge. Not only tradition said so: the marks left by its mount proved that it had been. Unless it was flawed, the value must be correspondingly high. How

---

14

could he or anyone else expect or persuade its present owners to give it back?

'Mary,' he said, though without enthusiasm, 'off the top of your head, do we have anyone in the diamond business among our donors?'

'They're only on the computer alphabetically and by where they live.' She thought about it. 'Anna might know.'

'Ask her, will you? I must read those Sudan project papers.'

Father Vaughan's job was running the Catholic Children's Relief Agency from a London office where enthusiasm constantly threatened to generate confusion yet from which aid flowed weekly, sometimes daily, to the children of the very poor in Africa and Asia. Before the Bishop's letter came he had been wrestling with a tricky question. Could a Catholic organisation operate in a Muslim country like Sudan? The snags were legion. They always were. That was why CCRA existed: to succeed where governments wouldn't even try. He turned his attention back to the Sudanese proposal.

'This project will provide immunisation for 25,000 children under five during the start-up period of three years . . .' A drop in the ocean of African humanity. Snag one: they'd have to send nuns to organise the programme. Male field workers were unacceptable working with young mothers in a Muslim country. Snag two: where could they recruit the nuns? Snag three . . .

At the moment he couldn't think straight. Reasoned analysis was dislocated by memories of that one unforgettable stay in Malabar and his old friendship with Peter Varishnan, now Peter Malabar, the Bishop. Peter, his senior by nine years, had been his mentor in his first vast parish in Hyderabad. Peter had taken him down south on that memorable trip. They still exchanged letters every Christmas. Peter was intelligent, compassionate and devout enough to have been consecrated a bishop at thirty-six. He might yet be elected to the College of Cardinals. How could his request be refused?

To his relief Mary returned, enabling him to put aside the Sudan project papers.

'We have a generous donor called Mrs. Luttrell. She lives in Wiltshire. Anna's pretty sure her husband is in the art business. That's as near as we can get.'

Luttrell. Lucy Luttrell? Could they be the same Luttrells he'd known as a boy, one of the staunchest West country Catholic families? Hadn't her father been an art dealer of some sort? A very up-market one, true, the kind whose firm ranked with Agnews or Colnaghi. He'd grown up with people like the Luttrells and recently, for the sake of the charity, he'd been renewing such contacts.

'Let's have a look at *Who's Who*,' he said, 'and check the addresses.'

Ten minutes later he dictated two letters. One was to Lucy Luttrell, the other his answer to Peter Malabar. He could promise nothing. But he would try.

While he was signing them, Mary's curiosity got the better of her. 'Father Gerry,' she asked, 'would having a diamond back mean so much to them? I mean, nowadays wouldn't a church rather have cash?'

He put down his pen and leant back in his chair to look at her. This was a question everyone he approached was bound to come up with.

'Money's very seldom a substitute for something treasured, is it? Say you're burgled. You lose your grandmother's ring. She gave it you for your twenty-first birthday. Can the insurance really replace it?'

'It's not quite the same.' She was still incredulous. 'You mean they'd put it back in the cross?'

'If they weren't going to, the Bishop would never have written. Asking for money instead would be no more than a refined begging stunt.'

'Wouldn't it just get stolen again?'

'Someone might try. I wouldn't care to be caught in the act myself, though. They take a very unchristian view of thieves down there.' He glanced directly at her. 'If the history is even half true, people killed in the past to defend that stone and they certainly killed to get it. Diamonds are not renowned for bringing out the best in people, whatever the advertisements may say.'

When she went home that evening Mary told the story to her mother, who always claimed that Father Vaughan must suffer from inner conflicts. She was into them in the way her neighbours were into yoga or health foods. A priest like him, she would insist, committed to celibacy and surrounded by attractive girls in the office all day, then going back to that house he shared with other priests! It was against human nature! He must suffer from conflicts.

'Well, he'll have his job cut out trying to get a diamond back,' she commented now.

'He's terribly determined,' Mary said, 'whatever you say. He has one of those silly mottoes on his desk. "The possible we did yesterday. The impossible we do tomorrow." He really likes a challenge.'

'Just like I told you. Inner conflicts, dear. He's trying to resolve inner conflicts.'

Chapter

4

The great rectangular diamond hung as a pendant from the centre of a magnificent necklace, itself formed of eighty-one diamonds, all mounted in white gold. James Constant, chief jewelry expert at Burnaby's auction house in London, had placed it over a black velvet–covered stand, shaped like a woman's neck. The linked brilliants sparkled in the strong overhead light, while the 1.5-inch-long central stone glowed and sulked on the velvet, as if wanting to lie on the creamy flesh between a real woman's breasts.

'A superb stone,' Constant remarked. He gently detached the pendant from the necklace to examine it through a chunky chromium mounted loupe, standing absorbed by the task, his concentration exuding expertise. 'It can only come from Golconda.'

Although Constant enjoyed such an English name and could invariably pass for an Englishman, especially in a hand-stitched Savile Row suit, his dark hair and olive skin derived from more exotic ancestry. His Lebanese father had been a diamond manufacturer in Antwerp before the war, who had fled the Nazis and never returned, eventually adopting the most reliable-sounding English name he could think of and settling down to business in London's traditional jewelry area of Hatton Garden. His mother was French. After an apprenticeship with

Cartier in Paris, he was now Burnaby's leading jewelry appraiser and auctioneer.

This morning Constant was intent on securing business, extremely valuable business. Two women, seated on the gilded French Empire chairs furnishing this private viewing room, were listening to his appraisal. Both were silent, though for very different reasons.

One was a fragilely attractive English blonde in her mid-thirties, who was a consultant to Burnaby's. Her name was Samantha Seebohm, and she stayed quiet because she was waiting in suspense for the reactions of her friend to Constant's evaluation. Her friend was the owner of this magnificent diamond, known as the Malabar Angel, and Samantha stood to gain very substantially if she agreed to sell it through them.

The owner, Helene von Brandenburg, was of a similar age, but fuller faced, handsomely strong featured and with long hair bleached blond only by the sun. Of the two, she was the more relaxed, sitting with one leg over the other, her expression dispassionate, saying nothing as if preferring to distance herself from a distasteful procedure.

'Without question a Golconda diamond,' Constant repeated, still peering at it. 'The smoothness and limpidity are unmistakable.' He removed the magnifying glass and half smiled at the owner. 'Tavernier called them "white and of very beautiful water". Do you happen to know if this came from Kollur?'

'How should I know!' Helene erupted with sudden irritation. 'How can you talk as if my diamond were found yesterday? This is an heirloom of my family.'

I'm sure James isn't denigrating it in any way, Helene,' Samantha intervened nervously.

'On the contrary, Baroness. The Kollur diggings on the Krishna River in India produced the Koh-i-noor. They were the source of the world's most historic diamonds, which took their genetic name from the Kingdom of Golconda.' He allowed this praise to sink in, then added, 'Kollur last produced a diamond of any size in 1701.'

Samantha breathed more easily. For a few dreadful moments she had thought this was going to end in disaster.

Constant held out both the stone and the magnifying glass to Helene. 'You can see for yourself, Baroness. It is white-white colourless and with a special fluidity. That is why we say the river runs through it. And why it was a subtle compliment for your ancestor to attach it to a rivière of brilliants.'

'My father did always tell me it was made into a pendant soon after it came into our family.' Mollified, Helene accepted the loupe and gazed at the diamond with conflicting feelings. Did she seriously wish to sell this last family possession? On the other hand, if Samantha was only half right about the value, could she afford not to? One of her problems was that because she was titled and travelled the world her friends—and the media—assumed she was rich. In fact her jet-setting was done on discount tickets and she seldom paid for a meal herself. Why should she? She had personality enough to be welcome anywhere. But it was degrading to be always short of cash.

'Look at the way your diamond is cut,' Constant went on. 'It is quite rectangular, as one would treat an emerald, probably because that was the heaviest shape they could obtain from the rough stone. Three hundred years ago they cut to keep the most weight, not to create a perfect shape. They hadn't developed the geometrically designed facets that reflect light within a diamond, although I should say this was recut in the nineteenth century. Originally it was much larger.'

Oh God, Samantha thought, be careful, James! Don't blow it. If you'd been at school with Helene you'd know how easily she explodes.

However, Helene remained equable, sounding almost impressed. 'That is correct. It was for my great-grandmother, my several times grandmother. The Angel was a present for her when she married and she wore it at the famous ball before the Battle of Waterloo. You know, the Duchess of Richmond's Ball.'

'And before it came into your family?' Constant's probing was careful, never implying anything so ugly as purchase. 'It's always useful to know the history.'

'The Angel was from the family of an Indian prince in Malabar.' She made a tiny dismissive gesture, as if her interest could not be expected to extend so far back. 'How should it have such a name otherwise?'

'It is certainly unusual. You don't know which prince?'

'There were thousands of princes in India!'

'There were indeed.' Cartier had continued selling to them

right up until the Second World War. Constant knew far more about princely jewelry than it was relevant to mention now: more than enough to be curious about this diamond's original ownership. The Kingdom of Golconda had been within the Moghul Empire and the Moghuls were Muslims, hardly likely to call a jewel an "Angel". Not that this would matter, provided the Baroness's title to the stone was good. 'We like to compile as complete a provenance as possible before a sale,' he explained smoothly. 'It can greatly improve the result.'

'And so'—Helene cut straight through to the reality of this discussion—'what is my diamond worth?'

'Do you have a gemological certificate, by any chance?'

'Why should we need a certificate for what we have owned two hundred years?'

'But you had a valuation for insurance?'

'How do you insure such a thing!' Helene laughed bitterly. 'You must be a millionaire to pay the premium.'

'I'm afraid we could not put it up for sale without a certificate from the Gemological Institute of America.' Constant had observed a blemish in the stone and could guess how this woman would react to hearing about it from him. But she would not be able to argue with the Gemological Institute.

'Sure.' She dismissed this bureaucratic nonsense. 'So we will get that. But what is the value?'

'Without a GIA report I don't like to commit myself.' He picked up the stone again and examined it, not because he needed to, but to give an impression of doubt. 'The colour grading—or rather colourlessness—is excellent. Internally I should say it is flawless. Externally . . .' He hesitated discreetly. 'Well, as you say it is an heirloom and any jewel becomes a little damaged with wear, even a diamond. Additionally, there is what we call a "natural" on the girdle.'

'I do not understand. We have always been told the stone is perfect.'

'A "natural" is a tiny part of the diamond's original dull coating which has not been polished off, usually to avoid spoiling the shape around the widest section, the girdle.'

'I have never noticed this.'

'Only an expert would, Baroness. Whether it constitutes a flaw is a matter of opinion.'

'And so what is the value? How often must I ask?'

Samantha felt her stomach muscles tighten. Last week in the course of persuading Helene to sell she'd quoted a few enticing figures, like the $140,000 a carat Christie's had recently achieved with a 52-carat diamond. She had risked oversimplifying the matter of valuation because she was sure that once they had her in Burnaby's building either James or Charles Luttrell, the Chairman, would win her round. Now she could see a tenseness in her friend's expression which promised fireworks if the answer was not what she'd been led to expect.

Constant saw it too, realised that Samantha might have quoted all the record auction prices in order to ensnare the client and instantly raised the figure in his mind to the maximum he dared. He had intended expressing certainty over a low figure. Instead he did the opposite.

'A great deal will depend on the GIA certificate. If they give it the third grading of flawlessness, I should hope for eighty to a hundred thousand dollars a carat. Perhaps four and a half or five million dollars.'

'Four and half only!' Helene turned on Samantha, furious. 'What is he saying, four? You were talking about seven million. Seven!'

'Please.' Constant became soothing, horrified at how far Samantha must have gone. Too greedy for her own commission, that was the problem. Charles ought to keep her in check. 'I must emphasise, Baroness, that we have to be conservative. It is more difficult for an old diamond, even one as historic as yours, to set records.'

'And next I suppose you tell me the necklace itself has no value!'

'Realistically, around thirty thousand dollars.' Constant could only see trouble ahead if he was not honest. 'But you should never sell it separately. It is part of the heirloom, part of the history.'

'That is true.' Helene was partially satisfied, until her inflamed imaginings broke through again. 'But if you think I sell my inheritance for peanuts, you are crazy.'

'Why don't you talk to Charles?' Samantha was only just able to contain her own irritation. 'He's the expert in creating public interest.' Damn Charles! He'd briefed her, once they'd confirmed that Helene had inherited the diamond. He'd sworn that all they had to do was string her along until they were ready to sign a contract, and Helene would be so keyed up to becoming a millionaire in cash instead of fiction that she would be unable to back out. Then they could erode her expectations so that the auction reserve was set at an attainable level. Why hadn't he alerted James? And why was James being so damned cool about it all? She could throttle the pair of them! 'I know Charles would like to meet you. Shall I call his office?'

'Maybe that is a good idea. I like to ask him myself.'

Three minutes later Charles Luttrell was with them, impressive as an ambassador with his thick greying hair, erect stance and courteous urbanity. As always he wore a red carnation in the buttonhole of a hand-tailored double-breasted suit. Erect was the word, Samantha thought, remembering him naked and randy on so many mornings. That's all over now, she reminded herself. Over, with no going back.

'This is a great pleasure, Baroness. I've heard so much about you.' He took her hand and raised it just close enough to his lips to display faultless German manners, instantly defusing the tension. 'So this is the famous Malabar Angel.' He stooped to admire the jewel. 'Well, I hope young James here hasn't been denigrating what is self-evidently a magnificent diamond.'

'I do think he is undervaluing it.' Helene was placated in spite of herself, though remaining detached enough to reflect that it was no wonder Samantha used to have problems with him.

'Without a certificate I prefer to be cautious,' Constant remarked, responding by edging his estimate upwards. 'I have suggested in the region of five million.'

Charles nodded, apparently evaluating this expert wisdom, while Helene's eyes made their own evaluation of him. If we could feed these crosscurrents into the grid, Samantha thought, we'd light up London. Furthermore, she caught enough of the look Constant was giving Charles to recognise the warning it contained.

'Five million is too little.' Helene insisted.

'I fear my colleague may be right, Baroness.' Charles had picked up the unspoken message. 'You can never be sure. Sotheby's have achieved three and a half million for a thirty-two carat emerald-cut diamond. But there are no guarantees in the saleroom. However,' he beamed at her, full of confidence, 'a lineage such as yours will always carry conviction. Nobility in the ownership and, if possible, romantic associations. The Duchess of Windsor's sale was the ultimate example. We also need plenty of time to generate serious interest.'

'You mean I must decide already?'

'Not immediately.' Charles's bedside manner would have done credit to a Harley Street doctor. 'But soon. We are now in June. This would be eminently suitable for our big October sale in New York—no really important jewelry can be offered any-where else—and even in these days of instant communications the lead time . . .' He smiled apologetically, a model of the patrician reluctantly harnessing technology to the cause of art. 'Frankly we ought to allow the full four months.'

'I cannot possibly agree that price.' Helene's aggression was returning.

'My dear lady, you do not have to. A reserve, eventually, yes. But there is a lot to do before then.'

'I do still like to think about this some more.'

Charles spread his hands in a gesture of generosity. 'There is no need to rush our fences.'

'Could we keep the stone overnight to make a more detailed examination?' Constant asked.

'That is necessary?'

'It will be safe in our strong room, I assure you.'

'I can bring it back to you myself tomorrow,' Samantha offered. Anything to smooth things along.

'What is twenty-four hours, after all?' Helene stood up decisively. 'Now I have a lunch. Can someone find me a taxi.'

While Samantha escorted her downstairs to the Albemarle Street entrance Luttrell turned to Constant, his manner com-pletely altered.

'Something you don't like, eh, James? Out with it, then.'

Constant picked up the diamond again, letting it lie in the palm of his hand.

'Tavernier mentioned having seen a cushion-cut diamond of eighty-nine carats which belonged to one of the Moghul princes, who gave it to a church when he was converted to Christianity. He was later executed for his apostasy. The diamond disap-peared. I think this could be it. Recut, of course.'

'In which case we have a major discovery!'

'If the Baroness can prove her ownership.'

Charles gazed at his subordinate with near incredulity. 'My dear fellow. We need hardly let that kind of detail worry us. Her family have had it two-hundred years, for heaven's sake. We need a serious coup for New York. This will make magnificent publicity. We must have Czernowski in on this.' Prince Czernowski was a public relations consultant whom they hired for the most important sales. 'What do you suppose it'll fetch?'

'Three million. Three and a half if we're lucky.'

'Well, don't tell her that until after she's signed a contract. For an auctioneer, dear boy, you have far too many scruples.' He winked at Constant delightedly. 'Can't be your ancestry, can it?'

Chapter

5

T h e y released her from the Stammheim maximum security prison ahead of schedule, at six on a clear June morning, after rousing her at dawn.

'No photographers this time, Nachtigal,' the wardress remarked with cold venom. 'The papers forgot you long ago, anyway!' She reckoned Nachtigal was a bad type whatever anyone said, despite the remission for good behaviour. The authorities must feel the same. Why else would they be freeing her early and at this hour? To make certain there was no publicity, that was why. No demonstrators and no TV cameras, just a soul-dampening ejection into deserted and unfamiliar streets. 'Down that way' she pointed, 'there's a bus stop. Take you into Stuttgart.'

So Ilse Nachtigal was left standing outside in the chilly air, wearing the cheap cotton dress they'd provided, her scuffed old suitcase dumped on the ground, recalling the wardress's directions and wondering whether to follow them or not. No one would be meeting her, that was a certainty. She hadn't known she was being let out herself until last night.

However, as the heavy gate crunched shut behind her it was the thought that she could now enjoy proper coffee that mattered most. Stupid. Despicably bourgeois. But compulsive. For eight years and thirty-two days her prison routine had started with a tasteless brew and black bread. Lately, as the days and weeks she crossed out on the cell wall calendar multiplied, she had begun to dream of fresh, strong coffee. Fresh coffee and the crisp, white rolls called *Brötchen*, spread with butter and jam, leisurely consumed at a table in the sun. So she stood outside the prison, hesitating, unexpectedly demoralised by being alone, wondering if a decent café would be open at this hour of the morning in such a godforsaken town.

'Ilse!' A woman's voice, a familiar voice.

She looked around, confused. There was not a soul in sight. Just a few cars parked in an orderly line down the street some distance off, all well away from the forbidding prison entrance. Then she realised the door of a black Mercedes was opening, a portly woman laboriously getting out. The woman hoisted herself upright, one hand on the driver's door.

'*Ilse, mein Liebling. Ich bin hier.*' A trembling voice, unsure, fearful. The once-loved voice of her mother.

Suddenly she felt trapped. The coffee, the *Brötchen*, the table in the sun, the things that had been associated in her mind with freedom, crazy as it was to expect them here and now, all evaporated.

'Ilse!'

She strained to see if her father was inside the car, but could not. Her mother started walking towards her, slowly, inexorably, arms outstretched in nervous welcome. She was wearing a cream-coloured summer coat, fully buttoned up. It bulged over her bosom and belly. She swayed slightly as she walked. As she came closer Ilse could see how lined her face had become: an old fat hausfrau with a silly smile, for all the world like a cream-coated hippopotamus. Why hadn't she visualised her as that years ago? It was so obvious! Maybe prison had clarified her perceptions.

The hippo stopped a couple of metres short of its quarry, breathing heavily from either exertion or emotion.

'You needn't have come, Mama.' Ilse spoke with all the composure she could manage, furious at being cornered, forgetting that up to this moment she had no plan beyond finding a café and then a telephone. 'I'd have been all right.'

Then she burst into tears, standing sobbing beside her battered suitcase in front of the jail until she let this waddling mother, who since she had become grown up had not understood one iota of what was passing through her mind, embrace her, kiss her and lead her back to the car.

Her father was not there, thankfully. But Ilse was nonetheless so unnerved that when they drove away from the jail she forgot to give any parting salute to the martyrs who had died in Stammheim and elsewhere: to Andreas and Ulrike and Holger and the others, the founding generation of the Red Army Fraction whose suicides she had never quite had the courage to follow. Twenty minutes later, as the Mercedes purred through the early traffic towards the autobahn, she remembered and was ashamed.

The journey was like an awakening from death. The blue and white autobahn signs prodded at her past, fingering memories all the way: Mannheim, Frankfurt, Wiesbaden. At the Koblenz turnoff they descended from the rolling countryside into the Rhine Valley, to cross the river, pass through the ancient town and take the twisting left bank route towards the home she loathed.

'It's so beautiful in summer,' her mother remarked lightly, hoping for some response. They had a view of the Rhine from their house—and that put the seal on the value of any property in the hilly southern suburbs of Bad Godesberg. What was more, their 'bit of ground', as her father called it with self-depreciating satisfaction, included a small vineyard, proving that the Nachtigals were a family of substance. 'You always liked this part of the river, didn't you?'

Ilse thought of the steamer trip past the castles and vineyards during which she and Horst had conceived the assassination that went wrong. They'd playacted his picking her up, then sat by themselves on a quiet part of the deck. Could they have been overheard? She might never know. But the pigs had used the new law to search his apartment—the same controversial law her father had welcomed in a TV interview—and shot him dead when he made a break for it.

'I never want to see the river again,' she said.

After that her mother made no more conversational attempts until they were in the driveway of the solidly built, imposing 1907 villa that Erwin Nachtigal had bought from the profits of his law partnership.

'Please, Ilse, remember something. Your papa loves you every bit as much as I do. He's just not good at'—she fumbled, knowing how apprehensive he had been—'at expressing emotions. But he telephoned Stammheim every day to find out when you were going to be . . . leaving.'

Scared stiff of what I might do next, most likely, Ilse thought. During the journey she had become more and more resentful at having allowed herself to be hijacked on her first day of freedom. And not even by secret servicemen: by her parents, this pair of bourgeois hippopotami, thick skinned and ambivalent, who pretended they'd always been the soul of virtue themselves. Well, she conceded, her mother might have been innocent. She was only seventeen when the Nazis were overthrown.

'I'll be as nice to him as he is to me' she said and got out of the car, just as her father opened the front door.

'*Meine liebste Ilse.*' He stood rotund and dark suited at the top of the stone steps. 'Welcome home.'

But his eyes were cautious, the words didn't ring true, he didn't hold out his arms to embrace her and the impression of falsity was reinforced by the way he stayed in the doorway. She had to walk up the steps to him and make the decision whether to kiss him or not, while her mother lumbered around behind.

'Hallo, Papa,' she said wearily, trotted up, kissed him with dry formality on the cheek and effectively forced him to move aside.

Indoors, the house appeared unchanged since she'd last seen it—the mahogany furniture gleaming; flowers in a vase on a side table beneath the ornately gilt-framed portrait of their most distinguished ancestor, Gustav Nachtigal, the nineteenth-century explorer; the mingled smells of wax floor polish and disinfectant. Everything as before: yet as unreal to her as a film set, the epitome of all she hated and wanted to destroy. She turned round to face the hippos, feeling inexplicably weak and faint.

'Your father must go to work now,' her mother said, with a decisiveness that must have been rehearsed. 'He is late already.'

'If the senior partner does not set an example . . .' His bulk was framed in the doorway, as he prepared to retreat. 'Until this evening, *Liebchen.*'

She groped for a chair and sat down. Why should she feel so deflated by his immediately going off? He'd only visited her in jail once. She'd refused to be repentant and he never came again.

'Are you feeling all right?' Her mother hovered. 'What would you like, dearest? Coffee? Torte? Something more substantial? Come through to the kitchen. I'll make it for you myself.'

She came close to refusing the coffee, because having it here betrayed the dream. Then the fragrance as the beans were ground overwhelmed her and she collapsed at the scrubbed pine table and burst into tears again.

'There, there, my darling. It's all behind you now. You'll forget all the awful things in time. What we have to do is get you healthy and strong again, don't we?' Her mother humped down beside her, putting a clumsily affectionate arm round her shoulder. 'It may take a little while, but we'll do it, don't worry!' She babbled on as if Ilse were fifteen not thirty-eight, brought her tissues, gently nudged her into drinking the coffee. She talked as if relieved that it was all coming out at last, like a bad go of fever. She'd been afraid her daughter would be as curt and composed as during those terrible prison visits, when they faced each other through a reinforced glass panel and wardresses listened to every word. The relief made her hardly notice that her daughter was saying very little and when she wanted to rest, she laboriously helped her upstairs.

Then came the most demoralising shock so far. Ilse had expected to be sleeping in her usual room, the bedroom that was hers as a girl. She had supposed a few of her old things might be around somewhere, if they hadn't been cleared out as junk. What she had never anticipated was finding every item of those possessions precisely as she had left them when she 'dropped out of the rat race' after university. The ornaments and stuffed toys she had adored as a teenager, the school photographs, the stiffly posed and reluctant graduation portrait with her parents, even her old hairbrushes and lipsticks—they were all there.

'You see'—her mother was becoming tearful too—'I always kept it for you. I always knew you would come home one day.'

Eventually the chattering and fussing stopped and Ilse was able to close the door and look around in renewed bewilderment. What had been in their minds, for God's sake! This was like the faithfully preserved room of a child who had been kidnapped or fallen into a coma: a museum of her early life! She wanted to break it up, to exorcise the pathetic hopes it represented.

Searching for a weapon, she actually had an old-fashioned cut-glass scent bottle in her hand and was poised to start with the graduation picture when something about her mother's words came back. "I always kept it . . . I always knew . . ." Not "we". Her stupid, devoted, mother must have fought to save this room. It was mad, it was an insult to her maturity and intelligence, but it rekindled a spark of affection. And it emphatically demanded solidarity against the Fascist pig, her father. She put the bottle down again, stripped off the cheap dress and went to lie on the bed, not even bothering to remove the coarse prison underclothes. She felt exhausted and defeated and tried to tell herself this was only because she'd been roused at four-thirty that morning.

When she woke it was afternoon. While she slept the suitcase from Stammheim had been silently placed on a stand. Some of the few clothes it contained dated from before her arrest. She decided to burn the lot. Hanging in the closet was her once favourite dressing gown, of brushed purple wool with a wide collar trimmed with braid. It had been cleaned and was still in protective cellophane. She ripped that off and felt the gown's softness, before undressing completely and slipping it over her bare shoulders, knowing instinctively that this moment was some kind of turning point.

The gown had always been luxuriously comfortable. Compared to prison clothes it was unbelievable. She began to feel like a person again, like someone of free will, like the student who'd enrolled with such enthusiasm for philosophy classes at the university all those years ago, when the world was hers. But accepting all the gown stood for had a price. Could she even pretend to be returning home, badly though she needed a place to live, not to mention the money her parents would provide?

Clutching the gown around her, she went down the wide, thickly carpeted corridor to the bathroom, where for almost an hour she lay in the hot water, letting the feel and smell of the last nine years soak away. She shampooed her hair and then, only then, with considerable trepidation, performed a ritual that prison conditions had made impossible, which indeed she had all but abandoned when she was living with Horst in the Düsseldorf 'squat'. She stood naked in front of a long mirror and asked herself how her body looked.

In jail you could only truly discover what femininity you had left by watching the warders' eyes. God, how she despised them: the ultimate capitalist lackeys. She'd lost sixty days remission because she spat at one who tried to touch her, and it had been worth every minute extra. The lovely, hate-propelled gob of sputum had hit him full on the cheek and dribbled to his collar before he could mop it up. She'd immediately challenged him to strike her, hoping for a double victory. But his nerve failed and all he did was shout out *'Verfluchte Drecksau'*. and hurry off to lay the accusation.

Well, she asked the reflection, what kind of face and body was she left with at thirty-eight, after eight years and thirty-two days of incarceration, not counting six months of being remanded in custody? Would Horst still say she was beautiful? She felt a chill as she thought of him, because of the way he was killed. She and Horst could never be repeated: they had such an incredible fusion of passion and commitment. Perhaps to him she really had been beautiful.

At twenty-one she'd been a vivacious, attractive brunette, quite capable of turning men's heads in a small town like Bad Godesberg. Socially acceptable too, which mattered. *'Aus einem guten Haus'* the phrase was: well educated, middle class, comfortably well off. The Düsseldorf apartment squat, with all the tension of the others not knowing there were weapons under the floorboards, had brought the first deterioration. Jail had done the rest.

She examined her face, close up in the mirror. Her complexion had become dull and sallow, her neck wrinkled, her eyes dark pouched. She looked horrifyingly middle aged. Where was the "inner radiance" that Horst used to rave about? She tried holding her lank, wet hair up behind her with one hand, turning her head this way and that, lifting her jaw to stretch the skin. With a proper hairdo, with make-up, could she pass for twenty eight? For her plan she would need to.

She ordered herself to be dispassionate. No, she could not pass for ten years younger. Her youth had gone. But she certainly wasn't ugly. Her features were okay: small nose, high forehead, good cheekbones, lips a little thin maybe. For once the old hippo was right. All she had to do was eat, rest and look after herself for a while. She could put thirty-one or thirty-two on a forged passport.

And her body? In prison one's flesh was a constant temptation to other women, a constant peril. Refuse toughly enough and you risked a single violent outburst. Give way and you were in for endless quarrels and fights. She had refused, ignoring the blandishments: the cigarettes and the suggestions that only sexual activity kept you sane. Her greatest fear had been that her morale might disintegrate; a gay relationship could cause it to do precisely that. Quite apart from this she was fiercely loyal to Horst's memory. So she had sought relief teaching revolutionary doctrine to anyone who cared to listen and otherwise bottled everything up, keeping her emotions to herself. She knew the strain of that discipline had paid off. But she had been able to do less to safeguard her appearance.

She cupped her breasts in her hands. They were still quite firm. Thank God she had never been heavily bosomed like her mother. She smoothed her belly with outstretched fingers. A trifle pudgy. Bad as the food was you could put on weight inside. But the work had kept her muscles in shape, though her legs were as scrawny as ever and they needed waxing badly. 'You're afraid they're too thin,' Horst always used to say with a laugh, 'but who wants to go to bed with a mare!'

Inevitably, as she examined the fuzz of mousy hair between her legs for crab lice, she thought about the abortion. She'd wanted the baby, but Horst had been adamant. 'Later,' he insisted, 'when this is over.' If she'd known he was going to be shot . . . She never would have a baby now. It was impossible to imagine whom she might want to have one with. She realised she was shaking her head at the memory and told herself to stop, to get a grip.

The question was whether she could stomach staying here, feigning respectability, long enough to regain the energy she needed, long enough to organise what she had to do.

The mere idea of staying with her parents jolted her. Yesterday she wouldn't have contemplated it. This morning she'd felt hijacked. And now here she was, humoring her mother, putting on her old dressing gown, going back to her old room. There should be a dialectical justification! Otherwise she would be betraying Horst in the course of avenging him.

When evening came she would have preferred to excuse herself from dinner and go back to bed, if it had not become a necessity of conscience to confront her father. Her principles made it inescapable. If she didn't do it straightaway, she never would. "Marxists can only be effective by telling the truth at all times." The English militant Ted Grant had written that. Horst had often quoted him.

'So,' her father declared solemnly, when the servant had cleared away the main course and the three of them were alone at one end of the long dark oak dining table, with the crystal chandelier hanging above, with candlelight gleaming on the solid silver racehorse statue that made a proud centerpiece. 'We are prepared to forget the past, Ilse, if you will also do so.'

Typical, she thought, never something for nothing, always a bargain. Typical *verdammter* lawyer. But it was progress that this time he hadn't asked her to be penitent: and she was feeling greater warmth towards her mother. She would take matters slowly.

'The past is part of me,' she said carefully. 'It can't be cut out like an appendix.'

'*Natürlich*, darling,' her mother temporised, displaying unexpected tact. 'What your father means is you must try to forget.'

'If they'll let me.' The cynicism flooded back. 'There'll be a social worker round tomorrow or the day after, checking up. You know how they operate.'

'I'll deal with that.' Her father was dismissive. 'The police won't bother you either . . .' He paused for effect, exactly as if he were in a courtroom. . . . 'while you're with us.' The power of Bad Godesberg respectability! 'But what I want to know'—he fixed his eyes on hers—'is whether you've given up all this Trotskyist nonsense. You were led into it, I'll accept that.' Now he was addressing a juvenile offender. 'You've learnt your lesson, I imagine.'

'Erwin, please! It is her first evening home.'

'Mother, it's all right, thank you. I can answer for myself.' Ilse turned back to the Fascist beast, her temper smouldering. He hadn't dared mention her organisation. Right then, she'd remind him. 'Trotsky wanted to send the Red Army in to help our workers keep Hitler out of power. I don't expect you knew that. If he *had* done it, the world would have been spared all the nightmares of fascism and Hitlerism.'

Her father's face flushed. 'That's irrelevant and you know extremely well it is. The Hitler days were long over in 1945. Why does your generation keep harking back to them?'

'Because we cannot accept that your generation was so reluctantly led.' She spoke matter-of-factly, masking her surprise at his walking straight into the trap, shrugging her shoulders, as if to add, Deny that you were a Nazi!

'I decline to continue such a discussion!' He slammed his fist on the table, making the racehorse rock on its plinth and the specially lit candles splutter. 'Your mother and I worked like slaves to recover from the war, we slaved to afford this house, we gave you the best of everything. My God, what do we find we have raised! A Communist, a terrorist, an accessory to the attempted murder of a leading banker! God give me patience!'

Absolution, you mean, Ilse thought, absolution from having helped drag the workers into the bloodbath of Nazism, from slaughtering twenty million Russians, from the massacres of the Holocaust and the return of Europe to the worst brutality since the Middle Ages. Absolution was what capitalists like him deluded themselves they'd been granted in return for the hard labour of reconstructing Germany after the war: and they imagined their children didn't know they'd been Nazis! Well, they were wrong. And the Red Army Fraction was fully justified in executing the worst of them. She didn't need to say so out loud either. He knew, even if her poor affectionate waddling mother didn't.

'Ilse, please.' Her mother was sitting up as straight and agonised as her corseted fat belly allowed. 'You must apologise to your father. He has done more for you than you will ever know.'

There was total silence. Her father glared. Her mother pleaded with watery eyes. And just as she was about to walk out, to cut her losses and leave, she remembered the dialectic that any action which contributed to the triumph of working-class democracy was justified. Well, she had an action planned, didn't she? Through those long prison years she'd plotted how to avenge Horst in a way he would approve. Better still, her father would contribute by keeping the social services and police off her back while she made her preparations.

'Forgive me, Papa,' she said contritely. 'I'm a little over-wrought and tired. I think I'll go to my room.'

Chapter

6

'I should like to speak to Father Vaughan.' A peremptory, old-fashioned, county lady's voice on the telephone.

'This is his secretary.' Mary was polite but riled by the tone. 'May I say who is calling?'

'Mrs. Luttrell. Mrs. Charles Luttrell.'

'I'll just see if he's available.' She cupped her hand over the mouthpiece. 'It's that woman you wrote to about the diamond.'

'I'll take it.' That was quick, he thought. She could only have had the letter yesterday.

'Father Gerard?'

'Lucy! What a pleasure to hear from you after all these years!'

'You are the Gerard Vaughan who lived at East Knoyle?'

'The very same.'

'Extraordinary. When I saw the signature on that appeal last month ago I wondered if it could be. But the world changes so much. Where have you been?'

'In India first. Then Africa. They brought me home last winter.'

'They?'

'My Missionary Society.'

'And your family?'

'My parents are both dead, I'm afraid.'

'I'm so sorry. Time does fly.'

'And you, Lucy? Are you well?'

'Well enough. The arthritis bothers me sometimes.' She always made light of her disablement. 'But I haven't rung to talk about myself. You say you're trying to trace a diamond?'

'On behalf of a church in India. The Bishop wrote to me. Someone had alerted him that it might be up for sale.'

'Is it a named stone?'

'We knew it as the Malabar Angel. Legend says it was the size of a pigeon's egg. That might owe more to the Asian imagination than fact. But it must be pretty large, because you can still see the outline of its mount on the processional cross from which it was stolen.'

'Stolen? How wretched! Of course I'll help if I can.' She sounded both shocked and dubious. 'As I expect you know, we also own the controlling interest in an auction house. The jewelry experts there keep their ears to the ground. I'm coming up to London tomorrow. I can easily ask. Most unfortunately I have a luncheon engagement. Would you care to meet me for tea at Brown's hotel?'

'You're being more than kind.' With his free hand he opened his diary. 'I have a meeting at three. Would a quarter to five be too late?'

'Not at all.' Anticipating that his knowledge of Mayfair might be scanty, she explained the location of Brown's Hotel in Dover Street, then said goodbye with a firm caveat. 'You must understand, Father Gerard, that if this diamond was stolen a long time ago it could be very hard to recover. However, one can always try.'

'Which is all the Lord Bishop has asked me to do. He is not expecting miracles, Lucy, only human effort.'

After he had put the phone down Father Vaughan sat silent for a while. How strange it was to hear himself called "Father" by the girl he used to play tennis with as a teenager. And stranger still that this mission should bring him back into touch with people he had never expected to see again.

Mission? he asked himself. Was that the right word? Yes, it probably was. After twenty-seven years of the all-encompassing demands made on a missionary priest in the Third World, he was finding it hard to settle into a job that finished for the day when the office closed, hard to go back every evening to the suburban house which he shared with three other ordained members of the Canonbury Society who also worked in the city, as religious and social counsellors. They all found the Society's headquarters out near Hertford, where they would normally be expected to live, too far out for sensible commuting. They were all happy to work whatever hours God demanded of them, and they all sorely missed the twenty-four-hours-a-day commitment of a priest's work abroad. Yes, Father Vaughan decided, he did have the time and the need for an additional mission in his life.

Chapter

7

The staff entrance of the Park Plaza was on East 61st Street, an eight-minute trot up Fifth Avenue from the 53rd Street subway stop, past the horse-drawn buggies lined up on the corner of 59th and the Park, away from the hot and windy chasm of midtown Fifth Avenue and out to a sense of space, trees and sunlight.

Unlike many lesser rivals, the Park Plaza deserved its name. Overlooking Central Park, the hotel occupied a chunk of land that had been hugely valuable when it was built in the 1930s, and it had been attracting would-be developers practically ever since. Luckily for the staff, the proprietor was a privately controlled corporation whose family members were proud to own one of the city's landmark institutions. They had modernised it in the early 1980s, yielding to fashion by designating the most exclusive upper floors of its forty stories the "Park Plaza Towers", but keeping the character of its old, rather ornate, public rooms. Most importantly, from Craig Clifford's point of view, they valued their management and preferred to promote from within. So he felt confident about what he could achieve.

The notices inside the staff entrance were in both English and Spanish. They reminded people of routines for emergencies or fire, as well as to collect their keys and make the obligatory change into staff clothing. But after Craig punched his card at the timekeeper's office and took his pass keys he just hung up his Burberry and put away the old shoes he'd worn for the commute, substituting more expensive, better-polished ones. The discreetly checked sport jacket and well-pressed slacks he already had on were his working clothes. On this swing shift, as the 4:00 P.M. to midnight evening stint was colloquially known, hotel guests would be shedding business suits and going out to restaurants or theatres. He aimed to look like one of them himself.

Craig took over his duties from his predecessor in the security office adjacent to the Park Plaza's main lobby, a room fitted with numerous video screens showing what was going on at various key points of the hotel and with its own access to the staff entrance. He read through the Incident Book, received a quick briefing and after twenty minutes was in the impressively vast space of the lobby itself. This would be his responsibility tonight, and one made distinctly more enjoyable by the Assistant Front Office Manager on duty being Barbara Andrews.

Barbara did wear a uniform: black pumps, a neat blue coat and skirt with a small gilt nametag pinned to the coat's lapel, a white blouse made less severe by a lacy frill at the neck. As he walked up to her, Craig thought she looked pretty good in the uniform, even though it was reminiscent of a stewardess's. But it wasn't her neatness that always caught at some nerve inside him. It was that clear, open face of hers, a face that didn't need make-up to look fresh and attractive. She had a generous mouth, only faintly touched with lipstick, and her eyes weren't calculating like Julia's. They were honest, intelligent, straightforward hazel eyes that seemed to say, Okay. This is what I am. I don't fool around, so please don't fool around with me. They didn't say it unpleasantly either—just naturally.

'Nice to see you,' Craig said. 'Anything much happening?'

Barbara was one of half a dozen assistants responsible to the Front Office Manager for controlling the room occupancy of the Park Plaza and a host of lesser details. The Front Office was the clearing house for the hotel: poor forecasting could result in overbooking. Celebrities might dislike the suites they were allocated. Honeymoon couples had to be sent welcome baskets of fruit or flowers. Complainers had to be humored. So her desk was prominently situated in the lobby, next to one of the white marble columns and looking directly across the reception area. Concealed in the desktop were a computer terminal and screen, which she usually operated standing up. It was easier to stay standing, both because it improved her view and because hotel guests were constantly approaching her with queries. The job wasn't designed for people with bad feet, but what hotel job ever was?

'Nothing much so far.' She smiled—a quick easy smile towards someone she'd enjoyed being on duty with before. Craig Clifford was refreshingly unlike the macho security stereotype. She'd heard he used to be in the Marine Corps, which was hardly a plus in her eyes, except that you could at least rely on marines being men. He'd knocked around, that was clear, yet he didn't seem to have any rough edges; and he had a nicely understated sense of humour. The truth was she couldn't quite make him out: and that intrigued her. 'Pretty much as usual today,' she remarked. 'Except Gloria Grace is due any minute. She'll cause mayhem if she can.'

'The old movie star?' He grinned. 'Takes me back.'

'Too far. Could be why she's always on such an ego trip.'

As they exchanged information a passerby could have mistaken Craig for a guest chatting up an attractive member of the staff: except that apart from those initial smiles neither looked at the other. They were too concerned with what was going on. This was one of the busiest times of the hotel day, when a high proportion of guests checked in. People were milling past. With jewelry shops, restaurants and public rooms all leading off the lobby, the area needed a lot of supervision. Handbag thiefs and prostitutes were only two of the nuisances.

After five years here Barbara had acquired an instinct about guests' behaviour. It was an instinct which her tutors at Cornell had warned her even the best university hotel management programme could never instil: and it was vital to success in the business. A good hotel manager never rested from observing and correcting minor details. Barbara was ambitious and she kept her eyes open all the time.

'Uh-oh,' she said suddenly, as a small procession came in from the Fifth Avenue doorways. 'What did I tell you? Lady Trouble has arrived.'

Surrounded by hangers-on, flashbulbs flickering, an over

made-up middle-aged woman, wearing a wide-brimmed white hat over long, flaming henna red hair was making an entrance. Her black silk dress clung to curves that were no longer voluptuous but simply fat and she glittered like a Christmas tree with jewelry: rings that caught the light as she waved her hands in theatrical gestures, a walnut-sized heart-shaped diamond brooch on her bosom, solitaire diamonds in her ears.

'Enough rocks to sink a ship,' Craig muttered. 'Are they real?'

'The biggest since Diamond Lil. Her hobby's finding men rich enough to buy them, even though she's a millionaire herself. I hope to God the champagne's ready in her suite.' She touched keys on her computer and scanned the details presented on the screen. 'Well, it's on the list.'

The entourage came to a halt in the middle of the reception area and a short, stout man in a dove grey suit that was almost as close-fitting as the star's dress detached himself and came across to Barbara.

'Miss Grace's keys, Mr. Boardman,' she said before he could speak and handed over a crisp white envelope. 'Suite twenty-three in the Towers as usual. We all wish you a very pleasant stay.'

'Hope you have orchids there this time. The right lousy orchids. Venezuelan orchids.' There was nothing conciliatory in Mr. Boardman's nasal tone. 'And I hope the wine's on ice. Miss Grace likes things done her way, understand?'

'If you need anything at all, Mr. Boardman, just call me.' Barbara smiled sweetly and gave him a card. 'We're privileged to have Miss Grace at the Park Plaza. Let me show you to the elevator.'

'Who's the heavy?' Craig asked when Barbara returned. 'I wouldn't mind having him for target practice.'

'Her press agent. Rumor is he has to pay the photographers to show up these days. Next thing she'll have a photo-call in her suite. And if one single thing is out of place . . . Zaroom! She's a bitch. Just wait.'

The phone on her desk shrilled. She took the call, then turned to him, slightly surprised. 'For you. It's Mr. Trevinski.'

'Clifford?' The voice was incisive, an archetypal police officer's voice. 'How are ya fixed tomorrow? I want you at a meeting.'

'No problem, sir.' Except that Julia would tear her hair out. Or his.

'Concerns an event you're gonna be responsible for. Some limey is hiring the Grand Ballroom for a jewelry auction. Millions of dollars worth. Security's gotta be hot.'

'What time d'you want me, sir?'

'Nine. You live in New Jersey, don't ya?'

'That's correct, sir.'

'No point going home. Have Miss Andrews fix a room.'

Although relieved at being spared the 1:00 A.M. bus trip, Craig knew just how Julia would react. Too bad. He must have shrugged his shoulders subconsciously, because Barbara noticed.

'Bad news?' she asked.

'Not exactly. Trevinski wants me here tomorrow morning. You're to give me a room. I guess I can tell you now. As of Monday I'm being named his Assistant Director.'

'Well, congratulations! That's great. That's really great.' Her enthusiasm was unaffected and spontaneous. 'I'd heard a rumor.'

'I preferred to keep it quiet. Who knows, they could have fired me instead!'

'Let's see.' She was consulting the computer. 'Can't allocate you the presidential suite tonight. Unfortunately it's taken. How about a room on the sixteenth facing the park? A give-away at only two seventy-five excluding room service and taxes.'

'Sounds fine to me.'

'Then it's yours. Compliments of the house.' She smiled again and tapped the keys. 'The simplest booking I ever made. What a pity you have to work. You should be celebrating.'

'I guess there's time enough.' He hesitated for a second. 'Say, would you like a quick drink later?'

'I don't finish until midnight.'

'Neither do I. Don't see how either of us can have a drink before.' No alcohol during duty shifts was a strictly enforced rule.

'Isn't that a little late?' All the old alarms began ringing in her brain. A guy as decent looking and straight as him was certain to be married. Why start something she couldn't carry on? Then

44

she saw the disappointment in his face. 'Maybe. Let's talk around nine. See how the evening's shaping up.'

The phone claimed her attention again. Craig could hear a strident voice shouting down the line, which he thought he recognised as the press agent's.

'I have to go.' Barbara shook her head and laughed. 'I told you that lady was trouble. She says the orchids aren't genuine Venezuelan. See you later.'

Chapter
8

'Listen, Sam,' Helene von Brandenburg was saying in her emphatic, slightly accented English, 'if I do sell the Malabar Angel I want enough that is worthwhile, for God's sake. It is one of the great historic diamonds in the world, after all.'

The two women were in Helene's studio, a long high room illuminated by a skylight and littered with travel mementoes and the bric-a-brac of a painter's life. Her paint-spattered overalls lay dumped over an antique ladderback chair. Un-framed canvases hung on the walls and were stacked around the floor. The overalls were a necessity, Samantha reflected, because her works looked as though she'd thrown the paint at them instead of using a brush: which would be entirely in character.

However, art was not uppermost in either of their minds this afternoon. A few minutes ago Samantha had handed back the Malabar Angel with its necklace and fitted leather case, the top embossed with the Brandenburg coat of arms in faded gold. Already she was wishing Charles and James Constant had not made quite so much of all that Tavernier and Moghul stuff. Until yesterday Helene had valued the diamond highly, that was true. But only as an heirloom. Now she was talking as if the old Baron had bequeathed her a stone as fabled as the Koh-i-noor itself.

'Of course it will be worthwhile, Helene.' Samantha's brittle rah-rah upper-class voice underscored the 'of course'. 'Burn-aby's estimates are always conservative. If James says five million, you can be sure it'll do better. Much better, probably. Look how well we did with Michael Carlisle's bronzes! You won't be making a mistake. That I promise.'

Samantha laid on the enthusiasm as thick as she dared in the face of Helene's unpredictable temperament, almost as thick as the clotted cream they used to pile on to jam scones during teatime outings from school. Anything to bring home this deal. She dropped names unashamedly, spoke as if socially they were still in the same set: and did it with all the fervour of a friend who stood to earn herself a fat commission at the end.

'Five million dollars in the bank, instead of the bank vault, could give you some very useful extra income. Not'—she forced a tiny laugh that came out uncomfortably staccato—'that you probably need it.'

'You have to be a fool not to like money in the bank,' Helene shot back at her. 'Sure I like to have more.'

At least that was honest, Samantha thought, having to stop herself from being grotesquely envious. The moment she had read the Baron's brief obituary notice in *The Times* she had rushed to the reference books, established that the great diamond was still in the family's possession, and had Burnaby's Credit Controller run a routine credit check on Helene.

The results had been revealing. This studio, for example, was part of a house in Bloomfield Terrace, a quiet backwater street of early Victorian houses in Pimlico, not actually in Chelsea but close enough to be fashionable. A few moments ago Helene had joked that it was the best investment she had ever made. But Samantha knew it was heavily mortgaged. Gossip columnist friends—to whom she leaked items and who repaid her in kind—had confirmed that the Baroness was renowned for never paying a taxi fare or tipping a waiter. Heirloom or not, she was likely to end up selling the diamond.

Accordingly, as soon as was decently possible, Samantha had rung and invited her to lunch, ostensibly to commiserate and not even mentioning Burnaby's until Helene asked what she was doing.

'It's not as though you're ever going to wear the thing,' she urged, making a sudden error of judgement. 'You told us yesterday the insurance is crippling. Far better to have the money.'

'The Angel is not a "thing"!' Helene snapped, tossing her head angrily. 'I have told you, my great-grandmother wore it at the Duchess of Richmond's Ball. Do you know what that means?' The anger became laced with scorn. 'You English do all think Waterloo was won by Wellington. But your precious Duke was saved by our Prussian army under Blücher. My long-ago great-grandfather was there two days before. He was the liaison for Marshal Blücher. Some woman, my great-grandmother to be with him and wearing her finest jewels, after all!'

'Well, of course, the history is fantastic.' Samantha back-tracked with speed. She had to clinch this before Helene flew off to Long Island or Saint Barthélemy or wherever and left matters too late for the October auction. 'It will read marvellously in the catalogue.'

'My father would turn in his grave.'

'Why not endow scholarships for young artists in his memory?' She smiled encouragingly, suppressing her irritation at these twists and turns.

'Now you are absurd! How well does that keep the family name, for God's sake!

That *was* a point, Samantha reflected: that was *the* point. Why hadn't she thought of that before! Helene had neither brothers nor male cousins. She was the last of the von Brandenburgs, the last direct descendant of the noble line. Like Charles's wife Lucy, in a way, only more so.

'A university fellowship, then. In politics.' An inspired suggestion. Hadn't the old Baron been a politician? Not that he had been so old, actually. Suddenly she was back on the windswept playing fields of that snobby school in Gloucestershire, shaking hands with him after a hockey match—Helene had been a holy terror with a hockey stick. Yes, he had been something junior and unimportant in West German politics. 'He was a famous statesman, after all, wasn't he?"

'Moderately.' Pride fought honesty in Helene's expression. 'Yes, in Niedersachsen, that was true. In the Bundestag, they admired him too. He was a Staatssekretär at the Ministry of the Interior for several years. Yes,' she confirmed as she thought back, 'they did admire his stand against the Baader-Meinhof. He was behind some of the strongest antiterrorist laws. He had guts, my father.'

'Secretary of State! Then for heaven's sake, that's the answer.' Jubilant at her own cleverness, Samantha piled on the merits of this marvellous combination of daughterly piety and cash-flow improvement. 'You honour him and have enough left to give yourself some useful extra income. Surely he'd approve of that?' If she could have claimed the idea would save precious lives as well, she'd have done so.

'I do still like to think about it some more. In Germany the titles are different. He was not the Minister. A fellowship may be overdoing it. I think about it.'

'I promise you, Helene. When Charles says five million dollars he's being ultracautious. He is the Chairman of Burnaby's, don't forget. He can't afford to exaggerate. They might get a much higher price.' Growing annoyance shadowed Samatha's carefully casual expression. Helene really was impossible! If she was to get a percentage of her school friend's inheritance she was going to have to lay the cream on even thicker. 'D'you realise this will be the fifth largest diamond ever to be auctioned? They may easily value it as six or seven million in New York. Anyway, you can rely on Charles to get the very most. Utterly.'

'I have not noticed he is so reliable for you, my dear.'

A nasty cut, very nasty indeed. Samantha didn't blush, as she used to do when anyone attacked him. But the muscles of her throat tightened and the skin strained around her jaw as she tried to laugh off the attack.

Helene noticed and relented a little. No one likes to hear her lover abused. But if Sam went on in this way she'd be haggard before she was forty. 'I'm sorry, Sam,' she said, suddenly feeling compassionate as she remembered that her friend only came from a very middle class background and never did have much taste in men, 'I didn't mean to be bitchy.'

'That was all over long ago. Five years ago.' Samantha did her best to recover her balance. How dare Helene say such a thing! Despite the arty facade, she was the archetypal German Baroness, damn her. And it showed how long they'd been out of touch. Worse, she'd contrived to change the subject! 'He was never going to leave his wife. So I left him. That's when I

---

changed to being a consultant instead of his art historian. It's purely business now.'

Helene wondered whether to believe this. In any case there was one related illusion she emphatically did not want fostered. 'I do think also,' she began, with unaccustomed circumspection, 'if I give my diamond for you to sell through Burnaby's it should be because that is the best way and nothing more.'

'It will be. I promise.' Samantha smiled edgily, guessing exactly what Helene had not put into words, namely that she might hope to restore her relationship with Charles by bringing in such a prize. Would she, hell! If she sidled up to him like a kitten waiting to be stroked and laid five million dollars of business on the carpet at his feet he would swear he'd never ceased loving her, open champagne, give her dinner at Les Ambassadeurs and obligingly take her to bed afterwards, just as though five years had not passed. But he'd only take her for granted even more.

Charles was a complete shit. He was maturely devastating in the way some middle-aged men managed to be: and he was a brilliant dealer. Everyone in the business admired what he had achieved. A few years ago, appreciating faster than most that the auction houses were stripping away the conventional art dealers' business, he'd bought a controlling stake in Burnaby's, then a minor auction firm with no renowned speciality. He'd fired old staff, hired experts, concentrated on high-quality jewelry and objets d'art, and rapidly carved out a niche in the market. Burnaby's auctions now made record prices.

What Helene failed to understand about Charles—and maybe it was just as well—was that he only respected things he had to pay for—and was he going to pay for having her as a client. Four percent was the standard commission that consultants took for introducing business.

'If you're afraid I might be trying to do myself a bit of good with him at your expense, don't worry. That's not the way he works.'

'Then if you don't do it for love, I hope you get a good percent.'

Samantha flushed as she prepared to be economical with the truth. 'You wouldn't mind?'

'I wasn't born yesterday, for God's sake. And he charges me a low percent, I hope.'

'Listen, Helene.' Samantha swallowed nervously. A few minutes ago she'd been manoeuvring her friend into thinking more greedily about money. Now she was apprehensive that she was quite tough enough to go straight to Christie's or Sotheby's if Burnaby's didn't provide some convincing inducements. 'Why don't I have another talk with Charles? Tell him he must only charge you a specially low commission, guarantee specific levels of publicity, that sort of thing? The more he has to give away, the higher a price he'll be determined to get for you.'

And Charles *would* want to clinch this deal. Every strand of his character would drive him to. He badly needed a truly major item for Burnaby's first New York sale and he genuinely respected women with titles or strong social connections. He'd only married Lucy and adopted the Luttrell name because she stood to inherit the family firm. Furthermore, once put on his mettle, no one would be better at making the Malabar Angel the most desirable diamond in the world.

'Okay, you talk to him. If you like, I come too.'

Samantha breathed relief. That was typical. Thank God that when Helene made up her mind, she didn't hang around.

'But it must be soon. Next week Otto invites me to Southampton. There is a party for his birthday. Everyone will be there.'

'Southampton?' For a moment she was foolish enough to assume this was the south coast port where ocean liners docked.

'Long Island.' Not exactly contemptuous, though the implication was clear: they definitely did not move in the same circles anymore.

'How silly of me. Of course.' Samantha giggled like a schoolgirl and accepted the rebuke. Four percent on five million! Two hundred thousand dollars for the price of a little embarrassment! It hardly bore thinking about! She would tell Charles this evening that Helene would back out if he argued the toss on the selling percentage. He could afford to cut it to the bone for a prize like this. After all, Burnaby's also took a ten percent buyer's premium on top. He was going to do what she wanted for a change.

Chapter

9

L e t ' s not be too late, Craig.' They were outside the Park Plaza on Fifth Avenue. It was twenty-five past midnight. Barbara felt a fluttering delight that she'd agreed to go out after all, because she'd warmed to him when they first met, but she intended to call the shots herself. At this time of night even the nicest guys started to get ideas. 'Let's go someplace close. You have any favourite?' She reckoned he wouldn't, he'd usually go straight home when he finished. 'We could have asked Gregory.' The concierge at the Park Plaza, Gregory O'Dwyer, was credited with being the most knowledgeable in New York.

'Maybe I should have. Except he'd gossip, he'd be taking a cut and his kind of place might not be ours.'

'So, where shall we go?' She disregarded Craig's distaste for the concierge and almost added, 'Don't ask me where, please! I've had enough of making choices for inadequate men.'

'There's a bar called Charlie's on Park and Sixty-third. Trevinski took me there once.'

'Okay. Mr. About-to-Be-Promoted.' She disliked hanging around outside the hotel. 'Let's go to Charlie's then. On the way she remarked quasi-casually, 'Gregory has a nose for everything that's going on. You ought to get to know him.' She reckoned Craig was going to need guidance occasionally. She liked the idea of providing it.

'If you say so.' he said, and that pleased her.

Charlie's had the olde English look. Its advertisements boasted 'the atmosphere of a London gentleman's club'. Translated, this meant the room was oak panelled and hung with English sporting prints, while a few pieces of Victorian furniture stood around, including a bookcase filled with imitation-leather-bound books. The price list was appropriately top heavy. Craig chose a corner table, adorned with an electrified antique oil lamp, complete with glass chimney, and politely pulled out a chair for her to sit down.

'Seeing this place a second time,' he commented, 'maybe it's not where I'd have chosen. It's as bogus as they come. Funny that Trevinski likes it.'

'He has his hang-ups, haven't you noticed? Socially insecure, I'd say.'

'I'll watch for it. What would you like?'

'A beer would be fine. Do they have Amstel Light?'

Julia's caustic remark about celebrating with Bud kicked back in his mind.

'The hell with beer. This is a celebration. How about wine?'

'Well . . .' She could guess what the wine cost and the last thing she wanted was a whole bottle, which he might feel compelled to order. 'I'll settle for a Sea Breeze.'

'That's new to me.'

'Grapefruit juice, cranberry juice and vodka, sir.' The waiter had materialised.

'I'll stick to whisky. Bourbon on the rocks.'

'Coward!' she laughed. 'I thought Marines drank anything.' She was curious about his background and exploited the chance to probe.

'I'm retired,' he said with a touch of prickliness, then quickly apologised. 'Sorry. It's still kind of a sore subject. Medical retirement wasn't what I had in mind when I applied for the Naval Academy. I was what the grunts call a lifer.'

'What happened?'

As the waiter returned with the drinks, interrupting them, she snatched a long look at Craig. He certainly was not the conventional image of a soldier, even if he did keep his hair shorter than most New York men. But what did Marines really do? When she thought about it she had no idea. He might as well have come from outer space.

'What happened?' she repeated. 'Why did you have to retire?'

He cradled the drink a moment before sipping it, then looked straight at her. 'Without giving you the whole life story, I was with some others in the hold of a small ship and we got rammed by a destroyer. Not a disaster. Just hard enough to send us all flying. I broke my ankle.' He grinned. 'Three years later it went again. The heavies threw me out and here I am.'

'Is that all?' Barbara's interest was whetted by the reticence of the account. 'I mean, do ships often ram each other?'

'Well, it's not—' He checked himself. Why pull all that secrecy shit, when any researcher using the Freedom of Information Act could find it out. 'Fact is, we were up in the Arctic on a trawler and the Russians didn't like that. So they warned us off. Gave me one experience I never expected, though. I got to wear a Russky uniform.'

'You did?' As she spoke Barbara realised she must be sounding like the original bimbo. It worried her even more that she almost felt like one. She'd only just remembered that Marines served on ships. This really was a segment of American life she knew absolutely zilch about—and she had a Master's from Cornell.

'Cut a long story short, the Russkie's forced us into port and arrested the ship. Then they got distracted. A Brit called Weston and I put on an act. I feigned sick, the guard came to the cabin and Weston slugged him with a wrench. Then I put on his gear, went up on deck and made a show of ordering the crew to cast off. The Russkies on shore were too busy to take much notice by then. We were damn lucky.'

'You got away?

'We did.'

'But Craig, you should have got promoted for that, not fired!'

'Officially none of us were there. Only the Norwegian crew were legal and they were supposed to be fishermen. An official nonevent. The guy who deserved the big medal was the Colonel and all he got was frostbite.' Craig took a slug of the whisky, as though dismissing the past. 'Now it's your turn. How come you're at the Park Plaza?'

'Nothing as exciting as that.' She was momentarily flummoxed and felt like backing off. That had been about the shortest account of his own exploits any man had ever given her. He'd taken a fraction of the time that an advertising man would have devoted to explaining a new cake-mix launch. Yet he'd revealed a lot about himself. He'd been entrusted with important missions, he knew what to do in a crisis, perhaps most significantly he didn't demand praise or bear grudges. She admired all of that. The trouble was, proud as she was of what she'd achieved, her past was drab by comparison. She did back off.

'Now I know why Trevinski hired you,' she commented. 'You're on to a good thing if he likes you. And that jewelry auction is going to be special. The hotel's had presidential banquets and charity galas. It's had some of the richest people in the world staying. But Gregory says we've never before had an occasion with so much portable wealth on show.'

'In other words, he's handing me a security nightmare.'

'Just about. It also means if it goes okay you'll have solved the problems on his worst day of the year. He won't forget that.'

'Here's to it, then.' Craig raised his glass and clinked it against hers. 'I hope you'll be around.'

'Off duty, if possible.' She smiled into his eyes. 'I'd like to look at all those things, even if I'll never be able to buy them.'

They were silent for a moment. It struck Craig that his wife would insist on being there too. A famous limey auction firm staging a social event cum sale would attract her like a bluebottle to a dung heap.

'Now, come on,' he said, breaking the unpleasant train of thought, 'it's your turn. How do you come to be where you are?'

'Well, at least I can keep it short because there isn't much to make it long,' she said reluctantly. 'My folks live out in Great Neck, I have a degree from Cornell in hotel management.'

She checked herself, reckoning he was about as likely to comprehend the uncharted territory of the post–women's lib generation as she was to understand the attitudes of the Marine Corps. Privately it worried her that the whole territory in which career women operated seemed to lack both signposts and role models. There had to be some middle path between rampant feminism and sitting at home darning a husband's socks. But that was the last subject she wanted to start discussing now.

'I guess the Green Machine had one thing going for it,' Craig said. 'We knew where we stood. The military have a cut and dried social system—if you can stand it. Can't be so simple for a woman in New York.'

'You can say that again!' She was surprised and delighted. 'And I'm one of the lucky ones. My first job was at the Ritz Carlton and I've been at the Park Plaza five years. The worst problem was finding an apartment I could even begin to afford.'

'You're not married?'

Now that, she thought, underlines what I like about this man. He's direct and he's deliberately making it easier for me to put the very same question. But she didn't go on to ask herself why she should care if he was married or not.

'Somehow haven't found the right guy so far.'

That was the understatement of the century. She was twenty-nine and in New York once you slid through twenty-five you hit the man-shortage syndrome. It was as if one month you were afloat on a sea of invitations and the next, almost overnight, the social scene dried up, especially if you refused one-night stands. Sure, she still went to movies and theatres: but nearly always with girlfriends.

'And you?' she asked.

'I married when I was in Europe. She comes from Chicago but she was working in NATO. We have a five-year-old daughter.'

Well, Barbara told herself, that had been inevitable. No decent-looking guy of his age could fail to be hooked up already, unless he was gay or some kind of neurotic. Craig's reactions to Gregory told her he wasn't gay and neither the Marine Corps nor Trevinski would have accepted him if he was a nut case. So he had to be married. She'd been wondering if he would try to skate around the fact: and now she was pleased that he hadn't.

'What's she called?' she demanded with false cheerfulness, referring to his wife. 'Is she pretty? I'm sure she must be!'

'Her name's Antonia. Yes, she is nice to look at. She's in school in North Plainfield.'

The way he had assumed she was asking about his daughter made things clearer. However, one thing she absolutely was not going to do was let him launch into the 'my wife doesn't understand me' routine. Men who took that line were self-pitying wasters of a girl's time.

'Does your wife like New Jersey?' She couldn't imagine settling down in the suburbs in the way her parents had.

'Not much. Things were okay with Julia when we were on the other side of the pond.' He made an effort to be dispassionate. 'I guess they were okay until I had to look for another job.' That was being charitable and then some. Anyway, why the hell was he ruining an evening talking about Julia? 'These things happen. If we all had hindsight we'd all be billionaires.'

'I'm sorry, Craig.' She would have liked to touch his hand, to reach out somehow, because he sounded trapped. But she held back.

'Let's change the subject.' he said abruptly. 'Would you like another drink?'

'I don't think so.' The empathy between them had melted away, the spell was broken. Suddenly all there was left to say was part of the original inevitability. 'I should be going.' She glanced around as if for the waiter, blaming herself for killing the evening, wishing she'd played safe by just talking about the hotel. She tried to laugh it off. 'I need my beauty sleep even if you don't.'

'That is one thing I do not believe. You look great. You always do.'

But the spell could not be restored and they both knew it. Craig signalled to the waiter and paid the check, anxious to cut short a conversation that had become stilted and difficult.

Outside, while the doorman sought a taxi, he offered to see her home.

She hesitated, not sure if this was ordinary, empty politeness, uncertain now what he really wanted: or whether she herself would wish to follow through the well-worn moves any further.

'That would be nice.' she said eventually, reflecting that he could always take the taxi back again. 'I don't really like cabs alone at night.'

The back seat was covered in worn and slippery plastic. At the first corner, as the driver turned to head north, she found herself sliding against Craig, put her hand out instinctively and found she was touching his. She let it stay there and after a moment felt him squeeze her fingers. Neither of them spoke.

When the cab stopped at the small apartment block on East 88th Street where she lived they both got out and Craig asked the driver to wait.

'Would you like a nightcap?' she suggested nervously. 'I made you rush that drink, I'm afraid. It's not how one ought to celebrate.'

'Are you sure?' He appreciated her uncertainty and made the decision. 'That would be swell. I can always get another cab back.'

'No problem around here, friend.' The driver added his ten cents worth in expectation of a larger tip.

'It's not exactly luxurious,' she said, 'but come on up.'

For a lady who liked to remain in control, Barbara reflected, she was in poor shape. Not to mention that she was tempting fate: and funnily enough she didn't care. But when they were in her studio on the twelfth floor she remained edgily unconfident and after pouring him a whisky sat right up at one end of the sofa, away from him.

'You know something,' she said, desperate to tread only on established common ground. 'If Jake Trevinski wants you to handle this auction it really will be quite a compliment.'

'You think so?' Craig looked around him, taking note of everything. This sofa they were sitting on must open out as a bed. There was a single deep armchair, upholstered in a rough oatmeal-coloured material. An out-of-date stereo system stood on top of a bookshelf. He scanned the book titles: *West with the Night*, *A Woman in Your Own Right*, *Our Bodies, Ourselves*, cookbooks, copies of the *New Yorker*, novels by Pilcher and Michener. There were posters on the walls in an angular gaudy style he couldn't identify. The decor suggested a wide-ranging, but self-examining lifestyle. She was damn right about the apartment not being luxurious, too. It had the minimum. Suddenly he realised she was still talking.

'I mean, there could be twenty or thirty million dollars' worth of jewels there and how do you stop people off the street just coming in? They don't have guest lists for auctions.'

She seemed so unable to stop chattering that he forced a change in the subject.

'How did you find this place? It's real nice.'

'I was so lucky. A classmate's mother lived here. She got married. But it's rent stabilised, so of course she wasn't going to let it go. She sublets it to me.' She knew she was talking too fast and with too much emphasis. This wasn't her at all, this wasn't

Barbara Andrews, college graduate, manager, cool, self-possessed. This man's mere presence just destroyed her.

'I should be going,' Craig said, putting his glass on the table and getting to his feet. He was becoming embarrassed.

'You really needn't yet.' She stood up as well, at a loss for words and annoyed with herself. The evening had gone completely wrong. 'I enjoyed our drink. Thank you.' She moved closer and kissed him softly on the cheek.

Craig unfroze, took her in his arms and kissed her long and properly. Then he sat her down on the sofa again and kissed her some more. She had her eyes closed but the world came back into focus.

'You're supposed to be in Room 1607, Mr. Clifford,' she said eventually, breaking away for a moment. 'At Jake Trevinski's request.'

'I'd rather be here. The hell with Trevinski.' And the hell with Julia too.

Chapter

10

Everything had started splendidly. Charles had begun by opening a bottle of Krug to celebrate Samantha's expected coup. That couldn't be better. He was being appreciative and she adored Krug. Next they'd gone to Langan's, which she preferred to Les Ambassadeurs. Brownie points again. But then came what she had feared. After devoting dinner to persuading him that he could not afford to fool around with Helene and must reduce Burnaby's commission, she had been idiot enough to accept going back to the flat for a brandy, thinking he would continue to talk business. Instead he had evaded discussing her cut and made an absurdly self-assured pass at her on the sofa, as if they'd never ceased to be lovers. What was that number Carly Simon used to sing? 'You're so vain, I bet you think this song is about you, don't you?' It could have been for Charles.

'So when did you say this kraut friend of yours is coming again?' he asked, recovering with easy grace from her rebuff.

'Helene's coming at eleven tomorrow. She knows I get a cut, by the way.'

'Does she indeed.'

'Not that it's four percent, of course.'

'On this kind of money, my love, no consultant gets that kind of percentage. Particularly not if we've scaled down ours.'

'On the Malabar Angel I shall.'

She stood up to distance herself from him and made a pretence of examining a painting above the mantelpiece. This place had a lot of memories for her. Although there were only two bedrooms, the large and well-proportioned drawing room gave it the luxurious ambiance Charles needed for entertaining clients. Some of his finest pictures hung on the walls, which, if offered enough, he would sometimes consent to sell. The more he wished to dispose of a picture, the greater his show of reluctance and the higher the price. She'd often helped him play that game. It was here, too, on one of the cream-upholstered sofas, that he had first kissed her. Well, not again.

'Charles, my sweet.' She cradled the brandy glass in her hand to reinforce her confidence. 'How often have I been "the only person you can trust"? Too bloody often. Now I've pulled a rabbit out of the hat for you yet again. I want our agreed commission, the full—'

She was interrupted by the phone, a gentle shrilling that nonetheless maddened her. Why did it always have to ring at the crucial moment? Charles lifted the receiver off the phone on the side table and she recognised the voice at the other end, faintly though she heard it. Lucy's county accent was both standard and yet raspingly individual.

'I'm coming up to London tomorrow morning. I presume you'll be there.'

'I'll be rather busy, darling. An important client. Are you free for lunch?'

'I suppose so. This does concern the business.' A momentary pause. 'Charles, I would like to know if we are being offered a diamond called the Malabar Angel.'

Luttrell swore under his breath and motioned Samantha further away. Her presence distracted him.

'Charles! Are you listening? Is there somebody with you?'

'No.' This was an idiot question Lucy often asked, as if one day he would accidentally tell the truth in reply. Nonetheless it confused him. 'I mean, yes, I am listening, my dear.' Unable to guess why his wife should be concerned about the diamond, he asked her directly. 'Is this Malabar stone of special interest to you?'

'To friends of mine. Are you trying to say that we have been offered it?'

'As it happens, that is what I shall be discussing tomorrow.'

'And who brought in this jewel?'

There was no point in evading the question. As a Director and major shareholder Lucy had the authority to demand information. 'A friend of Samantha Seebohm's inherited it recently.'

'So it came through her!' The hostile intake of breath was audible down the phone. 'Well, I must talk to you before we enter into any commitment. That is absolutely imperative.'

'Then you'd better have yourself announced as soon as you arrive.' Charles knew better than to argue when his wife was in such a mood and, besides, she wouldn't make this demand without good reason.

'Sam!' he called out as soon as he had put the phone down. 'You can come back.'

When she returned she had her coat on ready to leave, her handbag on her arm. 'And what wifely order was I not trusted to overhear?' she asked sardonically.

'I'm sorry, my love. But it was difficult with you in the room. She has some bee in her bonnet about your Malabar Angel. Is there anything wrong with it?'

'Not as far as I know. Why?' She was instantly suspicious.

'I think you'd better ask your Baroness to bring the diamond with her.'

'Keep your wife out of this, Charles. It's my coup.'

She walked out before he could reply, still unsure what had got into her. When she got home to her own flat she discovered she had lost an earring in that brief tussle on the sofa. It was a pearl earring she was particularly attached to. Damn the man. If he let Lucy screw up the Malabar Angel deal she'd murder him.

Down in Wiltshire, at the red brick Queen Anne manor house which had always been her family home, Lucy Luttrell asked herself—not for the first time—where the Charles she had fallen in love with thirty years had vanished to. Where was the amusing and uncannily perceptive young art historian who had been so tall and gangly thin that she longed to cherish and sustain him? Her father had rapidly identified the intuitively quick-thinking discoverer of 'lost' paintings as a potential heir to the chairmanship of Sir James Luttrell and Co. They had married, Charles had taken their name, he had revitalised the firm, earned wide respect and bought control of Burnaby's. But with the wealth and her childlessness had come the first affairs. Her young lover had totally disappeared, metamorphosed into a grandee of the art world famous for his unfaithfulness. And now this. Lucy might live in semi-retreat in the country, but she was worldly-wise enough to smell something badly amiss with the prospective deal which that obnoxious little tart had delivered into Charles's lap.

Chapter

11

I l s e approached rejoining the Red Army Fraction in a mixed mood, part nervous, part exhilarated, because she was forced to make the contact herself, in spite of being a veteran. Her premature release from Stammheim had ensured that, followed by being effectively incommunicado at home. She knew at least two phone calls had been intercepted by her parents. She'd overheard her mother insisting, 'Ilse is resting. She cannot talk to anyone.' So it had been left to her. But whom should she try to reach? Her lawyer's phone was bound to be tapped: there'd been a crackdown on lawyers who acted as intermediaries even before she was arrested.

Names swam through her head. Venerated names, names despised, names she couldn't even put faces to, because they were after her time. Of her own contemporaries Gabrielle, who had helped organise the raid on the OPEC meeting, was in jail; Susanne, who had set up Ponto's murder, was on the run; the other Gabrielle, from Dortmund, had escaped from custody along with Inge and they were hiding somewhere too. Angelica and Peter had turned traitor, sentenced to life but urging others to abandon violence and join the Greens. That left the so-called fourth generation: Christoph, Andrea, Birgit, all teenagers ten years ago. But, just like school, you seldom knew your juniors unless you'd recruited them yourself.

Would they even talk the same language now? Were young supporters still 'spontis' who hung out in campus cafeteria 'habitats' or 'chaos cafés'? She didn't know. Except that after eight years and thirty-two days imprisonment the jargon sounded inanely childish. That underminded her confidence as much as the reports the warders had deliberately let her read about the power of the Red Army being broken, despite its alliances with the 2nd of June movement, Action Directe in France and Autonome.

Then she remembered someone who was probably still around, because behind his boasting he was a coward: Hans-Peter, a mature engineering student Horst had recruited to run the info centre for the assassination that went wrong. Hans-Peter was the sort who'd be outwardly respectable, married perhaps by now, name in the phone book, keeping his nose clean, yet glorying in the secret power of belonging to Baader-Meinhof. Meanwhile he might still be responsive because he always had been torn between fear and bravado. One afternoon, when her parents were out, she rang him and ordered him to a coffee bar near the university next day.

When she reached the place, after a complicated bus and rail trip to avoid being followed, she was relieved to find that this 'chaoten cafe' where she and Horst used to meet before they went underground had hardly changed. A new, brightly chromiumed Gaggia coffee machine hissed steam on the counter, but the aroma was the same; so were the Formica-topped tables and the magazine rack stuffed with tattered old journals. She'd insisted on Hans-Peter coming here because inside herself she was scared of new and unfamiliar places and needed Horst with her in spirit. This had been their favourite recruiting ground, a place where they could mingle unobtrusively with students from the university.

Once properly inside, she realised to her dismay that the atmosphere had changed. The owner used to be an Italian called Rollo—the name outside was still ROLLO's—but an unfamiliar figure stood behind the bar, pulling the machine's handles while it hissed steam. He didn't smile or nod when she came up and the teenagers perched on the bar stools eyed her and giggled as she ordered an espresso. She retreated with the cup to a corner, her and Horst's old corner, pausing to take a magazine on the way, any magazine, just so long as she could pretend to be occupied while she waited.

How could she be a stranger in the place where they planned their first happening! It was incredible. They'd sat here, in this same corner, working it all out. Our info-centre, they used to call it, because this was where sympathisers came to report with the oddments of intelligence they needed, pulling up chairs, talking with the semisecretive enthusiasm of spontis who admired the hard core. Not that she and Horst were hard core then. But they did have plans. It was just after the toughest antiterrorist law yet had been passed, in February 1978. For years the Bundestag had been inching towards a restriction of liberties, about which Germans were sensitive because the dawn knock of the Gestapo was still an active ghost from the past.

'Okay,' Horst had joked, 'we'll celebrate the new law.' They had, with huge success, kidnapping the manager of a suburban branch of the Dresdner Bank as he opened up for the day and escaping with almost 350,000 marks. The mark was worth more in those days, too. Ilse gazed contemptuously at the chattering teenagers in their untidy long black sweaters and coats. Little do they know, she thought. Bank robberies and kidnap ransoms had netted the Red Army a good million dollars in funding.

But those days were how long ago? Twelve years! Rollo had gone. Horst was dead. Everything had changed. Even if Rollo had still been here he might have called the bulls the moment she came through the door. Everyone's sympathies could have shifted. Maybe Hans-Peter's objections to this place had been justified. She took cover behind the magazine, flipping through the pages and forcing herself to read, suddenly fearful that she might be recognised.

A photograph caught her attention, a blond woman, smiling, handsome, flashlit in a nightclub. Below was a staring headline: WHAT WILL THE BARONESS DO WITH HER DIAMOND? Below that was more text and a smaller picture of a funeral procession.

Ilse stared at the page, mesmerised, unable to believe what she was reading. Baron Claus von Brandenburg, onetime Staatssekretär in the Interior Ministry, had died suddenly of a stroke in May. What did his jet-setting only child, the Baroness

Helene, artist and gadabout, plan to do with the fabulous family jewels, including the great Malabar Angel diamond? It was typical society columnist blather: bitchy, speculative, name dropping. But it hit Ilse like a bomb beneath her chair.

She read it again, torn with pain and anger. Doubt was impossible. This could only be the same von Brandenburg who had served as a Secretary of State when Werner Maihofer was Interior Minister and they introduced the law of 16th February 1978: the law that let them murder Horst less than two years later. The article even said so:

'Herr von Brandenburg, as he was known in political life, quietly steered through the controversial legislation by the smallest majority Chancellor Schmidt's government ever experienced: a single vote.'

She needed no reminding of why the law had been controversial, though some Christian Democrats thought it did not go far enough. The law gave the bulls power to search all the apartments in a designated building, not just specific ones. They would never have found Horst otherwise. After the failed assassination he was moving almost daily between apartment squats and student hostels. By a miracle she'd been out at the time, only to be picked up later at a roadblock, another innovation allowed without a judge's permit, thanks to Claus von Brandenburg. Gradually during those eight years in Stammheim she had planned her revenge. And now the swine had cheated her by dying!

A tap on the café window disturbed her. She looked around, suddenly frightened. A face outside was staring at her, a man's face, with a hat pulled down almost over his eyes. He was signaling to her! A man in his late thirties. Who was this? Christ alive, it was Hans-Peter! She would never have recognised him, he looked so much older. She abandoned her coffee and hurried out, clutching the magazine. The barman shouted, but she took no notice.

'Are you mad, Ilse?' He grasped her arm furiously and pulled her rapidly away. 'We can't sit there with a bunch of kids. Things have moved on. If you want to talk we'll drive around a bit. Can't go to my apartment. Not safe.' He stopped by a black BMW. 'Let's go, shall we?'

'Well, one thing hasn't changed,' she said, recovering herself as he drove off. 'You always did like BMWs.'

'Correct.' He relaxed a little, as though a dangerous emergency had been averted, 'Sorry about the rush. Things aren't what they used to be. We're more on our own. Not so many veterans like you left and there seems to be less new talent coming up.'

'Or you're not looking for it anymore.'

'Not looking? Don't be absurd.' He was all indignation. 'I'm telling you, the action's tougher. We can't screw around in espresso bars anymore.'

'We blew up Beckhurts,' she argued, knowing this would prompt him into bragging. 'We executed von Braunmuehl and that General in Paris, didn't we?' Such successes had been crucial to her morale in Stammheim. 'We got that bastard Herrhausen of the Deutsche Bank. We only just missed the counter-terrorism chief in Bonn. He ought to be dead.' She spat on the floor. 'Filth!'

'That's true. Very true. I play my part. I may not be underground, but I do my bit as a militant. The world knows me as an engineer. That's what I am, too, in working hours. An engineer.' He laughed confidently, though the self-assurance sounded thin. 'Has to be pretty good, one's story, I can tell you. Since they took you in, Ilse, they've built up a computer profile of every citizen—one hundred seventy-two items of personal data in every profile. There's a special Office for the Suppression of Terrorism. Doesn't make life any easier, I can tell you. But we carry on. We keep going, even if the big happenings do have to be planned in Paris or Italy."

He drove on, letting her digest this for a while, hoping to cool whatever she had in mind and reckoning that without Horst she'd be a busted flush anyway. Most women in the Red Army were sexually dependent on a male, even if you might not think so from the cold-bloodedness of the operations they carried out. Why should this one be different?

'If you're the great organiser,' she said caustically, 'then you can help set something up. Now for God's sake stop somewhere. Your driving makes me nervous.'

Reluctantly he turned into a side road and stopped the car.

'Should be okay for a few minutes here.' he said. 'Not too long, though.'

She noticed that he was beginning to sweat. Excellent. She wouldn't need to warn him that his computer profile could always be added to anonymously.

'I wanted him executed,' she said, holding out the magazine, 'but look at that! The pig has dropped dead.'

'Von Brandenburg?' He glanced at her, increasingly frightened by her directness. She must have learnt that from Horst. He'd been scared stiff of Horst. 'You're not the only one who would have liked a shot at von Brandenburg. He was too well guarded, though.' He perused the magazine briefly. 'Nice bit of work, the daughter.'

'I wanted him blown out of this world, just like Herrhausen.' In her mind's eye the sequence she had planned night after night in Stammheim came to life. The limousine thrown across the road by the blast, the bodywork crumpling in spite of the armour plate, the tires bursting, the bodies broken and pouring blood on the torn seats inside, the first licks of flame, the glorious moment when the petrol tank exploded.

'But he's dead already!'

She wrenched herself out of the consoling dream, yet it still took a while for her to answer, because her reasoning was intuitive, not rational. 'The daughter will have to do instead,' she said eventually. 'It can be part of her inheritance. Who's available? Someone who isn't on the bulls' computer.' Then she made the admission she most resented. 'For obvious reasons I'm a little out of touch.'

Hans-Peter considered whether he needed to humour her and decided, quite rapidly, that he did.

'There's an Irishman at the engineering works. Real technician. He's known to us.'

'I'd like to meet him.'

'Is there any point? I mean, you seriously want to get the daughter?' He wasn't at all sure how the Irishman would react to killing a woman and he didn't want trouble at the factory.

Ilse gazed at the pictures in the magazine and trembled slightly. Hans-Peter thought it was from uncertainty. It wasn't. She was trembling from frustration. 'I'll decide if there's any point,' she said tersely. 'Now I must get back to Bad Godesberg.'

'Keeping your parents happy?' he sniped as he started the BMW. He didn't like being ordered around by a woman and he wanted to deflate her.

'Keeping out of harm's way, Hans-Peter, just like you. But for more purpose. Now, let's be clear. We meet this time next week and you'll have your Irish friend with you, *verstanden?*' This was a clear command and for all his bravado he didn't dare answer back. 'And find out about money,' she added. 'How much he needs, where we get it. If you're still a militant, then act like one for God's sake. And don't phone me. Be there.'

That evening she pinned up the photograph of Helene von Brandenburg on her bedroom wall, among the school and university mementoes. When her mother saw it, she waddled across to gaze at the picture with delight.

'Such a beauty,' she sighed, 'a real German aristocrat. I'm glad you still admire families of quality, *Liebchen*, I really am.'

'She looks quite interesting,' Ilse said unemotionally. 'I like to be reminded that such people still exist.'

Chapter

12

'S w e e t h e a r t , you have to get out of here. This is not Room 1607, remember?'

Craig rolled over and was instantly awake. Barbara was pulling at his shoulder.

'Wake up, sweetie.' She leant over and kissed him.

He nuzzled her breasts, then kissed her on the mouth. Finally he reached for his watch, which he had put on the table beside the sofa bed. Jesus Christ. Seven twenty-five.

'You can make it for nine,' she said, 'but you'll have to get your skates on. I should have set the alarm.'

'Not what was most on our minds.' He was astonished at her matter-of-factness. She spoke as if they been lovers for years, as if getting to work on time was a part of shared lives. He swung himself awkwardly out of the bed; this fold-out sofa thing was not the easiest piece of furniture to manage, though he had no recollection of difficulty getting into it. Then he went through to the tiny bathroom.

'There's a razor I use for my legs in the cupboard,' she called out. 'I'll fix you some coffee.'

The razor was not the greatest, but it was better than reaching the Park Plaza unshaven. When he was washed and dressed he found her in the kitchen, a brightly printed Kimono wound around her, pouring Grape-Nuts cereal into a bowl. A good aroma came from the bubbling coffee machine.

'Fantastic,' he said. 'I'm a new man already.' It was true, too. After a night as active as that he ought to have been feeling five cents on the dollar. But he didn't. He felt as though life was beginning all over again. This beautiful woman wanted him. She was the kind a man could depend on. He was going to find it hard to keep his mind on the business of the executive committee meeting.

'You'd better run, darling, or Trevinski'll have your head.' She kissed him lingeringly and then propelled him towards the front door. 'Call me later. Please don't forget.' She darted back and scribbled the number down, pressing the slip of paper into his coat pocket. 'Here. Hope it goes okay. Fingers crossed.' She held them up intertwined. 'Off you go.'

Craig found a taxi mercifully fast, but the morning traffic was thick. The twenty-seven blocks downtown were a slow, fume-filled grind of stopping and starting, the vehicle bucking on its springs at every intersection. When he reached the staff entrance the time was after eight-thirty. Thank God he'd collected the key of 1607 yesterday evening. The message light on the phone was blinking. He disregarded it, washed again, checked his shirt and tie and was knocking on Trevinski's door eight minutes before nine. He hoped his boss wouldn't ask if he'd slept well.

'Good to see ya, Clifford. Be right with ya.' Trevinski waved towards a chair and went on with whatever he was doing at a wide desk, equipped with a cluster of different-coloured telephones. He was a heavily built man in his fifties, thick necked, with a slit of a mouth and an oddly protuberant nose. His thinning grey hair was brushed flat on his head. He was working in his shirtsleeves and looked too much a caricature of an ex-police captain to be a senior executive in the sophisticated environment of the Park Plaza. But Craig knew he'd performed some never specified past service for the President of the company, which guaranteed his position. Nonetheless he tried to compensate for his lack of social polish when with clients. So he had two voices: an artificial one for clients and his own abrasive expletives for employees. In his book Craig was the latter, ex-major or not.

'Okay, Clifford.' He checked his watch and put on his coat. Its padded shoulders made him even more barrel shaped. 'I'm gonna introduce you at the start and you keep your mouth shut until the time comes. Could be ten minutes, could be an hour. Depends how Holtz feels, okay? Then you get your ass outa there. Let's go.'

He led the way along a deep-carpeted corridor to the general manager's office, where Craig had never been before. Brief introductions followed to the senior executives, who were pouring themselves coffee before taking their places.

Christian Holtz, the General Manager, was of Swiss origin, physically robust and chunky, like a more diet-conscious version of Trevinski. He shook Craig's hand firmly, said 'Glad to have you with us' and gave the impression of meaning it.

By contrast the Banqueting Director, Tom Garrison, gave him a minimal greeting. Garrison would have been distinctive anywhere: tall and always holding himself well, sharply dressed, not a single hair out of place and elegantly brisk with everyone except his special clientele, which included many New York society matrons responsible for charity dinners and balls. Craig would be in constant liaison with him and guessed that the reason for his perfunctorily limp handshake and nod was his dislike of security men intruding on his functions.

Others he knew by sight or to say hello to: Beth Symons, the head housekeeper; Martha Schneider, who ran the hotel's Sales and Marketing; the Food and Beverage Director; the Technical Services Director. Responsibilities were highly structured at the Park Plaza. But the third key player as far as he was concerned was the Resident Manager, who confusingly did not live in the hotel whereas Holtz did.

The Resident Manager was Steven Corley and he was in his early forties: thin, energetic, with a noncom's capacity for noticing details. If a flower arrangement had a single withered bloom, or a waiter needed a haircut, or an ashtray lay unemptied, he'd be after the executive responsible in moments. He was also Barbara's boss, via the front office manager.

'How did you like 1607, Mr. Clifford?' he asked with what sounded a contrived lack of expression.

'Good of you to let me . . .' Craig began, reckoning he'd better not risk praising its comfort, when Holtz saved his embarrassment by opening the meeting. Even so he felt like a schoolkid who'd been caught playing hookey.

'We have a lot to get through today, ladies and gentlemen. Let's start with the union problem.' Holtz glanced at the Food and Beverage Director. 'Is Local Six going to give us problems, or is what Gianni's been demanding only bluff?'

Craig listened with interest. Union disputes were totally outside his experience, but he knew they could present security nightmares as well as crippling the hotel's operation. The headwaiter, Gianni, was the delegate of the United Restaurant Workers union. If he did call the catering staff out, the management would be in trouble. The feeling was that he wouldn't. However, that still left plenty of other organisational matters more immediate than the auction in October and they were a full hour into the meeting before Holtz came to it.

'I put this event on the agenda so you should all be aware of what it means. Not only have we never hosted one before, it's going to be right in the middle of the peak season and multi-tiered, with at least one private reception linked in. Which room are you going to allocate, Tom?'

'They want the Grand Ballroom, where we have a charity gala that same evening. It can be cleared, of course.'

'They need space for fifteen hundred people? They seriously need that?'

'That's what they say, sir. Otherwise they'd want a room for nine hundred and at least one other for the overflow. They claim it's impossible to estimate the attendance this far in advance. I've told them the Grand Ballroom was booked months ago and they'll have to be out of it by five-thirty.'

'So long as they know, that's fine.' Holtz addressed the others. 'I don't want to emphasise the problem, ladies and gentlemen. But this is not going to be like a charity event. There is no guest list and there'll be no tickets sold. We'll have no check on who's entitled to be there, and we'll also have many millions of dollars worth of valuables being displayed and sold. Is hosting this event going to be worth the hassle?'

'The publicity will be.' This was the Sales and Marketing Director speaking, a woman in a tailored check suit with a string of pearls around her neck and pearl earrings, whose coolly restrained certainty carried conviction. Martha Schneider was well able to quantify what particular events or promotions could do for the hotel. 'Burnaby's tell me they'll be exhibiting the main items all around the world: Hong Kong, Tokyo, Geneva, Monte Carlo, London, Los Angeles and right here. They have one exceptional and historic diamond, which should fetch a record price. Every newspaper story will mention where the auction is and the celebrities expected to be here. I like it.'

'Anyone disagree?'

'Are they wanting a discount?' Garrison asked sardonically.

'No discount,' Holtz said. 'This is big business for them. If anything we'd should be charging more. How do you see the security, Jake?'

'Gonna need a lot of manhours, a lot of detail. I'll be giving Craig Clifford here responsibility.'

'You all know Craig has been named Assistant Security Director?' Holtz said.

There was a brief murmur of congratulation. Craig smiled and stayed silent.

'I could need extra men,' Trevinski said. 'We oughta check identities some way.'

'Let me have some numbers, please. And Martha, will you find out if there's any way these people can keep it exclusive?'

'By invitation only?'

'Invitation only would be the best. Now'—Holtz turned to the Technical Services Director—'these wiring faults we're having . . .'

'Okay,' Trevinski muttered under his breath. 'That's it. Come see me in an hour.'

When Craig left the meeting Holtz was speaking, but he raised his hand in acknowledgment and nodded.

Craig killed part of the hour by calling Barbara, though he felt stilted on the phone. Then he had some coffee in the security office and eventually went back to Trevinski.

'So we get the fucking auction and all its fucking hassle,' Trevinski exploded, as if he'd been waiting to get his feelings off his chest. 'I shoulda known Martha would go for it. She'll go for any goddam stunt that ain't on her own budget.' Trevinski's opinion of PR people was somewhere below sewer level. 'What happens when some gang tries a heist, eh? You start making a plan, Clifford. Work out all the angles you can. Where we're gonna need guys, what we oughta ask the goddam auction firm for, what security outfit's bringing all these rocks. They ought to hire men from Burns. Call them, will ya? Have them send a representative over. Talk to Lieutenant Bradley at the Midtown North Precinct. Tell him it may not be till the goddam fall, but we wanna be safe not sorry.'

He paused, checking in his own mind if he'd covered everything, the thought occurring to him that the Marine Corps might produce decision makers and organisers, but it didn't train a guy for this.

'Okay, Clifford, see you Monday. Have a nice weekend.' Craig was halfway to the door when he shouted an afterthought. 'And Clifford, Corley told me you never slept in 1607. We could have rented that goddam room, right? If you're screwing around that's your fucking business. But don't do it at the fucking hotel's expense, okay?'

Chapter

13

I f the Georgian facade of Burnaby's auction rooms could have been swung aside like the hinged front of a doll's house, it would have revealed a near comic contrast between the way Charles Luttrell liked to live and the conditions he considered adequate for his staff and clients.

On the first floor much of the building's street frontage was occupied by a high-ceilinged Chairman's room worthy of a nobleman's mansion. Elaborately swagged curtains draped the long sash windows. Portrait paintings of old Joshua Burnaby, the founder, and Sir James Luttrell (1829–1908) hung in heavy gilded frames on the walls. One end of the huge room was graced by an antique mahogany dining table, which served both for conferences and for client lunches while at the other a deep sofa and armchairs were arranged around a white marble Adam chimneypiece. The decor was designed to make the rich feel at home and the ambitious feel that they had arrived.

Charles Luttrell liked to think this room reflected his own patrician charm, though in truth he was himself nothing more than a talented upstart who had married intelligently and knew the value of employing men and women of good family in a saleroom. But no one disputed his approach and if it was bluff, what the hell? It worked. He entertained here as though in a well-staffed private house, keeping a smaller adjoining office for his desk and paperwork, and most of Burnaby's recent selling coups had been agreed on in this most uncommercial ambiance.

Just now, however, that carefully contrived atmosphere was failing to protect him from his wife's scorn. Lucy Luttrell was giving her husband a piece of her mind on the subject of the Malabar Angel; a diatribe given added force by her having discovered who had brought in the diamond.

At the same time, Father Vaughan was waiting in the downstairs entrance lobby, wondering why Lucy had summoned him so urgently. 'You must come at once!' she had insisted. 'We can't leave it until the afternoon.' Taxi rides were a luxury that he felt both missionaries and charity workers should manage without. But he had broken his rule, hurried here, and been directed by one of the doormen to sit on a hard leather bench close to a counter called APPRAISALS, where he tried to allay his impatience by watching what was going on. A priest has occasion to meet most kinds and conditions of men, but his vocation had never before taken Father Vaughan to an internationally famous auction house.

The morning session of a sale was ending in the great domed saleroom behind the main building and the lobby churned with a throng of people. Father Vaughan had no trouble spotting the dealers—there was a wary sharpness in their eyes no different from that of Indian bazaar wallahs. Would-be buyers waited at the reception desks for information or to buy catalogues, full of hope as they dug into purses and wallets. Burnaby's lavishly illustrated sale brochures were art history documents in themselves, if you believed what Charles Luttrell claimed for them, and in any case he never gave away anything that he could conceivably sell. Pinstripe-suited young executives with well-fed faces luxuriated in the high prices things had fetched. Neatly pretty secretaries hurried to and fro.

It was, he thought, absolutely no different from an Oriental bazaar, except that the surroundings were more salubrious and the participants had a higher opinion of themselves. At least, everyone except the amateur buyers and sellers did: and as he listened involuntarily to scraps of conversations he began to doubt if any cleric short of His Holiness the Pope would make an impact here. How on earth, if Lucy Luttrell had miraculously located the Malabar Angel, was he going to argue convincingly for its return to the bone-poor congregation of a small, weath-erstained stucco church in a part of India no one would have heard of? Well, my friend, he told himself, you're going to have to persuade them that theft is an injustice whether it happened today or three hundred years ago.

He remembered an incident that still amazed him. When he was first out in India a load of cement for repairing a village church had been stolen. The Indian parish priest announced that it had been provided for God's house and was therefore God's property. The villagers should be ashamed at such an affront to their deity. That night every single sack was returned: out of respect for God was the theory. In practice the thieves probably feared there would be a curse on the cement. Come to think of it, for all he knew there could be a curse attached to the Malabar Angel itself: the priest of the time might easily have called down God's wrath on the thief. But that was hardly relevant now. He had to invoke honesty, not superstition.

While Father Vaughan waited and pondered downstairs, up in the Chairman's room Lucy Luttrell was on the attack. She was a frail woman, dressed in a well-cut, slightly out-of-date linen suit, very much the country lady come to town. She leant on an ivory-handled stick, necessitated by her arthritis, as she gazed at the Malabar Angel and its necklace, laid out for her benefit on the Sheraton dining table and spoke to her husband with quiet determination. At least she had intended it to be quiet determi-nation, but she sometimes went over the top when she knew he was in the wrong, and on this occasion he was doubly at fault because of Samantha's involvement. Lucy Luttrell's future plans did not include liking his ex-mistress any better—and 'mistress' was the word she used in her mind, not some condoning euphemism.

'So you propose accepting stolen property?'

Charles laughed, a natural, man-of-the-world laugh, intended to reassure James Constant, a laugh bolstered by his having agreed on terms with the Baroness half an hour ago. A seven percent commission instead of ten and Burnaby's would pick up the tab for brochures and publicity. Dependent, of course, on the GIA certificate. Not a bad compromise. Samantha would have to take less. She would argue, but so what? He had a deal. He had the essential 'internationally important discovery' for their first New York sale. So he felt confident enough to laugh in his wife's face, even though she would not be deceived.

'Don't be absurd, my dear. The Malabar diamond has been in the Brandenburg family since the 1790s.'

'And why is it so named if it is not the stone taken from a church in Malabar a century before?'

'Taken? Or sold off by?'

'Stolen. I have it on impeccable authority that it was stolen.'

'The Baroness von Brandenburg can produce the 1791 receipt. Who are we to believe?'

'No doubt her ancestor did pay for it. But before that someone bought it from a fence. Or a looter. Morally it belongs to the church. Not that one could expect moral considerations to interest the people involved.'

'Lucy, please.'

'Well.' Her aggravation increased. 'If the church did not believe this jewel was rightfully theirs they would hardly have asked Father Vaughn to search for it.'

'Father who?' Charles was caught off balance. 'To search?'

'He is downstairs now. I think it's time we invited him up.'

Giving her husband a defiant look, she hobbled to the telephone in the corner of the room, spoke to the reception desk and then settled herself on an upright chair.

Accordingly Father Vaughn found himself confronted by a kind of *tableau vivant* when he was shown in: Charles Luttrell striking an elegant attitude by the long table, James Constant attentive to one side, a magnificent diamond necklace glittering on its velvet stand and Lucy, sitting as upright and composed as a queen, ready to stifle her anger and welcome him.

'Father Gerard,' she held out her hand, 'how very nice to see you after all these years. Charles'—she inclined her gaze towards her husband—'this is Gerard Vaughan, who was a family friend when we were children.'

The conversation-piece attitudes dissolved. Charles came across to greet him and Vaughn realised that behind the firm handshake and easy smile he was apprehensive. The feeling was confirmed when he went straight to the point.

'Well, Father, this is the Baroness von Brandenburg's famous jewel. Quite a coincidence that we should be arranging the sale for her, eh? I understand the Vatican has some possible interest in it.' He spoke as though the Pope was a potential bidder.

'Oh no. Not at all.' Vaughan was immediately embarrassed. What conclusions had Lucy leapt to? He must put his own role into perspective at once. 'Not the Vatican, Mr. Luttrell. The Suffragan Bishop of Malabar, who wrote after hearing that the diamond was likely to be sold.'

'Would you recognise the stone?'

'How could he, ' Lucy interrupted cuttingly, 'when it was stolen three hundred years ago?'

'May I look?' Vaughan asked politely.

'You'll find it easier through a loupe.' Constant produced his small chromium-mounted magnifying glass, handed it across and then held up the diamond for inspection.

Peering through the magnifier, Vaughan thought the rectangular stone less large than he had expected. Nor did it really sparkle. Rather it had a sulky, bad-tempered brilliance.

'It lacks the fire a modern diamond would have,' Constant said, sensing Vaughan's puzzlement, 'even though it was recut in the late nineteenth century to improve the refraction. If it's smaller than you were expecting that's because recutting must have cost a third of its weight.'

'And, if I may say so,' Charles prompted 'only an expert as knowledgeable as James would recognise it as being the same stone at all. If it is.'

'I don't think the recutting would bother the Bishop,' Vaughan said, disregarding the innuendo and handing back the loupe. 'So long as the faithful knew it was their historic diamond—that would be what mattered.'

'Rather unusual for a church to be given such a thing, wasn't it?' Charles was determined to undermine the claim. 'Surely Golconda was part of the Moghul Empire? This would have been a ruler's turban ornament: a Muslim ruler's.'

'You are absolutely right,' Vaughan said conversationally, as though delighted to acknowledge expertise. Two could play at verbal fencing. 'The stone was given by one of the Moghul Emperors to a Prince of Cochin, who became a Christian convert and donated it to the church to demonstrate his own subservience to God. Unhappily he was later kidnapped and put to death for his change of heart. That is one reason why the diamond still matters so much to Catholics there today.'

'And the other, I suppose, is that it also represents a huge sum of money that your Bishop would find extremely useful.'

'My husband,' Lucy cut in icily, 'sometimes displays a quite remarkable lack of sensibility. I apologise, Father.'

A moment of embarrassed silence followed, which Vaughan decided to break.

'The people there are poor, I admit. But their concern is not for money. It's as though someone had stolen their most precious heirloom. They still feel a deep hurt to their sense of dignity from the theft.'

'My dear chap, you might just as well say that Lord Montagu should have Beaulieu Abbey back to the Church, merely because a few monks still feel aggrieved at Henry VIII dissolving the monasteries.'

'There is absolutely no comparison, Charles.' Lucy intervened again with feeling. To some English Catholics the break with Rome was only yesterday. 'Much as we all loathe what Henry VIII did, he was the King. This was taken by a common thief. It ought to be returned to Malabar, just as those mosaics were sent back from America to Cyprus.'

'Frankly, Father Vaughan,' Charles said, now seriously annoyed, 'at this distance in time the church can have no claim for its return, even if you could quote chapter and verse for the theft, as you might put it.'

Vaughan got up, his own patience exhausted. 'The Lord Bishop has not instructed me to take legal action, Mr. Luttrell. He had hoped it would be enough that historically this diamond belongs to the church. Historically and morally. If Burnaby's is not prepared to help I should like to meet the owner.'

'That is the very least we can arrange.' Lucy rose haltingly from her chair, waving away Constant's move to assist her. 'I am perfectly all right, thank you. Now Charles, I am going to see Father Gerard out—we could do with a little more elementary courtesy in this firm—and I would like you to speak to your Baroness immediately.'

After they had gone, Charles Luttrell lit a cigarette, opened a cabinet at the side of the room and poured both himself and Constant a drink.

'Bloody waste of time,' he remarked. 'Helene von Brandenburg won't give an inch. However, if Lucy insists, we'll have to do that much. Catholics are all the same. They're a bloody mafia. At any rate, you've some good historical stuff confirmed for the provenance: Moghul Emperor, Cochin Prince. You can work in references to the Koh-i-noor being looted from the Peacock Throne. Build up the historic comparisons. We've got a real runner here, James. A very possible winner.'

'You think a claim is impossible, or were you bluffing?'

'No bluff necessary, dear boy. If he had documentary proof that the church ever owned the thing, he'd have produced it. Anyway it's centuries out of time and where would an Indian bishop find the funds for a legal action? No. The priest was the one who was bluffing. He all but snorted with puffed-up indignation. "Moral" ownership, my eye.'

'And if he gets publicity?'

'We laugh him out of court. Czernowski will see to that. We set to work the day the Baroness signs the contract. Next Monday, I should hope.'

'No contract until we have the GIA certificate, Charles. I'm not auctioning without one. And your Baroness won't like what it says about the flaws.'

'Promise her a top price in spite of that. You wrap this up, James. I want that diamond in our sale.'

'She'll have to bring it across. Will you pay her expenses?'

'If we have to,'Charles grunted. 'The hotel, perhaps. Maybe that damn priest will persuade her to hurry up. He could be a blessing in disguise. If his story got in the press she might find no one else was prepared to touch her precious heirloom.'

'But we would?'

'Yes, James. We would.'

'Then we'd better ask Czernowski in straightaway. I wouldn't trust our own PR staff to handle this.'

Although he employed a small in-house team of press officers, all young women whose parents were affluent enough to supplement Burnaby's notoriously meagre salaries, Luttrell regarded them as mere cannon fodder for the tabloids. When period jewelry was up for action he let them play at modelling the necklaces or tiaras; for bric-a-brac and oddments—now dignified as 'collectibles'—they were photographed cuddling rag dolls or balding teddy bears. But if millions were at stake he retained a professional PR adviser, and that professional, Prince Czernowski, was a middle-aged man like himself.

'We hardly want the Prince on the payroll before it's necessary.'

'It's necessary now, Constant said firmly, thinking how extraordinarily penny-pinching Charles could be at times, when at others his hospitality was extravagant. 'Shall I call him or will you?'

Outside, after Lucy had ushered him to the entrance, apologised for her husband's attitude and promised any assistance she could give, Father Vaughan paused on the street and looked up at the temple of Mammon. He knew that his chances of obtaining anything for the Bishop of Malabar were all but nonexistent. And in the same moment, he resolved to continue trying. He even had a most unchristian thought—a thought for which he later reprimanded himself—which was that if by chance a curse had been laid on the thieves of the diamond, he could think of no one better qualified to benefit than Charles Luttrell.

That afternoon Samantha took part in the first promotional conference for the October auction, one which Prince Czernowski comfortably dominated. Not for nothing was he a London legend for his combination of social connections and marketing flair. Furthermore, he invariably saw straight through Charles Luttrell's pretensions and did not mind saying so, which was precisely why Luttrell trusted him.

'What do we want most?' With punchy urbanity the Prince answered his own question. 'A damn good scandal, or a great love story, or two extremely rich women fighting for possession of the thing.'

Samantha smiled sideways at Charles. 'Why not start with the scandal?'

'My dear, one could hardly call this priest's claim a scandal.' He explained about Father Vaughan to the Prince.

'We'll have to watch out for that. Some people believe there's no such thing as bad publicity. Personally I do not agree. What else is there? Doesn't the Baroness have a story?'

'A bit of one.' Samantha became more cautious, as befitted the story's inventor. 'She's going to endow a fellowship commemorating her father. Would the media go for that?'

'If she's photogenic enough.'

'She quite beautiful in a way,' Charles began, caught Samantha's eye and modified the statement. 'That is, she has the ancestry.'

'One of the Friedland Brandenburgs? Her father was Secretary of State?' Czernoswksi had the Almanac de Gotha filed in his brain, ready cross-referenced. 'That will help. Ancestry always helps.'

'Intrinsically her diamond is more important than anything the Duchess of Windsor owned.'

'Charles, old chap, the duchess made history. Do not tell me this will match the Windsor sale. Nothing will match the Windsor sale in this century. I told you—a scandal or a great love story.'

'Great diamonds have their own personality. There's an almost sexual thing about owning them.' Charles walked across to the long Sheraton table and gently lifted the covering off an object there, revealing the necklace on its black velvet stand, the Malabar Angel shimmering as it hung beneath. 'What kind of person will buy this, James? A film star, some damn property developer, a sheikh, a Japanese museum?'

'Women don't buy jewelry over a million dollars. They prefer men to buy it for them, though I wouldn't rule out Donna Bradshaw, the store owner. That investment banker Walter Cranson could be keen. It's his wife's fiftieth birthday soon. He's been after something unique for months. The Kuroki Museum should be interested: the Japanese are into the historic jewelry market now. There's a German industrialist whose Swedish wife feels rejected by Frankfurt society—'

'Raeder, you mean?' Czernowski cut in.

'That's him. Wolfgang Raeder.'

'If you knew his wife you'd understand Frankfurt society's side of it. You have the obligatory sheikhs, I assume?'

'And film stars. Gloria Grace is one we'll be sending advance information to.'

'You'll be exhibiting around the world?'

'In the weeks leading up to the sale,' Charles said. 'Tokyo, Hong Kong, Geneva, here in London, Los Angeles and, of course, New York.'

'I'll handle it,' Czernowski decided. 'How long have we got?'

'Four months, all but. Today's June twenty-ninth. The auction will be on Monday October twenty-second.'

'There's never too much time. We ought to be supplying the magazines with material already. *Vogue, Town and Country, Connoisseur.*' Czernowski ruffled his thick, greying hair with his hand. 'We need a complete media plan. The weeklies, the wire services, the columnists—' He stopped abruptly. 'Why am I telling you how to wipe your own backside, Charles? Can't those Sloanes of yours downstairs organise this, or do they spend the entire day calling their boyfriends?'

'They are perfectly capable.'

'Which is why you brought me in I suppose? When can I have photographs?'

'Of the diamond, as soon as the Gemological Institute has issued a certificate.'

'Not only of the diamond, Charles. Of the Baroness. Preferably wearing the diamond. Or at home. Or doing whatever she does.'

'She paints,' Samantha said.

'In her studio then. When can I have them?'

'When she's back from New York,' Charles suggested.

'I'd rather have them before she goes.'

'She might feel we're jumping the gun,' Samantha warned. 'Actually, perhaps we should, because she'll be taking the diamond with her.'

'Will she, by God! I hope she won't find herself walking past Christie's or Sotheby's on the way. You have a binding contract?'

'A firm promise,' Charles said, reacting to Czernowski's alarm. 'Would she welsh on us, Sam?'

'I don't think so.' Samantha thought of her glorious four percent and shivered. She wouldn't trust Helene herself. But what could they do?

'If I were in your shoes, old chap,' Czernowski told Charles, 'I'd send someone with her.'

'I'm flying back tomorrow,' James reminded them. 'I could

delay a day or two, have us met by a security guard at Kennedy and take her to the hotel myself.'

'I'd do that if I were you,' Czernowski said. 'From what I've heard of your Baroness I wouldn't take a single unnecessary chance.'

Chapter

14

Hans-Peter was scared. Ilse could tell that from twenty metres away, He was shifting from one foot to the other and shooting nervous glances in different directions as he pretended to look at magazines in the Düsseldorf station hall. She had arrived from Bad Godesberg early and taken a stroll outside to spot whether she was being followed, before positioning herself to observe him.

After a couple of minutes she decided Hans-Peter wasn't only scared: he was a fool, a dead giveaway to any bull who happened to be passing and had eyes in his head. Why didn't he buy a damn magazine and then stand by the kiosk reading it, like a genuine passenger killing time? Probably too mean to spend the necessary couple of deutsche marks. Bastard! How she hated having to rely on men: and where was the explosives expert? Where was the Irishman? If Hans-Peter had failed, she'd kill him.

Suddenly, with a jolt, she realised that a man leaning against a pillar reading a newspaper was watching her. He was of moderate height, wearing slacks and a light fawn-colored windbreaker, and much of his upper body was obscured by the paper. He had thickly curling dark hair. As he lifted his head for another swift glance towards her, she caught a glimpse of a strong, young, somehow battered face. His eyes swept the area around her, then were lowered, the whole appraisal over in a split second. Who in hell, she thought. A bull? No, something about him wasn't German. The Irishman! He must be, because he was all the things Hans-Peter conspicuously was not: natural, unflurried, someone who if he was questioned would have a convincing story. In other words, a professional. She hoped to God she was right, emerged from the shelter of the pillar and walked boldly up to Hans-Peter.

'What a coincidence! How extraordinary to see you here! Are you living in Düsseldorf still?' She tried to sweep him up with the enthusiasm of a long-lost friend. If she didn't take the initiative he'd stand there paralysed. 'I've come over for an exhibition. Have you time for a coffee?'

Hans-Peter recovered a part of his nerve, managed to kiss her on the cheek, made a show of consulting his watch and said he had half an hour to spare. 'I know a café close by. Shall we go there?'

As he guided her out of the station building to the street the man with the newspaper folded it, shrugged his shoulders, visibly told himself that he'd have to abandon the girlfriend he'd been waiting for and made his way out, too. Five minutes later, having made certain he was not under surveillance, he casually joined the others at a pavement table in the sun.

'You must be Ilse. Nice to meet you. I'm Frank. Hans-Peter told me about you.' He leant across to shake her hand and caught the commitment and hunger in her eyes. He couldn't stand intense women, so he reacted by smiling broadly. 'The luck of the Irish to be always meeting pretty girls.'

'There's no necessity to say that kind of thing.' She liked the compliment and yet bridled at it.

'But I mean it.' Jesus, this was a prickly bird. She didn't deserve flattery either. There was a pallid, dried up, pinched look about her which told him instantly that she been inside, and for a long time. But he reckoned a touch of the blarney could only ease the eventual bargaining.

He sat down opposite her, waved to a waiter, ordered a beer and tried some small talk. They chatted edgily until the waiter brought the drink, after which Ilse wasted no time sending Hans-Peter packing.

'Nice to see you again. Thanks for coming. I'll be in touch.'

89

Hans-Peter took this dismissal with a poor grace, but he left nonetheless and Frank made a mental note of her ability to be forceful.

'Right,' she said. 'How much did he tell you?'

'That you're after making a bit of a bang.' He spoke with deliberate feyness. He always used to say that when a true Irishman died, he should die with a joke on his lips. Maybe that was why, in the end, he had parted company with the IRA and come to work in Germany. He was a professional, but he didn't like being too bloody serious all the time. Hans-Peter had warned him that although she had money, she was an ideologue and living in the past. So first of all he would have to get it straight that he only worked in his own way. 'Would it be a big bang that you're after, or just a little one?'

'It's not a joke.'

'Life's a joke. What kind of a bang did you say?'

She half scowled at him, then found herself attracted against her will by that wide smile and the world-weary look in such a young, tousle-haired face. She saw now why at a distance she'd thought it looked somehow battered. It was. He had a broken nose, with the bridge deformed and the tip twisted fractionally sideways. So instead of adding a remark to go with the scowl, she relaxed a little, delved into her handbag and produced a newspaper clipping. 'That describes the target.'

He took the news report. It was dated June 14 and came from the *Frankfurter Allgemeine Zeitung*. He had to labour a little over translating it:

BRANDENBURG DIAMOND FOR AUCTION

The Baroness Helene von Brandenburg is understood to have consigned her historic 53 carat family diamond for auction. The stone, attached as a pendant to a necklace of 88 small diamonds, is known as the Malabar Angel. It is the sixth largest cut diamond in the world, and the fifth largest ever publicly sold. Unconfirmed reports state that it will be the star attraction at Burnaby's October sale at the Park Plaza Hotel in New York and is expected to fetch over five million dollars.'

A photograph across two columns showed the necklace and pendant.

'This is only gossip at the moment, of course,' Ilse pointed out. 'But if it is correct, then we go ahead with the hotel.'

When he had read the story a second time Frank gave a low whistle. 'For Jesus' sake,' he exclaimed. 'Sure, I can make some kind of a diversion for you. But how in the name of God are you going to get away with snatching that? The place'll be crawling with guards.'

'This isn't a raid. I want to blow up the auction.'

For all that she had spoken very quietly, her words had been clear. Frank's problem was that he couldn't believe them. He took a long pull on his lager, then repeated back what she had said. 'You want to blow up the hotel?'

'So I need an expert.' She made it sound like going to a garage for a minor repair, something perfectly simple but which she was not qualified to do herself.

He finished the lager. 'Let's take a walk. I'll need a few facts and I don't care to be overheard.' The humor had gone from his attitude. Why in the name of God bomb the Park Plaza if it wasn't to nick the diamond?

They left the café and made their way slowly down the street, Frank stopping occasionally to window shop, using the reflections in the windows to watch for surveillance.

'To be exact,' Ilse said, as they paused appropriately enough outside a jeweler's, 'I want to destroy the room where the auction is held at the moment the diamond is being sold.' Her voice became more animated. 'I want to kill one particular class enemy who will be there, but I am happy to kill them all.'

'Any special reason?' He was recovering his sangfroid, now that he realised she was a nut case. He guided her on down the street. 'Like, I mean, what's it for?'

'Her father killed Horst and put me in Stammheim.'

'Horst?' Hans-Peter had mentioned a boyfriend who'd been shot.

'Horst and I . . .' For the first time she was without the right words. 'We were always together. The bulls shot him after we had a . . . a failed mission.'

'So you want to get even?'

'You could say so.' Quite suddenly she became dismissive. 'You have this kind of experience?'

'Sure, and of course I have.'

91

'We have to make a plan. A good plan. It may take several days to bring all the necessary explosive into the hotel. You will use Semtex?' She wanted to sound knowledgeable.

'Most likely. Depends what we can get. Depends how we're going to conceal it.' He wasn't going to bother with thinking out details on a job he had no intention of accepting. The bird was crazy.

'You will have to be away one week. How much do you want for the job?'

Frank thought, while they gazed briefly into a furniture emporium, its window stocked with overstuffed sofas in fancy colours. He tried to think of a figure high enough for her to turn him down, yet not so absurd that she would blame Hans-Peter afterwards. Hans-Peter had made him promise that.

'One hundred thousand dollars.' he said. 'One hundred thousand dollars fee plus all expenses.'

She turned and looked at him intently, worried by her own lack of technical knowledge. 'You won't cheat me?' she asked. 'You'll do it properly?'

'If I say I'm going to do something, I do it.' he said, reacting angrily by instinct, while his mind demanded to know what the devil he was going to say if she accepted. One hundred thousand dollars! Bloody hell! That was a lot of money. Whirlwinds of banknotes danced in his brain. For a week's work. Jesus Christ, he wasn't going to be able to refuse.

'Okay,' she said simply, 'it's a deal.'

The quickness of her acceptance brought reason back to his thinking. 'You're not after forgetting one thing, are you, me darlin'?' He drawled the words and laughed to make them sound an afterthought. 'A professional like me can be expecting money up front. Just for the security of the thing, as you might say.'

'How much?'

'Twenty thousand marks would be fine for starters. In used notes, remember, so there's no questions.'

'We shake on it then. As you say in England.'

'Ireland,' he corrected her. 'Ireland. The Emerald Isle, my dear old mother's home, the land of Guinness and potatoes.' He would have gone on, glib tongued and evasive, but he couldn't spin it out any longer. The figures still whirled in his brain. One hundred grand for a week seeing the sights of New York! He accepted her handshake and felt a tingle of electricity run into him, a tiny sexual shock vibrating from her fingers into his palm and straight into his blood. Oh Jesus Christ, he thought, what in the name of the Holy Virgin have I let myself in for and me supposed to have retired from this kind of thing! It also occurred to him that blowing up a skyscraper—or even only part of one—might not be as simple as demolishing the Imperial Hotel on the Brighton seafront had been. But a hundred grand for trying! 'Oh my boyo,' he told himself, 'why look a gift horse in the mouth?'

Chapter

15

T h e more reasons Craig had for talking to Barbara the happier he was going to be. This Wednesday he had one. Trevinski had ordered a review of the Park Plaza's emergency procedures and the Front Office staff were the key people to consult with. Steven Corley, the sharp-eyed Resident Manager, delegated Barbara to take him around.

'I'm sure Craig Clifford is no stranger,' Corley said, after calling Barbara to his second-floor office. 'Please introduce him to all the personnel he ought to meet.' Was there an extra dimension of knowingness in Corley's voice, a slight twist in the routine smile? Craig was uncertain. If there was, Corley could be a step behind events. These last ten days Barbara had been so elusive that Craig was afraid she was avoiding him. Had she been regretting that night together?

'I'll be happy to help,' Barbara replied, without a sign of pleasure.

'Maybe we should start with you, yourself, Steven.' Craig suggested.

'I can give you five minutes.' Corley eased himself onto a corner of his desk, one leg swinging casually, the absolute embodiment of the helpful superior who was shortly going to have to rush. 'The Duty Manager is the responsible executive in any emergency, of course.'

'We have his responsibilities listed. Assessing the threat, supervising the response, ordering evacuation of the hotel if necessary.' Craig handed a copy across.

Corley scanned it quickly and passed it to Barbara. 'If you were in the hot seat and a gunman was holding up the cashier, would you call the cops first, or me?'

'The police. Then you or Mr. Holtz.' She thought about it. 'Maybe a checklist for different kinds of emergency would be useful.'

'I think so, too,' Corley said.

'I'm surprised there isn't a report form for the Duty Manager,' Craig said. 'There is for the telephonists.'

'Sketch one out, then. Nothing too long. Clear and simple.' Corley checked his watch. 'I have a meeting now. You must excuse me.'

An hour later, when Barbara had shown him the operation of the entire front office, Craig suggested they break for coffee. She agreed, a little reluctantly, he thought.

'You know something?' He decided to stick with the business in hand when they reached the staff restaurant in the basement. 'This hotel has procedures for power failures, for fire, for burst water mains, for handling armed robbers. Yet there is not much about bomb threats. Don't you get those?'

'Hoax callers, sure. All kinds. Like you saw, the telephone girls have instructions to keep them talking while they alert the Manager and the police. So far as I know we never had an actual bomb . . .' She paused. 'Is this really what you want to talk about, now that we have a few moments?'

He shook his head and cut a quick look around to see if they were being overheard. 'I was worried I hurt you some way without meaning to. Did I?'

She stirred her coffee, fiddled with the spoon, then gave him a wistful smile. 'Are you serious about me, Craig? Or was it just a nice idea for a lonely evening?'

'It was a nice idea that became serious. You may not believe me, but I've missed you like hell ever since.' It was all he could not to take her hand across the Formica table. 'Like I hardly know what hit me!'

'Could you get away this weekend?'

'I'll do my damnedest.' He tried to sound cheerful, knowing

how hard it would be to escape from North Plainfield for even half a day. 'The snag is I now work regular hours and Julia knows what they are.' He saw no point in avoiding the truth.

'Irregularise the hours occasionally, sweetheart. If you want to see me you're going to have to break the mould some way.'

A squeaking noise from the beeper in Craig's vest pocket interrupted them. He swore under his breath. 'Guess I have to answer.' He went across to the house phone near the serving counter, listened briefly and came back. 'Trevinski.' He sat down again long enough to drain his coffee, then grinned hopefully. 'Maybe he has some smart idea for weekend duty.'

'I hope so,' Barbara said quietly. 'I hate sitting alone in the apartment all the time, just thinking.'

But Trevinski's demand was more immediate and less exploitable. 'Listen, Clifford,' he spat out, squat as a toad behind the desk with the red and yellow telephones. 'The hassle with this goddam limey auction's just begun. There's some German Baroness flying in tomorrow afternoon.' He checked a notepad. 'British Airways scheduled for 3:00 P.M. They want a limo and a security man at Kennedy to meet her. Fix that, will ya?'

'What's she bringing with her?' Craig decided to take a chair, even though he had not been invited to.

'No one's gonna say. You just be here when she comes, okay? If she needs stuff taken to a bank vault, you fix that, too. 'You come up with much on those procedures yet?'

'A few seem inadequate.'

He phrased it tactfully because Trevinski did not like criticism: but not tactfully enough.

'Inadequate?' Trevinski drew the word out, bristling as though this could be the start of a personal feud.

'Mr. Corey made a few comments about managerial reporting. In my opinion, there could be more detail on bomb threats. Searching for explosive devices in particular.'

'The switchboard supervisor calls me and the Duty Manager. We alert the precinct Detective Unit. You wanna tell me that ain't good enough? Bring in the experts, Clifford. Bring in the goddam experts fast.'

'We could train in-house search teams, surely?'

'I tell ya. The PDU gives the orders.'

'They don't know the hotel layout like the staff do,' Craig

persisted, aware of Trevinski's fanatical loyalty to his former police colleagues. 'Staff are more likely to notice what shouldn't be in washrooms and corridors.'

'Listena me, Clifford.' Trevinski straightened in his chair. 'We only ever had a coupla dozen bomb threats to this hotel and one hundred percent were hoaxes. Okay? One hundred percent! You don't know what you're fucking talkin about.'

'They've been real enough in Europe. We've had Air Force men blown up in Germany.'

'So that's goddam Europe. This is New York. When the precinct Lieutenant says to have staff guys trained, then we'll train 'em. Not before. I want professionals in emergencies, right? Next thing you'll tell me you don't wanna call fire crews for fires. We have bomb disposal problems, I want experts. Not a bunch of clerks and porters thinking they're Superman.'

Craig abandoned the argument. He had not suggested that hotel staff should try to defuse a bomb, only that they would be quicker at locating it. But there was no point in poisoning his relations with Trevinski any further.

'I understand, sir,' he said, wishing his boss had more brain inside that flat and ugly head. 'I'll go get myself briefed about this baroness.' If only she could have been arriving on Saturday or Sunday instead of Thursday.

Chapter

16

'A f t e r it is sold I offer a contribution, perhaps.' Helene von Brandenburg wanted to be rid of this disturbing priest. She had only agreed to receive him because he was of the cloth, and now he was making her feel like a thief. She hardly knew what course of action was best. What if all this was picked up by the media? She might have to defend herself against charges of trying to buy him off. 'The Angel belongs to my family. We have the legal receipt,' she insisted. 'If I do make a contribution from sympathy it is—how is the word in English? It is *exgratia*. As for giving the diamond to India, that is absurd to ask.'

The studio was in worse disorder than normal, with clothes strewn on the sofa and a small stack of her works waiting to be parcelled. She had to take twenty of them across with her to New York tomorrow. The morning had already been interfered with by a photographer, who had insisted that she pose first with the Malabar Angel and then with the paintings. If she had not appreciated the ultimate value of publicity she would have kicked him out. Then Father Vaughan had arrived, with absurd punctuality, and had not improved her mood by sitting resolutely on the only available chair while she continued frantically wrapping pictures, as if he were an island of sanity at the centre of a storm.

'It belongs to my family since two centuries, after all,' she repeated irritably, holding a canvas up to decide if she really did want to exhibit it, and wondering why she should be obliged to argue at all.

'Historically and morally, Baroness, the diamond belongs to the church.' As he spoke he realised, with embarrassment, that this had become his stock phrase.

'Well, morally it can belong to anyone. It can belong to the labourer who found it in a river originally. Morally you can say everything belongs to God.'

Father Vaughan rose to his feet. He had been warned he would achieve nothing. He saw no point in wasting further time.

'Thank you for seeing me,' he said a little wearily. 'I will inform the Lord Bishop.'

Helene stopped her activity, ready to say a relieved goodbye, when she realised he was paying close attention to one of her paintings. The nerve! Why should she be inspected like this? How would a priest understand what she was trying to express? She challenged him. 'You like what it is about?'

The picture was of a river valley, the natural images of water and trees distorted by crude colours and strong brush strokes, yet vibrant and alive.

'You paint with great feeling,' he said. 'I hope the exhibition goes well.'

She was so taken aback by his unaffected response that when she saw him out she repeated her offer of a contribution.

'I will tell the Bishop. But he is not looking for money, he is trying to restore his congregation's self-respect.' He shook her hand. 'I am sure that, being a creative artist yourself, you would understand their emotions if you could go there.'

After he had left, Helene felt in need of a stimulant. She was badly unnerved. She poured herself a brandy and gulped some down. Maybe publicity, which she hated anyway, was not so clever. She should never have consented to the photographs. Maybe she should just sell the jewel privately, without any fuss, as quickly as possible. And why had she even considered giving money to the church! Everyone would assume it was due to a bad conscience. Well, a few thousand dollars perhaps. Her father had always insisted on keeping faith with people: 'You cannot otherwise respect yourself.' Which was almost exactly what the priest had just been saying. Yes, she would do that. She resumed her packing, reflecting angrily and as though it was somehow the priest's fault, that she was going to be held to ransom for the excess baggage. And where would it be safest to put the diamond?

The phone buzzed and she answered it reluctantly. She really had too much to do at the moment. Samantha was on the line, sounding almost breathless with good news, as if an old schoolfriend had just won at Wimbledon, chattering it out nonstop.

'Helene? I'm so glad to have caught you. You remember James Constant, our jewelry expert. Well, I've just discovered he's on the same flight as you. It is Pan Am at ten tomorrow morning, isn't it? I thought it was. So isn't that marvellous! He can deal with all the security and customs problems. You won't have to worry about a thing. We'll send a limousine to collect you at Kennedy and take you to the hotel. We've booked you into the Park Plaza, with Burnaby's compliments, of course. Then you can get this certificate thing dealt with straightaway. Is that all right? Marvellous! James will pick you up at a quarter to eight tomorrow morning. Have a super trip.'

It was several minutes before the thought hit Helene that Constant would only now be booking his seat and wouldn't let her out of his sight until the contract was signed. She shrugged her shoulders, talking to herself. Too bad for them if she changed her mind. At least this would save her the cost of two taxis and a hotel—not to mention safeguarding the diamond. If she played it right they might even provide a limo to take her out to Long Island. She always had disliked avoidable expenses.

Father Vaughan was sitting on a Number 11 bus as it nudged its way through the congestion of Trafalgar Square en route to the Aldwych, where he would get off and walk the last few hundred yards to the Catholic Children's Relief Agency's offices. This particular double-decker moved so slowly and ponderously that it seemed to him like a huge red elephant: and like an elephant it preferred travelling with its own tribe, so it was huddled together with three others for protection. He had jumped aboard in a most unclerical way when it was stopped at traffic lights in the Pimlico Road and was now being given plenty of time to repent, because it would been a great deal quicker to have walked to the underground and taken a train. On the other hand, he needed time to think about what he should now say to the Bishop and at least the journey was giving him that.

Defeat would have to be his message. Without proof of ownership he could do nothing, although the idea of admitting defeat annoyed him when he was dealing with such transparently self-centred people. His only ally was Lucy, and he doubted if there was any miracle of persuasion that she could perform. He began to compose a letter in his mind. "Dear Lord Bishop, it is with the greatest regret that I have to report . . .'

A squall of rain began just as he stepped off the bus at the half crescent of the Aldwych, close to the building from which the BBC's World Service broadcast the news bulletins on which he had so gratefully relied in his years abroad. He unfolded an umbrella, poked it up against the gusting wind and trudged along to the CCRA, the letter still dominating his thoughts.

Mary would smile as he dictated it: the worldly-wise yet compassionate smile of a girl half his age who had a far better understanding of what made the world go round. 'Poor old Father Gerry,' he could hear her telling her mother in the evening, 'he really was a loser from the start . . .'

But when he reached the third-floor office, after labouring up the narrow stairs because the lift was out of order yet again, it was to confront an entirely unexpected situation.

'Thank heavens you're back, Father.' Mary leapt up from her desk as he came in. 'There's been a coup in the Sudan. Some General's taken over. The telephone lines are cut. How do we get in touch with the Sisters there? D'you think they're safe?'

'Speak to the Foreign Office first and . . .' He began thinking through all the possible means of communication. This was the devil's own luck. He'd sent out two Sisters from the Mildmay Mission only a week ago to discuss the children's immunisation project. Their task had been plagued with problems. Officials had made excuses for not seeing them. Their permits to travel were held up. Now this. He should have gone himself.

It was mid-afternoon before he was able to deal with the incoming mail and when he did it brought a surprise more intense in its way than the Sudanese coup.

'I quite forgot,' Mary said. 'You've had a packet from India.'

She held up a small parcel, her curiosity self-evident. 'It's been resealed by the Customs. Shall I open it?'

The package proved to be a tiny cardboard box, wrapped in brown paper. Inside, protected by some coarse cotton wool, was a bulbous-sided rectangle of dull gold. There was also a short letter.

My dear Reverend Father, I am more than grateful for your attempts on our behalf. After much consideration I have decided that you ought to have available the mounting from which the Malabar Angel was wrenched away. It may help you to know if the stone is truly ours. By tradition, this was found on the floor of the church after the theft. Your friend in Christ, Peter Malabar †

'What an extraordinary thing,' Mary said.

The mount was indeed unusual. Very broad at the base, it had not held the diamond in a conventional way. In fact, where it was split from having the stone forced out, the gold was revealed as not being solid, but filled with some hardened gumlike substance. Father Vaughan turned it over in his hand several times and then noticed an inscription on one side.

One of his idiosyncrasies was that he kept an old Swiss army knife either on or about him. In Africa one was constantly needing the services of a blade or a screwdriver and he was fond of joking that the corkscrew was invaluable for opening bottles of communion wine. He slid open his desk drawer, took out the old red-sided knife and flipped open another of its accoutrements, a small magnifying glass. Peering through this and twisting the gold to catch the light, he was eventually able to decipher the scratched inscription. He pencilled it on a pad.

'*Mene?*' Mary asked. '*Mene?* What on earth does that mean?'

'A well-known word. Part of the mysterious writing that appeared on the wall at Belshazzar's feast.' There were several versions of what it meant. 'I'll remember the significance in a moment.'

'Hadn't you better write back to the Bishop?'

Father Vaughan swivelled round to look at her, holding the battered circlet of gold in his palm.

'All in good time. Tell me something. Purely as a person, not as an expert. You know about the stolen diamond. Would you think possession of this proved who it had belonged to?'

'I'm not sure.' She was intrigued and slightly taken aback. 'If it fitted I suppose so.'

'And if it didn't fit because the diamond had been recut?'

'You could always argue that it used to. Would the inscription help?'

'I'm not sure. I shall have to look it up. It might.' He came to a decision. 'Mary, I must make a few phone calls. This is more complicated than I thought.'

The letter he subsequently dictated was very different from the one he had thought of on the bus. He also made an appointment to call on the Secretary of the Canonbury Missionary Society, to which he belonged. Father Vaughan was in a quandary. In the end he did not sign the letter at all, but left it undated in a folder until he had taken advice. He was beginning to feel out of his depth.

That evening Mary's mother, having been given a blow-by-blow of the afternoon's events, was forthright in her analysis.

'I told you all along, dear. He had inner conflicts. Why else should he make such a fuss about those letters? And don't you tell me he doesn't know what *Mene* is! Anyone who went to Sunday school knows that.

At the small house in Islington belonging to the Canonbury Society which he and three other ex-missionaries occupied Father Vaughan cooked himself a supper of soup and fish, then went to the bookshelf and took out the authoritative Jerusalem Bible. In the Book of Daniel, chapter 5, verses 25 to 28, he found 'Mene, Mene, Tekel, and Parsin. The meaning of the words is this: *Mene*. God has measured your sovereignty and put an end to it.' Whoever had incised the word on the Malabar Angel's mount would have known the Book of Daniel and decided that *Mene* was appropriate. But appropriate for what? To underline the Prince of Cochin's conversion? Or to threaten anyone who took the diamond subsequently? From his experience of India he suspected the latter. Either way, the mount was solid proof that the jewel had once belonged to the church.

Chapter

17

T h e Rhineland sweltered in high summer, driving secretaries
and factory workers to strip and sunbathe in their lunchbreaks.
For three days now Ilse had retreated to the end of the garden
in midmorning, always pausing to gaze down past the vineyard
at the wide river below. Industrial smoke from the Ruhr had
rendered the whole landscape hazy. The normally sharp out-
lines of pleasure steamers and barges were indistinct and their
colours muted. She would watch them briefly, a token silence in
memory of Horst, then return to her sunbed near the summerhouse and switch on a transistor.

Every day the weather forecaster, overzealous to sound
compelling and newsworthy, gave variations of the same statement. High pressure was persisting over Europe. The hot
weather would continue. A temperature inversion would cause
the haze to thicken. Et cetera. Et cetera. This Saturday Ilse lay
back on the sunbed and decided today must be the day. The
hippos would both be out; her father was attending a meeting,
and her mother would certainly go shopping. Today she would
retrieve the cash with which to pay Frank the 20,000 marks
advance he was demanding. 'Up front,' he had insisted, with a
cheerfully malicious laugh. 'In used notes, so there's no questions.' She'd given way for fear that otherwise he'd back out,

and she'd begun to appreciate that he was more grasping than he appeared at first sight.

When she told the hippos on Thursday that she could think of nothing more pleasant than to stay at home and soak up the sun her mother had been thrilled. She had lumbered off into Bad Godesberg in the Mercedes and returned with a brand-new bikini, straw hat and beach bag for her so marvellously appreciative daughter. The bikini had white polka dots on a blue material and its style was five years out of date. Ilse didn't care. She actually did want to sunbathe again. The skin of her body was still flaccid and pale from prison. She longed to luxuriate in the sun with almost the same intensity as she had craved for *Brötchen* on her release. So she had welcomed the bikini, and as for the beach bag, that was an inspiration. For that she had kissed her mother on the cheek, feeling almost fond of her.

'How thoughtful of you, Mama! I have nothing for towels and suntan lotion and things like that. May I take the sunbed from the terrace down to the summerhouse? I'd like to lie there and read.'

The summerhouse was a curious, neo-Chinese construction like a pagoda. It was painted white, with a double-tiered yellow tiled roof and imitation windows in the upper part. Inside it contained a single large room, decorated with bamboo screens and lights like Chinese paper lanterns, where during her childhood they used to have picnic lunches at weekends.

'Take the sunbed, of course, *mein Liebchen*.' Frau Nachtigal had been inwardly ecstatic that Ilse preferred to bask in their much envied garden, in their beautiful Rhineland, in their superb German sunshine, at home. 'No one will disturb you down there, my darling. You can rest and read to your heart's content.'

Ilse had smiled sweetly and thanked her mother again, because she needed to be undisturbed. Ten years ago she had concealed the residue of her and Horst's only bank robbery in the summerhouse. She needed to unearth the banknotes, sort them quickly and take what was wanted. However, she would not attempt that too soon. Things weren't like they used to be when she was under no suspicion. Now her actions were bound to be watched. Her family must become accustomed to her lazing in that part of the garden. She had reckoned three days would do, provided the weather held.

Sure enough, that first day her mother couldn't keep away. She came down with coffee, she came with cakes, she sat in a deck chair and tried to draw Ilse out on the future, she planned possible holidays together in places she had read about in magazines. Her mother was a pain in the butt.

On the second day Frau Nachtigal came down only in the morning, because it was Friday and on Fridays she always played bridge in the afternoons. The third day was Saturday and on Saturdays she equally invariably went into Bad Godesberg. So Ilse, presuming she had gone, lay listening to the radio and planned how to deal with the money even though there was not a tremendous amount of it.

On that memorable morning so long ago when she and Horst seized a bank manager as he unlocked the bank's back door and forced him at gunpoint to open the safe they had got away with close on four hundred and fifty thousand deutsche marks. It had been payday for a local engineering works, a small firm still retrograde enough to pay wages in cash. The money had been neatly stacked awaiting collection, mostly tens, twenties and fifties, with a few hundreds and five hundreds, all bound round with the Bundesbank's paper wrappers. She remembered her astonishment at how easily it had all fitted into a single suitcase, just like packing in paper bricks. When the case was full they'd hastily swept a considerable quantity more into a plastic trash bag, before making what the newspapers later glorified as 'an escape organised with military precision.'

The escape had actually been no such thing, except that they'd made an immediate handover. Horst had raced their stolen Volkswagen getaway car into the chosen side street, she had helped swing the heavy suitcase off the back seat into their colleagues' hands, they'd reversed direction and sped off again. When Horst discovered the plastic bag was still behind their seats he'd been livid. But she'd calmed him down eventually, pointing out that they'd been given no funding for the raid and might need some next time. When they counted the cash it totalled 198,260 marks, with an annoying proportion of new notes, all numbered in sequence, fresh from the mint. Those could only be spent slowly, carefully, and in different areas.

Horst wanted to bury the lot in a state forest. She had argued against that. Her arguments centred on tree-felling, on dogs, on poachers, on all the perils of a hiding place on government land. In practice she was afraid Horst might go soft and hand it over. Why do that when the Red Army could never know that the suitcase crammed with 250,000 marks was not the entire haul?

Then it came to her, as if by magic, that the summerhouse at home was the answer. Because whoever built the pagoda before the World War of 1914 had intended it for sophisticated entertainment, the single room had elegant chinoiserie display shelves and storage cupboards with bamboo-framed doors. Ilse had always been an inquisitive child. When she was ten she had discovered a rusting catch at the bottom of one of the cupboards. It released a carefully masked trapdoor, which came up to reveal a cobwebbed space in the brick foundations about two thirds of a metre wide and similarly deep. The space became her secret childhood hidey-hole.

Immediately after the bank raid she had feigned a desire to talk about the future to her mother, gone home for a weekend and dumped the plastic bag with its burden of cash. No one else knew it was there. No strangers could enter the garden. No burglar would bother with the pagoda. The only thing she failed to foresee was that Horst would be shot and she herself jailed.

And now, eleven years on, would the money still be there? She had calculated that it was worth around $117,000: just enough to pay Frank and fund the operation. But would it be intact, or eaten by mice? Would the notes be out of date and invalid? At around eleven, when her mother would be safely taking coffee in Bad Godesberg, she rolled lazily off the sunbed and pushed open the glass-paned doors of the summerhouse. They creaked. The hinges needed oiling. Now her parents were older they only sat out on the terrace by the house. She entered and looked around. The once fastidiously clean room had an air of desolation. The red paper lanterns were faded and one was torn. Cobwebs laced the bamboo-framed tables. She walked across to the cupboard and had to dig her fingernails around the edge of its door to pry it open.

'*Mein Liebchen*, what *are* you doing?'

She spun round. Her mother was standing in the doorway, holding a tray.

'It is so nice here in the garden, I thought for once I would not go into town. We can take coffee and torte here. What on earth are you looking for?'

'There was a deck chair I liked,' Ilse lied, 'an upright one. I was getting too hot on the sunbed.' As if to prove the honesty of her intentions she forced the cupboard fully open. It was empty, with a thick coating of dust on the floor.

'Oh, but we cleared everything out of here years ago. Didn't you realise? This old place has so many spiders. If you want an upright chair you'll have to fetch one from the house.'

Her mother sounded strangely irritated. Perhaps she felt guilty that the once loved summerhouse had become so neglected. Ilse took another quick look into the cupboard. Somehow she would have to find an excuse to clean the whole pagoda. Otherwise the disturbed dust on the trapdoor would be noticeable, and she would be unable to leave any of the loot behind. She couldn't possibly take it all at once. Damnation. This was exactly the sort of hippo idiocy that always upset her plans. She could have screamed. Instead, however, she closed the door again and went across to her mother, just managing a smile.

'Let me take the tray.' She led the way back to the sunbed. 'It was nice of you to think of coffee. How sad about the summerhouse.' Her tone sounded artificial even to herself. 'I used to love playing there as a girl. I think I might take a dustpan and brush to it this afternoon. Then I could sit there again.'

'The servants can clean it on Monday.' Her mother was touched by this domestic concern. 'There's no need for you to be bothered, *mein Liebchen.*'

'Oh, but Mama, I'd enjoy doing it myself.' She restrained her anxiety. 'In the afternoon I will bring down what's needed.'

She squatted on the grass and poured the coffee, while her mother sat uncomfortably on the edge of the sunbed.

'I thought this would interest you,' her mother said, displaying a magazine which she had also brought with her. There's a story about that Baroness you admire.'

'Really?' A renewed twinge of anxiety caught Ilse. She was a fool to have ever mentioned the bitch.

'She has an art exhibition in New York. They say she will sell her famous diamond there.'

'Well, good luck to her.' She didn't trust herself to make any further comment.

That afternoon Ilse made a show of playing the cleaning woman. She put on an apron, took down brushes and buckets and scoured the pagoda for an hour and a half. When she returned to the house fifteen thousand deutsche marks, thank God unattacked by vermin, were inside the beach bag. That night, after her parents had gone to bed, she checked one of the five-hundred-mark notes against one her father had given her. It was the same light brown colour. It bore the same date of issue. Would anyone reject it?

Chapter

18

Friday had come and Craig was still unable to devise any justifiable escape over the weekend. Julia had accepted a Sunday lunch invitation from the parents of one of Antonia's schoolfriends. Saturday was dedicated to mowing the lawn and clearing up the small garden: with July's burgeoning heat grass and weeds grew as fast as if North Plainfield were in the tropics. He had thought of inventing some unexpected duty at a hotel function, but dropped the idea for a variety of reasons. Basically he didn't want to get tangled in deception and total lying: certainly not when he did not truly know where he stood with Barbara and when Julia herself had become uncharacteristically inquisitive about what his new job actually involved. She'd been suspicious of his leaving early for work this morning. She must have sensed that he had other things on his mind.

In the late afternoon he was steeling himself to tell Barbara he had failed when she called him from the Front Office to come and deal with a guest's security problem. He was left unclear about the nature of the problem until he emerged into the great marble-pillared lobby and saw who Barbara had with her. It was that goddamn German with the diamond again.

'Thanks for coming, Mr. Clifford.' Barbara was cool and formal. 'The Baroness von Brandenburg would appreciate some advice.'

'How can I help this time?' Craig forced a smile. He had been learning fast since his promotion, taking his cue from the Banqueting Director's supple, unfazed reactions to difficult clients. He kept the smile in place, waiting for the Baroness's reply and thinking that whatever the downside of her character, she looked pretty good. She had changed since the morning and was eyeing him with casual self-assurance. Her sun-bleached, shoulder-length hair was neatly held back by a wide black velvet bow, and she had on a creamy silk dress, with a rope of pearls around her neck, while chunky gold bracelets glinted on her wrists. He could tell from the look she was giving him that she was about to demand even more attention than the hotel had already given her, which had been excessive.

'The Baroness will be leaving her valuables in our care again tonight,' Barbara said in a completely deadpan voice. 'But she is worried about taking them to Long Island tomorrow.'

Yesterday they'd sent a limo and a security guard out to Kennedy and Craig and the Front Office Manager had been on hand here to welcome her. Before she'd even checked in she'd bawled them both out over how long it had taken to clear her jewelry through customs, as though it was their fault. In any case what did she expect if she was declaring four million dollars' worth? He knew it was four million because she demanded a receipt stating the value when he took her jewel case down to the strong room.

Then the Baroness Helene von Brandenburg had demanded he be available at eight this morning to hand the jewel case back in person. So he'd had to leave North Plainfield very early, with all those attendant gripes from Julia. After that the Baroness had hijacked him into accompanying her and some ultrasmooth Brit from Burnaby's to the Gemology Institute of America fourteen blocks down in the diamond district at Fifth Avenue and 47th Street. And he'd had to take a cab there again at four to escort her back. 'Okay, okay,' Trevinski had ordered, 'You just do what the lady says. Without her rocks they ain't got no fucking auction in October, right, and we ain't got no publicity for it.' He must have been paying more attention to the PR angle than Craig had realised. 'Just keep the lady happy and bill every goddam cent of expenses.' So Craig had done as he was told: and now she was worried about taking the jewelry to Long

Island. In other words, she was going to want a security escort.

An escort to Long Island! Tomorrow, Saturday! How could he have not appreciated why Barbara had spoken in such a deadpan way, as if she had unlocked a secret but wasn't letting anyone into it. She must be through with her regrets.

'I stay with Prince Otto at Southampton,' the baroness remarked, as though she expected Craig to stiffen and salute at the name. 'You can arrange a limousine, I suppose?'

'The desk clerk will fix that,' Barbara assured her. 'Just tell us the time.'

'Is there anything further we can help with?' Craig asked solicitously. He caught Barbara's eye as he spoke and she gave him a mocking look, as if to say, '"Further," Mr. Clifford? Why the heck don't you volunteer to take her?'

'I do not like to take unnecessary risks, you understand? I cannot go alone with a hire-car driver I never meet before.' The Baroness half raised an eyebrow at him in a way that was part appeal, part seduction, part self-deprecation. 'You must think I am terribly stupid. But I like someone to come with me to Southampton.' As an afterthought, almost, she added, 'If the hotel does agree.'

'You can always leave your valuables here, Baroness,' Craig felt compelled to say, remembering Trevinski's warning about expenses.

She had class, okay, and the Colonel Brandenburg he'd been with at NATO must be some relation. The Colonel's first name was Heinrich and he'd always insisted that there were no titles in Germany anymore, so he didn't call himself 'Baron' or 'von'. He had been a decent enough fellow, always ready for a beer in the Officers Club. By contrast the Baroness pulled rank all the time. Yet behind her haughtiness he sensed an unease that Craig had only lately learned to recognise: the unease of people who hope someone else is going to pay. Like them, she jumped the gun in justifying her demand.

'Oh no. To leave my diamonds here is impossible. I have promised Prince Otto to bring them.' She smiled warmly at Craig. 'So, that is arranged. I must be there by midday. What time do we leave?'

'Gregory will know how long it takes,' Barbara said. 'You'd better check with him.'

While Craig crossed the lobby to the concierge's high mahogany pulpit of a desk, she glanced down at her computer and, as if idly, tapped in the number of the Baroness's room. 'I'll just put the limo booking into the computer,' she explained. She understood Craig's caution. If someone other than the Baroness was picking up the tab for his brief expedition into high society she preferred to know what had been authorised. The details flashed up. 'Charge to Burnaby's New York. Limit of stay two nights. Credit limit $1,000.' The total charged so far was $869, though that included tonight's room and taxes.

'Will you be paying by credit card, Baroness?' she asked politely.

'You send the account to Burnaby's.'

Barbara was about to make her routine reference to the need for authorisation when she remembered both that the Baroness was probably a millionaire and that Burnaby's would be spending tens of thousands hiring the Grand Ballroom. She'd get no thanks from Steven Corley or Holtz for offending her. So she kept quiet until Craig returned.

'Gregory reckons two and half hours on a Saturday,' he announced.

'Then we leave at ten. I see you here.' The Baroness smiled graciously and left them.

'Well, dig that,' Barbara laughed—a little nervously, Craig thought—'a day out in the Hamptons with Prince Otto. Shall I dare speak to you after tomorrow?'

He looked around them quickly, not wanting to be overheard. 'I guess I could be back by three and it could be a day in New York with Miss Andrews. If Miss Andrews would go for that.'

Barbara blushed. 'She just might. If her social calendar permits. You'd better call her tomorrow, though. She could have one of those last-minute invitations to the White House.' Her eyes kissed him, then she saw the spare, neatly dressed figure of Corley coming towards them. As usual the Resident Manager was glancing discreetly around him, a permanent half smile fixed on his angular face, as if to reassure people that his interest was purely beneficial. She covered up quickly, saying in a louder voice, 'Maybe we should check that Burnaby's will pay for the limo. I don't think Mr. Trevinski would want it on his budget.'

Corley seldom missed a trick. He'd already guessed something was going on between those two. Equally the Baroness had been smiling at them a moment ago. She'd already managed to establish a lousy reputation with the room service staff. If Barbara and Craig were keeping her sweet they should be encouraged. But he also noticed the doubt in Barbara's expression as she consulted the computer.

'You have a problem?' he asked, and after she had explained told her, 'Check it right away with Burnaby's.' Then he turned to Craig, who he noticed was not afraid to look him straight back in the eye. 'Will Mr. Trevinski want you doing this? Okay, then. Southampton gets one more summer visitor.' He smiled genuinely for a second, as though remembering something that he'd enjoyed. 'Seeing it's the weekend, have them take you to the Meadow Club. That's the place to go. Have a nice day.'

Nonetheless there was a sardonic quality about the 'Have a nice day,' as though he was investing the cliché phrase with double meaning.

'Well,' Craig said after Corley had moved on, 'I guess his specialty is making people think he knows more than he does.'

'He doesn't matter, Craig,' Barbara said softly. 'Can you really get away?'

'Sure. Julia won't mind at all.'

'You're joking?'

'She'll drink it up. A Baroness? Prince Otto? Only trouble could be she'll want to meet them herself—especially when she remembers the Baroness's cousin Colonel Heinrich.'

'She knew the family?' Barbara was astonished.

'She knew the Colonel, though not as well as she'd have folks believe.'

114

Chapter
19

S o , do we open champagne?' Helene von Brandenburg tried to sound flippant, but failed. She was more tense about her diamond's valuation than she cared for Constant to know and could not conceal it. 'Maybe, we have some in any case,' she added, 'since it is here.'

They were in one of the smaller suites at the Park Plaza. The champagne bottle stood on a table in a chromium ice bucket, swathed with a white linen cloth, two slim-stemmed glasses beside it. The Baroness did not believe in stinting herself. Courtesy of Burnaby's, naturally, James Constant thought, as he dealt with the bottle. He had his own way of opening champagne, grasping the cork and half twisting, half pulling it out. That way there wasn't an explosively loud pop, nor did the wine spray out uncontrollably. He liked things to be under control. Sure enough, the trick worked. He poured two glasses, let the fizziness settle down, topped them up and handed one to Helene.

'So. Do we drink to the sale?' Her anxiety filtered through again.

'I think we could.' There wasn't much choice. He raised his glass. 'To the Malabar Angel.'

In fact the Gemological Certificate had been less excellent than he hoped and the reserve price ought to be set well below the figures Charles Luttrell had bounced him into talking about in London. The Baroness was not going to like that. Conversely, failure to sell would cost her sixty thousand dollars, or two percent of three million dollars—assuming that was the reserve—and if Samantha was right she was unable to sign that large a cheque. She regarded Burnaby's as existing to make her richer, not the reverse. All in all he reckoned she might become quite emotional in the next few minutes. It would be prudent to deliver the good news first.

'Would you like to see the provenance I've roughed out? I envisage its being printed in a special brochure, devoted exclusively to your diamond, with a colour photograph.'

He extracted a folder from his briefcase and handed it across. The staff at the New York office had done their utmost in a very short time. The thick creamy card of the folder's exterior bore Burnaby's emblem at the top; below it was THE MALABAR ANGEL, followed by THE FINEST HISTORIC DIAMOND TO BE OFFERED ON THE INTERNATIONAL MARKET IN THE SECOND HALF OF THE TWENTIETH CENTURY. Below that again came a passable reproduction of the von Brandenburg coat of arms and, in less extravagant type, *Property of the Baroness Helene von Brandenburg*.

Helene settled herself composedly in an armchair, nodded appreciation of the folder's presentation and then took out the two sheets of linen laid paper it contained. She skimmed the first.

FAMOUS DIAMONDS

Nearly all the world's finest diamonds originate from the former Kingdom of Golconda in India. Among legendary stones from this part of the Moghul Empire are the Koh-i-noor, now set in the British royal crown; the Regent, once worn by Queen Marie Antoinette as part of the French crown jewels and now on display at the Louvre Museum in Paris; the Orloff, once the property of Catherine the Great and now in the Diamond Treasury of the Soviet Union; and the Wittelsbach, formerly belonging to the Austrian House of Hapsburg . . .

'For heaven's sake'—Helene stopped reading—'why do you say all this?' She sounded surprisingly antagonistic. "This is not about my family!'

Constant smiled. 'I hope to put the rarity of your diamond fully in perspective. I want potential bidders to appreciate that it is one of the very, very few large stones to have belonged both to the Moghul emperors and the nobility of Europe. By comparison even the Cullinan is nouveau riche.'

'Ah so!' Helene smiled, the start of a contented glow flushing her cheeks. 'I understand. That is good.' She picked up the provenance again.

Tavernier, the seventeenth-century French jeweler who made six expeditions to the Orient, reported this great diamond's existence after his visit to the court of the Great Moghul. 'I saw this Stone of exceptional fire, it being then set in gold as a turban ornament and of a reputed 89 carats weight.' New research has revealed that it was subsequently given by a Prince of Cochin to a church in Malabar and brought to Europe circa 1770 in a comparable way to the Orloff. It was purchased by the Baron von Brandenburg from a Berlin jeweler in 1791 and subsequently recut at the family's orders . . .

'But how can you know all this! It is more than we ourselves ever knew.' Helene's reaction was an odd mixture of admiration and aggravation.

'Oh, facts stick in one's mind.' Constant played down the extent to which imagination had leapt the barriers of proof. 'The moment I saw your diamond I remembered Tavernier's remark.'

Personally, he thought the comparison with the Orloff a stroke of genius. The Orloff had been stolen from a Brahmin temple by a French army deserter who had wandered southern India disguised as a Hindu, selling the jewel in Madras, after which it was taken to Amsterdam. Yet no one had suggested the Orloff be returned to the Brahmins. However, there were limits to inventing history. The Baroness would still have to indemnify Burnaby's against any possible charge of selling stolen property. 'Good title and right possession' was the agreed-on phrase in the New York art business, 'free of all liens, claims and encumbrances.'

'By the way,' Constant said, 'do you have the 1791 receipt with you?'

'We did have it, sure. With the jewels in the bank.' She became flustered. 'I have seen it myself. But no one can find it. I do think the bank people have lost it, the fools.'

'You can guarantee you have good title?'

'I can, of course!' Indignation replaced embarrassment. 'I mean, who will take any notice of this nonsense with the church? Everyone knows it is our diamond, after all.'

For a few seconds Constant wavered. The Baroness was evidently not aware of a landmark case in Indianapolis in 1989 when federal judge James Nolan ruled that sixth-century Byzantine mosaics stolen from a church in Cyprus fifteen years before must be returned by a local dealer who had bought them in Switzerland. That case had severely shaken the antique trade, quite apart from losing the dealer herself a cool nineteen million dollars profit on an agreed resale to the Getty Museum. Could Nolan's ruling apply to a theft possibly three hundred years ago? Charles Luttrell thought not. But the Baroness would still have to indemnify Burnaby's.

'Then all we need is the standard contract assurance that you have the right to consign the property for sale.' He made it sound as uncomplicated as it usually was.

'And now'—Helene shrugged off the awkwardness—'this wretched certificate. What does it say?'

Constant refilled her glass, then consulted another paper letterheaded GIA GEM TRADE LABORATORY INC., on which a diagrammatic drawing of the Malabar Angel's facets had been made.

'Not quite as good as we hoped, I'm afraid. The certificate confirms the rectangular cut, the weight at 53.28 carats, the dimensions and so on. Colour grading E, as I expected. But the stone does have that "natural" near the girdle and there are surface abrasions. For flawlessness they've only graded it S one-two.'

'Which means?'

'The sixth grade.'

Helene exploded. 'But you tell me before it is the third. How can they say this! Anyone can see it is magnificent!' Her temper rose rapidly. 'What is this damn certificate, after all? Who cares about it? Anyone can see what the Angel is worth.'

'I'm sorry, Baroness. The GIA laboratory is completely impartial.'

'And next you tell me the value is less!'

'Value is subjective. Any artefact is worth only what someone is prepared to pay for it. Ordinary engagement ring diamonds, for instance, are in regular demand. So they have an accepted trade value. We're in a different league. With a diamond like yours the auctioneer may be able to lift the value per carat astronomically above the estimate. What he cannot do is promise a price.'

'But you set one?'

'No, Baroness. We *advise* on a reserve. You decide whether to accept our advice.' There was no point in prolonging this, if she didn't want to understand. 'I suggest three million dollars, which will be confidential between us.'

'That is absurd.' She made as if to move. 'I go elsewhere.'

'I hope we shall actually sell your diamond for between four and five million.'

'Hope? What use is hope? You should be able to set a price. It's your job, for God's sake.'

'Baroness.' Constant could be as abrasive as diamond dust itself if he wanted. 'If you wish to know how much your diamond is worth to the trade in cash, then take it out to Harry Winston or Tiffany or de Graf. Take it to one of the Forty-seventh Street merchants. They'll make you an offer.' He handed her the certificate. 'You'd better have this, too, since you'll have paid for it. But don't expect five million. Don't expect three, because they won't be under any pressure to buy.' He stood up, then refilled her glass from the champagne bottle. 'With the compliments of Burnaby's. You will excuse me.'

'Wait!'

He stopped in the doorway. He genuinely had intended to leave. Charles would be livid at losing the showpiece of the October auction, but he had too much experience of troublesome clients to want this one ruining the occasion. She was exactly the sort who did a private deal a week beforehand and pulled out, sending in lawyers to countersue over the withdrawal penalties.

'Mr. Constant, I did not mean literally to go elsewhere. But this is a great disappointment for me.'

'If you wish to set a higher reserve, it is entirely up to you.'

'You think we get a better price than from a jeweler?'

'If we did not, Baroness, we would not be in business.'

He let her think about that. It must be quite a new experience for her, having a tradesman answer back.

'You have brought a contract?' She asked after a pause.

With some reluctance Constant reopened his briefcase, taking out a printed form. Burnaby's 'Conditions of Acceptance' had none of the glamour of the special folder. Helene read them through carefully, while he waited.

'You will notice,' he said, underlining what they normally left unemphasised, 'that various expenses are payable by the seller. Insurance and catalogue illustrations, for example. There is also a twenty percent charge if you withdraw after signing.'

'My God.' She made an attempt at humour. 'Is there anything I do not pay for?'

'Very little.' He couldn't recall being so blunt with a client before. The experience was profoundly enjoyable. 'Mr. Luttrell might meet the costs of the special brochure, as well as your present stay in New York, as well as charging only seven percent commission.'

'Tell him I now prefer six percent.'

'I doubt if he'll accept that.' Constant didn't give a damn if she dropped out right now. 'If you wish we can meet after the weekend, when you've had time to think about it.'

'I suppose Otto can bring me from Long Island,' she said, as if to herself. 'Where do we meet? Here?'

'The office would be easier.' He gave her a visiting card. The next thing they knew she'd be charging two more nights to Burnaby's account. 'If you decide to go ahead, would you bring the diamond with you?'

She gave him a sly, almost triumphant smile. 'I think about that too, Mr. Constant. And thank you for the champagne.'

As he left the elevator to walk into the lobby the attractive young Manager whom he'd spoken to before left her desk and approached him.

'Excuse me, sir. We just wanted to check something. Your guest has asked for a limousine to take her out to Long Island tomorrow. Can we charge that to the account?'

'Miss . . . ?'

'Andrews, sir.'

'Miss Andrews, you may bill the limo. Was there anything else.'

'We are providing a security escort, sir. With the compliments of the hotel.'

'That's very good of you. By the way, Miss Andrews, if the Baroness asks for a room again on Monday is there any chance the hotel could be fully booked?'

Barbara looked at him in astonishment and was rewarded with a perceptible wink.

'We should greatly appreciate the hotel being full on Monday.'

'Well, I . . .' She'd never had a request like this before. 'Well, sir, I could ask the Manager. But if she chooses to pay herself . . .'

'She won't,' he said. 'I promise you, Miss Andrews, that she will not.'

Chapter

20

I f it's personal advice you're after, Father Gerard, off the cuff as
you might say, I'll do my best as a friend but if it's a question of
conscience, then you know as well as I do it's your Spiritual
Director you should be talking to, not me.'

Father Fergus Crawburn was a plump, smooth-faced Irishman in his early fifties and if he greeted his brother priest
cautiously it was with reason. As Secretary of the Canonbury
Missionary Society he was an administrator, not a counsellor,
and primarily responsible for the everyday running of this
rambling Victorian country house on the outskirts of the county
town of Hertford, some twenty miles north of London, which
was the members' home as well as their headquarters. Gerard
Vaughan had lived here after his return from Africa: and
Crawburn vividly remembered how tricky finding him a suitable occupation had been.

'It is not then a question of conscience, I take it, Father
Gerard?' Crawburn confirmed.

'Not of mine, Father Fergus. Of other people's.' Fighting
words, Vaughan realised as he spoke them. But he always had
loathed bureaucracy. In Africa you rolled up your sleeves and
got on with things. But back in Britain! He supposed it would be
worse in Rome, so he shouldn't complain. 'To be exact, it's a
question of what I can hope to achieve and what I cannot.' He

handed out a sop to Father Fergus's self-esteem. 'You'll be better able to judge than anyone else I know.'

'Well, then, if we're talking practicalities, let's have the facts.' Although mildly flattered, Crawburn stressed the word 'facts', as if erecting a barrier against opinions, and while he listened he kept alert to signs of what he most feared from this particular colleague: actions that might bring discredit upon the Society.

Father Gerard, with his grey-flecked beard and stubby, calloused field worker's fingers, with his impatience of regulations and his perpetual itch to get things done, had been a crucial asset to the agricultural training school he ran in Africa. But the Society's discipline was liable to be insufficient for go-getters like him. Indeed that was one reason why missionary priests were required to be 'incardinated' into either a Bishop's diocese or a Society. And now he was straining at the leash again!

'Do you not think chasing after this jewel might be better done by a lawyer or some such professional man?'

'I doubt the Bishop could afford to hire lawyers. We were young priests together. Would you have felt able to refuse?'

'Perhaps not.' Crawburn knew he would have excused himself somehow. 'Nonetheless, even a Society as closely related to the Indian church as ours must set limits.'

That it did not set close enough ones was, of course, the snag and would probably be so about anything that truly captured Father Vaughan's enthusiasm. Crawburn still recalled with horror the blithe remark he had reportedly made when asked about retirement from the agricultural school. 'So long as I don't get any of the girls pregnant, I expect they'll keep me on.' The joke had gone down better in Africa than England.

The Society's relatively relaxed rules even allowed Vaughan to retain control of the salary he earned, though he voluntarily handed over part of it, as well as to live away from this their Mission House. However Canon Law, amongst many other things, did most emphatically forbid him from engaging in commerce.

'The, ah, negotiations you are conducting, Father Gerard. They are solely for the return of the jewel?'

'I'm not demanding a diocesan percentage, if that's what you're afraid of. The Bishop wants the diamond, not money.'

'I am relieved to hear it.'

'Do you think possession of the mount strengthens our case?' Vaughan had debated with himself whether to mention the curious inscription and decided against. It had an Old Testament quality of revenge, which would strike Father Fergus as dangerously fanciful and of which he himself was suspicious. After all it could have been engraved on the mount quite recently.

Crawburn steepled his fingers, as if in prayerful meditation behind his desk. 'In practical terms, I should say not.'

'Since the owner refuses to give back the stone, can you see any way of recovering it?'

'From an auctioneer or dealer, never.' Crawburn's reply was unexpectedly definitive. His Irish country upbringing had taught him to regard all dealers as horse thieves. 'A benefactor would be the only possibility, someone of the Faith who would buy it for you. But what would persuade someone to make such a gesture in this day and age, I can barely imagine.'

'A Prince of Cochin first gave it to the church for his redemption.'

'And maybe he did, Father Gerard, maybe he did.' Crawburn disliked being outpointed. 'But nowadays he'd be wanting publicity for his gift into the bargain. He'd be after recognition in this world as well as the next, would he not? I doubt if our Provincial would like your involvement being blazoned in the newspapers either, come to mention it. Our supporters might feel there were better uses for the money—for no doubt huge sums of money.'

'The congregation there prays regularly for its return.' In his mind he saw them kneeling at the evening service on the Saint's Day, the candles barely illuminating the crumbling Baroque decoration of the chancel, the incense heavy on the humid air, the priest holding the cross aloft, the sighs of veneration from the women tearfully audible. Half a world away, yet never forgotten. 'I felt obliged to help answer their prayers.'

'One can only wish all heartfelt prayers to be answered.' Crawburn had been caught out again, though he sidestepped neatly. 'And those must assuredly be from the heart not the head. Realistically, a benefactor would be an outside chance.'

'Should I accept conscience money from the owner? Would that prejudice a benefaction?'

124

'Possibly. Only the Bishop can judge. You must accept his directions.' Crawburn gave his brother priest a disturbed look. 'Frankly this distraction could occupy far too much time. Does the CCRA not keep you very busy?'

'At the moment, yes. The coup in the Sudan particularly. We've two Sisters under virtual house arrest with a diplomat's family in Khartoum.'

'They are at least safe?'

'Thank God. But the supplies we've shipped for them may be looted, there's no coordination. I feel I should go there myself.'

Visions of Father Gerard being thrown in jail or held hostage flooded Crawburn's mind. Why did the man see everything as a challenge? Perhaps, he tried to reassure himself, this was simply the true spirit in which the Faith had first been propagated. Perhaps Father Vaughan was of the stuff that founded Missionary Societies. Unfortunately that didn't make him any the more comfortable to have on the loose in a well-established one. 'Whether you should go is for the CCRA's Council to decide.' The last thing he wished to do was encourage more adventures. 'Personally I doubt if you'd get a visa.'

'Wish me luck if I do.' Father Vaughan stood up and shook hands. All the interview had achieved was to confirm his fears.

As Crawburn said goodbye the silver lining occurred to him. Being in Khartoum would at least prevent Father Gerard from making a further fool of himself over the diamond. Nonetheless he must leave his official attitude crystal clear.

'You do appreciate, Father, that any action on behalf of the Bishop must be purely your own. The Society cannot be involved.'

That evening Father Vaughan telephoned Lucy Luttrell at her home in Wiltshire. By his economical standards it was a lengthy conversation: all of eleven minutes.

'There's only one person I can think of,' Lucy concluded, 'and I don't really know her myself. Anyway she's in America.'

'I don't think I could manage the fare.'

'Would the jewel's return really mean so much to the church?'

Vaughan felt that if he had to reiterate this one more time he would go berserk. But how else did water make a hole in a stone? 'The Bishop and the congregation would regard its return as a miracle.'

'Then if I can arrange the introduction, I will pay your expenses myself.' There was an unexpected steeliness in Lucy's voice. She was damned if that bitch Samantha was going to profit from this immorality. 'It seems I cannot prevent Burnaby's from handling stolen property. But I can alert responsible people of the diamond's significance. Will you leave it with me, Father Gerard?'

'Of course. I may have to go to the Sudan for a few weeks.'

'There will still be time.' She was quite decisive. 'Believe me, if the miracle can be performed, then between us we'll perform it.'

A fortnight later, as Father Vaughan waited in a Khartoum hotel room for a summons from the Health Ministry that never came, and fretted at the impotent expense of the delay, he was still unsure why Lucy Luttrell had embraced the Bishop's cause with such fervour. He also speculated, against both his judgment and his theological training, on whether the acronym on the gold mount did constitute some form of curse: and whether, conversely, a benefactor could expect an equivalent benediction.

Chapter

21

B y the time the limo dropped Craig Clifford off on East 88th Street after his Saturday jaunt to Southampton with the Baroness, his mental state was less composed than a Marine Corps Major's ought to have been: even a retired Marine Corps Major who was trying to hold off going back home to his wife while stealing time with his girlfriend and was three hours late already.

He could think of plenty of men who'd be unfazed by this situation, guys who'd actually get a kick out of calling their wives from another woman's bed. But he'd never been in that league and anyway he was in near shock from half a day experiencing how casually the extremely rich expected to buy power over other people. Dealing with multimillionaire foreigners hadn't been on the course at Annapolis. Consequently when the same extremely rich had displayed their innate courtesy and charm towards their inferiors by insisting he should stay for lunch he'd not known how to refuse. Then they'd all but checkmated his plan for the day by courteously calling Julia—again that was the Baroness's idea—to say when he'd be back. So now the time was half past five and he was due home in an hour. In a phrase Prince Otto would not have used, this was an ass-kicker.

As he rang Barbara's apartment bell he didn't know precisely how he was going to handle her either. This was to have been the first day they'd had together since that initial, unexpected, night. He had desperately wanted it to go smoothly: and now one of the first things he would be compelled to do was get off the hook with Julia all over again.

'Don't tell me,' Barbara said as she let him in. 'The lady screwed you up.' She kissed him warmly. 'I knew she was going to. It was in her eyes. Don't worry. These things happen.' She hesitated. The last thing she wanted to be today was recriminatory. On the other hand if this relationship was going anywhere Craig would have to understand that she had her own life, her own independence, her own right to considerateness as well as love. 'You could have called, though.'

'I'm sorry.' Explanations were not going to help. Better to take the rap. 'They're pretty persistent people.' He stood back to take a proper look at her. She was in jeans and a plain red T-shirt that did her figure no harm, no harm at all. 'You look like a million dollars,' he grinned, relieved to be able to speak honestly. 'It truly is great to see you.'

'And you.'

They gazed at each other in mutual satisfaction, she happy beyond all expectation that though this man might not be too sophisticated, he wasn't loaded with the snobberies and social attitudes of the advertising executives and stockbrokers she sometimes found herself on blind dates with; he thankful that although she was ten years younger than he and could pretty well have any man she wished for, she had stayed cheerful and not launched into a tirade when the day went adrift.

'Well . . .' She didn't quite know what to do next. Not true. She knew exactly. She wanted to get him straight to bed, after holding him at arm's length all these days. But maybe that wasn't so clever. Maybe she should stick with what she'd planned and let things take their course. She still didn't know that much about him, for goodness' sake, except he was married and had gone through faintly mysterious times in Europe. Caution won, temporarily at least. 'You had something to eat, I guess.' She half laughed, dismissing the meal she'd carefully prepared. 'Well, I must have been crazy to think you'd be here by two. The pizza'll keep. You probably need a drink more than anything.' She steered him out of the tiny foyer and into the studio. 'What would you like? A beer or something stronger?'

'A beer would be fine.' The limo had been air-conditioned and this apartment wasn't. Even though Barbara had the windows open the July heat was sultry and oppressive. He took off his jacket and loosened his tie: that had been another mistake. Because he was technically on duty he'd dressed for it, while Prince Otto's friends had all been in polo shirts.

'Now.' Barbara had a knack of picking up his thoughts, not that it would have been difficult. 'Tell me all about it. How does the jet set live when they aren't making our lives a misery?'

Craig thought about the rambling three-storey clapboard house, with its white-columned porch, wide lawns, high hedges and imposing entrance gates. There'd been a seperate service driveway. Outside on the neat grass verge a Southampton Village Police notice warned against parking on the road: anywhere on Dune Road, which the Baroness had told him matter-of-factly was 'where the big money lives.' He thought about the oil paintings of racehorses in the hallway and the expanse of white-tiled floor in a kind of conservatory where they'd lunched at a long table made of thick smoked grey glass with arch-shaped chromium legs.

'It was pretty fancy,' he said, looking at her sofa bed and the posters on the wall and thinking that he'd been on a different planet. 'More like a movie set than a house. You know something, the Prince said it had three wells for water. He was very proud of that.'

'Crazy.' She shared his astonishment, though a little awkwardly because she was afraid her studio must seem more than usually cramped and uninspired by comparison, proud though she was of the way she'd decorated it. 'And what was he like?'

'Mid-thirties. The kind of suntan I'll never be able to afford. Not a bad guy, in his way. He works for a bank. I had a feeling the Baroness wouldn't mind getting promoted to Princess.'

'And was anyone else there?' She wanted to get more of a picture of the occasion that had fouled up their day together.

'A couple of other bankers. One was an older guy called Cranston, Walter Cranston. Typical Wall Street, what I guess they'd call the old school. Wasp. Silk cravat in the open-neck shirt and wearing a sport coat. But he was okay. I liked him.

And he knew just how to handle that goddam Baroness when she tried to sell him her diamond. I wish you'd been there.'

'Tell me.' She would have enjoyed watching that woman being put in her place.

'Come to think of it, the Prince must have set him up for her. As soon as the Baroness had done her patronising bit about "You never guess, Otto, this gentleman knows my cousin Heinrich," Otto really went to action stations. Made a big thing of asking me to stay for lunch—I guess that was to impress Cranston as much as anything—then started opening champagne.

'Nice for some!'

'I said I wished you were there.' Craig let that pass. 'The next thing, he was raising his glass and saying "We make a toast. Let us drink to Helene and her diamond." So we all drank to her health and I could see this old man Cranston was reacting. The word 'diamond' had a knee-jerk effect on him. Then the Prince said something about "Why don't you show us the Malabar Angel, Helene?" and she had the nerve to tell me to fetch the jewel case.'

'So you did?'

'Feeling damn stupid. Then she chased around a bit, found a dark-coloured cushion from a couch and laid the necklace out. It was pretty impressive to me. Cranston certainly thought so. "There you are, Walter," Prince Otto said, in an easy kind of way. "Just what you want for Sarah-Jane." Turned out she was Cranston's wife and going to be fifty soon and he was trying to find a surprise for her.

'"Of course, I don't like to lose such an heirloom," the Baroness said, as if she'd much rather not be selling it at all. "But I do want to endow a Fellowship in my father's memory." Then she delivered a long spiel about how legendary the diamond was, Indian Princes, her great-grandmother, you name it.

'"What do the auctioneers expect it to fetch?" Prince Otto asked.

'She cut a quick sideways look at Cranston, like she wanted to check if he was serious. "Seven million," she said. Maybe more. It is fifty-three carats after all and last year some dealer has paid three hundred thousand a carat for a rare blue stone. Burnaby's do tell me it is the finest historic diamond to come on the market since the 1950s." She'd been boning up on her statistics and she took another quick gander at Cranston. "What do you think of it?"

'"Magnificent," he said, but he'd caught that second glance and it made him cautious. "When is the auction?"

'"In October, if I do not make a private arrangement before." She was definitely measuring him for size. "If I should have a good offer, then I save myself ten percent commission and many expenses. My God!" She gave a despairing look at the Prince. "I can't tell you what they ask for, Otto. Ten percent commission, one percent insurance, a fortune for printing a brochure. To be honest, I would be better off with six million privately and we both save money."'

'And you and I get saved a lot of hassle too,' Barbara remarked. 'What did the banker say?'

'He took it in all right. Knew who she was aiming at: and stayed pretty cool. "It's a very fine piece of jewelry, Baroness," he said. "Sarah-Jane would appreciate a diamond like this. Do you have a GIA certificate by any chance?" She didn't like that. I guess whatever assessment they made of the thing yesterday, it wasn't as good as she hoped. "I do, of course," she said, as though he was asking unnecessary questions. "Do you like to see it?" Well, when he said yes she'd hadn't much choice.'

'And?'

'Cranston read the certificate and began to back off. "It is a quite exceptionally beautiful diamond, Baroness. But I should need an expert valuation before committing myself." She was furious, not openly, but she was. I guess she had worked this all out with the Prince beforehand. "Really, you know," she said, as if she'd now gotten bored by the whole business, "I don't like to wait until October. When I make up my mind, I like to do things at once. Pouf." She snapped her fingers. "Straightaway. I must go back to London on Tuesday. If you like to sleep on it and tell me tomorrow I accept five and a half." Well, that really blew it. I mean, she was down to ordinary horse-trading. Cranston just smiled politely, like he wished there wasn't a smell in the room, and said he was very interested but guessed he'd wait until the auction. Prince Otto rushed around with more champagne, trying to revive the party atmosphere, and

Joe Soap was left to put the damn necklace back in the jewel case. After that we had lunch.'

Craig sat back and finished his beer. He felt as though he'd talked for a long time. Christ, he was going to have to phone Julia. That was inescapable. 'Listen, sweetheart,' he said, 'I have to call my wife.'

'Or else you have to go? Is that it?' All the shared good feeling from his account of Long Island evaporated, as she'd feared it would have to. 'Which do you want, Craig? You want to stay with me, or you want to go?'

'What d'you think?' Perhaps that wasn't the most tactful way to put it. He put his arms around her waist and kissed her. 'Barbara, you're beautiful. I'm the luckiest guy in the world.'

She hugged him, delighted now that he wasn't wasting time. 'Craig, I like you very much. Don't start making phone calls at this moment. Please.' She kissed him back and then, with no hesitation now about what mattered most, pulled him down onto the couch.

For a time they just lay there after making love, she with her head on his chest while he stroked her hair and told her, in his own slightly stilted way, that she was all he'd ever dreamed of. She felt happier than she could have imagined. He was real, he was a proper flesh and blood man, a guy without hang-ups who didn't bore the pants off her with his ambitions and his plans and everything except what use he was going to be to a normal woman.

'You don't mind that I have a career of my own?' she asked at one point, not exactly nervously, yet probing towards what mattered. 'Not that I don't want to have kids like anyone else. But I wouldn't want to give up the hotel business either.'

'I wouldn't want you to,' he reassured her, thinking, Christ what a contrast to Julia. Then it struck him that if the divorce cost what he'd always been told divorces cost, and he had to go on paying the North Plainfield rent as well as alimony, they'd probably need all of their two salaries. He kept that thought to himself, but she sensed what was going through his mind.

'I don't want to rush into things, Craig,' she said. 'But on the other hand if we decide we're right for each other I'm not going to hang around being the other woman for years and years. I've seen what that does to friends of mine. We either get together, or we don't.' She reached up and kissed him, hoping she hadn't been too cut and dried, too self-analytical. 'Even if Manhattan does have a serious manpower shortage.' She sat up. 'Now you'd better call her. What are you going to say?'

'The Baroness could have had me run some other damfool errand. It's a miracle she didn't.'

'Okay.' Barbara had a gut feeling that she might yet bless the Baroness as well as cursing her. 'Just say you're held up. I'd love you to stay the night, but something tells me it's not a good move today.'

As he made the call, sitting on the edge of the couch, while Barbara tactfully absented herself in the kitchen, it struck Craig that he had now gotten into the league of guys who call their wives from other women's beds: and it wasn't a league he could stay in long.

Chapter
22

The Libyan was late. Only by half an hour, but that was enough to have Ilse covertly checking her watch and kill her already stilted conversation with Frank. She was nervous, and for reasons the Irishman had begun to appreciate were potentially dangerous. She was no longer accustomed to clandestine meetings. Nine years absence from action had dulled her sensitivity to what smelt right and what smelt wrong.

Frank noticed and was troubled. She'd lost what the Germans called *'Fingerspitzengefühl'*: the instinctive feeling for a situation brought about by a combination of inborn sixth sense, hard training and experience. He'd set up this rendezvous for her: and because she was apprehensive she'd insisted they arrive half an hour early at the pavement café the Libyan had designated. That was poor tradecraft, a bad omen. The making of contacts had to look natural and Ilse was about as relaxed as a laboratory mouse being fed to a snake. He'd have quit here and now if it wasn't for the money. Also, he was enjoying Paris.

The café was called the Mabillon, just off the Boulevard Saint Germain near the Sorbonne, usually hectic with student argument, but in early July more frequented by tourists. Ilse reckoned that was why the diplomat had chosen it. The Left Bank was awash with tourists. An Arab, an Irishman and a German woman drinking together would excite no curiosity. But where was the Arab? 'What's happened to him?' she asked in a stage whisper.

'He'll be along.' Frank wished she'd shut up. Just sitting here was good. He was basking in the late afternoon sun, watching the girls go by, bottoms wiggling and bosoms jiggling, happy in the knowledge that someone else was paying. A suntanned girl wearing high-heeled gold kid sandals and the tightest jeans he'd ever seen tottered past, every detail of her crotch made plain by the taut fabric. His eyes followed her, until he caught Ilse's sullen annoyance. Screw you, he thought, if you were human you'd have shared a room and I'd have less of a bloody ache in my own crotch. 'Arabs don't have any sense of time,' he said irritably. 'Don't you know that?'

Be patient, she told herself. Stay with it. This is crucial. If they give us the Semtex the rest will be easy. Frank swore they would deliver anywhere. But could she believe him?

'New York?' She'd not intended to speak out loud.

'And why not?' Frank said with stifled aggravation. 'Haven't they supplied us all up and down the coast of Ireland? In Holland? In Germany? Why should this be any different? Wait until the man comes, will you? And have another drink, for God's sake. You're a bundle of nerves.'

While she bit back her anger he waved to a waiter and, after some delay, succeeded in ordering another white wine with cassis for her and a Coca-Cola for himself. He never drank alcohol when negotiating with Muslims: though whether this respect for their principles made any difference he was unsure.

'This man had better come,' Ilse retorted eventually, leaving the implication unspoken, her fury fuelled by the humiliation she'd had to endure to get a passport for the trip. She'd had to convince her mother that a short stay with friends in Paris would do her good. Only then had her father been prepared to forward the application through his law firm. In theory it was unnecessary. She was not on parole, she was entitled to travel, but she knew there would have been delays if she'd applied herself. Having to depend on her parents rankled. She could only justify the degradation because it was for a greater purpose. Now she almost spat at Frank. 'If this man does not come there is no more money.'

'He'll come.' Frank shrugged off the threat. She was a mean

bitch, holding back half the twenty thousand marks until they had a firm deal, refusing to give herself to him as any warm-blooded woman would have done. He could have used a woman last night, any woman, even one as old as her, and he was still smarting at her curt refusal. She was turning out every bit as intense and unpredictable as he'd feared.

The white-aproned waiter returned, set down the drinks, deftly tucked the bill under an ashtray along with its predecessor and moved on. Ilse extracted the bill again and checked the addition. She felt cheated and vengeful.

'If you're so bloody tight with money,' Frank remarked tartly, 'you could have saved some by sharing a room.'

'When we have to pretend we are lovers, then it may be necessary. If we get that far. Until then, not. You say you know this man?'

They both fell silent.

'Hey! Look who's here!' The Arab caught them unawares, still enveloped in mutual antagonism. He was young and tall, wearing a polo shirt with an Adidas emblem and muscular underneath it, swarthy faced and pudgily handsome. He could have been a bit part movie actor and spoke with an American accent. In fact he had once been a junior oil rig engineer for Esso, doubling as a police informant. Another Arab was with him who was not merely older, but a quite different type: shorter, leaner and sharper featured with a hooked nose. 'Meet Ahmed,' the young one said.

Frank stood up and shook hands. 'This is Ilse,' he said simply. 'What'll you drink?'

They both sat down, asked for fruit juices and openly scrutinised Ilse, as though suspecting a potential enemy.

'My name is Rahman,' the younger one said, not impolitely. 'Tell us about yourself.'

'I have just spent eight and a half years as the guest of my government. There are things I would like to do.'

'You never came to Tripoli?'

'Some of my friends went.' She named two. 'We had a good connection with the PFLP.'

'Why didn't they contact us?'

'You should know.' She was beginning to resent this interrogation. 'They are in the Stammheim Hilton.'

For a moment Rahman was foxed, until Ahmed whispered something to him. 'Okay, okay,' he said abruptly, 'I get it.'

After this Ahmed took over the conversation. His English was less fluent, but he appeared more flexible, asking what it was Ilse had in mind.

'She would like to do a job on a New York hotel,' Frank said.

'This one.' Ilse scribbled the name of the Park Plaza on a slip of paper and handed it across.

Ahmed nodded. 'Zionist owned?'

'Partly. There is a function taking place. I want to do what the IRA did in Brighton.'

'Brighton?' The reaction was bemused.

'When they blew up the capitalist British leaders. I heard about that even in Stammheim. The bomb was in a bathroom.'

'We were not involved.' Ahmed said stiffly and suspiciously.

'But you understand the concept?' Ilse insisted. 'We take a room above the ballroom before the event. We conceal the materials. Then, when the event is in progress'—she snapped her fingers in the air—'Schuss.'

'And what is the event?'

She was ready this time and took a copy of a newspaper cutting from her bag. With it was a clipping of Burnaby's official sale announcement.

'For what reason?' Rahman enquired. 'Who will be there? Jewish dealers?'

'A lot of them.' That hadn't occurred to her until this moment, but it was obvious. 'Some of the richest Americans. It's a very famous hotel, too, a New York landmark.'

'Why should we go crazy about that?' Rahman cut in. 'What's in it for us?'

'Wouldn't it be easier than attacking the Sixth Fleet?'

Neither of them liked that. They said nothing.

'She has a point there,' Frank said relaxedly, as though it had only just come home to him. 'It would make a nice little bit of revenge for some reverses in the past. And we'd be doing all the work.'

'Perhaps,' Rahman conceded. 'But what's in it for her?'

'She has a score to settle, too.'

The Libyans exchanged glances, as though the conversation was at last making sense, when Ilse explained the background of Baron von Brandenburg and the law of 16th February 1978. 'We are all in the same revolutionary struggle.'

'We are not sympathetic to the cult of personality,' Ahmed said pedantically. 'But the fight against American imperialism is also our fight.' He turned to Frank again. 'What do you need?'

'The usual stuff. How much I couldn't be telling until I've seen the place. Maybe a hundred pounds. Maybe less. Depends on the structure.'

'For this date?' The Arab pointed to the newspaper cutting. 'October twenty-second?'

'For a week earlier. We'll have to take it in bit by bit.'

'And who will claim responsibility?'

'Responsibility?' The question caught Ilse totally unprepared. 'For me it is not necessary. I will know and that is enough. Retribution will have caught up with this family.' She looked at Ahmed and saw perplexity and mistrust in his cloudy brown eyes.

'This is done by your organisation?' He didn't want to say the name "Red Army" aloud.

'Natürlich.' Ilse scented problems and paused again while she thought ahead, like a chess move. 'We always work in small cells for security in the struggle. Against the capitalists, against the Zionists, against the pigs who jail our members. This will be a demonstration of our ability to strike back.' She prayed they would respond, because they had caught her out. The Red Army was not involved, and she was worried they might check up on her.

'This is a good opportunity,' Rahman said firmly, as if he had to convince his older colleague. 'We can take the war into the heart of the imperialist camp.' He didn't need to add 'at no risk to ourselves', because that was the assumption. The ease of keeping Libya's reputation clean if things went wrong had been Frank's strong card in getting him interested.

'We will convey everything you have said.' Ahmed got up. 'There are many aspects to consider.'

'We need a decision soon,' Ilse said, with a note of agitation in her voice that she failed to control. They had to help her. Didn't they understand?

'As soon as is practical, we will inform you,' Ahmed said.

138

'Through our friend here,' Rahman added. 'Don't worry, we'll be back to you.'

'Are you sure they will?' Ilse asked after the Arabs had gone.

'Sure and they will, in their own good time,' Frank said. 'Just leave it with me. And now they've agreed, me darlin', there's a little matter of ten thousand marks, if you please. Then we can be getting on with the planning and such.'

Chapter

23

'I must be honest with you, Mr. Kuroki.' Charles Luttrell was always at his most confidence-inspiring when being least truthful. 'I will pass on your offer, but I think it most unlikely that the owner will accept.'

He beamed at the diminutive Japanese seated with him in the great reception room at Burnaby's. Mr. Akira Kuroki might be dressed in a less than well-cut brown suit and a knitted cardigan that made Charles wince, but as Gakugei-In, or Curator, of the Acanthus Museum in Tokyo he commanded enormous purchasing funds. Such money would normally justify careful massaging of Kuroki's ego. Indeed the two men had done presale deals before. But this time it was out of the question. Unthinkable, Charles reminded himself. The Malabar Angel was the lynchpin of the New York sale, now only two weeks off, for which Czernowski had secured enviable publicity. Everything connected with it had rocketed into superlatives: in fact the publicity girls were running short of adjectives and had been forced into buying a thesaurus. So it was unthinkable Burnaby's should not sell the diamond by public auction on October 22, even though it might not make the price Kuroki was proposing.

'I think five and a half million dollars is a fair price, Mr. Luttrell.' Kuroki smiled as politely as if he were at a tea ceremony, his persistence studiously self-effacing. 'Only condition, as before, is that you do us favour of no figure announced.'

'I fully understand.' Charles leant back in his chair, clasping his hands together and intertwining his fingers, nodding slowly, creating a miniature pantomime of comprehension.

The international computer company behind the Acanthus Museum welcomed the cultural prestige which its generosity and Mr. Kuroki's taste had brought: the museum occupied the entire first floor of its headquarters building in the Minatu-ku district. But the Japanese tax inspectors' view of museum donations was rigorous. Unlike the IRS in America they allowed donations no tax advantages: in fact the reverse. The company stood to be taxed on the estimated value of its collection. Accordingly Kuroki's buying was as discreet as his personality. He knew precisely where the Malabar Angel would be exhibited in the museum: in his mind's eye the armoured plate-glass display case already existed, cleverly illuminated to strike sparks of fire from the diamond. He could visualise the announcement of its purchase, stressing the appropriateness of this Oriental treasure being returned to the East, and see admiring visitors queueing to gaze at it. But nowhere, ever, would the price be mentioned and Luttrell knew the money would not be paid direct from Japan.

'I think this is very fair offer,' Kuroki said. 'With much respect I suggest your client would be sensible to accept.'

Sensible! Charles thought. Thank God Kuroki could not know that in her present mood the Baroness would be round for the cheque this afternoon: if she knew, which thank God she could not.

During the three months since she had reluctantly signed the contract in New York Helene von Brandenburg's emotions towards the sale had swayed to and fro like an apple-laden bough in a gale. After first resenting the photographers her mood had changed. She'd been persuaded that her own ancestry, personality and good looks could do as much to boost the auction as the diamond itself. She had positively overindulged the gossip columnists and photographers. For weeks it had been impossible to pick up a newspaper or magazine without having her broad suntanned face and blond hair staring out at you. She had willingly conspired to have her name romantically linked with her charming Prince. She had told diarists how it broke her

141

heart to be selling the Angel, but to commemorate her father adequately she must: and darling Otto supported her. Darling Otto, Charles suspected, would not be interested in marriage to anyone without substantial cash at the bank. Continentals very sensibly made no bones about that kind of thing.

Then, at the end of July, she had vanished, remarking that nobody would be seen dead in London or New York in August. In September she was back and had briefly become excited at the prospect of the money again, but at the end of the month unwisely attempted a private sale to the banker Cranston and asked for the jewel to be returned. Charles had been forced to remind her of the penalty clauses in the contract: twenty percent of the three million dollar reserve they had so painfully agreed on, plus all Burnaby's considerable out of pocket expenses. Predictably, she had thrown a raging tantrum and stormed out of this very room, shouting abuse, calling him a con man and a shark and employing a number of German expressions which, perhaps fortunately, he could not understand.

So the Baroness would probably accept Kuroki's offer on the spot, if only from spite. Happily, however, she had vanished again and although Samantha had heard she was in the West Indies Luttrell was in no hurry to find out precisely where.

'Whether our client would be sensible to accept, Mr. Kuroki,' he pronounced gravely, unclasping his fingers and making a wide 'hands off' gesture to indicate his own complete impartiality, 'must be a matter for her. At the moment she is on holiday and out of touch, but I will do my best to pass on your offer. I'm afraid that is all I can do.'

The Japanese looked at him narrow eyed, suspicion tinged with respect. This could only be a delicately phrased way of demanding more. Auction houses did not lose contact with their most valuable clients in the run up to a major sale.

'You wish us to increase?' he said, managing to inject real incredulity into the words, despite his faulty English. 'When your sale estimate is only four to five million?'

'The estimate? Ah yes. I agree. But catalogues have to be printed a long time in advance, Mr. Kuroki. In the meantime very great interest has been generated. We expect some of the world's wealthiest collectors to be bidding.' To throw the Japanese off the scent he quoted a few names he would like to have attracted. 'The Aga Khan and Niarchos: I can imagine a saleroom contest between their agents! Baron Thyssen. Sheikh Makhtoum. Frankly, this item could go a lot higher than the estimate.'

Kuroki rose from his chair and shook hands, inclining his head just sufficiently to be polite without implying undue respect. He did not appreciate being spurned. 'I shall go back to my trustees,' he said stiffly. 'I must take advice.'

'I hope you will be at the auction. A diamond as legendary as this has not been seen in the saleroom for many decades.'

'I hope we can buy,' Kuroki replied carefully. He was far from certain that his trustees would permit him to. He had also noticed that whereas in the catalogue the Malabar Angel was 'historic' it was now 'legendary'. Luttrell must have supreme confidence to refuse a million dollars more than his own middle estimate.

In the small conference room downstairs, James Constant was showing the Malabar Angel itself to the press, seated at a table with three of the publicity girls and Samantha flanking him. He was nearing the end of his whistle-stop tour of the world. He had taken the diamond to Tokyo, to Hong Kong, to Monte Carlo, to Geneva. In each city he had displayed it to invited clients for one day and to the media for a morning, utilising Czernowski's associated PR offices where Burnaby's did not have one. The schedule had been gruelling, travelling with the necklace in a bag attached to his wrist, taking it with security guards to a bank vault each evening. He was thankful that only Los Angeles remained to be visited before the final pre-auction showings in New York.

'When can we interview the Baroness?' a reporter called out. 'Where is she?'

'She is away on vacation.' Constant was tired of the columnists, who wanted only to ask about the Baroness and her love life, tired of the paparazzi, afraid that publicising her might begin to backfire. The quality of the jewel itself was being neglected. He reminded his audience of that.

'Hold the thing up for us then, for Christ's sake,' a photographer demanded wearily. There was no mistaking that he was making do with second best. Constant obliged, then had the better idea of bringing Samantha into the act. So the flashbulbs flickered for her as well.

Then, mercifully, he was able to end the proceedings. The reporters picked up their press packs, weighty folders replete with statistics about Burnaby's history and sale records, about the world's greatest diamonds, about how this would be the first jewelry auction ever held at the Park Plaza Hotel. And there was the special Malabar Angel brochure, glossily bound in watered blue silk and lettered in gold. The promotion was costing a fortune.

As he collected his own papers together Constant noticed that not all the press representatives had gone. One, a dumpy woman in her forties, dressed in slacks and a vividly patterned Indian cotton shirt, had buttonholed Samantha. She was the saleroom correspondent of the *Dispatch*, who in Charles's telling phrase 'has her ear so bloody close to the ground that her nose is always in the shit as well'. Her having stayed made Constant apprehensive. He decided to tackle her himself.

'You know Victoria Stewart-Robinson, don't you, James?' Samantha was relieved to have some backup. 'You may be able to help her better than I can.'

'Well, I can't promise, but I'll try. What's it about?' He did his best to be forthcoming, not liking the way she had a notebook out and ballpoint poised.

'There's a story going round that the diamond rightfully belongs to a church,' she said in a rasping, common voice. Double-barrelled names were no guarantee of a pedigree, least of all among members of the Fourth Estate. 'From the Church of Our Lady in Malabar, India, to be exact.' She lifted the pen. 'Is that true or false?'

Constant was caught. If he said it was false, he could be accused of lying. If he admitted it was true, then he knew what the headline to her story would be. One of Vicky's specialities was catching out auction houses when they unwittingly offered artifacts illegally removed from Hindu temples, Egyptian tombs, or other exotic locations that the local inhabitants were only too happy to pillage. You needed your wits about you with ethnic Vicky.

'It has been claimed that it might be the diamond missing from an astylar cross since the seventeenth century,' he began

144

cautiously. 'I am personally in no doubt that before it was recut in the nineteenth it did belong to a Moghul Prince—as we explain in the brochure.'

'So it was stolen from the church in Malabar?'

'There is no proof whatever that it was stolen.' He would have liked to ask how the devil she knew the name of the church, but he wasn't going to let her get a rise out of him. The only way with ethnic Vicky, especially if she was on her 'theft of priceless treasures from the downtrodden Third World' kick was flat denial. 'It could have been sold off by a church functionary. We simply do not know. What we do know is that the Baroness von Brandenburg has secure legal title.'

'In words of one syllable, was it stolen or not?' This prevarication was not the stuff of which quotes were made. 'Yes or no?'

'In words of one syllable, Miss Stewart-Robinson, it belongs legally to the present owner and there is no possible legal claim on it from any other quarter.'

'That is not what the Bishop of Malabar believes.'

'I am not competent to talk about the Bishop's beliefs.' He cut into her as sharply as she was cutting into him: and did it matter? If this woman had her knife into Burnaby's she would disembowel them all in print anyway. 'Have you anything in writing about this?'

She gave him a look of perceptible triumph. 'I have a photocopy. Which I intend to publish in tomorrow's edition. With your comments.'

So she had somehow been talking to Father Vaughan! In which case he had seen the letter himself. 'If it is the document which I think it is, it does not constitute proof of the diamond being stolen.'

'Our readers will judge that better.' She stopped scribbling, though she did not put the notebook away in her handbag. The best quotes often slipped out when people were flustered, annoyed or thought an interview was over. 'Thank you for a remarkable lack of candour, Mr. Constant. I am sure that the group campaigning for this jewel's return will be most interested.'

Constant bowed ironically. 'You may give the group my compliments.'

She hesitated, almost decided to rough him up properly by

revealing that her informant was Charles Luttrell's wife, then decided against it. She would keep that for a later story. But her ill-concealed delight alerted Constant that there was worse to come.

'Bloody woman,' he commented to Samantha, in just the way Charles would have done, after the reporter had gone. 'What else d'you think she has up her sleeve?'

Chapter
24

'Antonia wants to meet that Baroness of yours.' Julia glanced up at Craig from the canvas chair where she was enjoying the last warmth of the sun in a turquoise towelling leisure suit that she'd bought by mail order from Britain. Her face glistened with sun lotion. The porch was a good place in the early evening: one of the assets he'd miss most if he left this house. A copy of *Vanity Fair* magazine lay open on the low table she'd brought out for her drink. Beside her, Antonia was playing with a Barbie doll. Craig noticed the doll had its legs wrongly attached, so it looked deformed and faintly obscene in its nakedness. Its clothing was scattered around the plank floor. Antonia immediately stopped sorting through the miniature garments.

'I want to meet the Bawoness. I want to meet the Bawoness,' she chorused obediently. 'Mummy says we're going to meet the Bawoness.'

Craig nodded without speaking. These days, Julia barely greeted him as he walked up to the house, unless it was with some domestic demand or other. Although it was early October, the city had been stifling. An Indian summer. The Indians could keep it. Great for his wife, luxuriating out here with her oh-so-English gin and tonic, ice clinking when she lifted the glass, the ultimate sound of cool leisure. The hell with her. His shirt collar was soaked with sweat. Although he'd bought an old Ford as a 'station car' three months back, which took some of the pain out of commuting, nothing was going to make the New Jersey rush hour trains less crowded or hot.

'Daddy!' Antonia ran up and hugged him. She was always welcoming. He adored her. She was the main reason he hadn't walked out on Julia already. He lifted her up, kissed her and got a wet, smacking embrace in return. 'Daddy! When are we going to meet the Bawoness? I've seen her picture in the magazine! Haven't you seen her picture in the magazine?' She'd been taught her lines and, like all five-year-olds, derived huge pleasure from repeating them over and over again, 'Daddy, I want to meet the Bawoness.'

'Why can't we, Craig?' Julia said with the whining edge in her voice that spelt envy. 'You've spent enough time running errands for her. Why can't we both be introduced? It's not as though I didn't know Heinrich Brandenburg, too.' She smirked in a way suggestive of intimacy. 'Quite well, in fact.'

'Let me get myself a beer.' Craig went into the house and through to the gadget-filled kitchen. He needed a cold beer and he also needed to think, even though he had seen this coming. Julia had long ago decided to be at the auction to capitalise on his frequent security assignments for the Baroness. The *Vanity Fair* article must have finally triggered the idea. But apart from having to act the guard dog one more time after the day at Southampton, the intermittent assignments that had punctuated the summer hadn't been on behalf of the notoriously unpredictable Helene von Brandenburg: they'd all been with Barbara, on occasions when there was no other excuse for not getting home. These last three months, as their affair matured, he had thrown away scruples and exploited major hotel functions and the auction preparation to the limit. Now he knew how an escapologist must feel when he's had himself roped up and thrown in thirty feet of water and finds he can't undo the knots. But he had one advantage over escapologists: he might be able to bluff his way out. He poured some beer and took the can back to the porch.

'I'm sure she'd be happy to meet you.' he said, bending the truth more than somewhat as he hefted out another chair for himself and knowing he'd be unable to play the Baroness card again for fear of Julia wanting to go along with him.

'I want to meet the Bawoness,' squawked Antonia. She'd seen the picture and she knew: the Baroness was like a super-duper Barbie doll, the very best. That was what her mummy had said.

'You will, sweetheart.' Craig reached out and chucked his daughter under the chin. 'Antonia specially. The Baroness told me she loves kids.' That was closer to reality. For some reason she had told him she'd always wanted children. 'Only problem is she most likely won't be here again until the auction.'

'What's an arkshon, Daddy?'

'Well, it's kind of a sale, when people get rid of things they don't want anymore.' Like five million dollar diamonds. He turned to Julia. 'That'd be the best day. She'll be there but without anything much to do. I tell you what, honey—maybe you could be shown the jewels before the sale starts. I guess I could fix that.'

Without any question he could sneak the pair of them in. Even Trevinski would sympathise. Trevinski, he'd discovered, had a soft spot for kids. Julia's meeting him was a risk that would have to be taken. She was so crazy about noble titles that she had never questioned why the hotel should be willing to make his services available to the Baroness. He edged towards firmer ground. 'God knows I've done enough for those auction people. Would you like me to ask?'

For the first time in weeks, Julia treated her husband to a smile that wasn't the prelude to a jibe. 'Wouldn't that be lovely, Antonia?' she cooed. 'We could see all the jewels and meet the Baroness.' A thought crossed her mind, regurgitating ideas from the magazine. 'Will Prince Otto be there too?'

'I guess so.'

'I'd love to meet him.' She savoured a sip of the gin and tonic. 'He looks so fantastic in the photographs. Is he really?'

'He's a reasonable-looking guy.' No point saying he'd been as condescending as hell. Say something she'd like to hear, then maybe she wouldn't probe too much. 'Plays polo back home in Germany. The Baroness told me he played against Prince Charles one time.'

'He did! Oh, I simply must meet him. Did you hear that, Antonia? He played polo with Prince Charles.'

149

Of course Antonia wanted to know what polo was. Craig, exploiting this diversion, began to explain that it was a game in which men on horses tried to hit a small ball with long sticks—a procedure the point of which his daughter found hard to grasp.

'But why do they have to be on horses, Daddy?'

'Because Indian princes invented it,' Julia cut in with aggravation. 'And it's the most aristocratic game there is. Really, Craig, you are useless.'

'Mummy, is Prince Otto an Indian?'

'You see the sort of dumb ideas you put into her head!' Julia snapped. 'How is she ever going to get properly educated in this dump?' She shifted gear back to the adoring mother's gentle guidance. 'No darling, Prince Otto is a German who plays polo. He is not an Indian. Now come on, it's time for your supper.'

She gathered up their daughter, the Barbie doll and her drink and swept into the house, leaving Craig to reflect on the decisions facing him. He poured the rest of his beer from the can and thought about them. 'Write down your problems, boy,' his father used to say. 'Write 'em down, the good things one side, the bad the other. Then you can make up your mind.' His father had been a foreman in a factory, addicted to books on how to stop worrying, how to make friends, how to gain self-confidence, all that kind of junk. He was pretty sure this advice had come from one of those thick-paged, large-printed volumes. Personally he reckoned the Green Machine had taught him most of what there was to know about making decisions. But his father's was still a sensible approach. Since he could scarcely sit on the porch and start writing columns with Julia around he began a mental tally, in much the same way he used to teach young officers to sum up a situation if they got themselves pinned down under fire: and, boy, was he pinned down!

After about three minutes he realised he didn't have to make any columns or any decision. Julia had made it for him. All he had to plan was how to lever her out of his life in the least painful way before she drove him completely crazy. He could not go on, as he had throughout this steamy summer, lying sleepless beside her at night, not even wanting to reach out and touch her, much less make love, while all the time images of Barbara tumbled through his brain. He reckoned Julia couldn't go on either, smoothing on the creams and lotions, examining

150

herself in the mirror, worrying at the onset of forty and all the time conscious that her husband didn't desire her any more. They were going to have to part.

There would be a cost. Christ, there would. A hell of a cost. Arguments, lawyers, alimony, dividing property. Would he lose Antonia? He'd heard a husband could get custody these days, if he was in a position to look after a child. But how could he and Barbara do that? Who would take Antonia to and from school? Where would she sleep in that trunk-sized apartment? For a moment he almost did start figuring those columns. Until he remembered that although Barbara joked about the Manhattan manpower shortage, about the weirdos and the gays and the lack of decent men, she wasn't going to hang around forever. Not for an invalided-out soldier trying to forge a second career and earning little more than she did.

So he made the only decision necessary: when he would make the break. His probation period as Assistant Director ended in three weeks, coincidentally the week of the auction. The day his job was confirmed, he'd move out. He'd just say he was going: and go. Leaving it until then would gain one minor bonus, too. Antonia would be able to meet the Baroness and watch the sale.

Friday evening. Barbara's shift had ended at four. She sat in her one comfortable armchair, sipping a cold apple juice and skipping through the pages of *Elle* magazine. How could anyone ever afford those clothes! Crazy! Two months' salary for a dress. The phone rang. It was a girlfriend suggesting they join up with a couple of guys for the evening.

'You'd like Joe's friend Steven. He's in PR, and he's looking for a night on the town. Could be fun.'

There was a distinct smell of delinquent husband in the description. Friday night and a blind date with a probably conceited, hard-drinking Madison Avenue executive who'd spend dinner boring her solid with descriptions of his fantastic new campaign, start fondling her thighs under the table and end up creating a scene if she didn't take him home. Thank you, no.

'It's sweet of you, Janet. I appreciate the idea. I'd have loved to come, but this evening I have plans.'

Plans? Who was she kidding? Friday night and she was going to sit here in the apartment, playing Mozart on the stereo, eating the salad she'd bought at the Korean deli and aching to be with Craig. She wondered what he was doing out in Plainfield. Being bawled out by his wife, most probably. Though he didn't speak about his domestic life too much, the picture she'd built up was clear. Julia was a bitch. But that didn't bring Craig any closer or make this Friday night any better. If he didn't either move in with her or clear out of her life pretty soon, she was going to have to make the decision for him.

Suppose he did move in? Could they survive in this tiny space? And how could they survive if they moved out of it? Rent-stabilised leases were like gold dust. Craig had told her he owned a house in Virginia. If that was sold he'd at the worst be entitled to half the cash and there were various military benefit details she hadn't entirely comprehended: like the extent of the disability pension he received. But it was clear he could get a mortgage at low interest through the V.A. Probably when the divorce was through, they would be able to buy an apartment big enough for his daughter to stay with them comfortably. In her mind she was very positive about that. She was going to love Antonia and enjoy taking her on excursions to the Natural History Museum and Central Park Zoo. The two of them would have good times together.

So, she concluded, it would be tough while they waited for the divorce to be settled, but it would be worth it. Light at the end of the tunnel. Hope coming with the spring. All the clichés, but so what? When she scrutinised what she wanted out of life, what she really wanted deep down, she wasn't so overly ambitious after all. What mattered was being with the right person and Craig was that person.

He wouldn't have to fool around deciding, though. She was sure he wouldn't, but there would always be excuses for delay. Mid-September to Christmas was the big season for events at the Park Plaza. Society dinners. Charity balls. This auction, which seemed to take up so much of his time and, she had noticed, caused the hotel's accommodations to be heavily booked, was only one function out of dozens. They would combine to keep him extremely busy. But she was not going to let them be an excuse for dodging the issue. Come to think of it, she was due three 'personal days' holiday. She just might take them over the time of the auction, go up to New Hampshire and stay with the Burckhardts, clear her mind finally and then—if it became necessary—deliver Craig an ultimatum. As she'd warned him, she was not going to be the other woman forever.

Chapter

25

W i t h i n herself Ilse Nachtigal seethed like a cauldron on a fire. Sometimes she had to dig her fingernails into her palms so hard to contain her frustrations that her hands bled. Four months had gone by since her release. Four months during which newspaper reports maddened her by glamourising her enemy and taunted her with the auction date when she must exact revenge: Monday, October 22. If she could be ready. If Frank did get the explosives. If, if, if! Four excruciating months with her parents throughout which she had pretended to be broken in spirit, the sorrowful prodigal *'aus einem guten Haus'* returned, the dutiful daughter who always preferred to stay at home when her parents went to parties lest she taint the bourgeois cream of local society.

The word had gone around Bad Godesberg, gossiped over coffee and cocktails: that Nachtigal girl certainly learned the hard way. Look what prison did to her! She's finished. Might as well go into a convent, if any self-respecting order would have her. Just shows what decent people her family are, standing by her after what she's done.

Throughout those summer months she had ground herself into continual subservience: and slowly it had paid off. Her trips to art exhibitions in Bonn and Düsseldorf—the occasions when she met Frank and Hans-Peter—shifted from being the cause of disquiet to bringing her mother quiet satisfaction. 'It's good for her to make these little excursions, Erwin dear,' Frau Nachtigal would say when Ilse was out of earshot. 'She is otherwise too introspective.' She had made a point of sending them postcards from Paris: pictures of the Louvre and Notre Dame. 'What did I tell you, Erwin. She is forgetting all that nonsense of the past.'

If her father wasn't so sure, he kept it to himself. While she lived at home he could keep an eye on her—and report on her weekly to the police. He'd always felt the Gestapo had been correct in principle: it was a family's duty to keep the authorities informed. He never suspected that she was counting on his doing so.

Exploiting this protection, she had gradually accomplished what had to be done. The money concealed in the summer-house had been moved into savings accounts under the false name she had chosen—Birgit Herbstein, the Jewish surname a deliberately ironic barb directed at her father's Fascist sympa-thies. She discovered Frank's surname was an alias, too, and also a twisted joke. He'd taken the name of a former British Chief of Police in Northern Ireland. A travel agent booked the airline tickets and a double room at the Park Plaza Hotel for seven nights. She gave Frank money for his visa, for travel cheques, for expenses keeping in touch with the Libyans. She had to pay out every time she met him. For all his incessant bantering she knew he was chiselling her and if he continued she might run short of funds, which in turn triggered fears that she might have genuinely lost her grip. She tried to put them aside.

Now, in the first week of October, all that remained were the visas—which she intended they should obtain in Paris—and her own passport. Hans-Peter swore he had that arranged and today she would be meeting him to collect it. Today she would also tell her parents she was making another visit to Paris. She went down to breakfast confident that they would not object.

'I so love Paris in the autumn.' She explained, 'The tourists have gone and with the season starting there are always new exhibitions.'

'Ja, ja. The Paris collections!' Frau Nachtigal read fashion magazines with reverent hopelessness. 'This time I may come with you, Liebchen. That would be nice, Erwin, eh?' She shifted her bulk around in her chair and bestowed a benevolent smile on her husband, a smile which shone like the silver on the breakfast table and said plainly, 'Look, you see, I really have brought our daughter back to appreciating normal life.'

'Oh Mama, that would be marvellous, of course.' Ilse very nearly screamed at this grotesque idea. 'But my friends have only a small apartment.'

'I am happy in a hotel, *mein Liebchen*. Don't worry about me. We can still spend the days together.' She beamed at her husband again. 'You could manage a week without me, couldn't you? Bertha and Franz will look after you.'

Ilse stared at the two hippos in disbelief. How could they do this to her? From Paris, using the alternative passport she was due to collect this afternoon, she would fly to New York with Frank. Everything was fixed and now her mother dared waddle in to wreck the plan.

'Paul and Irma may decide to go to the Loire,' she said, in desperation drawing on her future cover story. 'They often go for a few days.'

'*Wunderbar!*' Her mother breathed heavily with delight. 'I always wanted to see the chateaux. When are you going?'

'The eleventh. Next Thursday.' She was allowing Friday to Monday to obtain the visas and make a last contact with the Libyans. On Monday she would phone saying she was going to the Loire: and take the New York plane.

'So soon?' Her mother was disconcerted.

The conversation was broken by Herr Nachtigal announcing that he must leave for the office. 'Even on Saturdays there is work. Your generation doesn't know what work is!'

Anxious to avoid any more maternal planning, Ilse asked if she could go with him into Bad Godesberg, excused herself briefly while she collected her handbag, stuffed in a few five hundred mark notes in case she had to pay for the passport, though, God in heaven, the Red Army ought to provide one for a veteran, and for once was relieved to be with her father.

She sat silent during the short drive, until he broke into her thoughts with a single devastating remark.

'That Baroness von Brandenburg you're always reading about has an interesting legal problem.'

'Oh?' She didn't trust herself to say more. The swine must

have been spying on her more successfully than she'd realized.

'Wants to sell a family heirloom and now it turns out it was originally stolen from a church.'

'In what way, Papa?' If she sounded confused and phrased the question stupidly it was for good reason. She had instantly understood the implications.

'In what way is it a legal question, I suppose you mean? A reasonable point. An American court recently ruled that intermediate selling of stolen goods in another country does not make them irrecoverable. Your beautiful Baroness may have to return her diamond instead of auctioning it.' He always sat well back in the Mercedes' driving seat, his fleshy face impassive, eyes on the road, both hands on the wheel, retaining dignity at all times. So he did not look at her now. Just steadfastly sat there and said to the windscreen, 'It was her father's law that caught your boyfriend, wasn't it?'

'There were so many laws.'

'A fully justified law in my opinion.'

Why was he trying to provoke her now, after four months? Had he guessed? She must put him off the scent.

'That is in the past, Papa. I am trying to forget, right?' She took a colossal chance. 'About what Mama was saying just now: if she wants to come to Paris that would be nice.'

Her father grunted, perhaps satisfied, perhaps not.

She didn't speak again until he stopped to let her out in the town centre, and, she then felt constrictingly strained. Did he realise what a bombshell he had exploded underneath her? No, he couldn't. He must have been using the legal story to probe in a general way. She cursed herself for ever mentioning the Baroness to her mother, whom she suddenly saw had led her on. Informers. Spies. Pigs. If the worse came to the worst she would take her mother to Paris for the weekend, then poison her food to make her ill and have to return.

'See you later, Papa,' she managed to say.

'Please do not be late. We have guests tonight.' He drove off.

She walked to a café to kill time before taking the train to Düsseldorf and gradually recovered her composure. God damn it, why was she like this? Nervous. Unsure of herself. Lacking the sixth sense of experience. Frank had even told her as much. 'You've lost it, me darlin',' he'd said. 'No fucking *Finger-*

157

spitzengefühl, to coin a phrase.' Could he be right? In the old days she'd have fooled her father easily: and known she definitely had. She must get a grip before the rendezvous with Hans-Peter and the man he called Thomas who would provide the passport. What kind of a cadre member was Thomas? Of her own generation, or a later one?

When she and Hans-Peter reached the hide-out apartment soon after midday the place gave her an instant sense of déjà vu. It was in this kind of late-1950s low-income government-built housing that she and Horst had been sheltering when the pigs shot him. It was one of several blocks separated by littered waste ground in an industrial suburb, its drab concrete rectangle encompassing six floors of low-ceilinged apartments, with a number of communal staircases. Outside the once white concrete was grey and streaked, the decorative pastel panels under the windows faded and discoloured, the imitation balconies rusting. This was the best habitat for a militant: a nondescript rabbit warren, where new faces excited little attention.

Hans-Peter led her up one flight of a cement staircase, its walls a writhing scrawl of graffiti, to knock on a door. Then he stood back hastily, as if fearing he might be shot through the panel. He was more jumpy than usual. Ilse thought she saw the metal-rimmed peephole darken as someone peered out. Then the door swung inwards and there, standing well back in the gloom of an unlit passage, was a man in jeans and a dirty white T-shirt.

'Okay,' he said warily, 'come in. Close the door.'

Ilse went first, leaving Hans-Peter to obey the order.

The living room had the same effect on her as the whole building. Recognition. Empathy. Her spirits revived as though the past had returned to welcome her. This place had just the ragbag of furnishings she and Horst had so often lived with. An old brown settee, its fabric worn through, temporarily re-vamped with a blanket over the seat and back; glasses and bottles strewn around a stained carpet; saucers full of cigarette stubs on a stained teak coffee table, with simple rounded legs that would have been sold as 'Scandinavian' years ago. On this table, laid down apparently casually after Thomas had identified his visitors, was a treasure she hadn't seen since Horst died: a 9mm Beretta pistol, the same model they'd always used for their secret target practice in the forest. The Beretta was an old friend.

Seeing it keyed her up: and also aroused suspicions. What kind of bravado had prompted the man to leave it there? Was he expecting to impress her?

'This is Thomas,' Hans-Peter said unnecessarily.

In proper daylight Ilse saw that the man standing on the far side of the table was at least ten years younger than herself and somehow not what she had been expecting. He had greasy long dark hair and a saturnine, almost wolfish face. He was unshaven. All that wouldn't have counted if he had looked intelligent, if there had been some intellectual spark in his eyes. But there was none: only the craftiness typical of a petty crook. Could he be the new generation, a successor to Andreas and Holger and the other heroes? The habitat smelt right, the man did not.

'Hello,' she said coolly, deciding to waste no time. 'You have the passport?'

'Sure.' He was almost insolent. 'If you have the payment.'

'I have paid already. Eight years in Stammheim, remember?'

Hans-Peter shuffled his feet. 'Thomas took a lot of trouble,' he said. 'Things aren't so simple anymore.'

'Fucking right. Passports don't grow on trees. They cost money.'

'Let me see it,' Ilse demanded. 'Is it a proper one or a forgery?'

'What do you need it for? Hans-Peter told me this was a single trip.'

There was a shiftiness about the question that alarmed her further. Was he trying to sell her a badly executed fake? She glanced quickly down at the Beretta as she answered.

'An operation in America. "We are engaged in a war against the capitalist structure of Germany and its American allies." Have you forgotten?'

'I don't go for that idealistic crap.'

All the tension and anger inside Ilse exploded. This man wasn't a cadre. He was a fraud. She'd show the bastard who the veteran was. 'You little shit,' she said with an intensity of scorn that stopped him short, glaring into his face across the room. 'You dare call what Holger Meinz said "crap"?'

Then, as she stared him down and he recoiled instinctively from the elemental fury behind the dried-up complexion and mousy hair, she stepped forward and picked up the gun. The

159

stock slipped naturally into her right hand, her thumb slipped the safety off. There are techniques you don't forget.

'The passport,' she ordered, holding the Beretta pointed at his stomach and shooting a command sideways at Hans-Peter. 'Don't you move either, you creep. Now Thomas, the passport. And don't tell me it's in the bathroom.'

'Bitch. Give me that gun.' Thomas started to move forward until she shifted, faster than he could have imagined, into a slightly crouched firing position, body sideways to him, arm half bent, wrist level, the gun not quivering in her hand. It wasn't anything like the way gunmen acted in movies. It even looked faintly absurd carried out by a woman. But it was the way police marksmen drew a bead on a target. He recognised the professionalism and froze.

'The passport,' she ordered.

Thomas looked all around, exactly like a cornered rat, she thought. 'I have to fetch it from the closet.' His eyes flicked towards Hans-Peter.

'No. You don't move. Hans-Peter fetches it. If he tries anything, I kill you. Understood?' She raised the gun a fraction to aim at his chest. 'Hans-Peter, go around the side of the room.'

Out of the corner of her eye she saw Hans-Peter slowly edge round to the only closet, a door in the wall behind Thomas. He opened it. When he turned round he had a document in his hand.

'Stay there. Check the details. Read them aloud.'

In an unsteady voice Hans-Peter obeyed. 'Birgit Katerina Herbstein. Born Wuppertal. Profession: Artist.'

'Validity?'

'From July twenty-third this year.'

'Genuine or a forgery?'

'Genuine, I think.'

'Is it, Thomas?' The gun still didn't waver.

'What the fuck do I care, you bitch.' His eyes were searching for an escape. 'You'll pay for this, Hans-Peter,' he spat sideways. 'You'll pay for it, you prick.'

'Genuine or not?' She jerked the barrel up momentarily, then straightened her arm a little, as if about to fire. 'I asked you a question.'

'Doctored a little,' Thomas admitted. Jesus, he'd carve up

Hans-Peter for telling him this would be a push-over; saying she was just a deluded rich girl with a crazy obsession; claiming that although she'd been jailed, her dead boyfriend had carried out the attacks.

'Doctored but genuine?'

'Yeah. It's genuine.' He tried to mask his cowardice by being dismissive. 'Cost me a thousand marks before I put the picture on.'

'Bring it here, Hans-Peter. Come beside me. Show it to me.'

Hans-Peter sidled round again. He was shaking now. He considered trying to rush her, then abandoned the idea. If he failed and she shot Thomas he'd be in even worse trouble.

She glanced quickly at the passport and saw the photo she had provided. The pages that mattered looked all right. 'Okay, Hans-Peter,' she said, 'We go.'

'Filthy bitch. I'll get you for this,' Thomas shouted, adding a volley of obscenities.

'Buy yourself a dictionary,' she said. 'You could use some new words. And don't follow us.'

She backed towards the door, using Hans-Peter as a shield, opened it with her free hand without looking round and emerged into the passage. 'Close the door. We will walk slowly to the car.' She slipped the Beretta into her handbag, leaving it open and slinging the strap over her shoulder in a way that would enable her to heft the gun out fast. But she was confident there would be no pursuit. Thomas wouldn't want to get himself shot or even risk gunfire disturbing his sanctuary. She glanced back once and saw his face at the window. He had opened it. A further string of insults pursued her—but not Thomas himself. Her assessment had been correct. She hadn't lost her *Fingerspitzengefühl*. At the same time, there had been something wrong about him, like a person wearing borrowed clothes. Hans-Peter had some explaining to do.

'He's not one of us,' she accused Hans-Peter as they drove away. 'Where did you dig him up from? What is he, an ordinary crook?'

The answer was oblique. 'No one else was interested. I told him you could afford to pay. He'll kill me if he doesn't get the gun back.'

'Horst would have killed *him*,' she said tartly. 'And you, too, most likely. Who does the apartment belong to?'

'I borrowed it.' Hans-Peter became sullen. 'I tell you, no one wanted to be involved.'

What his contact had actually said, after also speaking to Frank, was that Ilse was old, burnt out, probably corrupted by those years in jail. She'd have lost that all-important instinct without which a militant got trapped and endangered others. Anyway, they weren't interested in massacring civilians. Their targets were businessmen, officials or military officers, men symbolic of capitalist authoritarianism for whom the public had scant sympathy. In a word, they wanted no part of this. If she succeeded, they might consider using her for something in the future. As for the passport, they needed all they possessed for serious operations. If she was prepared to pay he could try Thomas.

'You mean I'm on my own?' Ilse said.

'Just about.'

'So who was that runt?'

'He deals in things. I told him he'd get two thousand marks.' Hans-Peter's voice trembled as he thought about what had happened. 'I'll have to pay him. For God's sake, at least give back the gun.'

Before he dropped her off near the station she slipped the Beretta down the side of the car seat. She couldn't risk taking it on an airliner: and anyway when she arrived in New York she intended being clean of anything worse than a honeymooner's booking voucher for the Park Plaza Hotel.

'It's down the seat,' she said as she got out, then relented a fraction further and took a single five-hundred-mark note out of her bag. 'Give him that.' He was bound to have exaggerated the cost. A thought occurred to her. 'And tell Frank I don't like being cheated.'

'Don't call me again,' Hans-Peter said as she leant over to give him the notes. 'You're not wanted. Just fuck off.' It was the cruellest remark he could think of. 'And I hope you blow yourself up, too.'

But Ilse shrugged off the insult, telling herself on the train journey back that losing his help no longer mattered. She had the passport, now she could get her visa and travel cheques, her preparations this side of the Atlantic were complete; and above all she had proved herself. She had not lost her grip. That wouldn't be lost on Frank either. He'd realise he was going to have to earn his cash.

Frank had been stringing her along, even though there must be a basis of truth in his claim that blowing up the ballroom in the Park Plaza could be very much trickier than blasting open the old Imperial Hotel in Brighton. 'Its fine for you, me darlin',' he had said, with what she supposed might be Irish humour. 'But apart from the danger of your refusing to hand over the shekels if I don't do a proper job, I've a reputation to consider, have I not.' Now he'd have to reckon with her being a professional, too.

In the evening her good luck continued. Her mother had forgotten that they had an invitation from the Mayor for Friday the 12th.

'I am truly sad, *Liebchen*. I should so like to have come with you to Paris. Perhaps another time.'

'It's always possible, Mama.' Ilse felt so absurdly relaxed and happy at her day's achievements that she was quite encouraging. 'There is always another time.'

It didn't even occur to her until later that if her luck failed, 'another time' was precisely what there might not be.

Chapter

26

F a t h e r Vaughan sat waiting in the lobby of Claridge's Hotel in Mayfair, waiting to be called up to the suite where Lucy Luttrell had arranged an urgent meeting.

He'd thought he was accomplished at being patient until this summer. In his time he'd haggled with Indian moneylenders to help a widowed mother; he'd negotiated through an entire night with a Ugandan bandit leader to prevent an African village being machine-gunned and burnt. He'd thought he was acclimatised to field work. Yet this summer the Sudanese had taught him something new about nepotism, driving the Malabar Angel right out of his thoughts. He had spent many weeks trying to persuade one of the poorest nations on earth to accept medical aid for its children, refusing to give bribes for the release of supplies that the CCRA had itself donated, and finally being forced to leave by a 'spontaneous' Muslim demonstration outside the house where he was staying.

A lesser man would have returned embittered. But the swollen bellies and emaciated faces of refugee children had years before left a permanent scar on Father Vaughan's conscience. He had hastily arranged for a nonsectarian agency to take over the under-fives immunisation programme. After all, as he reminded his secretary when he got back to London, exhausted both by officialdom and an attack of dysentery, the objective was to help people who could not help themselves. The mechanism was secondary.

However, when Lucy phoned a few days after his return and asked him to come and meet a woman whose name, Donna Bradshaw, was faintly familiar, he wasn't sure he had the mental resilience to do anything more for the Bishop of Malabar. She had talked him round, persuading him that this American millionairess might help. Now, sitting in the quiet, deep-carpeted comfort of Claridge's lobby he was still uncertain. He decided to kill a few minutes by finding out about Donna Bradshaw.

'Mrs. Bradshaw, sir?' The senior hall porter at the desk noticed the clergyman's collar and felt able to indulge in mild confidences. 'Well, sir, we do not normally give information about our guests. But it's no secret that Mrs. Bradshaw owns a chain of boutiques in America. Not unlike our own Laura Ashley, sir. Fabrics and clothes. Very fashionable, they're said to be. She comes from California. Her husband is a Senator. Is that of any assistance, sir?' He had barely finished when the phone on his desk rang. 'Excuse me, sir.' He listened for a moment. 'Yes, madam, the gentleman is with me now.' He put the phone down and beamed as if he just backed a winner in the two-thirty race. 'Mrs. Bradshaw asks if you would go up, sir. The third floor, Suite 312.'

On his way up in the elevator, it occurred to Father Vaughan that the pursuit of this diamond was introducing him to more of the extemely wealthy than he had encountered in the rest of his life. He wished he could divert their attention to the many more important needs of the Church abroad. Possibly when this affair was over he would. Then, with a strange exhilaration at the way divine providence can work, he remembered why the name Bradshaw was familiar. It was nothing to do with boutiques. She was on the Advisory Council of the CCRA in the United States. He knocked on the door of Suite 312 with an unanticipated sense of purpose.

'Glad to meet you, Father.' The woman who greeted him was not the overbearing society lady whom he had half expected. Although elegantly dressed in clothes that he presumed came from her own shops, she was indisputably a businesswoman:

only lightly made-up, clear eyed, her hair firmly brushed back from her face and showing off simple pearl earrings, a cord looped around her neck unaffectedly preventing her spectacles from getting lost. He knew she must be in her mid-sixties, though she looked ten years younger. She was also, he knew at once from the way she had addressed him, a practising Catholic.

'Mrs. Bradshaw is an old acquaintance,' Lucy said by way of explanation. 'She's over here to open a branch in Knightsbridge. My husband took the opportunity of showing her the Malabar diamond.'

'Mrs. Bradshaw is also a patron of our Catholic Children's Relief Association, I think.' Evidently this was not why Lucy had asked him over, but establishing the connection could do no harm. 'I've just come back from a very frustrating time in Sudan on the CCRA's behalf.'

'Of course! That's right! It was you who's been trying to get our supplies released!' She was delighted, with a true California warmth overlying the briskness. 'Well, this is even more of a pleasure than I expected. I do apologise for keeping you waiting like that.'

Vaughan smiled. 'It's a pleasure for me. Mrs. Bradshaw. But I don't think you asked me here to talk about Africa.'

'I hope you will, though, when we're through with this diamond business. You'd like some coffee?' As if to make up for earlier discourtesy, Mrs. Bradshaw poured it for him, still talking energetically. 'Now, Lucy has filled me in about this and I have to say, it's quite a surprise. I could well have been a bidder at the auction. But if it rightfully belongs to the church, I'd obviously reconsider.'

'It should never have been accepted for sale,' Lucy remarked with a touch of venom. 'Unfortunately the stone was brought in by one of our less reputable consultants.'

Vaughan caught the hostility and decided this was a vendetta he should keep clear of.

'Let me get to the point, Father,' Mrs. Bradshaw said. 'Is the Bishop going to bring a legal action for its return as the papers have been saying?'

'I don't imagine so.' Vaughan didn't need to feign surprise. 'What have the newspapers been saying?'

'The Saleroom correspondent of the *Dispatch*,' Lucy said disingenuously, 'has heard of your correspondence with the Bishop. Goodness knows how. Could your office have told her? In any case, the point is that under American law the Bishop might be able to reclaim the Malabar Angel. Which is what we all want.'

'Yes, of course.' The undercurrents were now becoming confusing. Mary was most unlikely to have been talking to the press in his absence. 'I'm afraid I'm very out of touch. I can only say that the Malabar church could never afford to start a legal action. Not conceivably.'

'And if I paid the lawyers?' Donna Bradshaw said. 'How about it then?'

'Well,' he temporised, 'that would be an exceptionally generous gesture.' It did not surprise him. He was accustomed to the whims of human nature and the lengths to which people would go to obtain the blessing of the Church. An audience with His Holiness, for example, might not open the gates of heaven, but it was a sought-after distinction in mortal life.

'From what I know of these things my lawyers—our lawyers—could seek an injunction in the New York courts, preventing the sale. They'd need a deposition from someone of standing in the case: from you, if you have the Bishop's authority.'

'But . . .' Quite apart from his belief that legal action was the wrong way to approach this, there was another aspect that made no sense, no sense at all. He looked at Lucy. '. . . wouldn't that mean suing your firm?'

'Technically perhaps. The practicality would be an injunction forcing withdrawal of the diamond from the auction, after which we would be entitled to compensation from the purported owner.' Lucy sat more upright than usual, as if righteous indignation were a ramrod supporting her back. 'This collusion between her and some of our staff has been quite deplorable.'

'To be honest, Mrs. Bradshaw, I find it hard to believe that the Diocese of Malabar would succeed without documentary proof of ownership when the Greek government has been unable to recover the Elgin Marbles from the British Museum in spite of no one disputing that Lord Elgin took them from the Parthenon.'

167

'United States law is not British law, Father Gerard.' Mrs. Bradshaw disliked her ideas being rejected. 'We have ten days left. If you'll come to New York and make a deposition that'll be enough.' It occurred to Donna Bradshaw that possibly he wasn't accustomed to women taking the initiative so strongly, might even be suspicious. 'Listen, Father. I think this is the obvious route. But there are others.'

'Even if we obtained an injunction, would it prevent the diamond being brought back to Europe and sold?'

'I guess it would, but I should need to check. We can do that on the phone right now.' She glanced at her watch. 'Oh, dammit. No, we can't. Not for another couple of hours. Let's leave it this way, Father. I'll find out the legalities. Could you come across if need be? I'd be happy to fix the ticket and have you stay in our apartment.'

Vaughan gave this thought. He was being hijacked. On the other hand, it was in a cause he'd voluntarily espoused. He was due some holiday: although spending the time in New York was hardly the same as taking his intended Retreat in Devon.

'If I telex the Bishop,' he said eventually, 'I should have an answer by tomorrow or the next day.'

'Fine.' Donna Bradshaw extended her hand. 'Then I guess we can either get the lawyers on the road or not. But never fear, Father. We'll do something. There are other advantages we can utilise and I'd like to see your diamond back where it belongs. If the price doesn't go too high, that is.'

'With the publicity it's receiving,' Lucy said, the vitriol still in her voice, 'I doubt if it will make the reserve.'

When Father Vaughan left Claridge's he was convinced that the two ladies had told him only half the story at best. Lucy was clearly in a running battle with her husband. But Mrs. Bradshaw had a reputation for delivering what she promised. All he could do was wait. He did, however, ask Mary on his return to the office if she knew anything about the leak of information while he was away.

'Didn't you see the memo I left?' she asked, not entirely surprised that he hadn't read it yet. There'd been a mountain of nonurgent paperwork waiting on his return. She ferreted around his in-tray and came up with the slip of paper. 'I thought it was a little odd, but then she was the first person we asked for help, wasn't she?'

'Father Gerry,' the memo dated September 23 read. 'Mrs. Luttrell rang wanting copies of the Bishop of Malabar's letters. Have sent them. Mary.'

Chapter

27

'That bitch is trying to kill the sale.' Charles Luttrell was enraged at the Thursday art market column in the *Dispatch*. He was more or less inured to Victoria Stewart-Robinson's barbed comments on the art world, but these libels only eleven days before the auction had made him lose his temper. He glared across the table at Prince Czernowski, who had been called to join him and Samantha for an emergency conference. 'How do we stop this bloody woman?' he demanded. 'Sue the Editor? Seek a High Court injunction?'

'I'm not a lawyer, Charles.' Czernowski had forecast the outburst that would greet him. Accordingly he had matched Luttrell's habitual elegance with a red carnation in the button-hole of his own suit, indulged himself in a new silk tie from Harvie and Hudson on his way up from his Pall Mall office to Albermarle Street, and generally prepared himself to calm his client with a display of relaxed urbanity: a display the more necessary since Charles's own had audibly been on the point of collapse. 'This is exceptionally bitchy, I agree. But is it actually libellous?'

Luttrell snorted. 'Look at what she says, for God's sake. "High level representations by the Catholic authorities . . . the latest instance of British auction houses disregarding legal claims to works of art . . . possibility of court action in the

United States." Where did she get that from: It's bloody cod-swallop.'

'Hardly actionable, however.'

'What about this, then? "The most curious aspect of the Malabar Angel case is that Burnaby's controlling shareholder, Mrs. Lucy Luttrell, is herself a Catholic. Art world sources believe she is virulently opposed to the sale. Yet Burnaby's auctioneer, James Constant, has openly challenged the church's campaign for the legendary diamond's restitution.'

'She really is a cow,' Samantha commented. 'She manoeuvred James into making a sarcastic comment after the interview was over. But he never challenged the church.'

'Deliberate misquotation.' Charles exploded. 'As for that nonsense about my wife—' He stopped short, catching Samantha's eye. The look she cut him could have drawn blood. There would be explanations due later. He had an unpleasant suspicion that Lucy might herself be the 'art world source'. How otherwise could the newspaper have obtained the Bishop of Malabar's letter to Father Vaughan, a part of which was reproduced above the report?

'I doubt if any of it's actionable, my dear fellow,' Czernowski said amiably. 'It's simply designed to make you react. If I were you I'd issue the shortest possible statement, without mentioning either the reporter or her equally odious newspaper.' He doodled on a scratch pad with his gold pen, executing curlicues while he considered the wording, then wrote a few decisive phrases, tore off the sheet of paper and handed it across.

'Contrary to recent press reports, Burnaby's are unaware of any legal proceedings to prevent the sale of the Malabar Angel diamond. This uniquely historic 53-carat stone, the property of the Baroness Helene von Brandenburg, is expected to achieve a record price when it comes under the hammer at the Park Plaza Hotel in New York on October 22.'

'If you say so,' Charles conceded. 'We'll have it sent out on the wire service.'

'I would also fax letters to your most likely bidders today. What excuse could you use?'

'The final private showings next week?' Samantha suggested.

'Excellent. Make it a personal invitation, with a single sentence at the end telling them to take no notice of press rumours.'

Czernowski replaced his thin gold pen in his pocket and beamed confidently, the wizard who knew how to deal with the demons of the press. 'If there are any other problems, let me know. When will you be going to New York yourself?'

'The end of next week.' Charles could not avoid catching Samantha's eye again. She would be wanting to go if there was the slightest excuse. So would Lucy. He shunted that dilemma aside: it was not one on which he proposed consulting the Prince.

'Well, dear,' Samantha said tautly as soon as Czernowski had gone. 'We all know who's been talking to the press, don't we? Your beloved wife. Why the hell can't you keep her under control?'

'You know damn well why I can't.'

'You're supposed to be the Chief Executive!'

'And she's the major shareholder.' Charles grimaced and shook his head. Women! He was trapped in a cat's cradle of conflicting women's ambitions and resentments: Lucy's, Samantha's, that damn Baroness's—not forgetting the self-hyphenated Victoria Stewart-Robinson. Deal with them one by one, that was the only way.

'What precisely have you heard?' he demanded.

'Lucy was at Claridge's yesterday with Donna Bradshaw. Her precious priest joined them.'

'So?'

'So they're up to something.'

'Don't be absurd. Mrs. Bradshaw's a potential bidder.'

'She is also a prominent American Catholic.' Samantha shrugged her shoulders. 'Why should I be bothered? They can't stop the sale.' She looked at Charles, wondering just that: why should she care, why should she be bothered: except about her percentage. There was nothing as dead as a dead affair. But New York would be fun. New faces. New men. 'I'm looking forward to the auction. It should be quite an occasion.'

'It would be nice having you there, of course.'

'What exactly do you mean?'

'Well, my love, your presence is hardly essential.'

'You bastard!' She swore at him just genially enough to be jokey. 'When I delivered the star item!'

'And you get your percent, as the Baroness would say.' He

decided to disregard this petulance and concentrate on the next problem woman. 'Talking of which, where the devil is she?'

'How should I know. She's your client.'

'We may need an affidavit testifying ownership.'

'Find her yourself, then.'

'You'd better get her to New York,' he said, taking no notice. Money talks loudest, he reflected. Always has done, always will do. She'll do as she's told. 'Now,' he went on, strengthening the authority in his voice, 'you can help me write to the possible buyers. Get James on the phone, will you?'

'Charles.' She dumped herself on the corner of his desk. 'I am not your slave. Or your girlfriend. I am a consultant. Anyway it's hardly six in the morning in New York.'

'He works for us. Wake him up.'

She leant across, deliberately brushing her sleeve across his face, and took the phone. 'This is the final favour. No transatlantic ticket, no favours.'

While Samantha dialled through to James Constant's midtown apartment, Charles ran through the client list in his mind. Kuroki, the Japanese. He would want reassuring. Too many looted works of art had later been reclaimed from Tokyo museums. The Arabs? They might be less fussy. That Colombian export-import magnate? He'd be buying with laundered drug money anyway, and once the stone was in Colombia no law enforcement agency in the world would get it back. But the clients who mattered, who would contribute most to Burnaby's prestige, were the Americans. When Constant came sleepily on the line, those were the people he asked about.

'Is Cranston still interested?'

'Very definitely. He's already fixed a private viewing next week.'

'I'm told Mrs. Bradshaw's over here at the moment.'

'I believe so.' There was detectable caution in Constant's voice. 'I was told last night she's been talking to lawyers. Have you heard anything?'

'No.' A whole new scenario jumped into Charles's mind. 'Why should she?'

'I'm not in her confidence. Apparently she often does before making a major purchase.'

That didn't ring true. Charles made a mental note and

continued down his list. 'The film star Gloria Grace? Is she still on the cards?'

'Came to the viewing in Los Angeles yesterday.' Constant yawned. Yesterday had been a long day. 'We had a lot of Californian interest. So what's this all about?'

Charles explained.

'We'd better issue the same statement here. I doubt if an Indian church could bring an injunction in time. In that mosaic case they had testimony from both the Church and the Cyprus government. And quite apart from the time element, think of the bribes the church would have to pay the Indian bureaucrats.'

'A very comforting thought.' Charles laughed delightedly. If there was one thing likely to frustrate and infuriate Lucy it was corrupt officialdom: and the Indian government would become obstructive the moment its functionaries scented money on this scale. When the conversation finished he was a happier man, if still wary of the impact press comment could have on the auction bidding.

Chapter
28

Several miles away at the *Dispatch*'s headquarters in London's docklands, in a tower block built during the 1980s when many Fleet Street newspapers moved out to exploit low property values in the decaying eastern suburbs of the city, Victoria Stewart-Robinson was arguing with her Editor. The man whom Charles Luttrell would have liked to hang, draw and quarter was a prematurely aged forty-two-year-old veteran of circulation wars, a onetime provincial reporter with a knack for digging out scandal which over the past year had been skilfully adapted to the *Dispatch*'s relatively up-market, middle-class readership. His name was also Charles—Charles Cross—and he sat with his coat off and necktie loosened, sprawling back in a black leather executive chair behind a vast chromium-legged desk, a cigar in his right hand trailing smoke as he gestured.

'If you want a fare to New York, Vicky, fine. It's yours. Book yourself into the Park Plaza. Fuck the expense. But don't try to fill my paper with moralising about the iniquities of dealers.'

'They're sharks, Charlie. We ought to show them up. This diamond belongs to the church.' Beneath her ethnic dresses and stowed away in her Kenyan woven basket that served as a bag, the former Miss Vicky Robinson carried around a fervently earnest desire to discredit the Charles Luttrells of this world. 'They're shysters. They steal from countries too poor to safeguard their own heritages. This diamond ought to be back where it belongs.'

'Fuck the starving Indian peasants. The diamond's been lifted by filthy rich aristocrats. Go for this German bird. Take a hatchet to Luttrell. That's the line, Vicky. You're learning. You've got a nice veneer of expertise. Convincing. Good stuff. But this story's not some godforsaken church that no one's ever heard of. It's about a beautiful Baroness and an auctioneer's mistress and an embittered wife trying to screw her husband with the help of a priest. Pity you can't make him a Cardinal: this is a story about upper-class intrigue and deceit.'

'Print that, Charlie, and we will be in court.'

'You can imply it, though.' He sat up straight and flicked cigar ash on the carpet, his accepted way of indicating that an editorial session was at end. 'Get over there and screw them, Vicky. And remember: plenty of millionaires and not too many record prices per carat. And no starving Asiatics. Not unless a white man's responsible. Not in my paper. Enough basic facts to prove you're an expert and no more. There's only two things our readers want to know. How to spend money fashionably and how the rich come unstuck doing it.'

Chapter
29

O n e of the external lines in the Security Office shrilled. Craig picked up his extension. On the other side of the room Trevinski, who had come down to locate a document, affected indifference, while stopping what he was doing in order to listen. He always eavesdropped on his subordinates' conversations. This time he shifted his stance and stared at the row of TV monitor screens on the wall, as though something going on in the lobby had caught his attention.

'Is that you, Craig?' The voice was Barbara's. Quietly modulated, none of the penetrating nasal New York accent. He hoped Trevinski wouldn't recognise it and pressed the instrument close to his ear. 'It's a nice day and I'm off duty. Why don't we take a walk in the park over lunchtime?'

'Let me check the schedule.' He had nothing except routine until a pop singer was checking in. Rock stars—and their retinues—were a pain. But that wasn't until the afternoon. However, since Trevinski was here, he felt obliged to ask. 'D'you mind if I take an hour over lunch, sir?' He hadn't yet progressed to first-name terms with his boss and probably never would.

'Sure.' Trevinski twisted that flat, chunky head around, just as if he had not been paying attention and out of the slit of a mouth came the Commander in Chief's blessing. 'Make it early, will ya?'

'That's okay,' Craig said to Barbara. 'You know a place called the Coffee Palace? On Madison and Seventy-second. We could grab a sandwich first. Have to be early, though. Can you manage midday?' When she assented he put the phone down firmly. 'An old friend who's in town,' he explained, though there was no reason why he should account for his private life.

'Sure.' Trevinski accepted the white lie. Clifford's love life was his affair just so long as it didn't louse up the job. There was something between his Deputy and Barbara Andrews. Steven Corley had warned him. Corley was gay and had a fine-tuned sensitivity to sexual relationships. But he had more urgent concerns than Clifford's domestic problems on his mind. 'You had that meeting with the Precinct Detective Unit?'

'It's set for Tuesday.'

'Thirty million dollars of jewels oughta frighten the shit outa you.'

'Thirty's for the media. Fifteen would be more accurate. There may be four hundred lots, but most of them are small: ten to sixty thousand dollars.'

'Maybe small where you come from,' Trevinski said with unusual humour. 'Not in my book. That's the kinda small smells beautiful to a crook. Jesus, how many guys does Tom Garrison have on his banqueting staff? Seventy-eight! Candle men and linen men and guys who shampoo the carpets. You name it. They all have access and any one of them could be corrupted. How do we know some crook isn't checked in as a guest? And on top of that we could have a thousand goddam outsiders at the auction. Why can't they make it by invitation only, like a charity gala?'

'The Burnaby's people say there is no way they can do that. Entry by catalogue, sure. But they'll be selling those at the door. They only check the identity of bidders.'

'We have to bring in extra men, Clifford. Fix that, will ya? And ask the Precinct for special duty officers. You have any other ideas? If ya don't, ya should. You just rewrote the goddam procedures.'

The two men wrangled on for a further twenty minutes before

Trevinski went off, leaving Craig wondering if he had some underworld intelligence that he was keeping to himself.

It was with relief that he left the hotel to meet Barbara. The day was glorious. The heat of a few days ago had diminished and here, opposite Central park, you could catch the stimulating crispness of fall in the air, a scent that carried him straight back to Virginia and happier times.

When he saw her standing on the sidewalk outside the Coffee Palace, he rejoiced. She was fresh and beautiful, her hair blowing in the light breeze. Happy times could come again. He kissed her warmly. It was typical of Barbara that she didn't keep a man waiting as a matter of principle, didn't mind being militarily punctual when she knew he had only an hour.

'Sweetheart,' she said, still holding him, but leaning back, those hazel eyes gazing straight into his. 'Let's forget the sandwich, shall we? I'd like to talk.'

They walked across 72nd Street into Central Park and walked, not too briskly, towards the Mall and the lake, holding hands. Barbara listened briefly to what he'd been doing, commented that if Trevinski was so worried he ought to take charge of the auction security himself, then came to the point.

'Darling, you know I was going to spend a few days in New Hampshire? Well, Steven Corley says there's too much happening for me to take time off right now.'

'I'm sorry.' He knew she'd been looking forward to a break. 'Won't he even allow a long weekend?'

'I have a Saturday shift and again Monday. I can't even plan the weekend after.' She squeezed his hand and then halted. 'I wanted to get away to think.' She was loving, apologetic, ` challenging. 'Well, I spent last night and this morning thinking instead.'

'And?' He knew what was coming.

"Darling, I don't like being the other woman in your life. I hate it. If I can't be the only woman, then I guess we should break things off.'

Another couple passing by stared at them unabashedly. A man with a dog cut a curious glance, then looked away as if embarrassed. Craig took no notice. This was the crunch. Barbara didn't say what she didn't mean. All the material problems flashed through his thoughts, as they always said a drowning man sees his past go by. Money, divorce, access to Antonia, a place to live, the sunshine days of happier times. But he'd already made the decision and had no need to total the good and bad columns.

'I love you, sweetheart,' he said. 'Will you marry me when I'm free?'

'Of course I will, stupid.' She hugged and kissed him. 'Sure we'll have difficulties. Who doesn't?'

'There's only one thing. I'm not going to tell Julia for a couple of weeks.'

'Why not, Craig?' She frowned, fearful this might be the first of the excuses.

'Trevinski's on my back and he's due to confirm my promotion two weeks from today. I don't want Julia making life hell at the same time.' He kissed her again. 'That's the truth.'

'Not the first of the very good reasons?' She had her eyes levelled on him. 'Don't fool around with me, please. I don't ever want you doing that. If you have other reasons, please tell me right now.'

'None that matter, I promise.' He shook his head and grinned apologetically. 'Only one and it's crazy. I promised Antonia she could meet the Baroness. She'd be terribly disappointed not to.'

'Reason accepted, Major Clifford.' Barbara smiled. 'Funnily enough, that's a reason I understand a whole lot better than you might imagine.'

Chapter

30

The telex was elliptically phrased, almost evasive, although Father Vaughan understood immediately what was in the Bishop's mind: 'RECOVERY GOD'S PROPERTY ONLY BY FAITH AND PRAYING. OTHER METHOD INADVISABLE. † MALABAR'

The telex system had been unable to reproduce the pastoral cross before the signature, transmitting it as a plus sign. Appropriately, Vaughan decided. This was the right decision. The church going to law for a piece of jewelry could be misinterpreted as clerical avarice in a way that the suit over the Cyprus mosaics never could, even though they had been worth four times as much.

'What an odd message,' Mary commented over his shoulder. 'I mean how can praying get the diamond back?'

'It's through prayer that we enlist God's help to change our lives.' Although he suspected she had no thought-out religious beliefs he smiled encouragingly. 'For the better, one hopes.'

'I have to say, Father Gerry, I can't see prayer influencing your Baroness. Or stopping the auction.' Having been forgiven for her lapse in sending copies of the letters to Lucy Luttrell, Mary was now following the whole affair avidly.

'Possibly not. I wish I could have talked her into returning it. Since I failed I must do whatever else is possible.' He was still puzzled by what Mrs. Bradshaw's vaguely mentioned second line of attack might be. However, that did not mean he should reject it. 'God does move in a mysterious way,' he added, then fell silent for a moment, thinking about the curious inscription on the original golden mount that now lay wrapped in tissue paper in a drawer of his desk.

He'd been far from anxious to have the only solid evidence of the church's ownership produced in a court of law. In fact the idea had disquieted him greatly. There would have been no alternative to explaining that in his view the word *Mene* probably had been inscribed on the mount by a seventeenth-century priest and threatened Old Testament vengeance on unlawful possessors. That might well have convinced a judge about the ownership, but the headlines the next day would have been horrendous. Father Crawburn would have thrown a fit. He could well have been summoned to explain himself before the Canonsbury Society's Vicar General.

The animosities, the mysticism and, often, the horrors associated with the Malabar churches were explicable in their day. The original Syrian Christians there claimed to have been evangelised by the Apostle Thomas, who according to legend was speared to death at Mylapore, near Madras, where his tomb was rediscovered by the Portuguese in 1522. The donor of this very diamond had been crucified by the Moghuls. Less distinguished converts, usually lower-caste Indians, had suffered persecution and had their meagre property expropriated. If a priest's response had been to protect the church's treasure with a threat, Father Vaughan could understand why. But it was not how the church wished to be seen today. Rather than go to court, it was infinitely preferable to welcome whatever alternative Mrs. Bradshaw could offer.

'Well, Mary,' he said briskly, coming out of this reverie. 'I can't spend all day explaining the effect of prayer on our destinies. This telex means I have to make a reverse charge call to America. Could you get it for me, please?'

Even though he was, as it were, expecting the unexpected, the ensuing conversation with Donna Bradshaw caught him slightly off balance.

'If the Bishop feels that way, Father,' she said, her habitual energetic emphasis undiminished by the transatlantic line, 'I guess it may be for the best. Law suits can drag on an awful long time. We'll just have to take the tax-break route. Not a lot we can do over the weekend, but if I fix the ticket could you come across next Wednesday?'

'What exactly is the "tax-break route"?'

'We set up a charity to buy the stone and the Internal Revenue Service allows the cost against taxes. We'll need you here to sign a few forms. Nothing unusual. The Catholic Church is already recognised as a charity by the Attorney General's office. We just have to establish a special fund.'

'But we could never raise five million in a week!'

'You get the Bishop of Malabar's blessing. I'll find the money. Hopefully the Cardinal will accept to be patron. I shall be Honorary President. That leaves the executive role open for you.'

'For me?' The whole conversation was acquiring an Alice in Wonderland quality. How could anyone raise five million dollars so fast? She could only be going to donate the money herself: in which case she must be expecting to gain considerable prestige from this. Much as he had liked Mrs. Bradshaw at their one encounter, he was too shrewd not to realise she had personal objectives, as Father Crawburn had anticipated. Yet how could this single action earn her five million dollars' worth of image building? As for his coming across to organise it, she must have misunderstood what he was available to do.

'My dear Mrs. Bradshaw, I have a full-time CCRA responsibility here in London.'

'But you can take a week's vacation? Of course you can. Everyone knows you've earned it after that terrible time in Sudan.' There was absolutely no stopping her. 'We'll hire you a Manager and a secretary. By the time the auction's over all you'll need to provide will be occasional advice.'

'May I look at my diary?' With Mary's assistance he confirmed there was nothing on hand that others could not cope with. Yet he remained doubtful. 'I suppose I could come.'

'Then that's fixed. It will be a privilege to have you as our house-guest. Now we must agree on a name for our charity, so the lawyers can start work. It should include the word "injustice".'

'Injustice?'

'We're going to need ethnic support, Father. This should be a mixed-race committee. Definitely. A high proportion of New York's population is black or Hispanic Catholic.'

This time his agreement was less reluctant. She was talking political sense. Father Crawburn's reactions would not be enthusiastic, but he would hardly be able to gainsay a Cardinal. The idea of pulling rank on Father Crawburn had a certain humour.

'Fine. Excellent.' Mrs. Bradshaw spoke as though the diamond was practically theirs. 'So how about "New York Catholic Committee for the Relief of Injustice to the Church of Our Lady in Malabar"?'

Chapter

31

'S h e really is a beautiful woman,' Walter Cranston thought, watching his wife Sarah Jane walking round from the tennis courts at the Meadow Club in Southampton. She'd never been exceptionally slim and she wasn't tall, but she had always stayed neat and appealing, with hardly an unnecessary ounce on her. Just like the South Pacific song 'a hundred and one pounds of fun': always good-humoured, yet a miniature power-house. Crossing the lawns, dressed in a short white tunic, her breasts firm under the linen, her legs bronzed, she moved as grace-fully as an athletic half her age. What a woman—and as fine and devoted a partner as a man could hope for. They'd been married twenty-five years and she was coming up to fifty: a double cause for celebration. She deserved something very special.

Ever since Prince Otto showed him that diamond necklace in July he'd been chewing over whether it would be the right surprise for her or not. She might feel it was overbearingly historic, or that such a large rectangular stone, wearable only as a pendant, wasn't quite her style. How the devil could he be sure without asking her? And he was going to have to be sure because the auction was next week and her fiftieth birthday the week after.

Before he saw her approaching he had been gazing out from the Club's grounds across the great swath of beach, where the

Atlantic rollers were pounding in, though there were still a few hardy swimmers bobbing in the surf. The weekend had been one of the last of Southampton's summer. Most of the great white painted clapboard mansions along Dune Road and Main Street and First Neck Lane would soon be shuttered and closed up, the owners either fled to Florida or California or spending the winter season in New York, the local population finally dwindling from its sixty thousand August peak to around eight thousand. As he grew older Walter Cranston had come to appreciate the winter out here more, to savour the crisp air, derive a kind of exhilaration from the lonely feel of the sea fog drifting in, to enjoy the unpeopled walks around the ponds where a century ago Long Islanders cut ice for sale. From October onward it took an hour less to drive out from the city. This winter, he and Sarah Jane had agreed, they would not close up their own house just along from here in Meadow Lane. They'd continue coming out on weekends.

Waving to her, he started walking back to the clubhouse. Would she approve of that diamond? If she would, he was going to have to get moving. A serious bidder didn't just walk into an auction, any more than a bond dealer would walk on to a trading floor unprepared. He'd had research done and taken advice. When Walter Cranston spent substantial money, whether the amount was five thousand dollars or five million, he did it with his eyes open. The preliminary enquiries he'd instituted had shown nothing wrong: in fact had explained exactly why the gemological report was less than perfect. He'd arranged to be shown the stone again next week, privately at Burnaby's. But these last few days there'd been a story in the *Times* about a possible claim. That would need checking out. And the main question remained: would she actually be pleased to own the Malabar Angel?

One of the Club servants brought them tea on the terrace. That was a habit Cranston liked. Sarah Jane told him about her game and they chatted for a while, until a group of people came out among whom he recognised the Prince and his Baroness: unusual that, after the socialites had gone. But then there were at least a couple of hundred German residents in the neighborhood. They even joked about the place as 'Krauthampton'. They might even be across early for the auction.

'Isn't that the Baroness von Brandenburg with Prince Otto?' Sarah Jane asked, careful not to look directly at them. 'You know I do believe it is.'

'I guess so,' Cranston agreed cautiously.

'From what I've heard, that diamond of hers is spectacular. Too bad she has to sell a thing that's been in her family so long. I certainly wouldn't want to.'

'Appeals to you, eh?' He came as close to a straight question as he dared.

'Wouldn't it to any woman. Shall we ask them round for a drink this evening? We haven't seen the Prince for quite a while. I liked him.'

Cranston considered this. 'Well, why not?' he decided, eased back his chair and walked across. As he reached the group he heard the Baroness make a remark that caused him slight concern. 'If I do have to fight a case, Otto, then I fight it, after all.' He noticed, too, that although she was deeply tanned and her hair bleached golden, although she was dressed with casual elegance and could have stepped out of a fashion magazine, she didn't look happy or relaxed. There'd been a grittiness in her voice that was duplicated in her expression, particularly her eyes. Either she'd had a rough night or things were going wrong.

This observation came back to him when Prince Otto's white Mercedes crunched over the gravel driveway shortly after six that evening. Although Helene made a show of delight at the champagne he offered and the canapés the housekeeper had hastily prepared, she seemed no less tense than she had earlier.

Initially, the occasion progressed like any other small social gathering. Sarah Jane showed their visitors around the house, they exchanged conventional small talk and discussed the new season on Broadway. Then, quite abruptly and in a tone of confidentiality, Helene raised the subject of her diamond.

'I do like to ask you some advice, Walter. Really, you know better how Americans react than we do.' Leaning against the mantelpiece, she kept all of them fascinated with an account of the Church's claim on the Malabar Angel, concluding, 'Frankly, I think they never make this a lawsuit, you know. We have received nothing from lawyers, nothing at all.'

'They don't have a case, in my opinion,' Otto contributed.

187

'Yes, sure. I think we assume they don't.' Helene was impatient with him. 'But that's not what I want to ask Walter. What I like to know, Walter, is this. I am all the time pestered by the media and now they only ask one thing. Am I giving the diamond back.'

'In your shoes I wouldn't,' Sarah Jane said.

'I certainly do not!' The emphasis was harsh. 'But must I go on being interviewed? Burnaby's insist I should. For myself I feel like saying "To hell with it, I go away again." Does it do harm if I go away and refuse to talk? Or must I be there for appearances, because there is all this fuss?'

'Well . . .' Walter was keeping alert to his wife's reactions. 'What would you say, honey? Does it matter if Helene's there or not on the day?'

'It's not me they buy, after all,' Helene added. 'They buy my heirloom.'

'And a glorious diamond it is, too,' Sarah Jane said. 'I wish I'd inherited such a lovely thing. But that's not what you want to know, is it?' She paused to give due consideration. 'I guess most people would expect you positively not to be there. Quite legitimately. Who likes to see their own possessions sold?'

'In my own opinion, it would be in bad taste,' Otto suggested gravely. 'Only a dealer goes to watch how much his business makes. Helene is selling to endow a fellowship.'

'There's your answer, then.' Cranston laughed, glad to have elicited Sarah Jane's response so positively, yet uncomfortable about the overall conversation in a way he couldn't pin down.

'Even if Burnaby's make this a big social event?' Helene asked, keeping the pressure on.

'That's a different question. That I can't answer for you.' Cranston laughed again, this time not so genuinely. The Baroness was becoming tedious: furthermore, the final question had betrayed the game she was playing. He steered the talk away to less loaded topics. 'By the way, Prince Otto, have you seen the Newhouses lately?'

When the guests had left and Sarah Jane was having a word with the housekeeper about dinner, Cranston poured himself a final glass of champagne, sat down on one of the sofas and made an evaluation of what had been said.

Sarah Jane would very much like the Malabar Angel. So the

only question was whether he bid for it himself or through an agent, which would ultimately depend on his workload that day. Decision taken, barring unexpected considerations.

About the Baroness's remarks he was less positive. Just as on that previous occasion over lunch, she had been staking out a position for his benefit. Could the pair of them have hoped to run into him at the Club? Surely not. Otto would have simply phoned and invited them over. In that case Helene was superb at exploiting unexpected opportunities. But what had she and Otto intended him to remember afterwards? First that buyers need have no fear of legal claims. And second? Not so simple. Ostensibly she'd been asking if she ought to give press interviews or be at the auction herself. But her final question had given the lie to that. She did intend to be there. So what the hell had the song and dance been all about?

Chapter

32

'They have no credit cards? No credit cards at all?' Barbara
Andrews listened to the reception clerk on the internal phone,
at the same time taking note of the couple he was talking about.
From her desk by the marble pillar in the hotel's lobby she could
see both them and the caller himself. The couple were youngish.
The man had thick curly dark hair and wore a sport jacket over
fawn trousers. The woman was in a rather ordinary blue
woollen dress. They didn't look like Americans. They weren't
down at heel, but they weren't average Park Plaza guests either.
'They have reservations?' she asked.

It always amused her, this little pantomine of the desk clerk
telling a client he must consult about something when in fact
what he did was call the duty Assistant Manager barely five
yards away. She saw him nodding as he held the phone to his
ear, subconsciously supplementing his answer, while the couple
waited and a porter stood near the Bell Captain's desk with their
bags. The two suitcases didn't look any more distinguished than
their owners.

'Yes, they have reservations through a travel agency in
Düsseldorf,' the clerk said. 'They have vouchers for five nights'
stay. But they don't have any credit cards. What should I do?'

'I'll come right over.'

Barbara crossed the lobby and approached the couple. With-

190

out credit cards the hotel had no guarantee of payment for phone calls, meals, room service, theatre tickets: all the many extras that clients could charge to their accounts. Only two kinds of people had no credit cards: criminals and Europeans. As she approached these two she reckoned they were Europeans, the woman older than the man. Sizing up guests came as second nature to her the moment there was a query.

'Can I help you?' she asked politely. 'I'm one of the Assistant Managers.'

It was the woman who answered and if Barbara's blue uniform and gilt nametag reassured her she certainly didn't show it. Quite the reverse. It was as though the uniform antagonised her.

'We have paid our room in Germany,' she said in careful, stiffly phrased English. 'We have travel cheques also. Is there something wrong with German money?'

'I'm sure there's not.' Barbara smiled her routine 'Welcome on board, madam' smile. It was the best she could manage when she scented trouble: and the way this woman challenged her spelt confrontation. 'If you'd like to come across to my desk I'm sure we can fix the problem.'

As she guided them, she felt an all too familiar apprehension. As tourists her fellow Americans expected the rest of the world to accept dollars. Yet back home, shops, hotels and other places dealing with tourists, even many banks, would totally refuse to accept foreign currency. She herself had once been given a tip in Canadian dollars and had to waste an hour changing them. Anyway it was late afternoon and the banks were already closed. So this pair did have a problem, because she was going to want a one-thousand-dollar deposit plus fifty percent of the room rate before she allowed them in.

'May I just have your names again, please?' She tapped the entry key on her computer.

'I am Birgit Herbstein. My husband is Frank Hermon,' the woman said. 'We are married last week but we keep our own passports.' There was a kind of staccato defiance in the way she spoke that went beyond the distortions of a foreign accent. 'We ask for a double room low down in the hotel.'

'Birgit is afraid of being high up,' the man said, with an Irish inflexion, adding as what he apparently thought an amusing

191

explanation, 'It's ever since she saw that old film *The Towering Inferno.*'

Barbara did not laugh. The joke was too close to being sick. She tapped in their names and watched the display. Well, at least what they'd said was correct. A double room with bath. Six nights from today, Tuesday 16 October, prepaid American plan. The name of a Düsseldorf travel agent.

'I'm afraid I have to check your IDs. Excuse me,' she apologised for the slip, 'your passports.'

The woman took hers out of a leather handbag, which gave Barbara a moment of doubt. The bag had the distinctive Gucci dark green and red stripe. She knew what Gucci bags cost. Maybe this pair were more affluent than she'd thought. It was a fact of life that one had to be careful with the rich. They were easily offended, they always seemed to have friends who knew the company President and they had no qualms about creating hell.

'And yours, if you don't mind, sir.'

The man took his from an inside pocket. She checked them both, conscious of the woman's increasing hostility. His was issued by the Irish Republic, hers by the Federal Republic of Germany. She entered the basic personal details and passport numbers into the computer, noting with surprise that the woman was only three years senior to the man. He was twenty-nine and she looked more like forty than thirty-two. Then she handed the documents back and delivered the bad news.

'I'm afraid it's a company rule that if we don't have the guarantee given by a major credit card we must request a deposit.'

'But we have already paid,' the woman protested, her tone several decibels louder.

'That can't be right.' Hermon backed her up, though sounding more relaxed about it. 'What's the reason?'

'Extras, taxes.' Barbara didn't actually say 'people who skip without paying,' but Hermon's expression told her he understood perfectly. He had a broken nose and there was a kind of beat-up world-weariness in his expression, coupled with indications of humour that his wife evidently lacked. She decided to work on him. 'I'm sorry, sir. But we have to ask for either fifty percent of the room rate or a one-thousand-dollar deposit.' Their room rate was $350 a night so there was not much difference between the two figures.

'One thousand dollars!' Herbstein's reaction was close to a scream. She glared at Barbara, her head thrust forward like a snake about to strike. 'When we have paid already!'

Hermon reacted immediately to calm her down, remonstrating, 'That's not such a lot, me darlin', not much at all compared to what our honeymoon's costing.' He shot a quick question at Barbara. 'Refundable, of course?'

'When the extras have been paid, sir.'

'You see, love'—he smoothed over her agitation—'they'll be paying it back again, sure and they will. Now what would that be in proper money? Let me just work it out.' He did the figuring in his head with a speed that impressed Barbara, even though she was smarting at the 'proper money' crack. 'Twenty-four hundred marks or thereabouts. That's nothing to be worrying about.' He slipped out his wallet and removed five crisp pale brown banknotes. 'Here you are'—he peered at her nametag—'Miss Andrews. Here's twenty-five hundred deutsche marks, which is more than you've asked for.' His attitude became harder and more abrasive. 'Can we now have our room.'

Barbara flushed. The man's half bantering tone had ended with a clear-cut command: and she somehow knew the notes were genuine.

'I'll have to take these to the cashier.'

'If he'd prefer travel cheques, he can have those. But we've come straight from the airport and my wife is tired.'

The cashier was not enthusiastic. He complained at not being able to confirm the current rate when the banks were shut—as though he wouldn't have charged an extortionate one anyway. At the same time Barbara felt compelled to compromise, because the Irishman had so quickly damped down what could have become an embarrassing public shouting match. Besides, the vouchers were good. She returned to her desk with a formula.

'That's fine, Mr. Hermon,' she said, conscious again of the woman's dark eyes boring into her. 'We'll hold those for tonight until we can check the exact rate tomorrow.'

'Thank you, love.' he said. 'Then we'll be getting upstairs. Which floor did you say we're on?'

'The sixth. Number 609. A nice room. You have a view of the Park and it gets the afternoon sun.'

'Is that as low down as you have rooms?'

'The lowest bedroom floor is the fifth.' She was puzzled by such an unusual request but checked with the computer. 'There's nothing free there until Thursday. You really wouldn't like it so much. It's at the back and has no view.' She was going to say it was also cheaper, then thought he might be offended.

'I like to be as low down as possible,' the woman insisted. 'The view is not important. Please keep us that room.'

After the desk clerk had given them the key and Barbara had dispatched them to the lift with the porter, she tapped an entry into the computer about the fifth floor room and the thousand-dollar deposit, with certain temporary room service restrictions until it was paid, plus a notation about their being just married. It was company policy to send flowers and fruit to honeymooners' rooms. Come to think of it, they could have had a suite for one night for the price of a room if they'd asked. But then there was no suites below the tenth floor, so presumably they'd have turned the offer down. Altogether a distinctly strange couple: and he hadn't so much as taken her arm when they went to the lift.

'Control yourself, Ilse. You must bloody control yourself. Jesus, if you'd had a gun you'd have shot her.'

'Birgit.' she said, still taut and angry that the travel agent had never warned her about deposits. 'Birgit, I am called now. Don't forget that.' She went to the window and stared out at the trees of Central Park below. 'My God, we are high up. Where is the ballroom? We have to find where the ballroom is.'

Frank humped the two suitcases onto the wide bed, then made a quick survey of the room, assuming a fifth floor one would be basically similar. For a hotel room it was spacious, decorated in pastel colours, with a couple of framed pictures on the walls and elegantly furnished. A veneered cabinet concealed a TV, with brochures about the hotel's services arranged on top. There was a long built-in dressing table cum desk. A small refrigerator contained drinks. There were two internal doors.

He opened one, cautiously, as he always did in strange places. That revealed a tiled bathroom with a lavatory, a bidet and a shower above the bathtub. The tub itself interested him. He examined it, discovering that the surround had no removable panel. Whatever way one reached the plumbing, it wasn't from in here, which meant it would be difficult to use as a hiding place for explosives. Then he tried the other door. This one belonged to a large walk-in closet, with an old-fashioned lock for which they had been given no key; the room key was a plastic card, with a black strip of encoding. Presumably the closet dated from the early days of the hotel and had been retained despite modernisation. He was just levering up the edge of its carpet to inspect the floor with a knock on the room door disturbed him. He leapt up, while Ilse hesitated.

'Who is it?' he called out.

'Room service, sir.' He opened the door and a white-coated waiter stood there, holding a tray with a basket of fruit, a glass vase and a bouquet of flowers wrapped in cellophane. 'With the Manager's compliments, sir.' The man walked in and deposited the gifts carefully on the long table. 'Have a nice stay.'

'Hey.' Frank caught him before he could go again. 'Tell me something? Where is the Grand Ballroom?'

'On the fourth, sir. All the banqueting rooms are on the third and fourth.'

'Thanks.' Frank fumbled in his trouser pocket, could only retrieve a five-dollar bill, and handed it over.

'Thank *you*, sir.' The waiter closed the door quietly behind him.

'This room is no good for us,' Ilse said, edging on hysteria. 'We have to move more down, above the ballroom.'

'All right, all right. We'll do that on Thursday. We arranged it, for God's sake.' Creeping Jesus, she was totally unnerved. But nothing had happened! The scrutiny of the immigration official at Kennedy, when they were called forward in turn to the window of his little cubicle, had been thorough but friendly. They were on holiday. They had return seats booked. No problems. 'Hope you enjoy your visit. You ought to take a trip up the Hudson river. See the Fall colours.' The only thing they should have done, with hindsight, was change more money at the airport. 'Listen, me darlin'. We have six days. We have time.

We have to get the stuff from the Libyans and bring it in. Why panic?'

'In Brighton you put the explosive behind the bath panel, didn't you?'

'Sure we did, and these rooms have good enough cupboards.' He forced a laugh. 'But what's the floor like?' He resumed his investigation under the carpet, using a pocket knife to ease up a corner inside the closet. 'Shit. What I thought. Concrete.'

Ilse joined him. 'What does that mean?' It irritated her not to comprehend at once.

'It's what I told you months ago. All the floors in a skyscraper are concrete. If we put explosive here all the force will go up or sideways, not down. This may be an old hotel, but it's damn strong and solid.' He put the carpet back, pressing it into place with his fingers. 'We have to get a plan of the building or we're wasting our time.'

'How do we do that?'

'An architectural bookshop. A public library. How the hell should I know?' He would have liked to ask why the silly bitch hadn't done her planning properly, except that she controlled the money. 'I need a drink,' he said, becoming annoyed himself. He took a beer from the refrigerator, flipped the top off with his knife and swigged straight from the bottle.

What he now claimed to have warned her about he'd actually done no more than hint at for fear of losing the contract. The fact was that a skyscraper's construction was way beyond his experience. He'd blown up brick public houses in Ulster. He'd had a hand in the Brighton bomb that so nearly killed Mrs. Thatcher and her Tory Ministers: but the Imperial Hotel in Brighton was an Edwardian structure and basically brick. Because Ilse had a bee in her bonnet about how the Imperial in Brighton had been wrecked he'd kidded her along, pretending that since the Park Plaza dated from the 1930s the task would be comparable. It was not: and the only insurance he'd been able to take out was persuading her to arrive six days early.

'That's better,' he said, refreshed by the beer. 'And now, darlin', which side of the bed do you sleep on? Speaking personally I'm taking a kip.'

She stared at him, anger over technicalities she did not completely understand fuelled by his criticism.

'I sleep in the bed. You sleep on the floor.'

'You must be joking!' He was going to need some sex on this trip. He knew the electricity could spark between them. He'd felt it when they first met. She might even be good in bed—and what the hell if she was much older. In the dark all cats are black.

'On the floor,' she spat out. 'And I tell you something. If the ballroom is not destroyed you get no money.'

Around seven P.M. Frank woke, aching from the hardness of the floor. He cursed, told himself he was getting soft, realised Ilse wasn't there, cursed her again, showered and shaved and prepared to go downstairs. The faster he discovered how this building was constructed and laid out the better.

In the last few days before they left she'd become tougher and more self-assured. Hans-Peter had told him about that business with the gun. A woman as crazy as her was capable of buying another in New York. Everyone knew the United States was awash with weaponry and he didn't want her pulling a gun on him or anyone else. His aim was to place the explosive and get out of the city before it detonated. Jesus be thanked that he controlled the source of the stuff. But they'd only be able to carry in a limited amount and he had to know exactly where to place it.

Going down in the elevator he decided he should enquire about New York City tours, then steer the conversation onto the hotel itself. But who to ask? The lobby was crowded: a group of dark-suited men with nametags pinned to their lapels, presumably attending a convention, obvious tourists, women in businesslike clothes who carried no handbags, so he knew they must be prostitutes. He spotted the Assistant Manager and was hesitating when he noticed another woman in uniform, with a gilt tag announcing she was a lobby hostess. Relieved, he posed the question.

'The concierge is the person, sir. His name's Gregory.' She pointed across the lobby to a mahogany counter, many sided like a church pulpit, close to the Bell Captain's desk and not far from where the Assistant Manager sat. 'Gregory will advise you, sir.'

Frank threaded his way through the throng, reflecting that a bomb going off at this hour would cause real panic, and stood in line while the concierge concluded another conversation. Gregory was grey-haired, sveltely dressed in a version of the hotel's uniform that Frank guessed he'd had specially tailored and, from his well-modulated voice, was Irish too.

The compatibility was instant. 'You're from the home country? Glad to meet you.' Gregory didn't actually thrust out a hand across the small piles of guide leaflets on the countertop, but his pleasure was evident. 'So you're on your honeymoon and want to take the lady somewhere special? Never fear, I'll make certain you have the best there is.' He chuckled conspiratorially. 'This time of year the Hudson Valley is truly spectacular. You should visit the Beekman Arms at Rhinebeck, the oldest continually operated inn in the entire United States. Well,' he conceded, as though tactfully admitting Frank had superior knowledge, 'the White House at Newport, Rhode Island, is older . . . You'd rather start with New York? Well, sir'—Gregory swam easily with the tide of his client's preconceived opinions—"if the lady has never seen the city before you could do worse than the good old Circle Line boat trip around Manhattan Island. Takes three hours and there are still six sailings a day this month.'

To establish his credentials Frank bought tickets for the next day, adding a few dollars for Gregory himself, then edged closer to his objective.

'The Park Plaza is pretty historic, I've heard. When was it built?'

He'd hit Gregory's favourite topic. 'The site was bought from the Vanderbilt family right after the Depression. Building didn't start for four years, not until 1933. Architecturally it was highly advanced for its time. Now, if you're interested, we have a specially printed souvenir book on the hotel.'

Frank willingly paid out a further twenty-five dollars and, disregarding an impatient man in line behind him, said he'd heard the Grand Ballroom was one of the largest in New York.

'The largest in America, my friend, in its day. Both the main towers of the hotel are above, with only quite a narrow space between to give light to their backs. Believe me, constructionally that required tremendous strength. You could never tell from the outside, but the girders above the Grand Ballroom are as high as a room, in fact they could have rooms between them—'

An aggravated comment from behind him forced Frank to end the conversation. 'Is it possible to be shown round?' he asked quickly.

'No problem. I'll make arrangements with the banqueting office. Your room, number? My pleasure, Mr. Hermon. Have a very nice stay.'

As Frank moved away, holding the book and absorbing the key point that with huge girders above the ballroom and a concrete floor above them it would indeed be futile to plant the Semtex in a bedroom at all, one of those tiny coincidences occurred that change the fate of Empires. A workman passed by, easing through the crowded lobby towards the Bell Captain's desk. The workman wore blue trousers and a clean blue shirt with an identity tag and a necktie. From his leather belt, bumping against his thigh, hung a collection of tools; pliers, a hammer, screwdrivers, a wrench. He was an engineer and, most important of all, he was a white New Yorker, not a black. Frank stopped, transfixed, memorising details of his appearance. If there was a room-sized space above the ballroom ceiling no architect would have wasted it. That space would conceal air-conditioning ducts, pipes, cables: and the Park Plaza's engineers would necessarily have access to it.

When Frank left the lobby, as exhilarated as Newton must have been when he saw an apple fall from a tree and comprehended gravity, he was not unobserved. Barbara had returned to her work station and seen him waiting for Gregory. When Craig came along, doing a customary round of the lobby and stopped for an ostensibly routine chat, she discreetly indicated the Irishman.

'He checked in with his wife just after I came on. Gave me the only real hassle so far today. They had no credit cards.'

'Is that so?' Craig was only half interested. He wanted to feel close to Barbara, if only for a few moments, and he was also observing the clientele around them as part of his duty. There were a couple of women in business clothes over there who had no handbags and were quietly giving the eye to men: in other words, they were on the game. They'd have to be shown the door and warned.

'In the end we took the German banknotes. But they were an odd couple.'

Craig shifted his gaze to the man. He wasn't distinguished, definitely not Harvard or Wall Street, probably earned his living in some fairly hard business like engineering or a service station, but not a mobster either. 'Looks like a fairly regular guy to me.'

'He's okay, I think. She's something else. She did most of the talking and the way she stared at me!' Barbara almost shivered at the memory. 'She must be older than her passport says as well. At first sight she's nothing much, but when you catch her eyes you know she's burning inside. She was just furious about the deposit.'

'Could be he promised her the Park Plaza and they couldn't really afford it. People get angry if they lose face.'

An aspect of Barbara's impressions that hadn't quite locked into place before suddenly clicked.

'Now I know what was so odd! He paid the deposit, but it was she who got uptight. I'm sure it was her money.'

'Wouldn't be the first time in history.' Craig watched the man. He was a presentable guy, quite handsome in a way, though his face suggested he'd been in a few fights as a teenager. 'Nothing illegal about being a stud.'

'But he wasn't playing the lover boy.' Barbara shrugged her shoulders. 'Perhaps I'm imagining things. We have the thousand dollars, so why should we worry?'

'How long are they here for?'

She checked with the computer, just to remind herself. 'Till the twenty-second. That was another funny thing. They asked to be moved to a worse room, on a lower floor. On their honeymoon!'

'Like I said, they could be short of dough.'

'Not with a Gucci bag like she had. I'd have given an arm and a leg for that.'

To humour her, Craig went across to the concierge after the Irishman had gone, conferred briefly and returned with details of Hermon's enquiries, plus a delicately phrased hint that he tipped generously.

'Well, I have to say, that's all normal enough.' Barbara dropped the subject. 'How have things been with you?'

'Had a meeting with the Precinct Detective Unit about next

Monday. Went pretty well. They promised to detail some special-duty officers.'

'I'll be glad when that auction's over,' she said with feeling. 'It's completely monopolising you.'

He gazed at her with untroubled tenderness, not caring who noticed. 'After next week it won't. I promise. After next week you're going to be doing the monopolising.'

A client came up with a question for Barbara and Craig moved on. By the time the prostitutes had been discreetly escorted out and he'd gone through the security duty books he'd pretty well forgotten about the Irishman and his supposedly odd bride.

Chapter

33

'I presume this does not belong to you.' Lucy Luttrell limped across the drawing room of the Mount Street apartment, displaying a large pearl earring on her palm. She waved it in front of her husband, then crunched it down on the marble mantelpiece and swung round on her stick to face him again. 'Down the side of the sofa.'

'It is hardly likely to be mine,' Charles said caustically, though he had no energy for argument. The day had been bloody awful. The Park Plaza was insisting that for security reasons entry to the auction should be 'by catalogue only' and there had been a mishap over shipping the final batch of sale catalogues to New York. This being Wednesday and with only five days to the auction there was no time for a reprint. Every spare copy would have to be air-freighted across by courier. He had returned to the flat in a filthy mood, not even looking forward to Samantha coming round, only to find Lucy there: and apparently in her worst private detective frame of mind. Damnation!

His wife usually warned him when she intended staying in London. That was part of going their own ways privately, which made their childless marriage tolerable and usually courteous, if hardly loving. She would only have broken the rules if she was set on a confrontation: and that there was going to be. So he had settled himself on the sofa with a stiff whisky and soda and awaited developments. They hadn't been long coming, though he had not expected the discovery of Samantha's long-missing earring: at least he supposed it was Samantha's. It was typical of the day's general bloodiness that Lucy should unearth this reminder of an affair that had been dead until the Malabar Angel coup momentarily revived it.

'I'll bring some food and we can discuss what to do about Helene,' Samantha had said. 'She must be in the Caribbean somewhere.'

Charles was sure in his own mind that this unasked-for domesticity derived from Sam's concern for her commission and nothing else. The last time she stayed the night had been a sexual disaster: he'd been certain she'd only consented to keep him sweet and he had not been expecting her to stay this evening. Whatever their pretences the affair was finished. But how could he explain that to his wife?

'I take it you've been "entertaining" again,' Lucy said, launching into a mounting tempo of denunciation. 'As if it isn't enough that you accept stolen property and pander to that girl's insatiable greed, you have the unspeakable nerve to insult my Faith and a priest whom I've known since I was a teenager.' She moved a step forward. 'It's high time we decided precisely where we stand, you and I.'

'In a business relationship, my dear? Or a marital one?'

The remark silenced her. She stood by the mantelpiece, holding herself in for fear of dissolving into tears. Despite all the challenging bravado of a moment ago, the culmination of months of insidious discontent, she could scarcely bear to look at Charles. She wasn't as hard inside as she pretended to be and people imagined: she'd simply been forced to develop a defensive shell as he grew further and further away from her.

Her cardinal mistake, after the arthritis struck, was spending her time in the country and pretending they could behave like the French, treating marriage as a business contract in which the only sins were causing social embarrassment or damaging an inheritance. It was an escape that seemed justified because as a devout Catholic she could never contemplate divorce. But now, with this affair of the diamond, he'd committed both the sins—and done so for the sake of a brazen adventuress who'd been running circles around him for years.

'I've had enough of her, Charles. Do you understand?'

'If by "that girl" you mean Samantha Seebohm,' he said with as much conviction as he could manage, 'you are completely wrong.' He almost said 'out of date', but thought better of it. 'I doubt if she's been here twice in the last three months and then only to talk about clients. She is purely a consultant.' He prayed that when she arrived in a moment she would have the discretion to buzz the entryphone before coming up.

'"Consultant"!' Lucy spoke as though holding the word at arm's length because it smelt. 'So "consultant" is the euphemism nowadays! It used to be "model". This can't continue, it's too humiliating. She's left you once as it is. But what I cannot stomach is her publicly dragging our name in the mud.'

'So you want me to return the Malabar Angel to its owner? Forfeit at least six hundred thousand dollars in seller's commission and buyer's premium. Encourage Helene von Brandenburg to sue us.'

'We have the legal right to withdraw property if there are doubts about its ownership.' This was firm ground, unconnected with emotion.

'As gun licence holders we have the right to shoot ourselves in the foot. Don't be so bloody silly, Lucy. Do you want to destroy our first ever New York sale?'

'Then I insist that if the diamond is bought by a charity we waive the buyer's premium.' She knew she'd been sidetracked and compensated for it by throwing down a challenge. 'As the majority shareholder I insist.'

'Charity? What charity? What are you talking about?'

'Since you all refuse to behave decently Donna Bradshaw has established a charity to buy the stone. I shall be in New York myself helping her.'

'"Now I understand!' He got out of his chair to be on more level terms with her, his own annoyance overriding any feeling of guilt about the earring. God, what jealousy could do to a woman! 'So it was you who leaked the documents to that bloody saleroom correspondent. What's your next trick to preserve the Luttrell honour? A public announcement disassociating yourself? You must be mad.'

'I suppose I can forgive the Baroness for wanting the money.

What I cannot bear is your mistress taking her cut at the expense of my good name.'

'She is not my mistress, damn you.'

Lucy paused, out of breath, angry when she should have been calm, dreadfully afraid that yet again Charles would evade the morality at the heart of everything. As they both stood there and he picked up his glass, not even offering to mix her a drink, they heard the unmistakable noise of a key turning in a lock, followed by the font door opening.

'Darling?' Samantha's brittle voice came through from the hall. 'Darling, are you in?' A moment later she was with them, a bulging shopping bag in her hand. 'Darling, I bought a few—'

'How very thoughtful of you,' Lucy remarked acidly. 'Do take them through to the kitchen.'

Samantha stopped short, gave Charles a look of pure horror and dumped the bag on the carpet. Packages of groceries tumbled out.

'The drawing room,' Lucy said, quick to exploit this unexpected advantage, 'is not the place for those. Take them through, will you, Charles? And bring us both a drink. Samantha and I are going to have a little chat.' As he fumbled to gather up the packets, for once at a loss, she went to the mantelpiece and held out the earring. 'I assume this is yours.'

For an instant Samantha thought of disclaiming the thing: it would serve Charles bloody well right. How could he be so crass as to let her walk straight into this? Instead she decided the only way to handle it was by being as cool as Lucy herself: though she doubted if Lucy was cool at all. The room almost smelt of gunsmoke. She examined the earring as if to make sure, then accepted it without a word.

'In exchange,' Lucy said, 'you can give me the front door key.'

There was little alternative. As Charles returned she thought of appealing to him, then shrugged her shoulders, took the key from her handbag and threw it on the carpet.

'Charles.' Lucy's command was like a whip across his back. For the second time he was forced to stoop and forage on the floor.

'Thank you,' Lucy said, putting the key on the mantelpiece beside the ormulu mounted clock, where the earring had been. 'Now, shall we all sit down or remain standing up?'

'Let's behave in a civilised way, for God's sake.' Charles was only just controlling himself. He gave the women their drinks and, in an unaccustomed gesture of good manners, waited for Lucy to compose herself in the one upright armchair before sitting down himself.

'Now,' Lucy said, taking an appreciable swallow of the whisky and feeling a welcome glow of reassurance, 'there is really very little to discuss, isn't there?' She looked straight at Samantha, who avoided her gaze. 'I suppose you must hope that one day Charles will be free. If you do, you are quite mistaken, at least while I am alive. The Catholic Church does not welcome divorce and I have no intention of giving him one.'

Samantha lifted her eyes, saw that Charles was keeping out of this, the coward, and drank down her own whisky: a little Dutch courage would do no harm in a situation that could only end one way. Why hadn't he warned her? The hell with him, anyway. She was an idiot to have become involved again.

'It's nice to have that straight,' she said. 'But what ever made you suppose I want to marry him?'

Lucy blushed in spite of herself. The little bitch! But she wasn't going to rise to that particular bait. She held herself silent, forcing the wretched girl to speak.

'As a matter of fact,' Samantha said, 'he's not even very good in bed anymore. Not that you'd know much about that.'

'Sam, please!' Charles intervened at last, catastrophically.

'No!' Her temper broke through. 'Not "please"! Not "Some-day, I promise." No more bloody insincere half truths.' She rose to her feet and slammed down the glass. 'If you'd ever really wanted me, or needed me, or loved me you'd have left her long ago.' She turned on Lucy. 'There's smoked salmon and some steak. I hope it chokes the pair of you.'

Lucy didn't stir in her chair, but as Samantha reached the door she called out after her. 'You will no longer be retained by Burnaby's and you will not attend the auction in New York.'

Samantha's reaction was equally fast. 'On the contrary Mrs. Luttrell, your firm will honour its contracts. All of them! She spoke to Charles. 'I've tracked down Helene. She's in St. Barthélemy and coming back to New York at the weekend. She says if you must have an affidavit she'll swear it on Monday morning before the sale.' There was a fractional pause, just long enough for Charles to wonder what was coming next and Lucy to concentrate her attention and hobble alongside him. 'Withdraw her diamond and she'll sue you rotten.' She flung out of the room, banging the door behind her.

'Well,' Charles remarked, deciding that his wife was best left by herself to reflect on the chaos she'd created. 'I shall now do what English gentlemen did in your father's day. I shall go to my club.'

Chapter

34

T h e reception area of the Park Plaza's Banquet and Sales Office was intimidatingly luxurious, a world apart from the main lobby two floors below. Frank sat deep in a cream leather sofa, the soles of his carefully polished brown brogues lost in the pile of the oyster grey carpet, his eyes nervously flicking over gilded French furniture and, on the low table in front of him, heavy leather-bound albums of what he supposed were photographs of VIP guests. An ornate French-style ormolu clock informed him that it was seven minutes past ten. The appointment, made through Gregory the concierge, was for ten.

Ten o'clock, Thursday, November 18. He'd wanted it yesterday, but had been politely refused. Thursday! Jesus Christ. Their third day in the hotel and all he'd achieved was to make a telephone contact with the Libyans, surreptitiously study the hotel's layout and be forced to tell Ilse that until he knew where he would be placing the Semtex he couldn't judge what quantity was right. He had to make a survey of the ballroom and it would be dangerously stupid to sneak in hoping no one would notice: Gregory had told him there were as many staff as guests. He must behave and look like a normal visitor. So he'd cleaned his shoes, brushed his trousers, put on a clean shirt—and was still as apprehensive as a virgin on her first date. Trying to appear unrattled he picked up one of the albums to make a pretence of browsing through the pictures, only to find himself inspecting samples of banquet napkins.

'Would you like some coffee while you're waiting, sir?' The secretary's voice made him almost drop the book. 'I'm afraid Mr. Garrison is rather busy this morning, but one of his assistants will be with you very shortly.'

Recovering himself, Frank looked up at the girl. She was standing beside him, smiling the routine 'Have a good day' smile which he'd begun to recognise. Below the smiling face was a vision of swelling breasts straining the fabric of a white blouse. Below those came a flat stomach under an equally tight blue skirt. His eyes were just about level with her crotch. He fancied he could smell her sex. Oh Jesus! After two nights on the floor with a blanket and a pillow and that bitch Ilse squeaking and wheezing in her sleep it was more than a man could bear.

'Coffee would be just fine,' he said.

By the time she brought it he had developed his ideas. 'Couldn't you be showing me around if the bosses are busy?' he suggested. 'I'm really only after a peek for curiosity's sake.'

'I couldn't do that, I'm afraid, sir. It has to be one of the Managers.'

But the way she dimpled told him she would have liked to. He reckoned it was worth chatting her up.

'You have a lot of entertaining rooms?'

'Nineteen, sir. Some are dining rooms for twenty people to two hundred. Some can take five hundred. The Grand Ballroom holds nearly fifteen hundred.'

'The ballroom must be a hell of a size.'

'Wait till you see it.' She felt flattered by his enthusiasm. 'It takes up two floors of the hotel. Quite a few of the city's really big events are hosted there.' She smiled down at him, this time more genuinely. 'Those the Waldorf-Astoria doesn't get.' As she spoke a young manager in a grey suit came in. 'Here's Mr. Drayson now. He can tell you everything you want to know.' She made the introduction as Frank got to his feet. 'This is Mr. Hermon, one of our hotel guests. Gregory arranged for him to be shown around.'

'Glad to help you, sir.' Drayson was Frank's own age or younger. Pink-cheeked, sleek hair cut long over a white collar twinned with a purple shirt. He proceeded with a briskness suggesting there were other things he'd prefer to be doing on a busy Thursday morning. 'Would you mind signing our Visitor's Book, sir? Then I can take you around.'

'I'm not exactly your original VIP, you know.' Frank attempted to shy off. The fewer examples of his handwriting he left behind, the better. But Drayson was adamant.

After that, the tour followed a practised route, Drayson guiding him down long passages with a stylised commentary. 'Mid-September to New Year is our peak season . . . Over eighty staff respond to any event . . . Linen men, candle men, waiters . . . A hundred and fifty in the Chef's department . . .' He stopped in a further lobby, furnished with two gilt settees on either side of massive double doors, white painted with their panels outlined in gold. And this, sir, is our Grand Ballroom.'

The room was vast. Though not as high ceilinged as Frank had imagined he could see that it did indeed occupy two normal hotel floors. At each side there was a line of columns, which presumably supported the roof as well as effectively dividing the room into three areas. Many rows of white-clothed tables were set out, while at the far end a dais had its own higher table. Above hung four enormous cut-glass chandeliers, their gilded supporting chains emerging from wide rosettes in the fanciful plaster decorations of the ceiling.

'Quite a room,' Frank commented, thinking what glorious confusion there would be as that lot collapsed on an audience. He noticed that as well as the multi-tiered chandeliers there were flat glass illumination panels in the ceiling and no windows in the walls. 'Is it completely inside the hotel?'

'If you mean does it have external walls, the answer, sir, is no. Around three sides there are smaller reception rooms.' He indicated several doors. 'Some can be linked to this room in the unlikely event we required more space. For example, we have a major auction next week and as a precaution against overcrowding—just a precaution—there'll be TV monitors in an adjoining room.'

Frank picked up the unintended cue at once. 'When you have an auction, where would the auctioneer be?'

'On the dais at the end, sir. He'll be right up on the dais. And there'll be no tables or chairs set out, naturally.'

'And what's above there? I mean bedrooms or what?'

'Above the ceiling?' Drayson sounded faintly surprised. 'Well, I guess directly above there's just space. Can't say I've ever seen. There'd be sound insulation, for sure.' He thought about it grudgingly for a second. 'The ballroom's in the centre of the hotel. Right directly above us there'll be the well between the two main towers.' He checked his watch as a way of escaping questions he couldn't answer. 'Now, if you'll excuse me, sir, this is a busy day. We have a big charity gala here tonight.'

As they returned to the Banquet Sales Office a couple of distinctly English-looking businessmen were being welcomed by a tall, elegantly attired hotel official while another man stood listening and glancing around.

'Let me take your coat, Mr. Constant,' the official was saying. 'How d'you like your coffee?'

'That's our Banqueting Director, Mr. Garrison,' Drayton said, clearly with no intention of making an introduction. In any case Frank had become abruptly preoccupied with his book on the hotel. He knew the other man's face. Why?

The other man was stocky, mundanely dressed in a sports jacket and vaguely familiar. Where could he have seen him before? Frank gave him a second glance and realised he was being examined in all too familiar a way. Shit. Security. The same guy who'd been with that Manageress in the lobby. He hesitated in the doorway, holding the book.

'I'll be right with you, Mr. Garrison,' Drayson said obsequiously. He shook Frank's hand and propelled him out. 'Glad to be of service. Have a nice day.'

Frank retreated fast. He'd been noticed, which was dangerous. He hurried down the stairs to the mezzanine, then took the wide staircase to the lobby in a more leisurely way and after a quick precautionary walk around the shops, hopped in a elevator to the sixth floor. He and Ilse had to pack and have their gear moved for them to the less good room on the fifth: another reason why it had been impractical to collect the Semtex or even buy a blue-collar worker's rig yet. He also badly wanted to match up the hotel plans in his book with what he'd seen. He wished he could have had a compass in the ballroom. By the time they'd got there he'd become disoriented and it was crucial to figure out where the entrance to that space above the Grand Ballroom ceiling might be located.

'Thank the Lord that's settled.' Donna Bradshaw returned from escorting the Cardinal to her Sutton Place apartment's private elevator. 'And now, Father Gerard, I am sure you'd like a drink.' She crossed the wide, classically decorated living room to where a tray laden with bottles and glasses stood on an antique side table. 'What will you have?'

'A beer perhaps.' Vaughan drank only sparingly and particularly avoided the depressing heaviness of spirits at any time before the evening. 'If that's not a nuisance.'

'Not in the least. We have plenty in the refrigerator.' She departed to the kitchen, leaving him to reflect momentarily on the unabashed horse trading that had characterised the inaugural meeting of the New York Catholic Committee for the Relief of Injustice to the Church of Our lady in Malabar.

Two hours ago, before the others had arrived, Father Vaughan had been looking from one of the long windows across the East River when he noticed, of all things, a rabbit munching the grass of the apartment building's private lawn. The rabbit had hopped around, apparently undisturbed by anything, not even the muffled rumbling of traffic in the East River Drive tunnel below. Eventually it had disappeared behind a bush. After this Manhattan rabbit he felt prepared for anything: but even so, the Committee had proven itself a most unusual one.

His Eminence the Cardinal, ascetic faced, careful in his declarations, yet well able to put his foot down when things had gone far enough, had been the power broker. He had astutely held the line between the variously conflicting interests of a young black priest from the Bronx, a bearded Puerto Rican Father from a parish just the other side of the Lincoln Tunnel, a diminutive yet strong-featured lawyer and, of course, the ever astonishing Mrs. Bradshaw herself, clad today in a blue suit and a white silk roll-neck sweater, with a cluster of gold chains by way of adornment.

At Donna Bradshaw's bidding the lawyer had explained the basic proposition. It was simple. Bradshaw Enterprises, Inc., the holding company for her nationwide chain of boutiques, would put up the five million dollars or whatever was required to purchase the Malabar Angel and then donate it to the Committee. That was the main purpose for which the charity had been constituted and registered with the Attorney General. The subsidiary purposes included mandating surplus funds for the benefit of other listed Catholic charities: and there was going to be a substantial surplus, because once they had secured the diamond Mrs. Bradshaw would exhibit it around America at her stores, soliciting donations from the public.

No one present quibbled at the huge public relations bonus Donna Bradshaw herself would derive from this exercise and the clout that the restoration of the diamond would give her in Catholic circles. No one argued about the massive numbers of new customers her stores would attract as a result of the diamond's nationwide tour. What they had argued about was the percentages their own interests would get out of the secondary donations. The Cardinal had wanted money for his general New York funds. The Reverend Eugene Crisp from the Bronx had recently established a jobs program in his parish. The Hispanic Father had his 'Puerto Rican Abandoned Mothers Group'. Even for a missionary accustomed to the bazaar politics of India and Africa the in-fighting had been an education.

Donna Bradshaw returned with a Heineken for Father Vaughan and a glass of white wine for herself, then settled on a sofa in front of a grandiose fireplace that had fire irons and a grate laden with logs.

'I imagine it's the same in Africa,' she said cheerfully. 'Most of the ethnic charities here are a scam of some kind. There's no reason you should know it, but any jobs program is wide open. Father Crisp's operation is likely to support just about everyone except the unemployed.'

Vaughan recalled Father Crisp's aggressive assertions when the Cardinal's general fund had been canvassed by the lawyer—it was clear that the two of them had tried to favour general funding. 'We don't need general money in the Bronx,' the black Father had asserted, 'we need specific money. We need specific money in specific figures, like specifically one hundred thousand dollars.' His sleepy-lidded cloudy brown eyes fixed themselves on Mrs. Bradshaw's. 'This is a pretty nice apartment you have here. Not many people in the Bronx ever goin' to see inside a place like this. Mosta my people would just not be believin' five million goin' on a diamond for a church: however right that cause might be.' He continued to stare at her with cool impassivity. 'We need specific money, ma'am, for specific people who haven't got much to their names. Unemployed people, poor people, single-parent people. If I'm goin' to support this cause, it's gonna be for specific reasons.'

The Latino had make it equally plain, though in more civilised and restrained language, that the price tag on his membership on the Committee was similar. 'If you exhibit this diamond in fifty cities for a week each,' he had pointed out, 'you could surely raise ten thousand dollars in each. This isn't a dollar and a dream. It's a dream and half a million.'

'But,' the Cardinal had observed drily, 'whether it's a single dollar or a half million dollars, those monies can only be passed to charities that are on the Attorney General's list. On the list now and at the conclusion of the tour.'

Donna Bradshaw chuckled at the memory. 'His Eminence put them down pretty neatly there. He could have either the jobs program or the Puerto Rican mothers off the list any time he chose to investigate them. And not because those Reverend gentlemen are corrupt—because they can't control the others lower down. They know they can't, he knows they can't, we know they can't. I guess the end result was fair, don't you?'

The outcome had been thirty percent each for the ethnic charities, twenty percent for local Catholic charities in the cities visited and twenty percent for the Cardinal's own general fund.

'I have to take your word for that,' Father Vaughan remarked. Corruption could take many forms. He'd known missionaries who turned a blind eye to nepotism for unassailably humanitarian reasons. 'It certainly appears your Internal Revenue men are a lot more generous to charities than ours.' He thought of the tedious paperwork required to complete tax covenants in Britain.

'My company's donation for the diamond will be tax deductible and we can spread the relief over at least two years. All the expenses of travelling the diamond around will be deductible, too.' She chuckled again. 'Journalists like to say the IRS pays. That's not correct. I pay and they help. And believe me, if we did not have the Cardinal and those priests on the letterhead, they might do exactly the opposite. The only snag is that your Bishop is not going to have his stone back for a year.'

'Better late than never. Will you bid at the auction yourself?'

'You know, Father'—she had wandered across to the windows and was gazing out at the river and the ugly industrial mayhem of Queens on the other side—'I may go, but I guess I'll employ an agent to bid. And you? You're more than welcome to stay on here for the big event.'

'I suppose as an interested party I might.' He was far from sure.

She turned around, as if struck by a new idea. 'If you do, would you mind going on a talk show? You know, breakfast television. It's an idea my PR adviser, Janice, had. She'll tell you more over lunch.'

'What on earth would they want me to talk about?'

'About India. About the Malabar Angel's history.' She smiled with sudden wickedness, like a schoolgirl initiating a prank. 'Janice had a nice idea. She thought they might get Lucy's husband on, too. The two of them are coming across tomorrow, though not exactly in harmony.' She gave a small shrug. 'Well, that's their problem.'

'Go on the television with Luttrell? Merciful heaven, he'd tear me to pieces.' He remembered the hostility of the encounter in London.

'You think so? I can't say I do. I think you'd come across pretty well.'

Father Vaughan suddenly realised where this was leading. 'You mean this talk show might discredit his sale and keep down the price?'

'Something of the kind, Father Gerard. Something of the kind is not impossible. The IRS would appreciate your self-sacrifice. So would I.'

One of the reception desk clerks reminded Barbara about the odd couple's room change. 'We just had a cancellation, Miss Andrews. If you want to give those people a room on the fifth with a Park view, we have one vacant now.'

'Remind me of the room they're in, will you?'

'They're in 609, Miss Andrews.'

'Okay. I'll tell them.' Normally she wouldn't have done this

215

herself, she'd have left it to the clerk. But it was hotel policy that all honeymooners must be dealt with, so far as possible, by an Assistant Manager. A satisfied honeymoon couple both spread the good word now and could turn into regular future clients. Not that this pair were likely to come again. All the same she tapped 609 into her computer, verified their names and called the room. The Irishman answered.

'Mr. Hermon, I'm happy to tell you we have a better room on the fifth for you and your wife. One with a view across the Park like you have right now.'

Up on the sixth floor Frank spread his hand across the instrument, swore and said to Ilse, 'The bastards aren't giving us a room at the back, after all. What do we say, for fuck's sake?'

'Refuse. We have to be over the ballroom.'

'That's very decent of you and all,' he blarneyed. 'We don't mind being at the back, you know. We prefer it, as you might say. My wife gets the shivers just from the sight of a high-up window, she does. A room that's only looking down on a roof or something will suit us fine.'

Barbara couldn't believe this. What kind of a crazy couple were they? As a routine she checked the old reservation and realised she had made an error anyway, although with any normal guest it should have made no difference.

'I'm afraid we had a slight misunderstanding, sir. The room we had reserved is on the Sixty-first Street side of the hotel. We always talk about that as the back. There are no fifth floor rooms overlooking the building's interior space.'

'I must ask my wife.' Frank stifled the phone again and had just begun an altercation with Ilse when he appreciated what the woman downstairs was saying, although she didn't know it. 'Okay, okay,' he said hastily, waving at Ilse to be quiet. 'That'll be great, just great. We apologise for being a nuisance. When would you like to move us down?'

Barbara checked the computer. Room 538 should be cleaned and dressed with fresh towels and toiletries by eleven. It was nearly that now. 'I'll have the Bell Captain send someone for your bags in a quarter of an hour, sir.' Feeling considerably relieved at the odd couple's sudden swing from craziness to common sense, she fed this into the hotel's data bank. 'Right,

216

sir. Then you have 538 until Monday morning, the twenty-second.'

'Thanks a lot. That'll be fine.' When the conversation was over he could feel sweat trickling down his skin beneath his shirt. Shit, but that had been too close to arousing suspicion for his liking. And they'd been dead lucky. What the Manager had explained, without meaning to, was how the hotel was constructed. There were no back rooms on the fifth floor because what occupied the inside of the hotel on that floor was the space above the ballroom ceiling.

'Listen, Ilse.' She could bloody well take some of the risks for a change. 'When we've shifted rooms I want you to make a little investigation, okay? You go along the corridor and you try all the doors on the side opposite our room.'

'And what am I looking for?' She was doubtful and unwilling. 'You should do this. It is what I pay you for.'

'No. Just this once you're doing the dirty work. You open every door until you find one that leads to a service area. Then you go in and see if there's another door, on the side away from the corridor. Then you open that door. Beyond it should be like the inside of a house's roof—well, it is the inside of a bloody roof. Then you come back and tell me.' He spoke in a simplified way, as if to a child, because it enabled him to combine menace with a cloak of humour.

'And if this last door is locked?'

'You take a nice careful look at what kind of lock it is and come back and tell me. Then I go there and decide where to put the fucking bomb.'

For a few seconds she thought of refusing, then rationalised what he was afraid of. 'You think you ask too many questions here already?'

'I think, dearie'—he deliberately cut into her unhinged sense of self-importance—'that only a goddam bloody idiot would want to be wandering around like a lost hotel guest one minute and be back dressed as an engineer the next.'

An hour later, after they had transferred their belongings, Ilse set off down the long fifth floor corridor, ready armed with an excuse about needing a dress ironed. There were a number of doors on the internal side. Several did not yield and could have been storage cupboards. After that, about halfway down, she

217

found one open. She edged through and into a small service vestibule. On one side was a linen room, on the other a pantry: and straight ahead was what Frank had sent her for. A sign on the door announced NO ENTRY. The door itself had a conventional handle and also a mortice lock. She tried it, pushing gently.

'Hey! Excuse me, whaddya want?' A woman's voice, sharp and accusing.

Ilse controlled herself, didn't jump, didn't spin around, just eased up and half turned her head. A black hotel chambermaid in a blue coverall was standing there.

'I try to find somebody here. There is no one.' She removed her hand from the door. 'I thought perhaps you have gone through there.'

'There ain't nothin' through there. Through there's only for electricians. What you wantin', miss?'

'How do I have a dress ironed, please?'

'You shoulda used the phone, miss. You shoulda called the Housekeepin'.'

'I go and phone then.' The next thing would be a demand for her room number. 'Thank you for your help.' She managed to get past this thankfully unsuspicious maid and reach the vestibule door. 'I go straightaway and telephone. Thank you so much.'

'That's okay.' Once the stranger was out of her domain the maid was happy again. 'Jest call the housekeepin', miss.'

Back in Room 538 Frank received this intelligence with satisfaction. 'See what I meant?' he said victoriously. 'The bloody maid might be stupid, but she'd have recognised me the second time. Now, if you wouldn't mind opening that pretty little wallet of yours and providing the necessary, I'll be off for a spot of shopping.'

'What do you get now, for God's sake?' Frank's shopping requirements had been extensive already.

'Nothing that'll break the bank, me darlin'. Blue workman's clothes and a belt, tools and a small set of skeleton keys. And never fear, I'll be buying them all secondhand if I can. I wouldn't want to have people thinking I'm an apprentice, now would I?'

Chapter

35

J a m e s Constant was considering his auction tactics. He had
the Malabar Angel 'in the frame' now, firmly in the frame of its
quality, its provenance and who the serious bidders would be.
He and Charles Luttrell had long ago situated it as number 378
out of 394, to provide a climax minutes before the end. He'd
decided to open at $2.5 million, stride rapidly through the
reserve of $3 million and then manoeuvre into a two-five-eight
progression, accepting only those levels of the hundred thousands. He would give the impression that $4 million was the
floor price and only when he had broken that barrier would he
accept bids in simple hundred thousands—unless, of course,
the momentum swung into the kind of magic that shredded
estimates and manufactured headlines. With this stone it just
might.

He'd been hearing rumours of Donna Bradshaw's weirdly
titled charity—well, weird to him, perhaps not to an
American—and he knew from his conversations in Los Angeles
that Gloria Grace hated her guts. Two millionaires after the same
jewel was all he needed to shred the estimates into confetti.
Meanwhile he had plenty of lesser matters on his mind.

Today was Friday the 19th, the first of the three public
viewing days before the sale, but the last working day and
therefore the day everything had to be finalised. Over at the

Park Plaza a platoon of hired security guards were watching over the display of what the catalogue blandly called 'Magnificent Jewels', which had been brought in an armoured security van from a bank vault early this morning and laid out in bulletproof glass showcases in one of the hotel's smaller banqueting rooms. Constant had been there throughout the preparations, but now was back at Burnaby's Park Avenue office, where he had an appointment with Walter Cranston.

The intercom on his desk buzzed and his secretary asked if he would take a call. It was that fellow Clifford from the hotel. They'd only parted company half an hour before.

'Sorry to trouble you, sir. I have a couple more things we ought to settle.' Clifford mentioned some details of timings and how Burnaby's staff would be disposed around the auction dais when the sale began at ten o'clock on Monday morning. 'I have a small favour to ask, sir. My wife and our little girl are coming to the viewing today. Is there any way they could meet the Baroness herself on Monday? It would be a big moment for them.'

'I'm afraid I don't know if she'll be there.' Constant almost added that he hoped to God she'd stay away. 'Our Chairman is giving a lunch party during the sale interval and she's been invited. If I remember I'll mention it.'

'I'd much appreciate that.' Clifford thanked him again. 'I'll be around most of the weekend. Just call the hotel if you need me.'

The next thing Constant knew Walter Cranston had arrived. This was in fact a damn nuisance, but he knew why the banker insisted they meet here and not at the public viewing. Whereas Gloria Grace arranged everything for the benefit of photographers, Cranston was keeping his interest carefully private.

'Glad to see you again, sir.' He rose to his feet as the client entered, looking every inch a Wall Street seigneur in a dark single-breasted suit and discreetly striped tie. 'May I offer you some coffee?'

'Very kind of you.' Cranston appreciated good manners. 'Now I have a small problem,' he said, when the secretary had brought a tray with porcelain cups and an antique silver coffeepot with a high, curving spout. 'We have one heck of a day Monday and I may not be able to make the sale.'

'We can always bid for you, sir. There will be no charge.'

Constant knew what was coming next. Potential buyers, old money or new, rich or middle incomed, titled or upstarts, asked only one question.

'How high do you suppose the Malabar Angel will go?'

'There's been a great deal of interest. I expect in excess of five million.'

'Say I authorised you to five and a half?'

'In practice, sir, a round figure or half of one can easily fail.' He could not reveal that above the $5 million level he would still be angling for hundred thousand bids, nor mention the two-five-eight approach. But Cranston had been a good and reliable client before. 'I'd advise five six rather than five five.'

'But you're promising nothing, eh?'

'Nobody can.'

'Quite correct. Never promise what you can't deliver.'

'You could always bid by telephone, sir. We shall have six lines operating in the auction room. That could be a solution.'

'I guess it's always better to be on the dealing room floor, as it were.'

'There is no other way to get the feel,' Constant agreed. 'Would you like arrangements for a paddle in case you do come in person?'

'Paddle? I must be more out of date than I thought.'

'Allow me to show you one.' Constant went next door and came back holding an oversized table tennis bat, painted blue with a prominent white number. 'In theory you hold one of these up for every bid. If we know you it's less necessary, but no bids are accepted from people who have not signed for a paddle and proven their financial resources.'

'These must have sparked a few jokes.' Cranston waved the bright blue paddle vigorously above his head, then handed it back.

'Quite a few,' Constant agreed. 'Personally I hate the things.' They made it harder to judge the niceties of a bidder's mood: although in a place the size of the Grand Ballroom he'd be unable to see faces clearly anyway.

'Thank you, then.' Cranston moved to leave. 'Would you warn the telephone girls too?'

'I will indeed. We refer to this sale as "Iris" and you should quote that. Let us know in good time and one of the girls will call you before bidding for the Malabar Angel starts.'

As he ushered his client out, Constant overheard the tail-end of a phone conversation his secretary was having.

'The afternoon session starts with lot 201. Sales normally run at about seventy lots an hour. Your friend's item would be sold around four-thirty. Would you mind telling me who is speaking?' The secretary waited, listened, then perplexedly put the phone down.

'Something wrong?' Constant asked.

'No, not really. Just odd. Some friend of the Baroness rang about what time the diamond would be under the hammer. She sounded foreign. When I asked her name she hung up on me. Why do that if she was a friend?'

'Could be she doesn't want the Baroness to know. People are strange.' Constant dismissed it. He ought to be back at the Park Plaza and available to answer questions there.

'More importantly,' the girl added, 'I had one of the local TV talk shows phoning before that. Would you or Charles Luttrell take part on Sunday morning?'

'They say who else will be on?'

'Some lady saleroom correspondent and a priest.'

'Not me.' Constant was appalled. 'Emphatically not me. If the Chairman wants to feed himself to the lions that's up to him. Tell them he arrives from London tonight and will be staying at the hotel.'

And that reminded him. When was the Baroness going to swear the affidavit? Only Samantha was in touch with her. He rang the London office and learnt that Samantha was flying across tomorrow, though not with Charles: which left a number of speculations wide open, including that the Baroness herself was still being difficult.

Frank waited until after lunch, when he reckoned the cleaners and chambermaids would be finished with the rooms. He hung a DO NOT DISTURB sign on the door of 538 and changed into the workman's blue trousers and shirt, clipped a tool holdall to the leather belt and made sure the skeleton key was handy. At the same time Ilse sauntered down the corridor to spy out the land.

Obtaining the key had been easy. He'd gone to a locksmith

over on First Avenue, spun a yarn about a cupboard and later himself cut the wards off a standard key with a hacksaw, reducing it to the T shape that would open any rimlock. The one thing Frank had not managed to acquire was a hotel staff identity card to pin to his shirt. He had, however, with true Irish inspiration, asked for a business card when he went to an electrical shop to buy a flashlight and used that firm's name on an imitation identity disc, utilising a passport photograph, coloured cardboard, plastic wrap, and a safety pin. It had struck him that if he was challenged he'd stand a better chance producing the business card and claiming to have been called in from outside.

He'd barely changed when Ilse let herself in again. 'If you go now, it's all right,' she whispered, as though the room was bugged. 'I wait for you.' She began to undress. She would lie on the bed and feign sickness if he had to dodge back and hide. He eased himself out of the bedroom, checked in both directions, then softly closed the door and walked purposefully down the corridor. No hesitation now. He was Andy McClarry, engineer, sent to deal with a reported electrical fault.

The staff service area was deserted. He went straight to the central door, squirted a spray of WD-40 into the keyhole from an aerosol can, slipped in the key and presto! The door swung away from him. He shone the torch, caught a first glimpse of a cavernous space filled with girders and ducting, then concentrated on locating the working lights that must exist. No problem. The switches were inside on the wall. He tried one. Bare bulbs blazed into life around the cavern, creating pools of light and long, distorted shadows. He pushed the door behind him shut, leaving it unlocked, and rapidly took stock.

At first sight this structural space was an eight-foot-high maze of slanting girders, with huge dusty air-conditioning ducts suspended through them. Steel mesh catwalks threaded over the joists that must support the ceiling of the ballroom below. Above there appeared to be concrete. He flicked the flashlight beam around, stepped a short way along one of the catwalks and began to achieve a better comprehension.

The catwalks ran across a number of huge inverted T-shaped steel girders, each partnered eight feet above by its twin and coated in some fireproofing material, probably asbestos. Each pair was linked by thinner diagonals, which crisscrossed the space between them, constituting one huge lattice girder. And there was a series of them, stretching right across the cavern. Holy Mary, what a construction!

Somewhere out of his memory came the phrase 'collecting structure'. An architect's expression. This must be the collecting structure that spanned the ballroom and held up the two twenty-eight-storey towers of bedrooms and suites above. The concrete roof rested on the top of the structure, like the rigid top of a great box. It would hardly matter where he placed the Semtex, the explosion would be driven downwards by that concrete, down through the ballroom ceiling and possibly outwards through the thin walls of the service areas and storerooms. Fifty or sixty pounds of explosive would be enough to cause devastation. Thinking more about it, Frank realised that if the Semtex was placed in the angle of one of those T-shaped girders the explosion might cut right through the steel, like demolishing a bridge. The hotel wouldn't collapse: the rest of the collecting structure would ensure that. But the building would have to be completely evacuated for days or weeks while the damage was repaired. On the other hand, that would mainly drive the blast upwards and sideways, rather than directly demolishing the room beneath.

So where should he position the stuff? Ideally above the centre of the ballroom. He noticed a vertical cable hanging taut from the concrete roof and realised it supported one of the chandeliers below. Explosive could cut through that beautifully, sending the chandelier crashing onto the crowd as a terrifying bonus. But there was no hiding place. He went farther along the catwalk, ducking beneath pipes, sometimes bent double, as he searched for shadow and concealment.

Eventually he found a spot where a lower run of ducting lay across the intermediate joists that supported the ballroom ceiling. Taking extreme care not to push his feet against ceiling plaster, he crawled over the ducting. Beyond it was deep shadow. So long as he rested the container on joists he would be in business. He snaked back and after dusting himself down began his retreat to the entrance. He was almost there when he heard voices on the other side. Two voices. Women chattering. This was no time to hesitate. He swung the door back, stepped forward boldly and immediately tripped because the level of the sill was an inch or two higher than the catwalk.

The two Puerto Rican maids stopped gossiping in midsentence, startled and astonished by the tousle-haired apparition stumbling towards them. They gawped at Frank, his blue shirt and trousers streaked with dust, as he staggered, groped with one hand to steady himself and only narrowly avoiding falling at their feet.

'Sorry. Terrible sorry.' He managed to recover his balance, the tool kit swinging on his belt and thumping his backside. He grinned foolishly. 'Nearly had meself arse over tip there, all right.' Realising how unlike an American he must be sounding, he hastily tried to disguise his Irish accent. 'Sorry to disturb you, ladies. Been a fault reported in the ballroom lighting. Can't find nothing though, not that I can see.' He turned away from them to relock the door, trying to remember typical American phrases from movies, then grinned again as he realised they were still staring at him. 'Must have given you one hell of a fright. Guess I should be reporting there ain't nothing wrong.' He made as fast an exit as he could without actually running.

'Well, whaddya know!' exclaimed one of the maids, called Maria.

'One crazy guy.' Rosita giggled.

'Hey, look!' Maria stopped to pick a small object off the carpet. 'He dropped it.' She held up a small screwdriver. 'I go after him.' She ran to the passage door, then stood outside, hands on her hips, gazing down the great length of the corridor until Rosita joined her. 'How about that! He ain't there. Where's he gone to?'

'You know his name?'

'Never saw him in my life.'

'Hand the thing in at the housekeeping office,' Rosita said. 'They'll know what to do.'

Chapter

36

' A funny thing just happened, Craig.' The hotel's Head House-keeper, Beth Symons, was speaking. She was doing a Saturday morning stint because the union disruption of the restaurant a few months ago had now infected her staff. 'Two of my chambermaids reported something you ought to know about. Could be nothing. You'll be a better judge than me.' She liked Craig Clifford's approach to security. It was quiet and consid-ered, not like Trevinski's bull-nosed tactics.

'Please tell me, Beth.' He reached for a ballpoint and his personal incident book. He logged everything when it hap-pened, with the time.

'The two girls were in one of the service areas on the fifth floor. You know it has access to some kind of roof space?'

'I know where you mean.' He had been shown the door once. But what was the space beyond it?

'While they were there, an electrician came out and dropped a screwdriver. By the time they went after him he'd disap-peared. They handed it in later and we told Technical Services this morning. What's odd is this, Craig. They didn't have anyone assigned to that area yesterday.'

'Are you sure?'

'They double-checked the work sheets.'

'What did the guy look like?'

'That I don't know. And neither girl is on again until Monday. All they said was, he tripped up and got all flustered. They were laughing about it.'

'Thanks, Beth. I'll call back.'

Craig thought this through. Then he rang Technical Services, asked what was in the space and began to get alarmed.

'You mean all the lighting circuits for the Grand Ballroom are up there?'

'Not the emergency system. Everything else.'

'Meet me there in fifteen minutes. With a couple of electricians. Doesn't matter what else they're doing. Take them off it.'

He logged this order and hurried up to the Banqueting Department offices. The first would-be viewers of the auction jewelry were already arriving. The gems would be on display in a variety of armoured glass showcases from 10:00 A.M. until 4:30 P.M. He had arranged for Julia to bring Antonia at 3:00 and planned to escort them himself. But that was the least important matter on his mind at this moment. He needed to talk privately to Tom Garrison.

Fortunately the Banqueting Director was there and after a brief delay Craig was shown through the oyster-carpeted reception lobby to his office. Garrison's desk reflected his character: not cluttered with papers, well polished, adorned with an onyx ashtray and penholder, a thick leather-bound diary to one side. Weekend or no weekend Garrison himself was in a dark suit, a crisply laundered white shirt and black silk tie with small white dots. He nodded Craig to a chair. 'You look worried,' he said, not unsympathetically.

'I am, kind of. Have any of your staff reported faults with the lighting in the Grand Ballroom?'

'I don't recall any. Let me check.' He spoke briefly on an intercom, then shook his head fastidiously. 'Not that we know of.'

'There's been an unauthorised electrician at work in what they call the structural space above the ballroom. He was seen yesterday afternoon. Thus far no one can identify who he was or why he was there. Or how he gained access.'

'And so?' Garrison believed in letting others jump to conclusions. 'What possibility is the smart money on?'

'Jake Trevinski has thought all along that some gang could try a heist on Monday. If the lights went out there'd be a lot of confusion.'

Garrison chose to take this as a slur on his department. 'I disagree. My people are trained to switch the emergency lighting on immediately.'

'An experienced thief could snatch a handful of jewelry in a few seconds.'

'Why Monday for a heist? Why not today or Sunday?'

'These two days the stuff is only handled when being shown to a specific client with security guards watching. During the auction each lot will be held up in turn by one of Burnaby's staff, which means there's continual movement of the pieces. For all we know one of the guards they've hired could be a hood.'

'Hmm.' Garrison could see the sense in this. 'So what would you like us to do?'

'Be advised, basically. Be warned. We'll tighten the security so far as is possible. As soon as we find out any more I'll inform you. The engineers are going to test all the circuits now.'

'Better have them check the air conditioning, too. Suppose someone fed poison gas into the system? I mean, all things are possible.' Garrison gave a bleak, one-sided smile. '"Be prepared" as Tom Lehrer used to sing.'

Craig didn't know who Tom Lehrer was, but he came away aware that Garrison did not appreciate implied criticism from another department.

Nor did he feel any happier two hours later. He had put on overalls himself and the engineers had shown him the maze of catwalks, girders, joists, cables, ducting and pipes, explaining the functions of the various services routed through the structural space. They investigated them all, tested every lighting circuit and checked all the accessible wiring. There was no sign of anything having been tampered with.

'I can't figure that out,' Peterson, the senior of the two engineers, told Craig finally, scratching the back of his neck in perplexity. 'There's nothing we can see. Nothing wrong at all. Who was the guy that's supposed to have been nosing around?'

Nobody knew. Eventually Craig asked Beth Symons to call in either or both of the chambermaids as soon as possible. But this was not so simple. They lived with large families, few of whose members spoke English.

'She may come this afternoon. How should I know?' summed up the replies. All that could be done was to leave messages.

Craig logged a further entry and temporarily consigned the query to the back burner. He took no great notice of the man having 'disappeared'. The girls had probably not gone after him right away. No fault had been located and in his own estimation the dangerous day was Monday. He did, however, suggest that the Technical Services men should install a new lock on the door to the structural space by Monday morning at the latest and check the area regularly. Then, not unnaturally, he began to worry about Julia's visit in the afternoon. He had heard nothing from James Constant about the Baroness. Julia would go wild if he failed to arrange a meeting. He would have to stick his neck out and call Prince Otto at home in Southampton.

Frank and Ilse stood on the sidewalk close by a filling station on First Avenue and 33rd Street. This was where the Libyan had ordered them to wait, a few blocks down from the glass tower and multi-coloured flags of the United Nations buildings.

'Why don't you rent a car?' Ahmed had demanded angrily during his brief telephone conversation with Frank yesterday. That had been the original plan: to rent a sedan, park briefly alongside the Arab's vehicle, transfer the packs of Semtex into the trunk and subsequently park overnight in an underground garage near the Park Plaza. Then the explosive could be carried away piecemeal in shopping bags and Frank's black camera bag to their hotel room. Their lack of credit cards had scuppered that scheme and Ahmed was not pleased. His boss, Rahman, was inherently suspicious of outsiders forcing changes in their plans. The Libyans wanted their involvement minimal and strictly on the terms dictated by Tripoli. It had taken half the night to clear the alteration by coded diplomatic telegrams.

Ahmed swung his rented Ford into the filling station forecourt and bought gas while Frank and Ilse stood ten yards away. As the attendant worked the pump Ahmed watched the pair and the street around. There was no sign of surveillance. He paid, edged forward and stopped by them, leaning across the front seat to open the door and shout, 'Hey, surprise to see you. Jump in.'

As soon as Frank was in the front and Ilse in the back he drove on along the cross street, talking fast. 'The material is in bags in the trunk. Seven packets of ten pounds weight each.'

'We have shopping bags to carry them,' Ilse assured him.

'How you handle the stuff is your business. Where will you place it?'

'In the ceiling of the ballroom,' Frank said. 'It's going to make chaos like New York hasn't seen in a long time. If ever.'

'In the ceiling? You can do that?' A coarse respect crept into the Arab's voice. 'Difficult?'

'Not if you know how. Where's the detonator?'

'Right here!' Ahmed sniggered, reached into his pocket and handed across a partially empty Tampax box. 'Nice for ladies to carry, heh, heh. Appropriate. A detonator inside a tampon.' He sniggered again. 'Don't let her go off too soon, my friend.'

Ilse cut short a blasphemous reply. 'How is it operated?'

'He knows,' Ahmed said, still amused at his chosen hiding place. 'He has a way with women.' He turned onto Third Avenue, slowed and stopped the car outside a shop. 'Get out here.' He released the trunk's internal lock.

Frank didn't obey immediately. 'This isn't a fucking bank raid. You're a friend dropping us. No rush. No hurry.' He clambered out, opened the back door for Ilse with rare courtesy, then went round behind the car. They filled the three shopping bags. 'Don't make the weight even. I'll carry two, you take one.' He carefully laid the remaining pockets inside his camera bag and closed the zip. Then he slammed the trunk shut. Ahmed immediately accelerated away. 'Fucking Arabs.' he said to Ilse. 'And all that bloody orange juice I've drunk!'

The shopping bags felt as if they weighed far more than the twenty pounds there were in each. He was afraid the carrying handles might tear off. But action always elated him and this carried a hundred-thousand-dollar bonus. He slung the strap of the camera bag over his shoulder and began waving at passing cabs.

'Now for the tricky part, me darlin',' he said happily as a cab pulled in to the curb. 'Let's be nice and natural back at the hotel, with you looking as though you've been having the time of your life spending all me money.' He opened the cab door for her. 'Park Plaza, mate. We've just been on the spree.'

* * *

At her apartment in Sutton Place, Donna Bradshaw was hosting a small lunch party: herself, Lucy Luttrell, Father Vaughan and their special guest, Bernie Rissik of 'The Rissik Report'. They were in the blue-walled dining room, off the other side of the parquet-floored hallway from the long reception room that looked over the East River, seated around an oval eighteenth-century mahogany table that Mrs. Bradshaw had picked up at Malletts in London a few years back. The Polish maid, Danuta, was serving fresh salmon mousse, while they drank a lightly chilled bottle of Sauvignon Blanc.

'Your first time in New York, Father?' Rissik enquired in his permanently affable way, exuding innocence as his brain catalogued details of the Bradshaw family lifestyle. 'How d'you like our city? Quite a change from Africa, huh!'

'In some ways.' The horse trading over percentages in the charity had been completely tribal, while New York itself—with its street beggars, its glaring extremes of poverty and riches—struck Vaughan as having many elements of a Third World capital. He refrained from enlarging on that. 'A stimulating atmosphere,' he added cautiously, mistrusting this TV personality's facade of friendliness.

'You can say that again!' Rissik beamed. As a talk show presenter he had perfected this amiability, reinforcing it by always appearing in a blue blazer with gilt buttons, as though he were some Yacht Club Commodore. The giveaway—the deliberate giveaway—was his rug of black hair. This was trimmed long so that its curling edges covered his ears and swept his collar, framing the bland, snub-nosed face and roving eyes. The juxtaposition of mountain gorilla grooming and the impeccable blazer made him instantly indentifiable: which was what he needed to be. People might sometimes fail to recognise celebrities on his show, but they'd have known Bernie Rissik instantly if they encountered him on the subway, unlikely as that was. They also enjoyed the way he could put famous people on the spot. Behind the bland expression and the helmet of hair lurked all the jungle wiliness of the born columnist.

Right now he was mentally pinning down Father Vaughan, evaluating how he could be exploited. He had a gut feeling that this British priest, with his undemonstrative yet determined manner and his labourer's hands had the makings of a minor

231

cult figure: a three-day wonder that could soar like a comet out of 'The Rissik Report' into the headlines, explode in a shower of media sparks on Monday and be forgotten once the auction scandal was over. And there was this amazing intervention of Donna Bradshaw's! 'The Rissik Report''s slogan was "All you ought to know about next week". One thing New York emphatically ought to know about was the Catholic Committee for the Relief of Injustice to the Church of our Lady in Malabar. And, yet again, Bernie Rissik was the sleuth who'd discovered it. He had an absolute exclusive, a beat on all the others.

'The reason I wanted you to meet Father Gerard,' Donna Bradshaw said, guessing that what was going through Rissik's mind was exactly what she intended, 'is that up until we formed the Committee this really had been a one-man crusade.'

'What is more,' Lucy Luttrell chipped in, 'he has with him the diamond's original mount from Malabar.' She gave Vaughan a strangely defiant look, as if he would eventually understand she was acting for the best.

'I'd rather not bring the mount into this,' Father Vaughan said firmly.

'I would be interested to see it,' Rissik remarked, scenting a better story than they'd revealed so far. 'For background. Just background.'

'Surely showing it privately will do no harm?' Lucy urged.

'Come on, Father Gerard,' Donna Bradshaw weighed in. 'Fetch it for us.'

Vaughan agreed with reluctance. It was not easy to gainsay his hostess. He went along to his bedroom and returned to lay the walnut-sized chunk of hollow gold on the dining room table. Rissik examined it and immediately asked about the inscription.

'*Mene* is from the writing on the wall in the Book of Daniel.'

'The prophet guy in the Bible? So what's it mean?'

This was the exact question that had been bothering the priest on and off for many weeks. 'God has measured your sovereignty and put an end to it,' the Jerusalem Bible had said. But whose sovereignty? The crucified Prince of Cochin had voluntarily relinquished his earthly power to God. So should the word 'sovereignty' itself be reinterpreted as 'ownership'? The meanings were not so different: in which case was the word that Rissik was casually studying a threat to any 'owner' except the church? Vaughan decided to steer the TV prophet off the subject. A mysterious death threat to anyone who bought the stone was hardly going to help Donna Bradshaw's cause, even if she did intend donating it to the church later on.

'*Mene* was part of the famous writing that appeared on the wall at Belshazzar's feast. To be honest, no one knows its significance in this context. A professor of Middle Eastern studies might be able to help.'

'I guess we can pass on that.' Rissik put the piece of gold down again. Academic discussion of the Book of Daniel was not going to help his audience ratings.

'The essential point,' Lucy said, 'is that the existence of this mounting substantiates the Malabar church's claim. Personally I am opposed to the diamond being auctioned at all.'

Although she stopped short of naming her husband, Rissik was quick enough to pick up the corollary.

'If Mr. Luttrell agrees to come on the program—which I surely hope he will—would he dispute that proposition?'

'I should say so.' Donna Bradshaw chuckled. 'I should most definitely say so. Wouldn't you, Lucy?'

'He'll be hoping to promote the diamond's value, I think.' Lucy allowed herself a bitter, private smile, a trace of which surfaced on her lips and which Rissik noticed.

'Just what I'm going to offer him the chance of doing.' This could be built up into a very neat confrontation, especially when he threw that Brit art critic, the acid-tongued Victoria Stewart-Robinson, into the cake mix. She was the surprise ingredient. He had invited the Baroness herself, but had met with refusal. The researcher who'd said she'd do anything for publicity had it wrong. In any case, he needed someone to attack Luttrell, because Father Vaughan never would. He had the priest set up in his mind as the selfless saint, whom all communities in New York had united to assist.

'And you, Father? Will you be with us representing the Committee?'

'It would help our cause enormously, Father Gerard,' Donna Bradshaw half pleaded, half ordered.

'We couldn't have this to show the viewers, could we?' Rissik held up the mount.

'I'm afraid not.' Father Vaughan was emphatic. 'I'll appear, if you really feel your audience will be interested. But we are not claiming ownership of the diamond. Mrs. Bradshaw is most generously buying it to donate to the Committee.'

'Well, that has to be your decision.' Rissik sighed, shaking his head sadly and depositing a confetti shower of dandruff on the blue cloth of his blazer. He handed him the mount back. 'I'll look forward to tomorrow.' He had quite some story here. That goddamn mount was going to feature as well, whatever the priest said, and he'd goad Luttrell into spilling the beans on his wife's antagonism. This was going to be good television. His ratings would rise. He forked up the last of his salmon mousse. 'Delicious. My compliments to the chef.' He made a wide gesture, still holding the fork, which sliced the air in front of Mrs. Bradshaw like a pink-licked conductor's baton, and slid smoothly on to another element of the word picture that would introduce his TV guests. 'Quite an apartment you have here! What's the history?'

Barbara Andrews stood by her work station in the Park Plaza, feeling sick at heart at watching the man she loved pass by on the other side of the lobby with his wife and daughter. Anyone who hadn't known the truth would have commented that there went one lucky guy. The little girl was pretty. Very pretty. No wonder Craig adored her. Julia was . . . well, the kind of blonde she'd expected: aloof expression, very high heels, rather tight skirt, walking in a correspondingly strutty way, like a model on a fashion display catwalk. Halfway to being a whore, Barbara thought and then told herself that was unnecessarily bitchy. She'd just overdone dressing up to come here. The trio disappeared towards the Fifth Avenue entrance and Barbara wondered if he'd come back directly. Seeing them go past had exposed her to a bundle of conflicting emotions all at once: love, annoyance, fear, uncertainty. She needed to speak to Craig and be reassured.

While Barbara's eyes remained on the Fifth Avenue entrance another pair she recognised came in: the strange couple. The man had a seemingly heavy black camera case slung over his shoulder and was humping a Bendel shopping bag in one hand and one from Bergdorf in the other. The bags sagged from the handles. The woman had a Bloomingdale's one and that Gucci handbag she'd noticed before. They sure had been indulging themselves. She felt a twinge of envy. Money! They must have been spending as if it was Christmas. I was wrong about that, she reflected, they're more loaded than I thought. She watched them approach reception to collect their key. Loaded two ways! He was no weakling, but those bags were not light. He walked as though they were full of bricks and he was forcing himself through a physical fitness test. One of the bellboys ran up and offered to help. The woman shook her head violently. She seemed to be really on edge. The man shook his head, too, though in a more friendly fashion and mouthed words in a stifled way that Barbara couldn't quite hear. He nodded to her as they continued on to the elevator and she smiled back with the 'Welcome on board, sir' smile. Again it struck her that he made no polite acknowledgement of his wife's right to precedence as they stepped into the elevator. He almost hustled her in. A really strange couple.

Another client came up with a complaint and she was kept busy for a few minutes. Then, miraculously, without her even seeing him cross the lobby, Craig was with her.

'Hi, sweetheart,' he said softly. 'They've gone. I'm sorry you had to be here.'

She felt tears rising and blinked them back. 'Antonia looks beautiful,' she managed to say.

'She is. Inside too. You'll like her.'

'Are they going to meet the Baroness?' She'd heard all about that demand.

He laughed uncomfortably. 'We just don't know. I had to call Prince Otto in the end. He was not delighted. They may come to the auction, they may not. He couldn't commit himself.' Craig almost mimicked the accent, then didn't because there were people milling around. 'He's okay, I guess. She's the problem. She changes her mind five times a day about everything. If Julia wants to meet her she'll have to come along and take the chance.'

'Luckily I'm not on until four Monday afternoon. Maybe I won't see her.'

'I understand, sweetheart.' He wanted to hold and comfort her. 'I do truly understand.'

A commotion at the far end of the lobby interrupted them.

Camera flashbulbs were sporadically illuminating a woman with brightly hennaed hair and a dark blue silk dress that clung to every inch of her extravagant curves. A pudgy man in a grey suit detached himself from this advancing entourage and came towards them.

'Oh God,' Barbara murmured. 'Gloria Grace has arrived. All hands to the pumps.'

Chapter

37

T h e Indian summer had ended overnight. Gusting rain swept the city. Men in baseball caps and windbreakers huddled against the wind on street corners. What could anyone do on a filthy-weathered Sunday morning except stay home and watch television? Watch 'The Rissik Report'. Snort a line of pure white malice. Inject a fix for the coming week from mankind's sneakiest friend: the rug-haired Bernie Rissik.

As he strode onstage before the cameras and the invited studio audience Bernie knew the ratings were going to be good today: the highest since early summer, he hoped. Furthermore a story in this morning's *Times* heralding the Malabar Angel interview would have most of the art and auction world tuning in. Luttrell had his PR adviser, this Prince Czernowski character, holding his hand in the room where guests were served coffee as they waited. So what? Once a victim was on camera, seated in one of the small half circle of armchairs across which Bernie would trade banter, not a thousand PR advisers could save him.

As the first guest was ushered on, that flamboyant, overfleshed, henna-haired relic of Hollywood's prime, Gloria Grace, Bernie knew that Luttrell would be starting to sweat. Vicky Stewart-Robinson would have arrived in the waiting room by now. And Gloria Grace wasn't here for the reason she imagined either. He wasn't going to ask her about either her past successes—her very far past successes—or some judicious mar-riages or her future plans. She was here because she was a self-proclaimed bidder at tomorrow's auction and, wittingly or not, she was going to whet the audience's interest in that event.

'I suppose we have to watch this nonsense,' Prince Otto sighed. There were a hundred better ways to spend a Sunday morning when a mounting gale precluded riding or walking: listening to Mozart, for example, which was his favourite indoor relaxation. However, Helene had been insistent and, having come to realise how much she depended on him for advice, he gave way with relative grace.

'It may settle on one thing for sure,' she said. 'If this Rissik man makes fun of the priest, then I have no need to waste time with affidavits tomorrow.'

'There I agree.' He had driven to Kennedy to collect Helene from her flight yesterday and she had spent most of the evening debating with herself—and occasionally with him—whether it might not be better to negotiate a private sale with 'that absurd charity'. Otto had been strongly against.

'You admit you are wrong, that way,' he argued. 'And you throw away a higher price. You should now leave things as they are, in my opinion.' If he was going to marry Helene eventually, which it had crossed his mind to do, she would have to stick to decisions. As a banker he abhorred constant changes of plan. 'And I think you now have some obligation to this man Luttrell,' he added.

'He is a dealer.' Helene was instantly disparaging. 'One does not have obligations to people like that, for God's sake.'

'I have to say, Gloria'—Bernie Rissik was beaming at the aging star, his black hair shaggy over his eyes—'I can't think of a lady on whom this diamond would look more like the five million dollars it's expected to make.'

Gloria Grace sashayed happiness back at him, a red gash of a smile. 'That's nice of you to say so, Bernie. I so appreciate the compliment.' She had never intended to talk about the goddamn sale. She wasn't even certain she'd be able to bid that high. She might content herself with something lesser that would sparkle as much. But if the diamond was what Bernie insisted on talking about, well, it was better being on his show than not and she wanted to be invited again. 'I'm hoping to make that Angel mine tomorrow.'

'And it's not going to trouble you that it may be stolen property?'

'Whaddya mean stolen?' Her poise faltered, her carefully nurtured aristocratic accent lapsed, the red gash assumed a hard twist of horror.

'In a few minutes "The Rissik Report" will be interviewing Father Gerard Vaughan, a priest representing the Church of Our Lady in Malabar, where the diamond was stolen from.'

'Well, see here Bernie.' Gloria Grace almost snarled, she was so angry at having been set up. 'There is no way I or my husband would be party to any illegal transaction.'

Bernie beamed afresh. 'I have to say, Gloria, that is going to be good news for the charity your fellow Californian, Donna Bradshaw, has established to recover the diamond.' He stood up quickly, before she could react further, knowing how she hated Donna. 'It's been a real privilege having you on the show, Gloria, and to share your frank opinions on tomorrow's extraordinary auction.' He shook her hand and led her gallantly offstage before returning to the camera himself. He could afford a few seconds break after such a coup.

'Whose side is this man on, for God's sake!' Helene was beginning to lose her composure. She swung her legs off the sofa and sat up angrily, as though she could somehow influence what was going on in the studio.

'Not ours, from the look of it.' Otto remained relaxed. 'Let's not get too excited yet.'

Father Vaughan blinked in the floodlights as one of the attractive hostesses on the program brought him on. Charles Luttrell and a woman he didn't know were already seated in the armchairs. However, whoever she might be, she had on a costume he did recognise: a gold and red Ghanaian kente cloth, wound around her like a toga and held in at the waist with a gold kid belt. She had an angular face, swept-back hair and she wore large-framed red glasses that almost matched the lipstick on a meanly thin mouth. Watch out, Father Vaughan told himself.

Bernie Rissik advanced, all smiles, rescued him from the hostess and said quickly, 'Charles Luttrell you already know and this is Vicky Stewart-Robinson.' Then he moved on to the more important introduction to the audience.

'And here we have this morning's special guest, also all the way from London. Quite a British day we're having, eh?' The studio audience tittered obediently and clapped. There was no need for a sign to be held up ordering APPLAUSE. People favoured with tickets knew what was expected of them: and the flustering of Gloria Grace had honed their reactions. 'Father Gerard Vaughan is the unsung hero behind the campaign to return the great Malabar Angel diamond to its rightful home in India.'

'By purchasing it,' Charles said loudly, from the disadvantage of his seated position.

'By any means possible,' Rissik slanted at him, then resumed beaming. 'Glad to have you with us, Father Vaughan.' He motioned to the vacant armchair, sat down himself and leant forward confidentially towards Victoria Stewart-Robinson, the implacable amiability redolent of good news. 'Now Vicky—you don't mind my calling you "Vicky" do you? We're all friends on "The Rissik Report"—now Vicky, you're an art expert and a very well-respected one. If I told you I happened to know Father Vaughan has with him here in New York the original gold mount that held the Malabar Angel on its cross in the church, would you say a charity should be forced into *buying* back this legendary stone?'

Vaughan drew in his breath and kept silent. His instincts had been right. Even the opening gambit was a betrayal of confidence. Worse could only follow.

'I have also—' Luttrell began.

'Ladies first, sir.' Rissik cut him down. 'Now Vicky, tell us your views.'

'This typifies the rape of ancient moments in the Third World by unscrupulous Western dealers . . .' Victoria Stewart-Robinson's speech began to rival the lurid colours of her ethnic costume. ' . . . I intend on making my own personal demonstration of protest at the auction.'

240

'Do that and you'll be thrown out, my dear,' Charles said quietly—but not quietly enough.

'You'll have her thrown out, Mr. Luttrell? Do I hear you say Vicky will be thrown out if she protests? And you will throw out Mrs. Luttrell, too? Isn't your wife against this sale?'

'On personal grounds, yes, she is.' He kept his temper and followed Czernowski's advice to agree with Rissik if humanly possible. 'But because the present owners have legal title she has very wisely decided to support Father Vaughan's efforts.' He made an expansive gesture, hands spread wide, throwing the whole subject into the public arena. 'Who doesn't have occasional disagreements with his better half, Mr. Rissik? I am sure you do.'

Rissik eyed him suspiciously. This wall of virtue must be made to crumble.

'And doesn't Father Vaughan have morality on his side?'

'I am sure he has the entire heavenly host. I shall give them an appropriate discount on the buyer's premium if they win.'

This time the laughter was spontaneous, though there was less of it. The audience mostly didn't know that buyers at fashionable auctions were charged for the privilege of being buyers. But those who did enjoyed the joke.

'Father Vaughan',—Rissik managed to get his smile back in place and shifted the emphasis—'tell us what you're hoping to achieve tomorrow.' It was a weak question, but preferable to allowing Luttrell another opening.

'Whether the heavenly host will be helping, I can't say.' Vaughan took up where Rissik had backed off. 'I haven't been in touch with them recently.' Delighted amusement greeted this unexpected sally from a priest. 'People we do have on our side include His Eminence the Cardinal and the Reverend Eugene Crisp from the Bronx. By exhibiting the diamond around America we hope to raise substantial amounts for a jobs program and helping abandoned mothers here in New York.'

Rissik immediately led the cheering, stretching his hands out in front of him as he clapped enthusiastically.

'So you have a double mission, Father! Reclaiming the diamond and helping the underprivileged of this city.'

'Not so much reclaiming,' Vaughan insisted, 'as purchasing with the most generous aid of a private donor.'

'Are you sure you want to blow up this priest, now?' Frank enquired. He was with Ilse in their hotel room, assembling the timing mechanism that would activate the detonator and explode the Semtex. Originally he had turned the TV on to mask their conversation from eavesdroppers: even hotel rooms can be bugged. Then this talk show had begun and Ilse had watched with fascination as, for the first time, she identified people who would be among her targets. She had even stopped fussing around him as he did the work.

'If they are there,' she said, 'they get killed. What otherwise do you imagine? Don't tell me you want me to warn one man, for God's sake. Anyway the clergy are as much part of the forces of imperialism as capitalists and Generals.'

Frank bit back a retort. He'd suggested weeks ago that she could double the publicity impact by giving a telephone warning to a newspaper before the bomb went off, like they did in Ulster. Then there'd be panic before the explosion, a few people would escape and when she used some invented organisation to claim responsibility she could claim she hadn't wanted to take life, only to get across her message. She'd reacted to that idea like a nuclear meltdown. Phew! Unforgettable. An hour's tirade about world revolution. 'Violence is the highest form of class struggle.' It was museum stuff: and none of it had sounded like her own phrases.

Gradually, as they spent more time together he'd realised why. All the junk about attacking the imperialists was just that: junk. No organisation would claim credit for another blow at capitalism. There was no message. She might kid herself there was. In practice she was only after revenge: revenge for her boyfriend's death. Revenge on the Baroness, revenge on society. But he didn't like intentionally killing a man of the cloth. They would never do a thing like that in Ireland, Holy Mother of God they would not.

'You have a problem?' she asked suddenly, as he began soldering a wire delicately to the bell of the old-fashioned alarm clock he'd bought for a timer and a tiny wisp of smoke went up from the solder.

'For Christ's sake.' He had plenty of reasons to respond irritably. You're like a bloody hen. You think I don't know what

I'm doing? *Ich habe nicht problem, mein Liebe.*' He mocked her in her own language, hating her for her obsessions, for refusing to sleep with him, for being happy to kill a priest.

'*Kein. Kein problem.*' She corrected his grammar.

'You should have been a fucking schoolteacher.' He had soldered on one wire already and when he placed the bomb he would clip the other to the alarm bell itself. The rest of the circuit took in a battery and the detonator. When the bell rang it completed the circuit and the battery's power cord set off the detonator, the pencil-slim tube that had been concealed in the Tampax and which he would push gently into the plastic explosive. This was the most basic and reliable system he knew. Everything except the detonator could be bought in a hardware store. He'd experienced slight difficulty finding a twenty four-hour clock, then located a small traveling one that was ideal. It had to be a twenty four-hour clock so that they could set it tonight for 4:30 P.M. tomorrow. It had to be small, so it would fit comfortably into the box with the Semtex. The box was labelled as electrical fittings. He'd begged it from the shop where he bought the flashlight. This evening he was going to carry it quite openly down the corridor and through the service area into the structural space.

'This thing is good?' she asked dubiously. It was so cheap and simple, she could have made it herself.

'All we have to do is test the clock and the circuit.' He attached the wires to a miniature bulb holder instead of the detonator. 'When the alarm goes, the bulb lights up.' He snapped his fingers. 'Bingo! I'll give it two hours this afternoon. Better get it out of the way now. They'll be after cleaning the room any minute.'

He carried the assembly tenderly through to the old walk-in closet, set it on the floor and then locked the door with his skeleton key. The Semtex was in the closet, too, inside his suitcase. The detonator he kept well separate, hidden in its Tampax box in a drawer. Too many poor bastards had blown themselves up accidentally making bombs.

'But, Father, to go back for a moment to the point that interests ordinary folks like me.' Rissik was still angling for an admission from Luttrell. 'This mount you have in your possession, the diamond's original mount you showed me at lunch yesterday, isn't that still proof of the church's legal ownership? Isn't this auction wrong?'

'I think it is.' Vicky Stewart-Robinson interrupted, earning a grateful nod from her host. 'Tradition establishes ownership. If the boot were on the other foot and Burnaby's wanted to make the church's case they'd be saying so quicker than Jack Robinson.'

'And you agree with that, Charles?' Rissik beamed amiably.

'I most certainly do not.'

'That was how you authenticated the Harley family's tiara four years ago,' Vicky said. She looked at a notebook. 'May I quote you? "In the unusual instance of the Harley tiara being rediscovered one hundred and thirty years after its loss there can be no doubt that Victorian prints showing the tiara being worn by Lady Venetia Harley, coupled with contemporary reports of its ownership, constitute all that is necessary to guarantee the provenance and pedigree." Or have you forgotten?'

Charles flushed. 'The comparison is not valid. There is no contemporary illustration of the Malabar Angel diamond.'

'Don't you have an old saying in England, Mr. Luttrell?' Rissik suggested. 'What is sauce for the goose is sauce for the gander?' He swung round to face the cameras directly. 'Well, folks, that brings us to the end of this week's "Rissik Report": and leaves an unanswered question that I'm sure intrigues you all as much as it does me. Should the recovery of this historic church jewel be left to the untiring voluntary efforts of a single priest and the Committee he has inspired? Or is it time for the regulatory authorities to take an interest?'

As he spoke Charles Luttrell rose from his chair, bowed ironically to the audience and walked out. He wasn't on camera, so some viewers wondered what caused the tittering.

'This is intolerable. I sue them. We must phone the lawyers at once.' Helene rampaged in front of the television with such fury that Otto quickly switched it off in case she threw a book or ashtray at the screen.

'Calm down, *Mein Liebe*. Take it easy. Let's have a drink and decide what to do.'

He went through to the servant's pantry for the essential champagne. Outside the wind shrieked around the house, tearing small branches off the trees in the garden, sending whirlwinds of dead leaves into the air. Southampton had been hit by a tornado a few years back and this gale was starting to become a repeat performance. Quite appropriate to Helene's mood, Otto thought. He was going to have difficulty persuading her not to do something a lot worse than breaking the TV. The best course of action came to him as he was easing the cork out of the bottle.

'Have you accepted this lunch invitation from Luttrell tomorrow?' he asked, handing her a glass as he returned to the living room.

'Why should I expose myself to a collection of gawping Americans? I do have some self-respect.'

'I think we could use the occasion.'

'How?' She was in absolutely no mood for compromise on anything. 'Better to spend the time briefing attorneys.'

'If the Malabar Angel was sold privately to this absurd charity, as you call it, there would be no need for the auction or attorneys. The church would have the diamond, Mrs. Bradshaw would have her publicity, you would have the money.'

'And she beats me down because of the television nonsense? Half an hour ago you told me not to change my mind!'

'She is expecting to pay five million. I suspect that is the amount she has allocated. I agree I think differently now. You should accept that and withdraw.'

'You think so?' Helene didn't like being cornered. On the other hand Otto understood about money. He had a good sense of what was and wasn't too much. 'All right. If you advise me, I do that. But not myself. We make Samantha do it and then we tell Luttrell at the lunch. I am meeting her tomorrow in any case.'

'I think that's wise. Luttrell won't like it, but he still gets his percentages and after that performance you owe him nothing. He completely contradicted himself. He should never have let himself be interviewed.' Otto wandered across the room, sipping his champagne, marshalling his thoughts. There was something he'd been asked to do, something he'd forgotten. What was it? Oh yes, the ex-Marine major. 'I should have told you. That army acquaintance of your brother, the security man who drove you out here. He greatly wants his wife and daughter to meet you. Why not after lunch?'

'I have to do this?' Her tone emphasised what an exceptionally boring chore it would be.

'He's taken a lot of trouble.'

'That was his job, after all. The next thing you ask me is to tip him, I suppose.'

'Don't exaggerate, Helene.' This reluctance to consider others was a side of her character he found distasteful. 'I ask you to treat him as someone to whom you should repay a favour. It will take ten minutes.'

'If you insist, Otto.' God in heaven, marriage to this man could be an eternal round of obligations. How had she ever thought of it!

Chapter

38

'W h a t a creep that Rissik is! If I were the Baroness I'd go straight in and murder him. And as for that bitch of an art critic . . .' Julia Clifford had thoroughly enjoyed the vindictive interplay on 'The Rissik Report', adding her own spicy asides about Vicky Stewart-Robinson's outrageous dress and evident lack of ancestry. Her sympathies had lain entirely with the embattled Charles Luttrell. 'Such a lovely deep English voice! Will he be there tomorrow?'

'He's the head of Burnaby's,' Craig said, curbing his irritation at this typical 'Aristocrats can do no wrong' attitude. 'He's staying at the hotel.'

'How could I know? Don't treat me like a fool!'

The downside. There always was one. Julia's mental make-up required something nice to be counterbalanced by something negative. Already she had the full range of machinery required for Sunday brunch whirring and grating: the orchestra supporting the soloist. When his wife prepared a meal all of North Plainfield knew she was slaving over a hot stove. The definition of the downside continued, half shouted above the noise.

'You've only twenty-four hours left to fix for us to meet the Baroness.' There was no need for her to add that his life wasn't going to be worth living if he failed. She switched off the electric knife with which she was slicing potatoes and lowered her tone to the loving coo of motherhood as she shook out cereal for Antonia. 'And we do want to meet her, don't we, darling? Specially after hearing all about her fabulous diamond on the television.'

'Daddy! *Please* can we meet the Bawoness.'

'Don't worry, sweetheart. Daddy'll fix it.' How the hell, he had no idea.

'I suppose you must have bacon *and* eggs *and* hash browns?' Julia said, reverting to domestic martyrdom. 'They make such an awful mess of the pans.'

'You cook the eggs. I'll clean the pan.' Jesus, she only cooked him anything for breakfast once a week. How had their marriage gotten like this? Well, it had and it couldn't go on. He'd have liked to walk out on her today, now—to be able to tell Barbara 'I'm on my way.'

'Can I cook for you when I'm older, Daddy? I'll cook for you when I'm older!' The eagerness, the love. Oh Christ.

'Sure you will darling. Daddy'll like that very much.'

Subversion! Conduct prejudicial to good order and marital discipline! Julia frowned and cracked an egg into a bowl with such unnecessary force that flecks of yellow yolk spattered the formica worktop. 'Daddy will like cleaning up after very much, too. If he doesn't find an excuse to pull out fast enough.'

The phone shrilled. Julia jerked a thumb at Craig to answer. The call was from the hotel switchboard. He recognised the girl's voice.

'Clifford speaking.'

'Mr. Trevinski wants to know if you're coming in.'

'Around midday. Anything wrong?'

'I don't think so. We also have another message. The Baroness von Brandenburg can meet with you at two tomorrow in the hotel.'

'Thanks. Thanks a million. Tell Mr. Trevinski I'll be on my way.' He hung the phone back on its fixture and caught Antonia up in his arms, swinging her around and then hugging her. 'So whaddya know, sweetheart? Just guess what! You are going to meet the Baroness!'

The Park Plaza's telephone switchboard was located in a small room behind the reception desk. Four operators faced banks of room number indicators and lights. They wore spindly slender headsets, weighing next to nothing and projecting a tiny microphone in front of their chins. The design had been originated for astronauts. Occasionally they exchanged fragments of gossip, but mostly they were too fully occupied. They all found the confines of the windowless room claustrophobic.

One of them, Jane Runciman, a recently married girl of twenty-three, was dealing with messages this morning and feeling faintly nauseated by the closeness of the room, despite its air conditioning. Messages for guests were written out and passed through to the desk clerks, while a red light on the room telephone was activated. Staff members were spoken to personally if possible, because theirs were usually urgent. Jane had just called Craig Clifford. She reported the result to Trevinski's office, then dealt with the next request. Would the Banqueting Department please inform Mr. Constant of Burnaby's that there was a message for him at reception? After that she looked up Barbara Andrews' home number in the personnel directory.

'Miss Andrews? This is the Park Plaza. Sorry to call you on a Sunday. Mr. Corley wants to know if you can change your duty hours tomorrow. Mr. Harvey has been taken sick.' As she said the words it struck Jane that the explanation for not feeling too good herself could be that she was pregnant. Was that possible? Her period was late this month. It could be possible! How fantastic! But she must make sure before she told her husband. A boy? A girl? Names!

Up in her apartment Barbara groaned inwardly. She had scheduled tomorrow for getting a whole raft of things done that you could only do during working hours. That was the one advantage of the four-to-midnight swing shift. But if Errol Harvey, the Front Office Manager and her immediate boss, was ill she had no option. He was also Duty Manager tomorrow: in fact replacing him would be good experience.

'When would Mr. Corley want me in?' she asked.

'He'd like to have you stand in for Mr. Harvey the whole day.'

'Tell Mr. Corley I'll be happy to do that.' She could at least accept it as a compliment that the Resident Manager had selected her ahead of the other five Assistant Front Office Managers.

Jane Runciman informed Corley's office and then set about the problem call that had defeated them all so far: locating either of those two maids who worked the fifth floor, Rosita and Maria. After a laborious conversation with Rosita's family in stumbling Spanish she reached the same conclusion that her colleagues had. Either the family were afraid some accusation was going to be made or the obstructiveness was connected with the smouldering union dispute. She left word both with the Head Housekeeper and with Security that the girls remained unreachable. Then she took the short coffee break to which she was entitled, her head whirling with the idea that she could be carrying her first baby.

Up on 88th Street Barbara made herself fresh coffee and wondered about the intervention of chance. Tomorrow's shopping was to have been devoted to making this apartment more welcoming for Craig. Was that tempting providence? Counting chickens before they were hatched? All the mother-taught warnings? Suppose he didn't make the break with Julia at the end of the week? Then she'd look at the preparations she'd made and feel even worse. And if she didn't make them, when he came she'd be letting him down. She wished the week could be over, only a little consoled by his promise to get up here for part of this afternoon.

And tomorrow? Job-wise, tomorrow was Craig's big day. She was pleased she would be around throughout it. In fact, having watched 'The Rissik Report' and previously met the Baroness, she'd be quite amused to see what the rest of those people were like in real life, particularly the priest. Quiet and undemonstrative as he'd been, he really had something going for him. She hoped the church did get the diamond back. She'd been tempted to come early for her shift and watch part of the auction. That would no longer be possible. But, she decided, it would be an intriguing day to be in her boss's shoes, even though she was bound to be kept working late.

In the Grand Ballroom where the auction preview was reaching its final hours James Constant stayed at a desk in one corner, surveying the scene with satisfaction. A steady number of well-dressed potential bidders had been asking to examine items of jewelry and a pleasing proportion of those had gone through the process of establishing their financial credentials with his assistants.

Whatever effect controversy might have on the price the Malabar Angel itself achieved, the publicity had generated enormous interest in the sale as a whole. Hype spawned hysteria. For months James had told the Baroness that her heirloom could never rival the Duchess of Windsor's jewels in romantic appeal. He might yet be wrong. The media had managed to invest the Malabar Angel with a mystique all its own. This sale was going to break records. It was the same as with wine in a top restaurant. The presence on the list of a Premier Cru Château Margaux with an astronomic price tag would convince diners they were on to a bargain when they paid wildly over the top for lesser Bordeaux growths. Tomorrow he would get $100,000, may be $120,000, for a diamond necklace worth $80,000 because the standard of comparison had been set at $4 to $5 million. The same would happen all the way down the line to the smallest jewels. Superficially 'The Rissik Report' had been a public relations disaster: yet it had put the auction foursquare in the public eye more effectively than a thousand advertisements.

As Constant sat in the corner in his dark grey pinstripe hand-tailored suit and watched clients peering into the armoured-glass display cases he noticed the confidence with which they disregarded the security men. He absorbed the way they made notes in their $25 sale catalogues: and he knew that the smell of these preview days was the sweet smell of abundant spending.

He also speculated on how Charles was going to handle further press questions on Lucy's role in the charity committee and what on earth was going to happen if Samantha flew in this afternoon, as she had sworn she would. Lucy had, quite exceptionally, interfered with the conduct of a sale by ordering that Samantha was not to be allowed into the auction room. What if she came with the Baroness and was confronted by Lucy herself with all the TV cameras focussing on them? It would make the gunfight at the OK Corral look like a tea party.

251

This minor reverie was interrupted by a flunkey from the Banqueting Department approaching with a number of telephone message slips. 'These are for you, sir. Mr. Drayson had them brought up from reception.' He tipped the man and read them through: 'Please call Mr. Cranston at his apartment.' 'Mr. Wolfgang Raeder called from Germany.' 'The Baroness von Brandenburg accepts the lunch invitation.' 'Dr. Kuroki called.' 'Miss Anneke Los will be arriving on KLM this afternoon.'

The first ones, annoyingly, meant he would have to return to the office. Cranston, Raeder and Kuroki would all be reacting to the TV show, demanding yet more assurances that the sale was legal. The Baroness: well, she must have a reason for changing her tune about attending. He'd discover what it was in due course. But the final message made his pulse quicken in the right way. He re-read that one with delight. Anneke had made it! She would be here. As a KLM air stewardess she could roam the world during her frequent rest spells after long-haul flights: but only on what amounted to a stand-by basis. She'd promised to be here for his first New York auction if she possibly could: and she'd made it! That put the seal on James Constant's day. He'd met Anneke at a London party two months ago, stolen a long weekend with her in Hong Kong after the showing there in September and been pining for her ever since, unable to escape from New York himself.

As he stuffed the messages in his pocket, Trevinski and Craig walked into the room, spotted him and came straight over. Trevinski pumped his hand and then got down to business, speaking in a low voice out of the side of his mouth.

'We wanna double-check security tomorrow, sir.' His concern was eradicating the polish he affected for hotel guests. 'We got reason to believe there could be a heista some kind. Attempt at a holdup. You seen anything suspicious?'

'No. What sort of suspicious?'

'Wrong kinda guys around. Guys checking out what's here.'

Constant scratched his forehead in perplexity. 'The opposite if anything. We've had a lot of serious potential buyers during these three days. Why do you think this?'

'Explain, Clifford.'

'Well, Mr. Constant.' Craig took it more relaxedly and drew up a chair as he ran through the meagre information he had, though Trevinski remained standing. 'The engineer can't be identified or traced. All the wiring and air conditioning for the Ballroom has been checked. But the man wasn't a phantom and he must have been up there for a reason.'

'Which coulda been to kill the lights, plunge the place in darkness, have accomplices seize a load of jewelry,' Trevinski emphasised. 'The Precinct Detective Unit is on alert. But they don't have any leads. We'll do all we can. Sure. But you oughta triple-check the credentials of every person you employ tomorrow.'

'Could you tell Mr. Trevinski how you handle items before and after they're sold?' Craig asked. He had discussed this in detail before and had never been entirely happy with the arrangements.

'It's a routine. The same in London or anywhere else. Several of our girls have the auction lots ready. When I come to an item my assistant holds it up in her hand for bidders to see and a colour photograph is projected on a screen. After being sold it's passed back and held for collection. In London that would be in a separate office. Here it'll be in an adjoining room under very strict supervision. Items for which payment is not made immediately will be taken by a security van to a bank vault.'

'Wide open,' Trevinski muttered. 'Thirty seconds'd be enough with no light.'

'We rely on the hotel to provide lights that do not fail.' Constant became acid. 'Are you asking me to cancel the whole thing? Because if you are, believe me you're going to be paying compensation in millions. The Park Plaza signed a contract for the staging of this event.'

'Cancel, no way,' Trevinski said hastily. 'We just ask you to be extra alert. Thank you, sir.' As he preceded Craig out of the room he said over his shoulder, 'This fucking phantom engineer. How does he get in, for Christ's sake? Through the Fifth Avenue entrance in working clothes? Through the staff entrance with no ID?' He strode on along the corridor to take the elevator down to their office. 'You gonna tell me he brings a blue shirt and trousers in a bag and changes in the bathroom? Any guy so much as takes his overcoat to a bathroom gets the once-over.' Trevinski stopped, aware of where his reasoning had led. 'I'm gonna tell you something, Clifford. This guy is no fucking phantom changing in bathrooms or walking through locked doors. This guy is a guest in the goddam hotel. He has to be. And you're gonna find him.'

Chapter
39

T h e time was 4:27 P.M. Frank catnapped in an armchair. Ilse lay on the bed reading an old book that had long been her bible. The cover stated *Road Traffic Ordinances*. The contents dealt with the revolutionary armed struggle and the concept of the urban guerrilla. This was the Gospel according to Ulrike Meinhof, the inspiration for Gabrielle, Inge, Sigrid, Susanne and Ilse herself. Frank had said she was mad to bring it, but his kind had no intellectual basis for their actions anyway. She'd insisted that the title and the German language text made it safe enough. She'd won that particular dispute. Now she was so absorbed with the familiar and cherished slogans that she had almost forgotten the time. At 4:31 the alarm went off.

Frank woke, jumped up from the chair and ran to the closet. The clock was still beating its tinny call. The light bulb wired to it flickered continuously. He knelt and silenced the alarm, Ilse now standing behind him. He picked up the clock gently to avoid breaking the solder joint of the wiring.

'One minute slow,' he said ruminatively, almost to himself. 'One minutes after six hours. Start it again at five-thirty to be safe. Twenty-three hours. Just about four minutes.'

'Four minutes is a long time.' She made it sound four years.

'You don't know exactly when you want it anyway. So the thing goes off early! So what? The place'll be packed. If your bloody Baroness is going to be there at all, she'll be there then.'

'This is the best you can do?' She could have done as much herself. Here was this man claiming to be a technician and using an ordinary alarm clock. 'You told me you could make a detonation through radio control.'

'Not in this hotel. Not when we'll be at the airport.'

'This is the best technical way? With a clock that loses time?'

'No, me darlin'.' He'd had enough of her nitpicking. 'If I'm to be honest and all, it is not. There's another way entirely. I'll fix you a press button and you can sit up in the ceiling with it yourself. That way you'll be certain sure of the time and may be a place in Ahmed's Paradise on top.' Muslims only had one use for women and he couldn't see Ahmed the Libyan wanting her as a concubine in Paradise or anywhere else, but never mind.

'That's not funny.'

'Then do things my way, for Christ's sake, and stop complaining. It's basic but it works.' He rewound the clock. 'In one hour we place it, okay?'

'No!' She seized the clock. 'This must have an adjustment.' She examined the back, found the *Fast–Slow* lever and shifted it a fraction. 'Now we test it two more hours.'

'For crying out loud. You've broken the sodding wire off.'

'Then you put it on again. That is what I pay for.'

She was livid. For months he'd made her feel inadequate, wishing she was a scientist, by talking about the explosive being detonated by radio or a call to the telephone in the room. Now he said the construction of the building made all that impossible: and relied on an eight-dollar alarm clock! It was more than she could bear.

'I go for a walk.' She all but spat at him. She had to vent her feelings somehow.

'No, Mrs. Luttrell is not available. I'm sorry. I don't know when.' Donna Bradshaw hung up on the reporter and sighed regretfully. The TV show must have sown all the right seeds of doubt. But she should have known better than to trust Bernie Rissik. He'd betrayed Father Gerard's confidences about the mount and Lucy's about her opposition to the sale. Now the paparazzi were after both of them. She abandoned trying to take a Sunday afternoon rest and went through to the reception room. In any case it was time to offer her guests their traditional refreshment. Lucy looked as though she needed a restorative. Initially 'The Rissik Report' had seemed a triumph for their cause. On reflection Donna wasn't at all so sure.

'That was another reporter, I'm afraid,' she told them. 'Let's forget about the media and have some tea.' She rang the bell and asked Danuta to bring some. Teabags were not what the English preferred, but at least they were Earl Grey.

For a short while no one spoke of anything significant. Father Vaughan asked politely about the CCRA's fund raising in the United States and wished he could take his coat off: he was finding a conventional English tweed suit uncomfortably hot even in late October. Lucy sat, as always, in a hard-backed chair, drank her tea and expressed polite interest. Then, unexpectedly, she made a declaration that cost her evident emotional pain.

'I went too far with that dreadful man yesterday, Donna. I do believe most profoundly that the diamond should be returned to the church. But I should not have attacked my husband in public.'

'It was not in public, my dear. It was in private. That so-and-so broke the rules.'

'And we've had newspapers telephoning every moment since. They must be hounding him as well. I was wrong to do that. He has many faults and we did have a terrible row a week ago.' That confrontation had begun to haunt her more and more. Charles had not returned from his Club and had remained there ever since. She'd pretended to Donna that it was quite normal for her to stay with friends if he was working. Now this had crumbled the subterfuge. 'But even if we do quarrel we do not actively set out to harm each other.'

'Don't blame yourself unduly, Lucy.' Father Vaughan was sad that his old friend seemed set on self-abasement. 'That newspaper woman knew, too. It was all over her face. If Rissik hadn't said what he did, I am certain she would have brought it up.'

'Very possibly, Father. Unfortunately that doesn't alter the facts. I'm going to be hounded so long as I stay here and it would be out of the question to attend the auction.' She shifted to face her hostess. 'Donna, you've been marvellous. Generosity itself. But I ought to go home.'

'You're determined to?' She saw that Lucy was. 'Well, why

don't I book you on the Concorde in the morning. You can take a helicopter out to Kennedy from the East River Terminal. It's no distance.'

'I think that would be for the best.' She paused a moment, undecided about something further. 'Should we ask Charles round for dinner tonight?' She almost added, 'He'll be by himself'—except that he seldom was.

An olive branch?' Donna saw an intensely uncomfortable evening ahead. And what if he then declined? 'Unfortunately, my dear, we can't. We have an invitation ourselves.' Mercifully that was true. 'And now, Father Gerard.' She forced cheerfulness. She was even less happy at the way her ploy had developed than she had been fifteen minutes ago. Rissik had managed to harden everyone's attitudes. 'I trust you're not going to desert me, too?'

'I shall stay and see how the auction goes. Most definitely. If I didn't I should be completely hung up on the suspense.' Father Vaughan laughed indulgently. 'If your bid succeeds I ought to be here on the Bishop's behalf. It if does not I shall have to commiserate with the Cardinal. Either will be quite a new experience for me.' And also, in the least vengeful way, one in the eye for Father Crawburn.

'I'm sorry, sweetheart.' Craig felt like a louse, yet what could he do? 'Trevinski's sure we have a gangster resident in the hotel.'

'So what else is new?' Barbara tried to mask her disappointment. 'We must have had hundreds through in the past.'

'They weren't planning a jewelry heist.'

'Some of them were. A few succeeded.'

'Then Trevinski could be right. Either way I'm about to take the records of every male guest we have here to the Midtown North Precinct. Checking them could take half the night.'

A moment's silence. Should she say it? For goodness' sake why not?

'If it does take only half the night, you know where to come. I have no White House invitation for this evening.'

'I love you, Barbara. I'll call later.'

At 5:45 P.M. Craig reached the precinct with a computer printout of the names, age and credit card details of every man staying in the hotel. As the Police Lieutenant pointed out, with no physical description, they didn't have a heck of a lot to go on.

'Could you send an officer to interview those two maids?'

'I guess so. If that's what Jake Trevinski wants. He still has credits in the favor bank. But, I tell you, those Hispanics are as likely to keep their traps shut for us as they are for you.'

Charles Luttrell was changing in his suite. He always changed for dinner and he hated dining alone. His original plan had been to entertain James Constant and Samantha. There were invariably last-minute things to discuss before a sale. However, as Robert Burns had so memorably remarked, the best-laid plans gang oft agley and he hastily invited James's freshly arrived girlfriend Anneke instead. Quite apart from not wanting to challenge Lucy gratuitously by being seen dining with Samantha, she herself had left a message saying she had gone straight out to Long Island. That disturbed him: the Baroness was unlikely to be swearing affidavits on a Sunday evening, so something else must be up. The only certainty about those two was that neither would want to lose money unnecessarily. Even so, he was continuing to make an appalling job of managing the women in his life. Whether Burns had written verses about the lack of a woman in one's bed after dinner, he didn't know. Probably. It was a frequent constituent of the male condition.

A few minutes ago Donna Bradshaw had telephoned, ostensibly to confirm that she would be at the lunch party tomorrow, actually to tell him something quite different.

'Your wife and I were both of us upset by the Rissik interview,' she had said.

'Join the club.' He could afford to release a fraction of his resentment. Nothing he said or did now was likely to inhibit Mrs. Bradshaw's bidding tomorrow.

'I guess you have every reason to be sore.' Unknown to Charles, she had then gone beyond her brief. 'Lucy never dreamt your personal disagreements would be aired by Bernie. That was never her intention. It's made her almost ill. She's decided she ought not to play any further part in this. She apologises and she's flying home in the morning.'

The apology had been the fictional part. Donna felt it was justified, even though Charles in no sense deserved it, because

Lucy was so obviously worried that she might have destroyed what was left of her marriage.

'Thank you for letting me know, Mrs. Bradshaw,' he had said with little warmth. 'Please wish her a safe journey.'

He hadn't been deluded by the apology. Lucy believed he was in the wrong and would never change her mind. At the same time the message signalled more than it appeared to. It meant Lucy was ready to resume the outward appearances of marriage, though she wasn't risking saying so herself, in case she was rebuffed. So for the moment the situation was on hold, as the Americans put it. At least there would be no scenes at the auction, which was what he had feared even more than the publicity. Czernowski insisted that bloody TV fiasco would ultimately do no harm. He hoped Czernowski was right.

As the evening began to darken Ilse returned, having walked off some of her anger. Frank was asleep on the bed: her bed. She shook him awake furiously, smelling whisky on his breath. A couple of empty miniatures from the refrigerator stood on the table.

'Have you been drinking, you fool?' She shook him again.

'Just a dram. Nothing to do any harm at all.'

'You think hotel staff are allowed to drink on duty!' She could have hit him. She was already as tense as a spring. 'Where's the clock?'

'Don't go near it.' He came fully awake. 'The whole thing's ready, wired up, packed in a box in the closet, set for 4:30 tomorrow afternoon. All I have to do is carry it along to the roof space.'

'But . . .' She'd never thought he would assemble the bomb without her there. 'Is it keeping time?'

'After one hour it gained about twenty-five seconds.'

She calculated quickly. 'But that is worse than before!'

'Sure. And who interfered with the fucking thing? The Rhineland's own mechanical genius! Now I've had to set the alarm late, for 4:38 P.M. Let's get going for Christ's sake, before some chambermaid comes barging in tidying the room.' He stripped to his underclothes, disregarding her, and dressed in the workman's blue shirt and trousers. 'Okay,' he said, strapping the tool belt round his waist, 'I take the box with me, you go along and if the coast's clear, you signal. If it isn't, you bring the maid along here. Tell her you've spilt fruit juice on your dress and the floor. Here'—he took a carton from the fridge, ripped it open and before she could protest, slopped orange juice on her skirt and the floor—'off you go. Come back if there's anyone out there.' He propelled her to the door. 'No arguing. Let's get this done.'

'You bastard.' She was nearly in tears.

'Out you go!' He pushed her through the door. 'Is it clear?'

'There is no one,' she called back, agitatedly, choking on the words, and went down the corridor.

All right and proper, he thought. A girl would be fussed and all, spilling drink on her dress. He stepped into the corridor with the electrical components box in his arms and went the opposite way from Ilse. Sixty pounds felt like a ton. After turning a corner he eased it to the carpet, not needing to pretend he was resting a moment, praying no one would ask questions. A couple passed, gave a sideways glance and went on. Then, echoing along the passage, he heard what he'd hoped for: Ilse's broken English beseeching help. He took a quick peek round the corner, saw her and a maid going into their room and marched down past to the service area. Had she been alone?

She had. The service area was deserted. Grunting under the weight he lowered the box again, unlocked the access door and switched on the light. The cavern stretched before him. He hesitated a few seconds, checking for movement, then hefted up his burden and managed to close the door behind him.

This was where the earlier reconnaissance paid off. He had made careful sketches after being shown the ballroom and spent hours relating them to the layout of the fifth floor. Without question the entrance to the structural space was over the left wall of the ballroom as you looked towards where the auctioneer would stand on the dais. The dais itself was located close to the end wall, while above and in front of it hung the first of the huge, ornate chandeliers. Up where he now was above the ceiling the cables supporting those chandeliers were ideal reference points, descending from the concrete roof in a straight line through the confusion of girders and ducts. There was no mistaking them. The spot he had found for the bomb was partway between the first and second chandelier cables. He had not seen the actual seating in the ballroom, but it was a certainty that VIPs would be given honoured places near the front: directly beneath the bomb. If Ilse's hated Baroness sat anywhere, it would be there. A lot of people were going to be killed in those rows as slivers of metal and glass and heavy chunks of plaster cascaded down with as much slashing momentum as if they were bombs themselves.

Not that anywhere in the ballroom would be safe. When the Semtex detonated its blast would destroy the ceiling and bounce back down off the concrete floor, sending an almost instantaneous second whirlwind of explosive gases around the structural space and out of any weak point like this access door.

Because of his reconnaissance he worked fast installing the box. Three minutes after he went in to the cavern he had it wedged between the joist and the ducting. With the flashlight gripped in his teeth he opened the lid and clipped the second of the two wires to the clock, which rested on top of the packets of Semtex. The hands were showing 6:58. He rearranged the blanket he was using for sound insulation so that the clock was covered. Anyone who did hear that alarm go off would be hearing the last sound of his life. Finally he partially closed one half of the lid and attached a third wire to its inside. This was a simple booby trap. If the lid was fully opened the wire would yank the alarm bell striker and complete the circuit. After he had fully shut both cardboard flaps he wriggled back to the catwalk, took the flashlight from his teeth and was out of the structural space at 6:59.

The maid had not come back. Thank Christ for that, though without the box he'd have been confident of bluffing his way through: had fully assumed he would have to. He left the Service Area and suddenly realised he'd been a bit too clever. He couldn't return to the room in case the maid was still there. He would have to kill time. How? The only answer was to behave like an engineer who'd finished a job: amble not too briskly along the corridor or go up and down in the elevator until Ilse's dramatic performance was through. He started to walk.

'Say, excuse me.' A woman was gesticulating at him, standing in a doorway in a quilted dressing gown. 'Are you an engineer?

I need help. I just plugged in my rollers and something's wrong.'

What could he do? Pretend he was going off duty? Use her room phone to call someone else? A hell of a risk.

'They're not heating up like they should and I have to get ready.' Who said Ilse was the only agitated woman on the landing! Hell, he was an engineer. The easiest way out was to mend her rollers.

'Strictly speaking, ma'am, I'm off duty now.' He had the American accent better this time. He'd been practising in the bathroom. 'But I'll be happy to do what I can.'

She led him into her bedroom. Lacy underclothes hung over a chair. An evening dress was suspended on a hanger from the closet door frame. The defective rollers stood on the table, a faint smell emanating from them. He touched them lightly. Just warm.

'They began to get hot and then . . . finito.'

He swivelled around to take a small electrical screwdriver from his holdall. It wasn't there. Shit. The one tool he needed and he must have dropped it. He made do with a larger one and began checking systematically, the wall plug first. He was in luck. When he took the back off he saw the internal fuse was burnt out. Did the kit he'd bought secondhand include a spare? He was pretty sure it did. He knew what a kit like this ought to contain and had been insistent at the shop. Bingo! One tiny metal-capped glass tube fuse. He clipped it into place and plugged the rollers in again.

The woman stepped forward and held her hand over them. He looked at her properly for the first time. She was around forty, slim, and the front of her gown was swinging loose, revealing soft white thighs. He realised she had nothing else on. A warm, near-burning smell rose from the rollers.

'You miracle man! You've saved my life.'

'All in the line of duty, ma'am.' American actors said that in war movies and westerns.

'How can I ever thank you!' She had begun to notice his physique and she liked what she saw. She didn't have to be ready for her friends for an hour and a half yet. Her husband was in Baltimore. She squinted at his nametag. 'If you're finished with working, Andy, join me for a drink? Just a quickie.'

He knew another kind of quickie was on offer and, Christ, after a week with Ilse he could use one. But the risk!

'That's real kind of you, ma'am. Nothing I'd like more.' He bestowed his most Irish of smiles on her. 'We're not allowed alcohol on duty.'

'My dear boy'—she moved closer—'if you haven't had a whisky in the past hour, I'm the First Lady.' She touched his arm. 'Come on. Relax.'

'I have to go. I'm truly sorry.'

'If you say so. If you really say so.' She leaned forward and kissed him on the cheek. 'If you're at a loose end around midnight, you know where I am.'

When he escaped into the corridor again he was trembling: not from fear, from frustration. He hurried back to 538.

'Where have you been, for God's sake?' Ilse threw at him. 'What has gone wrong?'

'Nothing. I had to mend a fuse. For real.'

'The box, you cretin. What about the box?'

'The box is where it should be, all hunkydory.' He stripped off the work clothes. 'Now give me a whisky, will you, and stop yattering and then we'll go down to eat.' Not in the hotel, he realised. That woman might spot him. He faked enthusiasm. 'A celebration, me darlin'. Tart yourself up and we'll go on the town. We've done what we came for, after all.'

'This is Gloria Grace. Do I have to spell the name for you? Gloria Grace. I want a bottle of Dom Perignon right away. And one glass.'

'A single glass, ma'am?' The night butler had been having trouble with the film star earlier. Now it was 11:15 and she wanted champagne by herself. What a pain in the ass.

'Just bring a single glass, d'you hear me?'

'A waiter will be on his way, ma'am.'

'And another club sandwich. You sent one with beef just now! Beef! Was that some kind of a joke? I want a club sandwich with turkey. D'you hear me? Turkey. I want someone up with it right away.'

The Night Butler wrote the order down and passed it through

to the night cooks. 'Make it snappy, will ya?' he called out. 'That Gloria Grace is having another of her evenings.'

The whole department was having one of those evenings, come to think of it.

The night reception clerk who handed Frank and Ilse their key reckoned the man was the worse for wear, but at least he was happy, not unpleasant.

'Have a good night, sir,' he said. He noticed that the woman took the man's hand as they walked to the elevator and the man seemed at first to resist, then changed his mind and put his arm clumsily around her shoulder. He wondered what a decent-looking guy was doing with a broad like her. Either he was a stud or she must be pretty hot in the sack. The night clerk had plenty of time to study such quirks of behaviour.

'And now, me darlin'.' Frank swayed a little as he closed the bedroom door behind them. 'How about a kiss for your husband, eh?'

'You're drunk.' She pushed him away from her. 'You don't know what you're saying.'

'Oh, but I do. Indeed I do.' He'd always been aware of her suppressed sexuality. She'd dolled herself up and looked better than usual. His sudden lust was sparked by the acute frustration of his experience along the corridor, fuelled by relief at having planted the bomb, several whiskies and most of a bottle of wine. 'Oh yes, I do, me darlin'.'

He seized hold of her, tried to kiss her and got a resounding slap on the face in return.

'You little bitch.' He spun her round, whipped her left arm up behind her so hard that she screamed and began tearing the dress off her back. She screamed again. He threw her down on the bed, pushing her face into the cover, ripping off her underclothes. Then he pulled off his own trousers and began to rape her from behind. She went on struggling. He yanked her over, clapped a hand across her face as she screamed some more and started to rape her in earnest. Her arms, now free, flailed at his back, her nails digging into his skin. He just went on, hammering into her, venting weeks of repression. But the thing he expected never happened. She did not succumb. She did not start to enjoy the sex. She went on fighting until he was through with her and still he had to hold her down as she cursed and swore.

The night waiter was on the fifth floor, delivering steak and French fries to yet another importunate guest, when he heard muffled cries from down the passage. He walked along and knocked on the door. The number was 538. The cries ceased, though he could hear something happening. His knock was not answered. He reported this to the Night Butler when he was back down in the pantry.

The night reception clerk remembered the couple from 538. They'd come back less than an hour ago. After the night butler's report he called their room.

'Are you having any trouble, sir?'

'No, no, no,' the Irishman answered. 'My wife and I had a little disagreement, that's all. No problems. You want to speak to her?' He put his hand over the mouthpiece. 'Tell him everything's okay.'

'That's not necessary, sir.' The night clerk was embarrassed.

'Who is that, please?' The woman sounded shaky.

'The Reception, ma'am. We had a report of, er . . . noises.'

'There is no problem. My husband and I have a little row, that is all. Can you wait a moment, please.'

Ilse did as Frank had done with the telephone, at the same time heaving herself upright and away from him on the bed. 'You get on the floor, or I ask for help.' When he had removed himself she told reception, 'Everything is all right. Good night.' She looked at Frank with the purest hatred, memories of Horst and her abortion pulsing through her brain. The body she had consecrated had been defiled. 'I get you for that,' she said. 'One day I get you.'

Chapter

40

'T h o s e girls would tell the cops anything, sweetheart. They'll tell them what they think they want to hear.' Barbara poured Craig the last of the coffee. 'We should be on our way. This is my great day. You're speaking to the Duty Manager, remember?'

'Temporary, acting, unpaid, as they say in the military.' He gazed around her cramped kitchen, taking everything in, fixing it like photographic developer does film. So this was what it was going to be like from next week. No bitching. No pounding machinery. Just Barbara and going to work together. No Antonia, either, when he came home at night. The downside, and a big one.

She picked up his thoughts, but askew. 'I had been planning to buy a few things today to brighten the place up. Think of it as improved.'

'I want to remember it as it is.' He leant across and kissed her. 'So far as I'm concerned we've started today.'

In the hallway she gave him a tender hug. 'I'm glad you came after all. I would have felt very left out.'

He had rung the bell at 1:00 A.M., long after she'd gone to sleep, and was completely bushed himself. There were over a thousand male guests at the Park Plaza and when the police officer came back from interviewing the chambermaids it had been with the sketchiest information.

The engineer had been not too tall, not too short. Rosita recalled he had dark hair. Maria thought it was mousy. He was young. He was more like thirty-five. Basically the girls hadn't wanted to talk. Craig himself knew there was a scam going on with maintenance contracts in the hotel. They were probably afraid of putting themselves in the firing line. The computer records showed over three hundred male guests in the twenty to thirty-five age bracket. Only one was both a mechanic by profession and known to be short of cash. He was an English honeymooner.

'Isn't that the guy who won the Green Queen prize weekend?' Barbara said, as they rode the Lexington Avenue train down to 59th Street. 'Those promotion winners never have any money. You might just as well argue it was the honeymoon pair, because they have no credit cards. Be reasonable. Anyway, if my memory's right, both those couples are checking out today.'

'If they were doing the groundwork for a heist, this morning would be the time to leave.' Craig held her affectionately round the waist, as the train jolted and swayed. 'Gregory put a note in the computer that the Englishman is very antagonistic to the hotel.'

'So was the strange lady.' Barbara thought she would never forget those eyes. 'And how! There was something going on there.'

'I'll check them again. The main point is, there'll be new locks on that access now and there were no faults yesterday.'

'You mean you're wasting your time?'

'Most things have a logical explanation. They used to say in Intelligence that getting to the bottom of things is like building up a newspaper photo. It's actually printed as thousands of dots. Until you have enough dots you can't make out the picture.'

'Well, go to it, you good old logical male.' She laughed both at him and with him. 'Have fun with the dots. Rather you than me. I prefer working on instinct.'

James Constant stood on the dais at the end of the Grand Ballroom behind a high mahogany desk, not unlike Gregory's semi-pulpit down in the lobby. The time was 9:55 A.M. He was facing some forty rows of seats, the front ones reserved for VIP clients, all rapidly filling. He was ready to open the auction and supremely confident, a red carnation in the buttonhole of his dark grey suit, his presence as dominating as any maestro's.

On the front of his desk a blue and gold sign announced BURNABY'S. On either side were tables staffed by Burnaby girls, across which the sale items would be passed. One had a computer in front of her. Behind the dais a computerised display flashed up prices in seven major currencies. At the moment the green liquid crystal digits all read zero. A high display screen closer to Constant would show vastly enlarged photographs of each jewel as the real thing was held up on view.

On the right, between two of the cream-painted pillars that formed an arcade down each side of the ballroom, in fact disguising steel architectural supports for the massive collecting structure above, a further table accommodated four telephone clerks. These were the girls handling the special lines installed for telephone bidders like Cranston. Auction house girls were a standardised product in both New York and London. Burnaby's mostly wore shirtdresses of the kind you saw advertised in the *New Yorker* and had their hair held back by velvet bands.

Between the pillars opposite the telephone girls was an improvised press gallery, politely restraining some fifty journalists. Their enclosure was elegantly sectioned off with thick white rope held in gilt supports. The video cameras were between the next pair of pillars on a low platform that projected a short way out from the line of the pillars to give a better view. The crews had been arguing vehemently with Czernowski earlier about their camera angles. Constant saw that he was still talking in asides to one of the journalists. Bernie Rissik had put a highly competitive edge on the reporting—just as the 'phantom' had on security.

Uniformed security guards were stationed all around the room and Constant knew plainclothesmen would mingle with the clients standing behind the rows of seats and at the sides. The security men hated the media and the media hated them. He prayed the reporters didn't discover the reason for all the extra guards. All in all the occasion had taken a lot of setting up, right down to Constant's own New York Department of Consumer Affairs Auctioneer's Certificate hanging in a black frame by the main entrance doors at the back. The Certificate carried his photograph in colour and cost him four hundred dollars every twenty-three months.

Constant took stock. Auctions always began with the less expensive and exciting items and the room was barely a third full. But during the afternoon session it would be packed. The chandeliers glittered down on fashionable women and a growing contingent of recognisable dealers. The nearest chandelier, Constant realised, was going to have to be dimmed. It was a monstrous creation, fully six feet high and looped around with cascades of heavy cut glass and it hung just low enough to be a distraction to his vision. When its multitude of bulbs had been subdued he felt happier and resumed his observation of the clientele.

Looking at the women present, Constant decided most would have come from curiosity. The morning session was going to be dominated by dealers. Several groups of Hassidics from the diamond district were particularly noticeable, in their black hats, long black coats and beards. They held their numbered bidding paddles awkwardly, as though this were an intrusion on traditional practices. At ten o'clock precisely Constant raised his auctioneer's gavel and tapped the desk top for silence.

'Ladies and gentlemen, welcome to Burnaby's first ever New York auction. We have entitled this a Sale of Magnificent Jewels. They come from a number of notable private collections and magnificent they are. We are proud to be offering them today.' He cut a quick glance to his left, where the girls had the initial lots lined up, gave a barely discernible nod: and he was off.

'Lot One is a pair of diamond, emerald and ruby cluster earclips, the property of a lady from Palm Springs.' He deliberately took this first lot at a slowish tempo. 'Very attractive as you can see.' A girl held one high in each hand. A screen showed them magnified a hundredfold. 'What am I bid for these most attractive clips? A thousand dollars?' He saw a paddle raised at the back as a man called out 'Fifteen hundred.' Another paddle, another voice. 'Two thousand I am bid, two thousand. Thank you, madam, two thousand five hundred. Three thousand.' The lot was up and running. He'd keep it going in five hundreds. 'Three thousand I am bid. Three thousand five hundred. All done at three thousand five? Against you, sir, the bid is four thousand. Four thousand five hundred.' His pace slackened a fraction. This could be the end of the run. 'Four thousand five hundred dollars.' A minuscule pause. 'Four thousand five hundred to number twenty-three.' The gavel crashed down. The liquid crystal lights flashed the final currency conversions. The girls passed on the earclips to colleagues as the next Lot came up. Going slowly Constant had sold them in under forty seconds. 'Lot Two, a diamond and yellow gold flower brooch . . .'

The reporters gossiped. This was kid's stuff, not worth switching the cameras on for. Prince Czernowski and the hotel's PR Director departed for a discussion about handling Vicky Stewart-Robinson's threatened demonstration if it materialised. She wasn't here yet. Near the back a woman in a Chanel suit commented, 'I just adore jewels, however small.' Anneke Los, standing near her, overheard the remark. She was longing to clap, because James was so smoothly in control, but eventually became slightly bored and went to have coffee. Maybe she would do some shopping this morning and come back in time for the lunch. Charles Luttrell was standing casually to one side, getting the feel of the sale. The momentum was building nicely. James had this really up and running. The security guards kept their eyes open for a nondescript man of about thirty, acting in a suspicious manner.

'Lot Ten. A diamond and cabochon emerald necklace. Eight thousand am I bid? Nine thousand. Ten. Eleven. Twelve thousand dollars . . .'

Luttrell decided he could return to the major clients' questions—and the redoubtable, thrice-cursed Baroness, who wouldn't be coming to his lunch without a reason. And where was Samantha? He hoped to God they were together at the lawyers, having that affidavit sworn.

The couple had not exchanged a word. Frank took breakfast in the restaurant. Ilse swallowed down aspirins with her coffee. She was physically hurt, horribly sore, degraded and angry. She intensely wanted to see a doctor, to swab out any possibility of pregnancy, or worse, of catching AIDS, if it was not too late. Even the knowledge that the bomb had been successfully planted and, with luck, her enemy would soon be spread-eagled under a pile of masonry did nothing for her morale. She just did not trust the bomb to go off.

271

However, while Frank was downstairs she did search the room. The Tampax box she discarded in the bathroom waste bin. The Bendel and Bergdorf bags she left in the closet. Frank had packed before he went down, keeping a single shopping bag for the disposal of his blue shirt and trousers. Typically, he intended to resell the tool kit, which was hidden in his camera case.

When he returned she spoke for the first time since the night before. 'We take a taxi to the Grand Central Station and I deposit the luggage. After that, do what you want.'

She would never pay him. Never. She'd arrange a rendezvous and kill him. She would drop the suicide pill she always carried into his beer. 'In Germany, I pay you,' she said. But there was one disgusting task still to perform jointly. 'When we go, you carry my bags. You deal with the bill. You behave like a husband. You hold my hand.'

'Sure and it'll be a pleasure, me darlin'.' But the banter was bluff. She was a killer. He should have taken more account of that business with the passport. He picked up the two suitcases, wondering if anyone downstairs would notice how little they were leaving with after all that apparent shopping.

In the lobby he did as Ilse had ordered. He remembered to call her Birgit. He tallied the check, settled the extras at the cashier's counter and obtained a refund of two hundred and thirty dollars from the deposit: though not without that tight-assed Manager emerging from the back office and giving them both the once-over.

'I hope you've enjoyed your stay with us,' she said, with as much enthusiasm as a warder letting a man out of jail on parole. And he sensed some reluctance, too. Mistrusting the look in her eye, he tried to crack its meaning with a joke. 'Lucky we paid that deposit and all!' he said, waving the bill in her face. She didn't react, just disappeared to her office again.

'We've no time to waste, Birgit me darlin',' he said briskly when he returned to where Ilse sat waiting like a cat on hot bricks by one of those fancy marble pillars. 'We'll be missing the train and all. Let's be going.'

He took her arm as the bellboy carried their bags to the Fifth Avenue entrance. He couldn't quite bring himself to hold her hand. Then for the benefit of the boy he asked loudly for a cab to Grand Central Station. He wanted it known they were catching a train, after the way that bird at reception eyed them. She was the one who'd given them the trouble at the start. He wouldn't trust her not to cause problems again.

'The change,' Ilse demanded in the cab and for once he lacked the nerve to keep it.

'See you later,' he said with relief at Grand Central, where he deposited his bag separately from hers. 'But don't wait for me checking in.' Later, hell. What she did was her affair. He would sell the tools, junk the overalls and take the next available flight. The Holy Mother be praised that he'd insisted on having a full fare ticket, not a cheapskating APEX like her own. She was stuck with the 6:30 P.M. Lufthansa schedule, two hours after the bomb would have gone off. It had sounded fine back in Düsseldorf. Now it was unnecessarily dangerous.

Craig had excused himself from the Monday morning staff meeting. He read the overnight incident book—as if he hadn't been here most of the time himself—and noticed a comment on a disturbance in 538. That was Barbara's bizarre couple. But no follow-up had been necessary. Then, as he ran through the auction security arrangements with Drayson, the pink-cheeked Assistant Banqueting Manager, a tiny incident caught at his memory. Who had the man been with Drayson last Thursday, the man who had hidden behind a book? He had known the face, but couldn't place it.

'That was an Irish guest.' Drayson consulted his diary. 'Name of Hermon. Room 538.'

'What were you showing him?'

'The Grand Ballroom. He was interested in the hotel's period aspects.'

'May I use your phone?' Craig rang Technical Services. 'Have you anything further on that electrician in the structural space? Anyone else back from the weekend who saw him? Any working clothes reported missing?'

'That the so-called phantom you're talking about? Funny, we just had a call from a lady on the fifth floor about an engineer who repaired her rollers last night. She wanted to know how she could thank him in person.'

'And he had no name?'

'He had one, sir. She remembered it. Andrew McClarry. Only snag is, we don't have no Andrew McClarry.'

'What time was this?'

'You'd have to ask the lady that, sir. Early evening from the sound of it.'

Bad ankle or no bad ankle, Craig Clifford could shift when he needed to. He located a Mrs. Wellbeloved from Room 559 having coffee in the Yacht Club Salon downstairs. She described the electrician she had found so compellingly helpful as being Irish American and tousle-haired. There must be high odds on McClarry being Hermon. But at reception he discovered Barbara's couple had checked out barely thirty minutes earlier.

'Miss Andrews was looking for you,' the desk clerk told him and he went straight round to the office.

'I tried to find you, Craig.' She saw the concern on his face. 'I kept leaving messages. Don't you have a beeper?'

'Sure. No one used it, though. I was with Drayson.'

'What have you found out?'

'That guy was the phony engineer. I have to search their room. Would you warn Trevinski for me? He's in the Monday meeting.'

He went straight up and entered their room with his passkey. After that he had to take things more slowly.

Fortunately the maids had not yet cleaned up yet. The bedcover was stained; apparently with blood and some other fluid. In the bathroom waste bin there was a Tampax box, with an unused tampon. There was also a pair of dirty cotton gloves. Those finds did not make sense, but they hardly constituted a crime. The closet contained two large shopping bags. He searched carefully and picked up several small lengths of copper wire, neatly snicked off at the ends. Finally, under the bed he came upon a business card. It was from an electrical supplier on Third Avenue. He picked up the phone, was delayed briefly because the room was empty and the dialling line had been disconnected, then obtained his call through the switchboard.

The shopkeeper was puzzled. He audibly sifted his memory. 'A young guy with thick dark hair? We have so many customers fit that description. Now if you could tell me what he purchased here.'

274

'Copper wire. Possibly a flashlight.' Craig tried to think what else was probable. 'You sell engineer's tool kits?'

'No, sir. Place on Thirty-third Street sells those. Sorry I can't help you more.'

Craig wrapped the visiting card in his handkerchief to preserve any fingerprints. He had found the phantom electrician. No question. But what had the guy been doing: and doing again last night? How far would the cops be prepared to go on so little evidence? Where had the couple headed for from here? Before hoisting Trevinski out of the meeting he consulted Barbara.

'I had the impression they were flying back to Europe. Let's ask the desk clerk. Too bad I was in the back office then.'

Eventually the bellboy recalled that the pair had taken a cab to Grand Central Station. From there they could take the Carey bus to Kennedy or La Guardia, or a train to just about any eventual destination. The dots of half the picture were in place: the phantom had a face and a name. But achieving that, Craig realised with a faintly sick feeling, had taken all morning and they still didn't know what this was all about. So where do we go from here, he asked himself: and the answer came back, fast as a ball off a wall. For a start we go over that structural space again. To top it all in an hour or so he'd have Julia bringing Antonia to meet the Baroness. He'd have to just introduce them and leave: if he had time enough to do that much. And, for Christ's sake, if anything dangerous was about to happen he did not want them in the way.

Chapter

41

T h e lunch party was a gamble, albeit a civilised one. In London or Saint Moritz Charles Luttrell would have made the auction a black tie affair in the evening with drinks available privately for favoured clients. He couldn't do that in New York because city regulations forbade auctioning gemstones after dark. He could scarcely offer only drinks at lunchtime, so he had compromised with a buffet. The gamble lay in exposing the main bidders to each other when controversy over the Malabar Angel had become so superheated. He had compensated for this by extending invitations to more people.

They began arriving before the morning session was finished. Around one o'clock Gloria Grace made her media-anticipated entrance, in a sheer dark green dress with diamond-shaped panels cut out of the back and sleeves and long black gloves, their wrists liberally adorned with diamond bracelets. The photographers waiting outside were delighted, demanding she stop and pose.

'That woman has absolutely no taste.' Donna Bradshaw, standing with Father Vaughan, reacted less enthusiastically. 'It would hurt me, it would cause me actual physical pain, if she succeeded in getting your Angel.'

'It would be a pity,' Father Vaughan agreed, observing this apparition of flaming red hair and dark green silk. 'However, something tells me she will not.' His own view, after a few days spent with the extremely rich in New York, was that the high bidders would not be here in person.

'She's the wit who said people only go into Tiffany's to get out of the rain,' Donna Bradshaw commented, 'when she's wearing half Forty-seventh Street herself. I ask you!'

James Constant, a couple of feet away, overheard and took note. He was surprised at the priest's assessment of the film star, because it was precisely his own. By contrast, once Donna Bradshaw decided to buy anything, from a shop site onwards, she usually got it.

'Where the devil is Samantha?' Luttrell asked him. 'She can't have just vanished.'

When she did arrive, very late, it was with the Baroness and Prince Otto and it was evident from the different ways the two women were dressed that they were united in being here for the kill. Whereas the Prince had clearly snatched time from work and wore a regulation banker-dark suit, Helene had on a high-necked black silk blouse, her favourite rope of pearls glistening against it, her wheat gold hair cascading down to her shoulders, telling the world that there is nothing quite so stunning as a beautiful aristocrat. But Samantha was dressing with a different message, in a sharply cut little dress that announced her as a shrewd businesswoman, nobody's fool, the person who really engineered this auction. While the other two accepted glasses of champagne from a waiter, she motioned Charles and James Constant aside.

'I've just had a nightmare morning and all because of your wretched talk show interview.' She was making no secret of her anger with Charles even though her voice was subdued. 'Helene absolutely refused to sign an affidavit and spent the time at the hairdresser. She's accusing you of total bad faith and for once I agree with her. If she does withdraw the Angel you have only yourselves to blame. She knows what the penalties are and she doesn't care.'

'If she sells to a client of ours and through us the situation is slightly different.' Charles was taken aback.

'I really don't mind what you arrange. As for that nonsensical attempt of Lucy's to ban me from the auction: I brought you this deal, I have a legitimate interest and if I feel inclined I shall be

there in the front row with you. Or I may not.' She noticed the
Baroness moving towards them. 'Well, here Helene is. You can
damn well deal with her yourself!' She turned away, leaving
Charles as near speechless as she had ever done. Until this
moment he had been buoyed up by the success of the morning
session. Only fifteen lots out of the two hundred had failed to
make their reserve prices. Some had vastly exceeded them.

'One piece of good news.' Prince Czernowski materialised at
his elbow, urbane as ever. 'I've struck a deal with that damned
reporter.'

'With whom?' Charles's mind was on Helene, now launching
herself through the crush towards him like a blond torpedo, the
essential life-saving glass of champagne in her hand.

'Ethnic Vicky. Told her she would not be allowed into the
session this afternoon unless she agreed not to create a scene.
She can't afford not to give an eyewitness account. So she
capitulated.'

'At least that's a relief.' Luttrell had barely thanked his PR
adviser, when the Baroness was with him and Constant.

'I must speak to you.' She made no attempt to draw them
towards a more private corner of the room. 'After this terrible
publicity I do think we should make a private sale.'

'My dear Baroness, you have left this a little late, haven't
you?'

'And look what you have done on the television! Otto thinks
it is better we ask Mrs. Bradshaw if she will buy for five million.
Finish. No more argument.' She read refusal in Luttrell's expression and instantly challenged it. 'If you do not, I will. It is my
diamond, after all.'

Charles felt his equanimity collapsing. 'James,' he said in an
undertone, 'would you like to cast a fly over the stream? See if
the fish'll bite?'

Two minutes later Constant was back. 'She doesn't reject the
idea. She doesn't accept it. She will let us know before the lot
comes up.'

'There's your answer, Baroness. It will be the lady's privilege
to make up her mind in her own time.' He smiled at Helene with
ironic satisfaction.

'You mean I have to wait here all afternoon?' Helene was
shocked. This outcome had not occurred to her.

'It is entirely up to you.' He absolutely did not wish to withdraw the Malabar Angel. Cranston had already made arrangements for the telephone clerks to call him. Kuroki of the Acanthus Museum had an agent acting on his behalf. All the indications were that the diamond would comfortably beat the estimate. But one could indeed never tell.

'Should I have accepted, Father Gerard?' Donna Bradshaw was saying. 'Five million really is as much as I want to pay and surely some potential buyers must be nervous.'

'The Baroness evidently is.'

'I think I'll hold on for a little. If that Grace woman buys anything else that matters, at least I'll know she's out of the running.'

Julia left the banqueting area disgruntled. Craig had behaved as though he were in the middle of some emergency, first insisting Antonia would hate the auction and then deserting her as soon as he had caught the Baroness after her lunch party. And the Baroness herself had been short to the point of rudeness.

'What a darling little girl.' She had patted Antonia's head. 'How lucky your husband is. He has been very helpful to us. You know he was in NATO with my cousin Heinrich.'

'I worked there too,' Julia began. 'I knew Heinrich well.'

'Ah, so!' The Baroness had darted a glance at her watch. 'You must excuse me. There is so much to do today.'

And that was it, as though she had somehow offended the wretched woman. Antonia hadn't understood at all. For a while Julia thought of attending the auction, but she couldn't find Craig and it was absurd to pay twenty-five dollars simply to get it. She left a message for him at the reception and took Antonia for a window shopping spree on Fifth Avenue. If they'd come all this way they could at least have some fun.

Ilse had killed time in Manhattan for four hours. She was relieved to be rid of Frank and would avoid him at the airport. The thought of being next to him in a plane for eight hours sickened her. She didn't wish to be with him another eight seconds. But without a companion the waiting had become interminable.

She was feeling worse and worse. She had taken painkillers

and bought antiseptic ointment, which she applied to her vagina in the washroom of the Fifth Avenue Public Library, where she had taken refuge for a while. The result was excruciating pain, yet she didn't dare go to a doctor. She might not have enough cash for one of America's famed medical bills, nor could she brave the inevitable questions. She had ordered a frugal meal at a small restaurant nearby on 42nd Street but had been unable to swallow it. The agony did not subside. Depressed, xenophobically angry at all things American, she decided to check in very early for her 6:30 P.M. flight. She retrieved her suitcase and caught the Carey Bus out to Kennedy, reaching the East Wing terminal at 2:30.

A few minutes earlier the engineers reported to Craig that they had again found no faults in the wiring. Every single circuit running through the structural space had been tested.

'Only one guy knows what this is all about,' Trevinski growled. 'He has to be brought in, even if all we can tag him with is impersonating a member of staff and entering an unauthorised area.' He rang the Midtown Precinct and put his case. 'They're gonna cooperate. They'll alert all the airports, train stations and bus depots. For the both of them. The man Hermon and the woman Herbstein. But what the fuck was the guy trying to do?'

'Whatever it was, it has to happen soon,' Craig said. 'The auction will be over in a couple of hours. I'll go take another look in that structural space myself.'

In the Grand Ballroom James Constant's pace was being slowed by the high prices he was achieving. At 3:00 he had only reached Lot 264. Not that he minded. The room was packed. The atmosphere was fantastic. He hadn't experienced anything like it since he went as a spectator to the Duchess of Windsor's sale in Geneva. He worked through into major items: a mouth-watering pearl choker, a rope or *sautoir* of diamonds with three massive rubies suspended from its casual knot, an art-deco pearl and diamond necklace made by Cartier back in the 1920s. The bidders were going mad. The Malabar Angel would break carat-price records. If it was not withdrawn.

Chapter

42

' I am not with him anymore. I don't know where he is.' For the
first time in years Ilse was protesting the truth to an official: and
being disbelieved because she'd stumbled over answering to her
alias.

'Miss Herbstein?' the police officer had demanded as he came
up to her while she was drinking an orange juice at the cafeteria
in the East Wing terminal. And she hadn't responded as fast as
she ought. She had disregarded the pig at first, then answered
him confusedly.

The police officer was called Ed. He and his colleague, Stu,
had kept the woman under observation for some minutes after
the Lufthansa ground stewardess had pointed her out. She was
the only passenger who had checked in so far for the 6:30 flight,
nearly four hours before departure. It was now 3:30. The two
policemen did not know she had been killing time in any way
she could, still suffering agonies of pain. They merely saw her
swallowing down pills with the juice. Now, at close quarters,
they reckoned she was suspiciously agitated as well as hyped
up. She seemed unaware of the bustle of the airport around her,
of the announcements, of anything. She could be on another
planet.

'Listen, lady,' Ed insisted, pressing his question, 'you just spent a week with a guy called your husband and now you don't know where he is?'

'It's true.' She was distraught. 'I don't want to see him anymore. Never.'

'What were you doing at the Park Plaza?'

'We have a holiday.'

Ed towered over her. He put his hands on his hips. The gun holster swung slightly on his belt. 'Your husband has a holiday going around as a service engineer?'

'I am sorry. I do not understand.' But she did now. Something had gone wrong which that bastard hadn't told her about. 'In Germany he is not an engineer.'

'I didn't say in Germany, lady.' Ed reached for a chair, swung it behind him and sat down. 'I said here in New York. What was he doing?'

'I tell you, we have a holiday.' Out of her whirlpool of emotions came a single realisation. The hateful truth was the only escape. 'We think perhaps we will get married, but I am not sure. I am older than he is. We decide to take a holiday together, to see how it works.'

'Yeah.' This could be the truth. She was no chicken.

She averted her eyes. 'But, well, I like him, but I don't always like . . .' She let the sentence trail off, confident the meaning was clear.

'And so?' The other officer asked. He was becoming intrigued.

She took a deep breath. 'Last night he . . . he forced me.' The tears that came to her eyes were genuine. The pain was still excruciating. 'I never want to see him again.'

'He raped you?' Ed said, disbelieving. 'He rapes you and you don't do anything? You don't tell anyone?'

'I have to get home.' She let her self-control collapse. 'What happens if I call the police and say I am raped? They have investigations and I have only a ticket for this flight.' She sounded desperate. 'If I miss this flight I have to buy a new ticket.'

'The ticket.' Ed held out his hand. She extracted it from a handbag that looked like Fifth Avenue to him. But she was telling the truth. It was an APEX ticket. No alteration permitted. Not refundable.

'What are those tablets you been taking?' She handed him the foil-wrapped painkillers and he saw what they were. 'This guy raped you?' he repeated. 'And you didn't call for help?'

'I like to kill him.'

'Would you be examined by a doctor?'

'Be examined? Of course I would.' In her agitation she let her English improve. 'I have not dared to see a doctor in case I have not enough money to pay him. Of course I want to see a doctor! I have used an antiseptic and the pain is terrible.'

'Stu,' Ed ordered. 'Go get the doctor and I'll bring this lady along.' He spoke with something like compassion. He wasn't in much doubt that she was telling the truth. Maybe she really didn't know where her boyfriend was or what he'd been playing at in the Park Plaza.

The auction going on below was audible up in the maze of the structural space. This time Craig had entered it alone. He carried a powerful flashlight, which would be more use if he had some idea of what he was looking for. His investigation was going to be limited by the number of expanded metal catwalks bridging the joists. But whatever Hermon had tackled must have been similarly limited. Up until this moment the day's events had been so hectic that he had not been able to apply any quiet, deductive reasoning to them. Jake Trevinski had decided that it had to do with a heist, with cutting the power to the ballroom lights at a crucial moment. He was not a man with whom subordinates argued. Trevinski was an ex-Police Captain and Trevinski knew the answers.

Well, did he? As Craig edged along the first catwalk, shining the flashlight into shadows, he thought it all through. Muffled clapping from below announced what must have been a dramatic sequence of bids. So when would the auction reach a moment suitable for a heist? The most valuable lots were saved for the last half hour or so, when there were be most bidders and spectators. Pickpockets worked in crowds. Could a snatch thief succeed here? He'd have to leap up onto the dais and grab what he could from the girls handling the jewelry. Or try at the end. It was already nearly 4:00. The whole thing would be over in forty-five minutes. The thieves, if there were any, didn't have long.

Apart from knocking his head on a duct as he squeezed through a section of one of the lattice girders, Craig achieved nothing on the first catwalk. It was an eerie place to be by oneself, a maze just waiting for sabotage. He never realised before how architects utilised hidden space to conceal essentials: these huge square sectioned air-conditioning ducts, electric cables, water pipes for the ballroom's fire sprinkler system and other, thicker ones that he figured must be carrying waste and sewage from the back rooms on the sixth floor. The back rooms! Why hadn't that struck him before?

Hermon and his woman had asked for a room at the back on the fifth and Barbara had been unable to assign one because at this level there were none. They had wanted to be over the ballroom. Why? What could they achieve from a room above this space? He swung his flashlight around. The concrete roof showed there was no possibility of doing anything from above, which must be why Hermon had bought himself blue work clothes and pretended to be an engineer to gain access here. But he had not interfered with any of the systems. Therefore Trevinski could be wrong.

Okay. Suppose Hermon was not involved in a heist? What connection could he have with an international jewelry auction? Maybe there was no connection. So what the hell had he been doing?

Craig made his way along the second of the catwalks, crouching to get beneath girders, frequently finding his way obstructed and now reminding himself of those search procedures for staff that Trevinski had been so cool about. 'If a suspicious package is found, the finder must report its location to the Duty Manager immediately.' He laughed to himself, in spite of the seriousness. It would be no pain reporting to Barbara. But what the hell was he looking for? When the technicians had found nothing, could untrained common sense hope to do better?

At a spot where he could stand upright comfortably, he began directing the flashlight at longer range towards the next catwalk, rather than in his immediate vicinity. The beam reflected back from a run of tin ducting that was lower down than the others, apparently resting on the subsidiary joists. He traversed the light, probing areas of darkness and shadow left by the naked

bulbs overhead. What had he himself written for the staff? 'You
are looking for something that is out of place.'

A few yards away a shape that was not logical, even in this
confusion, caught his attention. He couldn't identify it or get
close from where he was. He retraced his way to the access door
and started along the third catwalk. What was the thing he'd
seen? The ducting obscured his view. He crawled on top of it.
The tin made hollow, creaking protests at his weight. He
directed the light along its length. Well, of all the damnedest,
most ordinary things. The shape was a discarded cardboard
box.

Pretty damn lazy of some engineer, junking a box out of sight.
In the military they'd discipline a man for dumping rubbish
anywhere round a barrack. Craig shone his flashlight again,
discerned lettering and squirmed closer to read it. 'Third Avenue Electrical Supply Inc.' Holy shit! The name on that visiting
card in Hermon's room! He must have used that box to bring
something in and then discarded it. He needed to know more
about this box. He edged even nearer until he could grasp one
of the top corners with his right hand, the light wobbling in his
left. The box did not budge.

Craig was straddled across the duct now, his chest on its flat
surface, the metal complaining, his feet off the catwalk. He
moved very gently, fearful of damaging the ceiling plaster, until
he felt something solid. His right foot was against a joist or a
girder. Too bad that was his bad ankle. He pushed himself a few
inches farther across the duct, placed the flashlight beside him,
though its beam then illuminated upward, not down, and put
both hands to the task of lifting the box out. He heaved, the foot
he was using to give himself purchase slipped, he caught an
excruciating twinge in his ankle and had to let go, subsiding
onto the duct. This was crazy. The box was as heavy as lead. It
could not be removed without help. What the hell was inside?

He was about to lever the lid open with his fingers when all
the indicators coalesced; the dots resolved into a picture that
Trevinski was unlikely to recognise, but anyone with European
Intelligence savvy would. An Irishman, a German. Attacks on
Rhein-Main. The Red Army blowing up an Air Force sergeant's
car. 'Do not touch or move the object. Don't open things you
can't identify.' And he'd been crazy enough to think he had

identified this as a junked box, probably full of discarded material from whatever Hermon had been working on. He felt chilled and isolated. Another few seconds, a single yank with his fingers . . . Phew! He slid back very carefully over the duct and manoeuvred himself onto the catwalk again, slightly twisting that damn ankle. He hobble-ran back to the access door. Why anyone should want to blow up the Grand Ballroom he could not figure out. The management was going to have to believe that Hermon did.

'Lot 357. An exceptionally fine solitaire diamond, unmounted, of 24.2 carats, graded G1 flawless.' The image of a magnificent stone appeared on the screen. Constant's gaze flicked rapidly across the front rows. Gloria Grace was seated right under the chandelier that irritated him. He could tell from the strain on her face that she was after this one, drew conclusions and opened the bidding. 'One million dollars. May I have one million?' This stone belonged to a dealer who had only recently had it cut and set a reserve of $80,000 a carat: a fraction below $2 million for the stone. Constant would be there in seconds. 'Thank you, sir.' A jeweler had lifted his paddle. The race was on. 'One million. One million two. Do I see one million five?'

'Thank you, ma'am.' Gloria Grace had raised her gloved and diamond-bedecked hand. No goddam paddle for her. But she was instantly outbid. 'One million eight. One million eight on my left. Yes, this is against you, madam. Two million. Two million three. I'm sorry, sir, I can't take one million four.' He took the risk of brushing aside an intermediate bid. Two million five. Thank you, sir.'

An elderly man on the left by a pillar had raised his paddle aloft and waved it like a flag in a way Constant recognised. It was Walter Cranston, bidding in person. When had he arrived? Gloria Grace flushed and determinedly lifted her index finger, as though the more of a contest this became, the less of a gesture she was prepared to make. 'Two million eight?' Constant asked. She nodded. 'Two million eight in the front.' Cranston shook his head. 'All done at two million eight. Two million eight.' Down crashed the gavel. 'Sold to Miss Gloria Grace for two million eight hundred thousand dollars, a record per-carat price for this auction house.'

'Well, at least that woman is now out of the running,' Donna Bradshaw commented to Father Vaughan with satisfaction. She and the priest were sitting farther back out of choice. 'I guess this is the time to accept the Baroness's offer. Would you do that for me?'

Father Vaughan looked around for someone to convey the message to. His own judgment was that she had left the decision too late. He saw the well-fed, rubicund face of Charles Luttrell near the doors and guessed that he was more than satisfied with the prices being obtained. The psychology of the auction was fascinating. Bidders seemed completely carried away. As he threaded his way through the pack of curious onlookers filling the back of the room, he heard a woman say to her companion, 'Imagine owning a thing like that! I'm allowed to dream, aren't I?'

The woman had hit the nail on the head, Vaughan thought as he moved past. The peasants of Malabar dreamt of their diamond's return, probably because they attributed semi-magical powers to it. The rich dreamt of the distinction it would confer on them. Donna Bradshaw would probably admit, if challenged, that her charitable purposes contained a substantial vein of desire for public recognition. Of all the potential buyers he was aware of, the banker Cranston appeared to have the least complicated motive. He reached Luttrell and delivered his message.

'A little late in the day, don't you think?' The response was languid and predictable.

'It was the Baroness's suggestion originally.'

'If you insist. Would you wait here?' Luttrell edged his way along the arcade of pillars towards the front where Helene had a VIP place reserved. He would not be sorry to see Lucy's favourite defeated: and he was relieved that Samantha had not challenged his wife's ban on attending.

The priest saw him occupy a vacant seat beside the Baroness in the second row and start whispering.

Frank decided to telephone his warning from the American Airlines departure lounge, partly on a final impulse, partly from more devious motives.

Everything had gone his way since he parted with that bitch

287

Ilse. He had left the tool kit by a construction site, dumped the working clothes inside the Macy's bag on a garbage pile, taken a cab to Lufthansa's Manhattan sales office, and had his ticket made over to American Airlines for their earlier Frankfurt departure. In these things his reasoning had been clear and sound. The tool kit would be resold to someone, the clothes appropriated by a vagrant, his removal from the Lufthansa passenger list not be remembered by anyone at Kennedy. Always insert intervening stages between one's movements and a potential pursuer: that was the game. Anyway it was too risky to leave from the same terminal as Ilse, let alone on the same flight.

Not that he anticipated immediate pursuit. He just knew, for an absolute fact, that the sex-starved woman's rollers would blow a fuse again. When they did, she'd complain, if she was still at the hotel, and she'd be able to describe him. Accurately, too. Jesus, her eyes had stripped him to the buff. Then the security men would start coming to conclusions: not that they'd be too interested in even the Queen of England's rollers after the Semtex exploded.

Thus far his reasoning was logical. The telephone warning idea was compounded of different elements: disgust with Ilse herself and a fair certainty that he would never be paid, inborn respect for a Catholic priest's presence, a belief that if he was ever arrested he could plead the warning in mitigation.

Accordingly at 4:10 he went to a telephone in the corner of the departure lounge, stood facing outwards in case anyone approached, pressed a quarter into the slot, dialled the newspaper he'd chosen and slurred out three short, quiet sentences.

'Listen carefully. There's a bomb in the Park Plaza Hotel. They should evacuate the building.'

He clicked the instrument back on its rest, cutting short the girl's agitated response and went to the duty free shop to buy some whisky. Irish whisky, to remind him of home.

'The woman has been raped, Officer. Not gently either. She got badly bruised as well. The antiseptic ointment she applied only inflamed her vagina more. She's been in a lot of pain. I've done what I can for her.' The doctor was young and he'd been alarmed at the state she was in, mentally and physically.

Ed nodded. 'I didn't think she was lying. Should we take her to the hospital?' That would be a way of detaining her on humanitarian grounds.

'The hurt is as much psychological. Psychologically the last place a woman wants to be after an experience like that is among strangers. She ought to get home.'

'Thanks, Doc.' Ed said. 'She can get dressed.'

When Ilse emerged, the policeman made a last attempt to extract information. 'Okay, Miss Herbstein,' he said kindly, 'you can go. But we'd sure like to catch the guy who assaulted you.'

'So would I!' She felt she could be vengeful now, almost without restraint. Apprehension had been transformed into relief at having been attended to by a doctor, at her claims being vindicated. Her performance was becoming fine-tuned. She would go as close to helping them trap that bastard as was safe. 'He will not dare to travel on the same plane. He knows when we get to Germany I have him arrested. He will take a different flight.'

'You never saw him in blue-collar clothing?'

'Blue collar?'

'Workman's clothes.'

'No. I told you. He wears sports clothes. But I don't know what he did all the day. I was so unhappy I went for long walks by myself.'

'You went for one yesterday?' The request from the Midtown Precinct said the man had been acting suspiciously late yesterday afternoon.

'Ja. I was walking in the Park until it was nearly dark. When I come back he was having a shower.'

It crossed Ed's mind to detain her just the same. Then he thought what a sensation a good attorney could make of that in court. He could hear the questioning. 'So, Officer Perelman, you have this woman who'd been raped, brutally raped. You have medical confirmation right there at Kennedy. The doctor— the doctor *you* called in, Officer Perelman—the doctor advises she be sent home to her family. So what do you do? You can't catch the rapist, so you lock up the victim.' Oh boy! He was going to have to let her go. How the hell could she be involved in a robbery when she was at the airport, eating painkillers and hardly able to sit on her ass.

'Sorry we had to question you, Miss Herbstein. Have a good flight.'

Above the Grand Ballroom ceiling the eight dollar alarm clock had shifted when Craig heaved at the box. The movement nudged the *fast-slow* lever and tautened the wiring to the detonator, straining the solder joints.

Chapter
43

Jane Runciman at the hotel switchboard saw the indicator light flashing and took the call from the newspaper.

'We don't know if this is some weirdo or not,' the reporter said. 'But a guy just called us and said a bomb is due to go off in your hotel. You have a big auction event today, don't you?'

'One moment, sir!' Afterwards Jane felt amazed at her own calm. She reached for the bomb threat checklist, laid it by her hand, activated the emergency system bleep and asked, 'What exactly have you been told? Would you mind repeating that message.' She wrote it down: "'There's a bomb in the Park Plaza Hotel. They should evacuate the building." Thank you, sir. And that was ten minutes ago?' She noted the time. 'Did this man say where it was? Nothing at all. What kind of voice did he have?'

'The guy was Irish.' Unbelievably the reporter began asking questions himself. 'Anyone famous at this auction? We pay good money for your kind of help.'

'This is important, sir. Do you know where he was speaking from?'

She had a point there. A good one. He'd heard an announcement in the background. 'I guess he was at an airport. He didn't sound drunk, either.'

'May I put you on hold for a second?' Jane saw that Barbara

had come through. 'We have a bomb threat, Miss Andrews. Made through a newspaper. You want to speak to them.'

Thirty seconds' conversation didn't leave Barbara much wiser. The reporter callously started asking her questions, too. She cut him short, put down the handset and told Jane to call the Precinct: and bring in any officers out on the street.

What next? Craig had told her that if you did not know precisely where a bomb was located you could lose lives unnecessarily by evacuating a building, because bombs were usually placed in public areas. When you knew where it was—and that the threat was not a hoax—then you could use the fire alarm and have staff direct guests away from the danger area. But the priority at this stage was to find the thing. Craig would be attending the auction. She rang Trevinski.

In fact Trevinski was busy throwing water on Craig's theory. 'I just don't believe ya, Clifford. You're telling me this phantom guy fixes a bomb in the ceiling? What for, for Chrissake? We oughta have a coupla men bring down the box. It's probably nothing worse than junk.' The phone distracted him. He picked it up and went pale. 'We have a warning? Okay. I'll handle it. Have the Precinct send a bomb expert. Fast. Yeah, we know where it may be.' He put the phone down.

'We should clear the ballroom, sir.' Craig insisted. 'Right now.'

'The whole fucking hotel, don't ya mean?' This was unimaginable. Over two thousand guests out on the street. The General Manager would go nuts. 'If this is some kinda hoax, Clifford, you'll be on the line. I want an expert to check that box.'

'We have a warning, sir. The fact we never had this for real before doesn't mean it can't happen.'

'I don't want no panic, okay?' Trevinski took the middle way. 'You go get those people outa the ballroom. The goddam auction must be almost over. I'll consult with Corley about whether we evacuate the rest of the building.' As Barbara Andrews had reminded him, the fire alarm was the fastest way. He just didn't want to use it without serious cause. To Trevinski's credit it did not cross his mind to do anything except initiate routines, even though he was directly beneath the ballroom floor.

* * *

'All done at three million three?' Constant delayed a fraction before bringing the gavel down on the auction's second-most-valuable jewel. Walter Cranston was the bidder and that meant he would drop out of the competition for the Malabar Angel. But the auctioneer wasn't on the dais to do favors either to buyers or rival sellers. 'At three million three.' A final hesitation. Crack. The polished wooden hammer hit the desk top. 'To you, sir, at the back. Another record price for Burnaby's here today.'

A record by a whisker, but he wished Lot 376 had gone to anyone other than Cranston. He used the brief pause to survey the room. The field for the Angel was perceptibly narrowing: even though, thank God, the Baroness had evidently decided against withdrawal. She was in the front row now with Charles, her mane of blond hair inclined towards him, discussing something in an undertone. Charles rose and walked back along the side of the room towards where Mrs. Bradshaw was positioned.

So who was left in contention for the stone? Gloria Grace was still here, but could not have the funds after her purchase. He hadn't seen Wolfgang Raeder, though he was definitely in New York. Kuroki was seated halfway back beside his agent. A woman's hand suddenly bobbed up near the back, thumb extended in a good-luck gesture. It was Anneke. Constant gave her a quick thumbs up in return. Then it was time for Lot 377.

Walter Cranston was mightily pleased at securing the 31.3 carat diamond solitaire ring for his wife. Various remarks she had made about owning someone else's heirloom, not to mention the adverse publicity, had persuaded him to bid for a more straightforward present. He'd paid a top price, which would please Sarah Jane secretly, but not an absurd one. He thought about staying for the Malabar Angel out of curiosity, realised the time was already 4:30 and decided to get back to the office.

From the side Donna Bradshaw saw Luttrell's return blocked by the press of spectators. He caught her eye and shook his head. There wasn't going to be any presale deal. A moment later a well-dressed, very English-looking blonde joined him, touching his arm for attention and bringing a look of distinct embarrassment to his face. Mrs. Bradshaw didn't need to be told who the girl was and wondered how she had such nerve. Thank heavens Lucy wasn't here! Luttrell wasn't telling his girlfriend to leave, either. She evidently said something peremptory and he shrugged his shoulders, as though he had too many other matters on his mind. After that she followed him as he eased a way through the crowd, up to where he had been sitting at the front of the room. There must have been a vacant seat, too, because the pair disappeared from sight as soon as they got there.

'Well, Father,' she said to Vaughan, restraining herself from comment, 'I guess we'd better move a little closer ourselves, so the auctioneer can see us. I suppose I shall have to use this wretched thing.' She twisted the blue paddle to and fro in her hand. 'It makes me feel such a fool! You wouldn't like to bid for me, would you?'

'I doubt if I should be very effective.'

'Then wish me luck.'

As the two of them edged to a better vantage point and Cranston squeezed his way out past the security guards, the sale of Lot 377 was concluded. The Malabar Angel's image, hugely magnified, appeared on the display screen. The assistant held the rivière of brilliants and the great diamond itself high in front of her. There was a moment's complete hush.

Seated halfway back, Kuroki whispered to his agent, 'I authorise you to bid five and a half.'

'Five six would be better, sir.' The agent, a noted dealer himself, was older than his Japanese client, but he respected money. If this bidding succeeded he could expect further commissions from the Acanthus Museum. However the round figure was unsatisfactory.

'The Trustees authorise five and a half. Very sorry.'

'If it goes past that figure, sir . . .' The agent was interrupted by the start of the bidding.

'Ladies and gentlemen. It is Burnaby's privilege to be offering here today the finest ancestral Golconda diamond to have come on the market since the 1950s.' Constant could allow himself a few seconds buildup for his prize item. 'The Malabar Angel, with its rivière of eighty-two brilliants, was worn at the Duchess of Richmond's celebrated ball before the Battle of Waterloo. Ladies and gentlemen, three million dollars would be a modest start.' His eyes darted around the room. A paddle was raised. 'Three million dollars in the centre. Do I hear three million five?' One of the telephone girls lifted her paddle. 'Three million five on the telephone.' He guessed that was Raeder. No need to bid himself for the house any longer, despite the Baroness, tricky as ever, who had insisted moments ago on raising the reserve. 'Three million eight? Thank you, sir.' This to a well-known dealer, expansively corpulent in a dove-grey suit, seated a few rows back. 'Three million eight.'

Craig Clifford reached the double doors, having taken the stairs two at a time in spite of his ankle. He realised the auction was approaching its climax and it would be near impossible to halt the proceedings except through the auctioneer. He made his way as quickly as he could down the extreme side of the room, less crowded because the pillars obstructed the view.

'I'm sorry, I can't accept that.' Constant rejected $3,900,000. 'Four million. The lady at the back. Thank you, ma'am.' Donna Bradshaw had entered the contest, taut and excited in spite of herself. 'Four million dollars I am bid. Four million at the back.' The rhythm was good, the feel was good, he risked a substantial rise. 'May I have four million five?'

Kuroki nudged his agent. 'We should begin. Give what he asks.'

'If you say so, sir.' Knowing he was positioning himself wrongly, the agent raised his paddle. The auctioneer could not maintain this momentum. It might be a problem getting the $5,500,000 bid.

'Four million eight,' Constant announced. 'On the telephone four million eight.'

'We have to get hold of this," Donna Bradshaw muttered, more to herself than Father Vaughan. She gesticulated with the paddle in a far from ladylike manner, calling out, 'Five million.'

At the front Helene von Brandenburg chuckled delightedly, the figures dancing for her, all the possibilities they promised coming alive. She wished Otto could have been here. 'You see,' she whispered to Charles, 'I was after all correct. We do make more.'

'We receive what we earn, Baroness.' If Charles was oblique it was because he had endured enough of her playacting. But Samantha merely smiled contentedly beside them, as her commission ratcheted upwards.

During the same minuscule pause which followed the five million bid Craig reached one of Burnaby's assistants by the dais. He noticed the dozen remaining pieces of jewelry laid out on the tables, the girls' cool expressionless faces and sleek hairstyles. Two security men were standing behind them.

'I have to speak with Mr. Constant,' he told the nearest girl. 'Urgently.'

'I'm afraid you really can't.' The tone reminded him of Julia.

'Security.' He showed his badge. 'We have to clear the room.'

'But it's almost over anyway.' Incredulity in the girl's eyes, then sudden fear. 'I'll tell him.' She moved away, as if Craig was diseased.

'I'm sorry, I cannot accept five million one.' Constant was finessing this. So long as he did not lose the momentum he had time. 'Five million three I'll take.' No response. He wondered if he had overplayed his hand.

Craig surveyed the packed room. Jesus, it could take ten minutes to clear. He spotted Gloria Grace's fireball of hair in the centre and was somehow surprised she was there. For that matter, where were Julia and Antonia? Pray God, not here. He scanned each row and could not see them.

The telephone girl raised her paddle.

'Five million three.' Constant hoped no sign of relief coloured his voice. 'Five million three I have. Will anyone say five million five?'

Both Kuroki's agent and Donna Bradshaw lifted their hands. This was definitely now a three-horse race. All the others had dropped out. Personally, Constant wanted Mrs. Bradshaw to win. He knew in his gut that was the right ending. But Kuroki's man had been quicker to raise his paddle, by a whisker.

'Five million five in the centre. I'm sorry, ma'am. The gentleman was ahead of you. Five million five.'

'Damnation,' Donna Bradshaw muttered. 'I'm half a million over the top already.'

'I'm sure that was the Japanese man's last effort.' Vaughan had been studying Kuroki, who seemed to be countermanding his agent and now appeared fatalistically calm.

'Five million five. Is everybody done at five million five?' Constant raised the little wooden gavel a few inches. 'At five million five . . .'

At the front of the press area, hard up against the silk rope, Vicky Robinson scowled, about to shout her protest, despite her promise not to demonstrate. It was iniquitous that a multinational conglomerate like Acanthus should defy all morality. As she craned forward she felt a firm hand on her shoulder.

'No, my dear,' Prince Czernowski said silkily in her ear. 'Not today, thank you.'

'Five million six.' The snow-crisp clarity of Donna Bradshaw's own final bid was heard all over the huge room.

Constant absorbed Kuroki's impassive reaction and received the tiniest shake of the head from the telephone girl. Nonetheless he would make an attempt to reach six million dollars.

'Five million six in the centre. Five million six. Do I hear five million seven?'

'You'll get it at seven, Sir,' Kuroki's agent hissed, bitter at having secured the half million position after all, only to be losing out.

'I regret not possible.' Kuroki's Board would not congratulate him for overstepping their limit.

'Five million six.' All bidding had to stop somewhere. Constant scrutinised his audience, always alert for surprises, certain that but for the appalling publicity, he could have done better. 'Are you all done at five million six?' He raised the gavel again and this time rapped it down without hesitation. He liked clean, decisive endings. 'Sold to Mrs. Bradshaw for five million six hundred thousand dollars. My congratulations.'

The camera crews panned their lens round onto Donna Bradshaw, as she and Father Vaughan backed away from their vantage point. Flashlights caught her. At the back Anneke applauded wildly. Kuroki was quickly filmed excusing himself to his neighbours as he too rose to go. Luttrell and the Baroness smiled for the cameras from the front row. A second before Helene had been complaining, 'I do think six million should be possible.' Luttrell had disregarded her, delighted that the ordeal with this bloody woman was over, though he was still uneasy at having Samantha beside him in public and being photographed.

In the press stand Czernowski asked Vicky Stewart-Robinson if she was now content. 'Fuck off, you creep,' she said, stepping over the rope to make a quick exit and be able to catch Mrs. Bradshaw for an exclusive.

On the dais Constant paused for the photographers, then caught a low, agitated voice from beside him.

'James. The security man wants the room cleared.'

He turned and saw Clifford standing at the end of the row of tables. Clifford made a curious gesture, levelling his right hand, palm downwards and drawing it across his throat. The meaning was macabrely evident. What the devil was going on? Constant swung back and addressed the audience, holding up his hands for silence.

'Ladies and gentlemen. I'm afraid we have a slight delay.'

He saw puzzlement on Luttrell's face as he stepped down from the rostrum to speak to Clifford. Suddenly the high-pitched buzz of the fire alarm shattered the comparative silence. People stood up, confusedly looked round, jumped to conclusions and began to push to escape. The panic Craig feared had begun.

At that moment the entire room shook, the great chandeliers swung crazily, a skull-numbing bang tortured and burst ear-drums and an all-enveloping blast of hot air swept around the room like a firestorm as the ceiling collapsed. Lumps of plaster crushed anyone directly in their path. Shards of glass flew into scalps and shoulders with the cutting force of spears. A fog of dust swirled around the ballroom. Then as more debris fell, the screaming of those trapped began: and a steady rain descended on everything from the sprinkler system.

Out at Kennedy Airport Frank Hermon passed in through the aircraft door and was welcomed by a stewardess stationed just inside the cabin. She checked his boarding card. 'Fifty-six E is down on the left, sir. I hope you enjoy your flight.'

Chapter

44

T h e way people heard the explosion in Manhattan was freakish and arbitrary. In some buildings as close as the Trump Tower or Hunter College it sounded so distant that no one paid much attention to the dull thud in a notoriously noisy city. At other locations in midtown it could have been just an unfamilar noise that wasn't immediately explicable and that you forgot about until the wail of the sirens began.

On Central Park it sounded as if a quarrying charge had gone off and along midtown Fifth Avenue itself startled passersby saw the entrance facade of the Park Plaza vibrate like a sleeping giant about to waken. A shock wave coincided with the shuddering bang. The stonework above the hotel's main entrance bulged outwards. Clouds of dust blossomed from the fifth floor windows. Then, in the same split second, this extraordinary, dreamlike spectacle became carnage as the incredulous watchers on the sidewalk were showered with razor-edged shards of splintered window glass, slicing into heads, shoulders, faces.

The brief moment of silence—or what seemed like silence after the roar of the explosion—was broken by cries and shrieks. The injured collapsed onto the sidewalk, already wet with blood. Others ran in panic. The main doors of the hotel burst open and a press of screaming people spewed out, fighting and struggling in their anxiety to escape, crunching through the broken glass and adding to the bloodshed if they tripped or fell.

In the Grand Ballroom itself Craig saw the plaster of the ceiling start to crack a millisecond before the continuous buzz of the fire alarm was swamped by the explosion. Almost alone among the crowd, he had not been pushing towards the doors, but had been waiting at the side for Constant to come across and unconsciously looking up in anticipation of disaster. In the next seemingly endless seconds the whole ornate structure above him disintegrated. A storm of hot air swept around the room and he felt a stab of agony in his left ear as the drum burst.

As the entire room trembled he thrust himself back against the protection of a pillar. Sheltering there dazedly he watched a massive chunk of ceiling crush the auctioneer's desk that Constant had just vacated, while Constant himself, a step away, was covered in smaller debris and disappeared beneath the continuing cascade. The nearest of the huge chandeliers, its myriad bulbs still illuminated, swung crazily until its gilded chain snapped and it plunged in front of where the Baroness, Luttrell and Samantha had risen from their seats. All the lights around the sides of the room went out, yet there was not complete darkness. From above a ray of daylight shone down into the murk, like a single car headlight in fog. He was unable to figure it out. He felt the rain of the sprinkler system start and dust choked his nostrils. As he fumbled to get a handkerchief over his mouth, the screaming began.

Charles Luttrell, faster to appreciate that there had been an explosion than the women he was seated between, had leapt to his feet, glanced up to identify the shape cavorting in the swirl of dust above their heads and realised the chandelier was about to fall. They were hemmed in both ways by the rows of chairs and the panicking people. Blood was running into his eyes, though he felt no pain. Helene had either been knocked down or was deliberately crouching. Samantha stood beside him shrieking, her hands to her ears. He tried to lift her bodily out of harm's way. As he did so the chandelier crashed down on them, flailing glass and metal.

On the fifth floor the two Puerto Rican chambermaids were drinking coffee in their service area. The blast blew off the structural space door, flinging them across the room with such force that they were dead within seconds of being stunned by the noise. The insubstantial walls between the space and the corridor collapsed, the blast sweeping everywhere like a tornado, bursting into bedrooms, sending windows flying into the street, collecting dust from its destruction and whirling that out, too. By a freak of the direction in which the concrete roof directed the blast it did not affect the office floors alongside the ballroom so badly. But Trevinski's ceiling flapped like a sail and collapsed seconds after he left to meet the police downstairs.

Barbara was at the reception desk briefing a police officer on the location of the ballroom as the whole building shook and the lights failed. A great rush of air came past them. When the emergency lighting switched on a sweeping cloud of dust was rolling into the lobby. Distraught people appeared out of it, their clothes whitened, shouting for help as they ran and colliding with the first fire crew dragging hoses in. She hastily organised the reception staff to form a line, showing the way out to Fifth Avenue and clearing a passage for the emergency services. She only remembered that Craig was up there too when Trevinski pounded up and began giving orders to the few security men around.

At the back of the ballroom, near the double doors that led in from the small reception lobby outside, Father Vaughan recovered consciousness, struggled to his feet and tried to work out what had happened. Lights were shining dimly in a thick haze. He could hear groans and cries for help. For some extraordinary reason it was raining: a continuous and persistent rain that had already soaked his clothes. In the half light all he could see was devastation. There must have been an almighty gas explosion.

Still dizzy and feeling sick, he began searching for Donna Bradshaw. It did not take him long to find her. She was lying a yard away against the pillar that Vaughan realised must have saved their lives. He scrabbled to throw the debris off her, finding his fingers coated with a sticky mix of dust and water, but her body was inert and her head hung to one side. He heaved her up, one arm round her neck, the other beneath her knees and staggered out through the shadowy opening of the doorway to the little lobby. He was not the first to get there. People were propped against the walls and they all seemed to be bleeding from their scalps, rivulets of blood staining the dust caked on their faces. He searched for the pulse in Mrs. Bradshaw's wrist and found to his immense relief that it was beating, though weakly.

Out at Kennedy Airport's East Wing terminal, Ed, the police patrolman, answered his office phone and swore under his breath. 'I know where the woman is,' he assured the Midtown Precinct detective, 'and I'll bring her in. But we never found the man. Okay. We'll alert every airline here. Yes sir. He could be on a plane right now.'

The first fireman on the scene had forced his way up to the ballroom against the cascading human tide, telling people who grabbed his arms that help was coming. In the great marble-pillared lobby, familiar to him from inspection visits, he had found order slowly being restored although part of the ceiling had fallen and only the low-power emergency lights were functioning. By the time he reached the area of the banqueting suites and saw in the gloom how devastated the area was he became more concerned about structural collapse then fire.

The doors of the Grand Ballroom were off their hinges, blown outwards and skewed across the foyer. Badly injured men and women were lying on the carpets, others hobbled around or helped each other while two dust-caked hotel staff members tried to establish order. The fireman pushed through into the huge ballroom itself, filled with swirling dust through which a single shaft of daylight drove down like a spotlight from a hole in the roof. Now he had to take stock, make an appraisal of the fire risk and what immediate action was needed. Ambulances he knew would be coming.

Inside there was a weird confusion of fallen ceiling plaster, twisted galvanised ducting, shards of glass and wood. Pinned beneath were the worst injured and the dead. Jesus, there must have been hundreds of people in here. He paused to look up again, scanning for signs of fire or further masonry falls. The skeletons of three chandeliers swung grotesquely from attachment points high above where the ceiling had been, all stripped of their glass lustres. There was a huge space up there which he knew had been a maze of air-conditioning ducts, piping, electrical wiring, catwalks: and the massive lattice girders supporting the towers of the hotel. The ballroom lay beneath the well between those towers. The blast had blown out a vent shaft, through which the beam of daylight was coming. But had the main structure been affected?

He peered up against that single ray of daylight, shining his flashlight, and saw that one girder was kinked downwards, as though a giant had struck it with a hammer. The bomb must have rested on that girder, which had deflected the explosion upwards and sideways, blowing out the vent shaft cover and sending shock waves towards the street side of the hotel. The fireman knew how freakishly blast acted, instantaneously exploiting the weakest obstacles in its path. This one had expended most of its force on the far end of the room. The majority of the people here might be concussed or wounded, but they would not have been killed unless directly hit by a large piece of the ceiling.

Was there a fire risk? He could see no smoke and although the fire-protective coating had been stripped off some of the girders and electrical cables were severed and dangling the sprinklers had dampened everything. There should be no serious hazard, provided the current was kept switched off. The tin ducting, hanging precariously from the girders was a danger. But that could not be dealt with until the injured were removed. Then a terrible thought struck him. Could there be a second bomb?

He was giving orders on his radio when a dishevelled man carrying a young woman in his arms came from the devastated far end of the room, stumbling over debris as he tried to follow the side wall.

'Hotel Security,' the man said. 'It was a bomb. There are quite a few dead up there.'

'Could there be another bomb?'

The man seemed bewildered. 'I don't think so. I'd found that one. We just had no time to get disposal men.' He shook his head. 'No, I'm sure there isn't another one. The guy only operated up there.' He jerked his head at the roof. 'Anything else would have detonated too. I have to take this woman out. She's hurt bad.'

Craig carried the inert body on down to the lobby. Should he have warned the fireman there was a load of jewelry up there? Probably not. Saving life came first. When the injured were out, then he'd have to start searching. He saw Barbara in the lobby,

---

303

but didn't stop. In the street there must be ambulances. When he staggered out into the daylight there were more than that.

Fifth Avenue was pandemonium. Patrol cars, ambulances, fire tenders: sirens, whistles, radios crackling, bullhorn orders. Firemen running, axes on their belts; bewildered hotel visitors wandering disoriented on the sidewalk among the stunned and bleeding passersby; women in tears, parents carrying children and shouting for help.

Medics spotted Craig and hurried over. As he laid the girl down on their stretcher he recognised the bloodied and dirty face. It was the Burnaby sales assistant who had been holding the Malabar Angel aloft for the bidders to see before the bomb detonated. He realised she was dead.

Ilse Nachtigal sat quietly in the departure lounge. She had just overheard a newsflash on another passenger's transistor. A huge explosion had severely damaged the Park Plaza Hotel. Hundreds were feared dead. Ambulances were attending from all over the city. Police spokesmen refused to speculate on the cause. More details in a special report shortly. She rejoiced in her heart, knowing Horst was avenged at last. The bomb had worked. She could hardly believe it! And in ten hours she would be back home in Germany. She was so delighted that she decided to spend the last of her dollars on a drink.

As she crossed the lounge to the bar area she noticed something that made her freeze. Those two pigs who had questioned her were standing in the entrance. One pointed. They had seen her. She looked frantically around, saw the women's room sign and walked as fast as she dared to a sanctuary the men wouldn't enter. She locked herself into a lavatory cubicle and sat on the seat, shell-shocked, trying to think. There was no escape route, no window. Even if the pigs had not seen her go in, the only way out of the lounge was back through the Customs and Immigration. She was cornered in her moment of triumph.

She wrestled with what to do until there was a hammering on the outer door, she heard it open and Ed's voice shout, 'Come out, lady, come out with your hands in the sky.'

'Give me one minute,' she called back. 'I will come.' She opened her handbag, slipped the cyanide pill from its concealment and swallowed it down with water cupped in her hands from the toilet bowl. For a short while the agony in her gut was terrible. But she didn't scream. She was joining Horst and Horst . . .

Ed heard her collapse, the lumpy sound of a body falling. By the time he broke down the toilet door she had died.

When Craig returned to the lobby Trevinski was with Barbara. He walked up to the desk and asked if his wife and Antonia had left the hotel.

'They went hours ago. They're not here,' Barbara said.

'Thank God.' He wiped his face with his handkerchief.

'Clifford,' Trevinski cut in, 'you're responsible for those goddam jewels. You know that?' He relaxed a trifle. 'I shoulda listened to you about the bomb.'

'Are you all right?' Barbara asked anxiously.

'I'm okay, sweetheart. I'll see you later.' For once he didn't care what anyone thought or knew.

Chapter

45

W h e n are you coming home, Craig? I'd like to know.' Julia was becoming anxious, sensing that something more than clearing up was keeping him at the Park Plaza.

'I lost two of my guys killed. We've had looting. We still haven't located all the jewelry from the auction. It's a mess here, I tell you.'

'So when do you come home?'

The crunch at last. In a way he welcomed it: except he should have gone home to North Plainfield and said this face to face, like a man. But he was bone tired and he had problems.

'I'm not coming back. I'm sorry, Julia, for a whole raft of reasons I'm leaving you. That's just the way it has to be.'

'What do you mean?' Alarm and fear. 'You're not coming back? What is this?'

'There are things we have to talk about,' he said wearily. 'I'll come out the moment this job is done.' He put down the phone: and did not much like himself for doing so. Maybe there wasn't any good way to break up a marriage.

And when would the job be done? It was now Wednesday, two days after the bomb, and although he had a twenty-four-hour security cordon on the ballroom area from the first moment that order was reestablished he knew some of the sale items would never be recovered. The auction dais end of the room was where the main force of the explosion had hit and where the casualities had been worst. The blast had been both vicious and mystifyingly selective. Both security men supervising the salesgirls had been killed outright. Of the girls themselves two were only scratched and shocked, while colleagues standing a few feet away had suffered dreadful injuries. James Constant himself had moved to talk to one of those girls a split second before the detonation: saving himself from a huge chunk of ceiling decoration which demolished his auctioneer's desk. The girl, Craig had later discovered, was the one he had rescued only to find she was dead. The falling chandelier had killed the Baroness and Luttrell's girlfriend, yet left the dealer himself with nothing worse than a broken arm and concussion.

Craig knew from battle experience how random shells or bullets can be even when carefully aimed. Yet this blast struck him as so irrational in its effects that he had begun to wonder about it. He'd had no time to do more than glance at the papers, but he knew rumours were going around that there had been some kind of a curse on the owners of the diamond. A pretty irrational curse too, he figured, if it killed the Baroness and spared the new owner. Then again, Donna Bradshaw had been standing right by that priest. Hell, he hadn't the time to waste on this kind of speculation. His problem was that another thing the blast had done was to collapse the tables holding the auction items, sending a load of the world's most valuable jewelery flying into the general debris. Right now Constant was helping identify things as they were recovered: and so far those did not include the diamond all the fuss had been about. Personally Craig doubted if it would be found.

For the past twenty-four hours they had been sifting a ton or more of debris from the dais area, sifting the glutinously wet sludge by hand, a bucketful at a time, on plastic sheeting. Somewhere in there, Constant insisted, were the two most important diamonds in the sale: Cranston's thirty-one-carat solitaire diamond ring and the Angel itself. The rivière of brilliants making the Angel's necklace had been found. Examining the stones' damaged mountings, Constant remarked that something very heavy must have smashed onto the necklace, rupturing the clasp which held the great diamond to it. Craig's worry was that the 'something' could have been wielded by one of his own staff. The temptation to exploit the chaos and slip several million dollars' worth of gemstones into one's pocket would be extremely strong: and who searched the security men? Whether it proved embarrassing or not, Joe Soap was going to have to.

By the time Julia rang late Wednesday afternoon Craig was acutely concerned. Four major items of jewelery remained missing, to a value of at least $10 million. Trevinski believed the hotel would be liable, having a duty of care to its clients. 'We made a deal over that goddam auction. We gotta find them fucking things. You're on the line, Clifford. You're on the line!'

After speaking to Julia, he went back to the ballroom to check on progress. The place was a shell, a warehouse with a few fancy light fittings dangling in the centre, stripped of their glamour. 'Why in hell did the guy do it?' he kept asking himself. But so far nobody knew.

The media, from the tabloids to TV, were mixing fact with speculation hourly. Luttrell had wanted a media event and, Jesus, he'd got one! Yet the only real facts about the foreign couple were that they were both terrorists. The woman's wailing mother had been filmed, until her father slammed the door in reporters' faces and put their house under guard. The Irishman was wanted by Scotland Yard in London but would be extradited here: he'd been arrested as he walked off an American Airlines flight at Frankfurt. Most oddly of all someone calling himself the Commando Holger Meinz had phoned a Düsseldorf newspaper claiming responsibility. It would need a team of psychiatrists to figure out the motives for such indiscriminate killing.

This was a field day for the shrinks. The moment of the explosion was unlikely to quit Craig's own dreams easily, but he was mentally resilient enough to cope. Others would need counselling for years, just as many of the survivors would carry fragments of glass or metal embedded deep in their bodies for life. The debris had flown around like shrapnel in a bombardment. It had been like a bombardment in another way, too; the casualties were not so high. Of close to nine hundred people, only nineteen had been killed outright, mostly at the top end of the ballroom. Another twenty-three were seriously ill in the hospital. The great majority of some four hundred others had been cut or bruised in ways worse to look at than long lasting. But that wouldn't stop them from suing. The complaints the hotel had been besieged with included the loss of three men's toupees and, the damn stupidest of all, over thirty sets of false eyelashes.

Craig knew the details because one of his burdens was building a dossier in preparation for the negligence lawsuits that would fester until a trial case established whether the hotel could be held responsible for the actions of terrorists whose access to most of the building had been legitimate because they were staying there.

As he supervised his staff sweeping the last of the debris from the sodden and filthy carpet Craig felt a touch on his shoulder.

'How's it going, sweetheart?' Barbara leaned against him affectionately for a second. 'You look bushed.'

'I told Julia.' He took her hand unobtrusively. 'Not about you. I'll do that when this is finished. Just that I'm leaving her.'

'We'll make a go of it, don't worry. I love you, Craig.' She kissed him quickly: though not fast enough to escape raising a grin from one of his men, which made them move slightly apart.

'You sure were right about that couple,' he remarked.

'Instinct. I told you!'

'It's so crazy who got hit and who didn't.' This would probably be part of the nightmares. 'That girl I brought out first, but not Constant. The Brit reporter who was scheduled to make a scene. She tried to leave ahead of the crowd and got a one-way ticket. The PR guy, that other Prince, and all the media got away with scratches. And what kind of chance had Martha Schneider being called out of the room ten minutes before? I guess she was the luckiest of the staff: her and Trevinski.'

'Craig!' Barbara still had her hand on his arm and he felt her fingers suddenly grip him. 'That man of yours over in the corner,' she said softly. 'Just watch him.'

The security guard was in protective blue coveralls and crouching as he gathered dust and fragments into a bag to be taken to an other room, spread out on plastic sheeting and sifted. It was a primitive method akin to sieving river gravel for diamonds, but Craig had been unable to devise a more effective one.

'It's the way he just turned his back to us,' Barbara said.

The guard stopped fingering through the debris and fumbled in his pocket for a tissue, blew his nose loudly and stuffed the tissue back.

'It's not what he just took out,' Barbara commented, 'it's what he could have just put in.'

'One way to find out,' Craig said and strode across the room to tap the man on the shoulder. 'Hey, Joe. I'd like a word.'

Joe stood up reluctantly. He was middle aged with careworn features, an ex-army sergeant who had drifted into security work because it was all he was qualified for. 'What is it, sir?' he asked.

'I'd like to know what you put in your pocket just now.'

Joe produced the tissue, but the story was written in his face.

'Is that all?' When he got no answer Craig ran his hand over the coveralls and felt a lump the size of a piece of wrapped candy at the bottom of the pocket, protectively close to his groin. 'Let's have it,' he ordered.

'I have five kids, Mr. Clifford.' The pleading began as he dug deeper than before into his coveralls. Was this going to be Cranston's solitaire, or the Malabar Angel, or what? Craig knew it wasn't candy. 'It was too much temptation.'

Joe held out the object on his open palm. Craig took it carefully between his thumb and forefinger. It was a lump of something caked in a mess of damp plaster dust. The man must have worked up the coating with his fingers: there was no way the explosion could have done that. Very gently Craig scraped it away with a fingernail. The gold of a broken clasp appeared and when all the muck was off he was looking at the Malabar Angel.

At her Sutton Place apartment Donna Bradshaw was recovering well. She had been released from the hospital that morning and was being tended by a private nurse. Her bedroom overlooking the East River was crowded with flowers and 'get well' cables. Piles of newspapers lay on a table and on the bed. A secretary was due in shortly to deal with urgent correspondence. It would take more than an explosion to disrupt the onward march of Mrs. Bradshaw's life.

Meanwhile Father Vaughan had joined her for tea, sitting close to her bed on a silk upholstered chair which might be standard equipment in an American lady's boudoir, but left a

310

fair amount to be desired for a gentleman visitor's comfort and ease. It did, however, tune in well with the frilly pink bed jacket Mrs. Bradshaw herself was wearing.

'What I cannot get over,' she was saying, 'is being sucked clean out of my shoes. That was the weirdest thing: and I have no memory of it at all! I'm just thankful I don't wear a wig!' She laughed at herself—a clear sign that she was on the mend, Father Vaughan thought—and then became more serious. 'It's really a miracle we weren't both killed.'

'I've been thinking about that,' he admitted. 'We talk about "Acts of God" and "Fate". But this was an act of the devil not of God, or of man's devilry, which is the same.'

'It is hard to see how the Baroness being killed or the auctioneer saved could serve God's purposes.'

'Or the Japanese curator having a heart attack,' he agreed. 'But we are all subject to divine providence.'

'Father Gerard, tell me something.' She tried to sound half joking but her concern showed through. 'Do you believe there was a curse on the diamond? It does sound absurdly superstitious.'

'On balance, almost certainly. The priests of primitive congregations in the seventeenth century took a very direct view of how God's wrath should be applied. Whether it was necessary is another question. We all carry enough burden of evil to destroy ourselves, terrorists and their victims alike. Covetousness, envy, greed and, I assume, revenge.' He paused. 'I think you and I may have been overambitious ourselves. And I do not believe that my cloth saved me. Or you. We happened to be in one of the safest parts of the room. Divine providence, if you like. Not special protection.'

The telephone by Donna Bradshaw's bed buzzed. 'Have you now?' she answered with delight. 'How extraordinary! Well, well. Legally you should return it to Burnaby's, I think, since I haven't paid them yet. Thank you, Mr. Clifford. Thanks for all you've done.' She spoke to Father Vaughan. 'They've found it! Can you imagine, a security man stole it! That stone certainly has inspired amazing greed.'

'Your exhibition tour should draw enormous crowds.'

Was this disapproval or cynicism? Donna Bradshaw didn't much care. She had already made up her mind.

'It might be better for all of us,' she said, 'if the Malabar Angel goes directly back to India.'

Father Vaughan drank a little tea, mainly to conceal his relief. Illogical as it might be, he did not want his benefactor to be the owner of the diamond for too long.

'The Bishop will be over the moon,' he said unaffectedly, 'and I suppose I shall have to commiserate with your Cardinal?'

'That's about the size of it, Father Gerard.' She was delighted at having so obviously made the right decision.

'I think it would be better if one item is not returned, however.'

'What do you mean?'

'That ancient gold mount with the inscription. I might take a short walk and consign it to the East River.' Father Vaughan gave her a most unpriestly wink. 'We can say it was lost in the explosion. It will be quite enough for the Bishop's congregation to believe their diamond has come back through a perfectly normal miracle.'